the COAT CHECK GIRL

the COAT
CHECK
GIRL

a novel

LAURA
BUCHWALD

RADIANCE

RADIANCE

An imprint of Roan & Weatherford Publishing Associates, LLC
Bentonville, Arkansas
www.roanweatherford.com
Copyright © 2024 by Laura Buchwald

Library of Congress Cataloging-in-Publication Data
Names: Buchwald, Laura, author.
Title: The Coat Check Girl/Laura Buchwald | The Ghost Table Trilogy #1
Description: First Edition | Bentonville: Radiance, 2024.
Identifiers: LCCN: 2024936970 | ISBN: 978-1-63373-943-7 (hardcover) | ISBN: 978-1-63373-944-4 (paperback) | ISBN: 978-1-63373-945-1 (eBook)
Subjects: BISAC: FICTION/Ghost | FICTION/Fantasy/Paranormal | FICTION/City Life
LC record available at: https://lccn.loc.gov/2024936970

Radiance hardcover edition October, 2024

Cover Design by Casey W. Cowan
Interior Design by Staci Troilo
Editing by Staci Troilo & Lisa Lindsey

"To her whose heart is my heart's quiet home, to my first love, my mother."

(from Christina Rossetti's "Sonnets Are Full of Love")

Dedicated to my mom, Maggie
my first and favorite reader and friend

Prologue

❧

IT RAINED NINETEEN inches the summer they hired a coat check girl. For people who love rain, it was cozy and romantic. For everyone else, it amounted to little more than wet clothes and broken umbrellas and plans. And for the girl in coat check, it was a chance to work exactly where she needed to be.

On a quiet block of West Ninth Street, in the heart of Greenwich Village, Bistrot filled up nightly with regulars and tourists who didn't mind venturing out in the weather. The restaurant was a neighborhood favorite and a draw for people in the know with a flair for the macabre, those who wanted the badge of dining in a place with checkered history. The space had been transformed many times over the decades. In the summer of 1999, it was a throwback to an era when dark oak, red leather booths, and smoky mirrors were in vogue.

For two people who worked there, it was as close to home as anything they'd experienced in a very long time.

What neither realized at the start of the summer was that their home was in trouble. Bistrot was going down fast, and nobody knew that except for Chef.

And me.

Chapter One

✦

JOSIE STEPPED OUT of the West Fourth Street subway station and stood in the rain. She was grateful to it for cleansing her of the heat and grime she'd collected underground. She was grateful, too, that it masked the tears she didn't want to shed in public. What she didn't like was its weight on her clothing, but it was her fault for overdressing in summer. Now the rain clung to her clothes and her clothes to her skin, just as the heaviness of her grief enveloped her and refused to let go.

She had just returned from Keene, New Hampshire, where she'd said goodbye to her grandmother and supported her mother, as best anyone could support Alice Gray, through the pomp and circumstance that follow death. Nanette's death was neither unexpected nor a blessing, despite the sentiments of earnest well-wishers who cited a long life and peaceful departure as evidence of something beautiful.

Who could say whether her death was peaceful? No one. Not even Josie, who for the thirty-two years she'd been alive had shared an inextricable bond with her grandmother. Her lightest, dreamiest childhood memories included Nanette, as did some of her most difficult. In those, Nanette was her solace.

In her final hours, while in and out of consciousness, Nanette brightened at the sound of Josie's voice calling her by the nickname she'd given her. Josie the toddler had rejected "Nana" and created her own moniker.

Until Nanette's stroke in late winter, they'd spoken nearly every day. Josie prayed to her nameless gods that Nanette's death *had* been painless, but she'd never know.

No, as far as she was concerned, if you were still alive, you weren't yet an authority on death. When the Greek chorus of mourners murmured their platitudes of a better place, Josie felt guilty, as though her skepticism were judgmental and unkind.

"Excuse me!" a woman behind her huffed, and Josie jumped. She was blocking the subway's entrance—a rookie move, especially in bad weather.

"Jesus," the woman added unnecessarily as she passed.

Josie's eyes filled with tears. It wasn't personal, but today she was raw and vulnerable. It took little to make her cry. She pulled out her sunglasses. She'd just have to be one of those people who wore them in the rain.

In the final few blocks of her commute, she refocused on gratitude, the importance of which Nanette touted long before it was trendy. Bistrot. She was grateful for the refuge the restaurant provided after six years of staying in a job that was supposed to be temporary. There was comfort in the familiar, even if that familiar bore a striking resemblance to stagnation. And there was comfort in employment.

"Lady!" Curtis swept her into a bear hug when she walked inside. "I'm so glad you're back!" He pulled away as her wet clothes seeped into his. "Girl, do you need me to buy you an umbrella?"

"I have one at home. I'm so tired, I'm surprised I remembered pants."

He blotted her with the back of his sleeve. "Well, we're all glad you did. How did it go?"

"It's a blessing. She lived a long life. She's in a better place."

"Ugh. Don't you just want to slap those people?"

"Kind of, but no. They mean well. Whatever gets you through the night." She blinked back tears. "What did I miss here, my love?"

"What did you miss? The new guy quit."

"Drunk Philip?"

"No lady, Drunk Philip left in May."

"Right. Cory Who Never Pushed the Specials?"

"Girl, he was, like, five months ago. This was Gregory!"

"I've never even heard of a Gregory."

"Well, then, the answer is you didn't miss much. His replacement is Justin. Don't get too attached."

"I never do."

"True dat. Let's get on with this beautiful mess that is our livelihood." He took her hand and led her through the bar toward the main dining room, where the staff gathered for its weekly Tuesday meeting.

Bistrot's building dated back almost one hundred years to the early twentieth century, once a meeting hall, then a speakeasy with an unmarked door before it became a restaurant. In 1999, it was a respite from modern living, a time capsule where cellular phones got poor reception. One could hide out from the looming anticipation of a new millennium and all the paranoid talk of Y2K and the "millennium bug." It was also, for better or worse, a departure from the year's culinary trends—Asian food fused with every other ethnic cuisine, tepid vegetable foams, overly artistic plating.

It was a beautiful space. In the front room were a long, L-shaped oak bar with a mirrored back bar, a pressed tin ceiling, and a half-dozen café tables and chairs, all reminiscent of a spot on the Left Bank where Hemingway might have held court. The larger, more formal dining area was lined with red leather banquettes, mirrors, and Art Deco sconces that shed soft light on the twenty-table room. In the middle of the dining room's two-story ceiling was a large skylight. The rain continually pelting it that summer provided a percussive backdrop to the classic jazz that played throughout the restaurant.

A private twelve-top, accessible by the restaurant's back staircase, lorded over the masses from its balcony perch near the kitchen doors. Groups reserved the spot for its intimacy and view of the room. At no additional charge, they were treated to the erratic showmanship of Chef, the tortured madman who owned the restaurant. Chef was Eriq Villeroy, but no one called him by name. He was Chef, and he didn't attend staff meetings. Instead they were led by Andy, Bistrot's manager. Tonight, Andy was weary.

"Okay folks, a couple more things," he said. "Who wrote 'Unhinged Bitch' next to Missus Guilfoyle's name in the reservation book?"

Derek Magnus, legs stretched out, occupying one side of a booth, let out a laugh. People looked at him. "Come on!" He pulled the toothpick he was chewing—in lieu of the cigarette he probably wished he were smoking—from his mouth and stared at Andy, grey eyes unblinking. "I didn't write it. But it's true!"

"People." Andy grimaced. "Please act like the adults you're supposed to be."

"Seriously," Josie said as she slid into the booth across from Derek. "Don't write that stuff in my book. It's right out in the open. Anyone can see it."

She looked at Curtis, who shrugged and mouthed, "*Sorry*." He'd been at the restaurant for eight years, longer than anyone except Chef, and his patience for difficult customers was thin.

Andy stood. "Josie, welcome," he said in his somber voice. "We're happy to have you back."

Josie blushed. She didn't like being the center of attention. "Thank you. And thanks for the gifts. We appreciated them."

Andy had sent flowers to the funeral on behalf of the restaurant and a tray of cookies to Josie's mother's house for the post-service luncheon. They'd arrived broken, and Alice didn't serve them. Josie binged on the crumbs after everyone left. It was the most she'd eaten for several days.

Derek reached across the table and squeezed her hand. "Welcome back, sister. It's good to see you." His tone was contrite, which Josie expected. He knew better than most how close she and Nanette had been, yet he'd been distant in the aftermath of the news. This was the opposite of Curtis, who wept with her and called to check in every day.

"Okay," Andy continued. "Second order of business, we're going to be closed for a couple of weeks at the end of summer to renovate the basement."

"A couple of weeks?!" someone shrieked.

"Yes!" Andy made a motion as though snatching a mosquito from the air. "No pushback, people! This is not negotiable! We need this whole place to be ADA compliant, and that includes the basement! You will be compensated for your time. Most of you."

"Most—" Josie started. The idea of looking for a new job while mourning Nanette was paralyzing.

"Wait. Andy, do you have confirmation from up top on this? That most of us will be compensated?" Derek asked.

"Yeah, this would hardly be the first broken promise you've made," Curtis said.

Josie shot him a look. This was not the time to challenge Andy, even if he was a man of many an unkept promise and unrealized plan. If he were, in fact, trying to figure out who would still get paid, it behooved everyone to stay on his good side.

"Thank God we're renovating that dump," Johnny the sous-chef said. "There's cobwebs older than my pops down there. Fuckin' fire hazard."

"Well, we *have* a ramp," Curtis said. "And an accessible bathroom on this floor. Are there a bunch of wheelchair-bound patrons clamoring for a tour of the cellar?"

"Finally." Andy's voice rose over Curtis's. "Third order of business, people, we may hire part-time coat check."

His words hung in the air for a moment.

"In summer?" someone asked.

"So, now we have to share tips with anoth—"

"Hush!" Andy cut them off. His right eye twitched. Frustration and fatigue, the two main elements in a restaurant manager's life, made this happen. Though he acted beaten down by his work, Josie suspected that he loved it. She theorized that he'd been picked on as a kid and overcompensated by managing Bistrot's crew of misfits with authority that stemmed from deep insecurity and a Napoleon complex. Josie had empathy for him the others often lacked, though today she was too thin-skinned to access it.

"First of all, folks, I said *might*."

"You said *may*," Curtis said.

"I've yet to hire anyone, and if I do, she will be part-time and keep her own tips. She won't work the whole night, just through dinner service, and only on the nights she's really needed. Second, have none of you people noticed the extra amount of gear dripping all over the floor? It's raining, folks, and it's going to keep on going for forty days and forty nights." He scanned the room as though he'd said something clever and waited for the complaints to die down. "This can only help."

"Speaking of hiring extra help," Derek said, "remind me what happened to that second weekend bartender you mentioned a few months ago?"

"I'm still working on that. It's hard to find good help. And besides, we're not that busy in summer. Everyone's in the Hamptons."

"Not this year they're not," Curtis said, shaking his head. "Ain't nobody hanging out on a sopping wet beach."

"Anyway, people," Andy said with an exaggerated sigh, "we're all in this together, and we have jobs to do now. Let's roll."

THE DOWNPOUR CONTINUED as the afternoon waned. Josie watched the sky grow darker and the raindrops trickle down the windows.

At 5:00 p.m. she perched at her hostess stand, absently leafing through the reservations. Her mind filled with phrases she'd heard for years—the "stages of grief," the "new normal," "survivor's guilt." She knew intellectually that she had no reason to feel guilty. She was *supposed* to outlive her grandmother—but the idea that the world still spun without Nanette in it made no sense. Nanette was her lifeline. Yet here she was, back at Bistrot, in a city full of people who never knew Nanette existed, a city that hadn't missed a beat despite the fact that the world had grown so much darker.

On top of this all-consuming turn of events, news of the restaurant closing for a few weeks unnerved her. If she weren't one of the people compensated, she'd be in trouble. Living in New York on what she made meant living constantly at the limit of her means. Some weeks she had twenty dollars to her name and others she had a few hundred. Money was never anything she could take for granted.

And if she were compensated, what would she do with so much free time? The last thing she needed was idle hours alone. The idea terrified her.

Live in the moment, Nanette would advise her. *Replaying the past and worrying about the future erases the present.*

For tonight, she was back in the sanctity of the place she felt most safe.

Derek stood behind the bar, polishing glasses and inspecting them in the light before sliding them into their overhead racks. Curtis and the other servers learned the dinner specials—rack of lamb *au jus* with rosemary new potatoes and *haricots verts*, monkfish Lyonnaise with ratatouille and pureed potatoes—and joked with the busboys in restaurant Spanish. The pre-dinner rituals were comfortable and familiar. These people, these servers, cooks, food runners, and bartenders, were Josie's family.

Just as Mario, the head porter, turned on the outside lights against the darkening afternoon, the front door opened, sending a gust of humidity into the air-chilled room.

Someone stood inside the vestibule, shaking a mess of umbrella spokes and running her fingers through damp hair. Josie recognized her but couldn't place her. Her long, mermaid waves were tousled by the rain. She had pale skin, kohl-lined eyes, and wore a pastel yellow raincoat over a short dress and shiny white rain boots.

Manhattan was filled with beautiful women, but this one was a different animal. Josie looked over to the bar. Derek had disappeared down the trap door to the subterranean liquor room.

As the woman approached, Josie realized she didn't know her after all. Yet there was something familiar about her, as though she'd had a cameo in a dream, or they'd made eye contact on the subway. And what eyes she had, like a cat's, irises a mosaic of green, gold, and violet. Her lips were pink and glossy.

With her utilitarian black uniform, her makeup-free face, her hair a messy knot on top of her head, Josie felt dowdy. Dressing up, though, would have been an affront to her grief. At least that was how she'd justified her choices that morning.

The woman stood in front of Josie, seemingly awaiting a greeting.

"Hello. May I help you?" Josie slipped easily from grieving survivor to hostess mode.

"Hi, Josephine?" she said with an easy smile and thick southern drawl. She extended a hand. "I'm Mia Boudreaux."

Josie shook her hand and wondered why Mia Boudreaux knew her and knew her as Josephine. Few people called her by her full name.

"I'm sorry—have we met?"

"Oh!" Mia's eyes crinkled when she laughed. "We have now. I'm here about the coat check position. They mentioned how you'd be the first person I'd see."

Andy emerged from his office in the back of the restaurant, rolling down the sleeves of his pink Oxford, and slid into the first booth, where he conducted interviews. He started scribbling furiously on a yellow legal pad.

"Of course. Let me introduce you to our manager." Josie walked Mia to the booth.

"Well, hello," Andy said.

"Hi, Andy. This—"

"I'm Mia Boudreaux," Mia said. "Thank you for seeing me." She took the seat across from him with a quiet confidence that impressed Josie.

"Josie, tell Mario to turn down the air," Andy tossed her way without looking up from his notepad. "It's like the North Pole in here!"

"*Please,*" Josie mouthed, and rolled her eyes.

Mia gave her a conspiratorial smile, a tiny gesture of solidarity that Josie, at times suspicious of the motives of other women, deeply appreciated.

She walked back to the front as Derek trotted up from the cellar, his head emerging from behind the bar, followed by the rest of him. He carried three bottles of Malbec and a jug of Jack Daniels. He looked over to Andy's booth, and then winked at Josie. She got it. He liked women.

"You, my dear, are becoming a caricature of yourself," she said.

"What do you mean?" he asked, all big eyes and feigned innocence. "Can't a guy appreciate beauty?"

"You're nothing if not consistent, Magnus."

SHORTLY BEFORE DINNER service began, Josie climbed the front staircase to the ladies' room and stared at her reflection in the mirror. There were dark circles under her eyes, and her irises were muted, as if all depth had drained from them. She found a dull-tipped brown pencil in the bottom of her bag and attempted to make herself prettier. She wrestled her dark hair out of its bun and ran her fingers through it. Ignoring the sign asking people not to do this, she opened the complimentary Listerine and swigged from the bottle, then felt guilty and wiped it down with her sleeve.

A creaking sound came from one of the two stalls, startling her. Mia was downstairs, and there were no other women on staff that night. But the building was old, and strange noises came with the territory. She continued to scrutinize her face. Grief was exhausting. Her lips were chapped. She tried to exfoliate them with a paper towel and heard a set of keys clatter to the floor.

"Hello?" She bent down to check for shoes in the stall. There were none. She bolted upright, the hair on her arms and the back of her neck standing up, and stared at her reflection with eyes like saucers.

"*Shit,*" she whispered, as a long-dormant sensation washed over her.

As a little girl, Josie learned that she and her grandmother shared an unusual trait—the ability to connect with the spirit world.

"You and I are lucky, Josephine. We see more than most people, and not just with our eyes," Nanette would explain when something intangible frightened Josie, when she couldn't bring herself to enter a room, or when she heard voices where there shouldn't have been any. The problem was, Josie didn't *want* to see more than most people. She wanted to be normal.

She learned early on to keep these experiences to herself. Besides Nanette, most people didn't understand. When they did, it meant there might actually *be* such a thing as ghosts, and this was equally inconvenient. Josie's mother, a staunch disbeliever, thought it was a cry for attention on her daughter's part. To avoid such accusations, Josie learned to compartmentalize her experiences and developed a protective, wild imagination to explain away the things that didn't make sense.

Nanette urged her to see her ability as a gift. "Spirits only make contact because they have a message for us or need our help. It's a good thing."

It had been a while since a spirit had needed help from Josie. In her younger days, she mustered all her willpower to consciously ignore even the clearest signs that one was present until, eventually, the signs tapered off and then disappeared altogether. She did not need them to come flooding back now, did not need fear to join the list of complicated emotions she was juggling. She left the ladies' room and ran down the steps to her post.

With an unobstructed view of the coatroom from her station, Josie watched the evening unfold. Mia greeted people as the restaurant filled. Several of the male customers, unaccustomed to anyone occupying the coatroom and clearly pleased that the one who did looked like Mia, crowded in and helped themselves to hangers, while their wives and dates glowered beside them. Mia seemed to take it in stride, she and Josie flashing each other amused looks throughout the night. The new girl was always a hot commodity. Josie had enjoyed that status once.

By nine o'clock Bistrot's dining room was nearly full. The muted din of conversation and clinking of glasses and flatware to plates echoed throughout the restaurant.

"Eighty-six the lamb!" someone announced.

"That's too *baaaad*," Curtis said.

Josie swatted him with a menu as she led a group of four—parents, son, son's new girlfriend, she guessed—to a circular table in the middle of the room.

As she wove her way back to the front, a voice that could shatter glass pierced the room. It came from table nine.

"Miss!" Mrs. Guilfoyle shrilled, though she knew Josie's name. "Excuse me!"

Josie prided herself on her ability to soothe even the most cantankerous customer, but she was hardly in the mood for it tonight. "Is there something I can help you with, Missus Guilfoyle?" She plucked part of a straw wrapper from the tablecloth.

"Well, someone had better. I ordered the tuna medium. The thing practically bit back."

"Tina." Her husband glanced at the nearest table and offered Josie the silent apology he had so many times before.

"Stanley!" Mrs. Guilfoyle was a screecher. "This is *not* medium!"

"Fine, but there's a way to—"

"I'm sorry it's not to your liking," Josie said. "I'll have Sam take it back."

"Ha!" Mrs. Guilfoyle snorted. "Good luck! Haven't seen him since I ordered my tuna. *Medium.*"

"Tina!"

"I'm sorry about that, too," Josie said. "I'll have him take care of you right away." As she walked through the dining room she muttered under her breath, "*Unhinged bitch.*"

A quiet giggle echoed in her ear. She darted her eyes back and forth between the tables, but everyone was engrossed in conversation. She swallowed hard. She'd only imagined it.

Sam stood by the coat room, no doubt trying to impress Mia with the fact that he was "really an actor." Josie had heard his spiel so often she could deliver it for him, and still his starry-eyed naivete struck her every time.

"Sorry to interrupt, guys." She put her hand on Sam's shoulder, and he jumped. "Sam, Guilfoyle's unhappy. Please go do your job, my love."

"Josie, hey. I'm real sorry about your grandma."

"Thanks, honey."

"Are you okay? I mean, I know you're not okay—"

His earnestness touched her. "I am. Or I will be. I really appreciate your asking. And Missus Guilfoyle is really unhappy with her tuna." She patted his arm. When he walked away, she turned to Mia. "Was he regaling you with tales of thespian life?"

Mia laughed, a sparkling windchime of a laugh. "He seems darling. All y'all do."

"Don't let us fool you," Josie said. She returned to her post wishing she hadn't been so flippant.

As food service wound down, the dining room emptied, and the barroom was just getting started. Exhausted though she was, Josie couldn't face going home to emptiness. She'd hated having roommates in the first years after she'd landed in New York. Now she'd give anything for the idle chitchat and constant companionship she'd once found so tiresome.

When she had tasks to do, she was fine. She was even grateful for the small talk her job demanded, the tired jokes about the rain, references to the great flood. When she had time to think, the rawness of her loss hit her so fully she forgot to breathe.

She headed toward the stairwell to the ladies' room and paused. Being busy had also kept her from having to think about what had happened earlier.

Derek came trotting down the steps. "Josie." He put his hands on her shoulders. "How are you holding up?"

She blinked away the threat of tears. "I had no idea how much grief could physically ache."

"I'm so sorry." He pulled her in for a hug.

"It keeps me up at night." Her voice was muffled against his chest. "And if I do fall asleep, I wake up in the morning, and it hits me all over again. It sucks."

"I know it does. I'm sorry, sister."

"Thank you." A tear slid down her cheek, and she stepped back. "How do I have any goddamn tears left?"

"Why don't you take a little time off? Just a couple days. You only got back last night, right?"

"I can't take time off. For one thing, I just took ten days, and for another, and do what? Sit around my apartment feeling sorry for myself?"

"You're not feeling sorry for yourself. You're grieving."

"I'll be okay."

"I know you will. It takes time though, and no one expects you to just stop being sad because you're back in New York. We love you, we're here. But now I have to go serve a bunch of people who really don't need that last drink. At all."

"Well, it is your responsibility as a—"

"Don't say it!" Derek held his hands up in mock horror.

"—mixologist."

Mixologist had become the it word of the cocktail scene, and while it had a specific meaning, denoting someone who created specialty cocktails, some people used it as a synonym for *bartender*. Derek was adamant that he was the latter, and took a no-frills approach to the job. In fact, in his younger, cockier days, he'd famously charged more to patrons who referred to drinks by name, Greyhound or Cape Cod, and less to those who called them what they were, vodka and grapefruit or vodka and cranberry.

"*Ich bin ein* bartender!"

Josie smiled. "I'll join you in a few. And if you need a hand behind the bar, I'm happy to help."

"I should have it covered, what with the invisible backup Andy's provided."

"I think it's time to let that one go," Josie said, patting his arm. "Andy is a man of many talents. Growing the staff is not one of them." She climbed the stairs and stood outside the ladies' room, steeling herself.

"Hey, Josie." Mia came up the steps behind her.

Josie exhaled with relief and pulled the door handle. "Good first day?"

"It sure was. I'm just gonna freshen up before I leave."

"Don't leave yet. Join us for drinks!" It felt suddenly, urgently important to Josie that she connect with Mia. In the void left by Nanette's absence, she craved feminine energy. She knew Mia was technically done after dinner ended, but theirs was an industry where people stuck around the job off the clock.

"I don't think so, girl. Tonight took a lot out me. It's been an awful long time, and I'm fixin' to get some rest."

"Of course." Josie blushed at having sounded so needy. "Maybe another time, then."

They stood in front of the mirrors, Mia wiping at the smudges of kohl on her eyelids, and Josie applying the wrong shade of lipstick—it was all she had in her bag. She watched Mia in the mirror. Small talk didn't come as easily to her when she wasn't working.

"How long have you been in New York?" she asked finally.

"Too long, girl. I've just about overstayed my welcome. I come from New Orleans."

"Well, that's why I like you! That was one of my grandma's favorite places. I grew up eating her versions of jambalaya and gumbo."

"Is your grandma from there?"

"No, but she lived there for a bit. She's from New England."

"Interesting, 'cause you look like you could have some Creole blood in you."

"Really?"

"Wouldn't surprise me if your grandma had roots there dating far back."

"She loved that town. It sounds magical. The architecture, the music."

"The ghosts."

Josie froze.

"I didn't mean to scare you, girl! I just figure it's a well-known fact how they come with the territory."

Josie waited for her to elaborate.

"Have a good night, Josie," Mia said with an easy smile. "Thanks for welcoming me into the fold." She pushed open the door, leaving Josie intrigued.

Maybe this was why Mia seemed familiar, this New Orleans connection. Maybe it was no coincidence she had come along when she did.

"Thank you, Nanette," she whispered. Her face tingled, and she smiled her first genuine, unforced smile in weeks.

At 10:00 p.m. the crowd was all drinkers, and Josie joined Derek behind the bar. Though they had their designated roles, the Bistrot staff functioned as a collective to keep things running, pitching in when and where they were needed.

A couple from the neighborhood offered Josie their condolences.

"Thanks guys. I appreciate it." Their names were Javier and Daniel, and no one knew for certain which was which. They were the same physical type, bearded and bespectacled, slim-fit, colorful shirts stretched over lean torsos with zero body fat. And they each had a signature drink—one a Bulleit Manhattan, hold the fruit, the other a Boodles martini with two olives. They traveled frequently, so while they'd been coming to Bistrot on and off for years, there was not enough continuity to keep their names straight. People referred to them instead by their drink orders. To make matters more confusing, they'd swapped cocktails a few years back, the one now known as Boodles having decided the brown liquors were making him fat at the same time Bulleit decided gin gave him terrible dreams.

"How did everything go in New Hampshire?" Bulleit asked, surprising Josie with the specificity of his knowledge.

"You know how these things are." In fact, she knew nothing of his experience with funerals. "Bittersweet, exhausting, glad it's over, and wish it had never been in the first place."

"Did the boyfriend go with you?" Boodles plucked an olive off its toothpick and bit it in half.

Josie squinted at him. "Um, no, on account of there is no boyfriend...."

They gasped and talked over each other.

"You broke up?!"

"We love you together!"

"Oh, honey!" they said in unison.

"Fellas, I think you have me confused with someone else," she said, pouring herself a seltzer from the soda gun. "I'm thoroughly single."

"What happened?" Bulleit whispered, gesturing with his head to the left side of the bar, where Derek chatted with a customer.

Josie laughed. "Derek? He's not my boyfriend! He's like my brother!"

The men looked at each other, crestfallen.

"Impossible," Boodles said, shaking his head.

"You two are so great together," Bulleit said. "So much chemistry!"

"And you laugh a lot."

"Well, that's because we're good friends," Josie said, putting the conversation to rest. "Period. Never been anything else."

This was a lie. When Josie and Derek had first started working together six years earlier, they'd bonded easily over a shared love of jazz, old movies, and spicy food—all things Nanette had introduced her to. Derek was smart and well-read, and Josie was as taken with his mind as she was his disheveled good looks and crooked smile. He was a writer who had optioned two screenplays in the years before they'd met for a modest but respectable sum of money. He'd let her read them, and she was impressed. She loved people who could create things.

Their nascent friendship soon devolved into a slew of boozy late nights and sleepovers. Neither was looking for a relationship. Josie was twenty-six and hadn't been in the city long. Derek was thirty and, she soon realized, had his share of admirers.

Things ground to a halt the night she finished her shift and entered the bar to find a tan blonde in a short denim skirt sitting in her seat.

"Josie," Derek stammered when he saw her. "Look who came in to surprise me! Kate's in town."

His cadence suggested he'd told her about Kate. He hadn't. And though she knew they weren't bound for longevity, this wouldn't do, the Kates of the world stopping by, so she broke things off. When Derek told her there was something different happening, that he felt a real connection to Josie, she squelched the conversation.

"Methinks the lady doth protest, etcetera," Boodles said.

Bulleit nodded in agreement, and Josie moved on to tend to another customer.

Later she relayed the conversation to Derek with a laugh that sounded forced to her own ears. He smiled and nodded, but withheld commentary, so Josie kept babbling.

"Boodles was on the verge of tears. And Bulleit was trying to be stoic, but you could tell he was really rooting for us crazy kids."

"They're good men, those two. I like them."

"I like them, too, even if they have wild imaginations."

"Not that wild."

"They don't need to know about our sordid past."

"Christ," Derek said when the front door opened. "Trinkets."

The Trinkets were a trio of girls in their early twenties, one of whom was in feverish pursuit of Derek and had not learned the subtleties of the dance. They traveled in a pack, and for a while Josie couldn't tell them apart either. Now she knew one had a tiny nose ring, one a bad complexion covered up by too much spackle, and the third—the girl who liked Derek—had exceptionally long eyelashes. With their matching dark jeans, metallic heels, and tiny purses, they looked like characters in a sitcom about New York written by and for people who'd never lived in New York. They wore copious amounts of body and face glitter, which had led to their nickname. To Josie they looked like sparkly trifles.

Derek's girl pouted as she scanned the bar for seats. The one with the bad complexion methodically applied lip gloss, and the nose ring puffed up her chest and chomped on gum in an effort to attract the attention of a couple of Wall Street guys drinking tequila.

Eventually Derek's girl elbowed her way to the corner of the bar and looked at his back as he rang up a tab.

"What can I get you, hon?" Josie asked, sliding a couple of coasters toward her. By this time of night the glitter from her eyeshadow or lip gloss had migrated across her face, giving her the appearance of a sexy alien.

"Oh, hi, Josie." Flustered and disappointed, she couldn't come up with a drink order.

Josie turned toward another customer who was snapping his fingers and waving a twenty-dollar bill over the bar. "Aren't you charming," she muttered as she fixed him a scotch on the rocks.

When she looked back, the Trinkets were colluding. The spackled one looked worried.

"We're out of Mandarin," Derek called over his shoulder, disappearing through the trap door like the Wicked Witch of the West.

"Are we really moving that much orange-flavored vodka?"

"Josie?" Derek's Trinket squeaked in her breathy, little girl voice. A speck of glitter hovered dangerously close to her eye.

"Do you know what you want?" Josie asked, a bit more warmly now.

"Three Cosmos please?"

The Cosmopolitan had been made famous by *Sex and the City*—likely required viewing for the Trinkets—and was exactly the kind of drink Derek loathed making. Josie didn't mind drinking them, but making them on a crowded night in a busy bar was another matter. She felt compassion for the girl as she mixed a batch of drinks. She'd fumbled her way through her twenties too. This girl was harmless. If Derek had a fling with her, it would never last.

When she slid the glasses across the bar, the Trinket over-tipped, looked around longingly, and retreated.

Derek returned, bottle of Absolut Mandarin in hand. "Thanks, sister. I owe you one."

"Be nice," Josie said, ducking under the bar. "Yours isn't actually that bad."

"Mine?"

Curtis jogged down the staircase from the restrooms. "Train in fifteen?" They lived off the same subway line in Brooklyn and often left together.

"Okay. Did you see anyone go into the ladies' room?"

"Yah, some young thang."

Josie took a deep breath and headed upstairs. The Trinket with the spackle was at the sink stubbing out a cigarette. Smoking was still allowed in designated areas in New York City bars and restaurants. The ladies' room was not one of them. She looked startled at being caught.

"I'm sorry—I wasn't—"

Josie waved her away. "Just go outside next time, okay? You could get us in a lot of trouble."

The girl ran the faucet to rinse the ashes from the sink. "Bye, Jody!" she said, scurrying out the door.

Josie shook her head. She untangled her hair and wiped the smudges of liner from her lids. "Jody," she muttered, ignoring the fact that she didn't know the girl's name either. "Get my name straight, girl."

"*Josie*," someone said quietly, then followed it with a giggle.

Josie spun around. The room was empty.

Chapter Two

JOSIE SETTLED INTO a new phase of mourning, a quiet resignation made bearable by the crew at Bistrot. The comfort she derived from them, though, was offset by the unwelcome visitor—or visitors—she'd encountered her first night back, no matter how vehemently she tried to shut down those thoughts. Her ability to do so had taken time and practice all those years ago, and she was rusty. She remained on high alert, and while she wished it were Nanette coming to visit, she knew, somehow, that it wasn't.

Wednesday and Thursday passed without incident, and by Friday her fear had dissipated. The bar filled quickly after dinner service ended, and the right-hand corner held its usual core—Curtis, Johnny the sous-chef, Sam, and Sylvie.

Sylvie was a regular who had lived across the street from the restaurant for decades. She'd regaled everyone with tales of her years as a burlesque dancer and a magician's assistant "back in the day"—though which day she meant was anyone's guess.

The restaurant had changed hands several times in the years she'd been a fixture there, beginning with Dave's Continental in the early seventies, then Ménage, a fondue spot—which Josie and Derek were certain had been one giant key party—and finally *Blush!*, complete with italics and punctuation, a pioneer of the nouvelle cuisine that plagued New York in the eighties. Chef took over the lease in 1989, and later that year Bistrot opened.

Several nights a week, Sylvie sat at the bar drinking champagne. Since the beginning of the year, it had become clear that her memory was slipping. It started small, mixing up people's names, forgetting whether she'd paid her bill. But lately it had grown more extreme. She'd begun to confuse Bistrot with the space's earlier iterations, asking after staff members no one had heard of, ordering items that were never on the menu. She mistook strangers for friends, which led to awkward exchanges.

Outwardly the change was more dramatic. A woman who had always put great effort into her appearance, meticulous lips and lashes, platinum hair shiny and styled, she now shuffled around with a missed button or lipstick on her teeth. Tonight her hair hung limp and dull.

"Poor thing. She's getting worse," Josie said. She sat at the other end of the bar talking to Derek.

"Yeah, she's changing fast."

"It makes me so sad. Not that everything doesn't right now. Is that the Oregon Pinot?"

He pulled two glasses from the rack and filled them. "To Nanette," he said, raising a toast.

"To Nanette." Josie's eyes filled. "I'm sorry."

"For what?"

"For being so weepy."

"Josie, you just lost your grandmother! Stop apologizing for crying. Come on!"

"It feels self-indulgent. As far as deaths go, it was pretty much what one would hope for. An elderly woman slips away in her sleep with her loved ones around. We got to say goodbye. It's not a tragedy."

"I'm pretty sure the death of a loved one is, by definition, a tragedy."

"You know what I mean."

"Of course. There are more senseless deaths. Another NYU kid just leapt out of his dorm a few weeks ago. That's textbook tragic. But Nanette was your anchor, and that's huge. That's life-changing. You're supposed to be heartbroken."

"There are just so many layers to it all." Her voice caught. She twirled her glass on the bar and watched the wine spin.

"Talk to me."

"One of the things I can't stop thinking about is how awful her birthday was."

"What happened?"

"Ready for this one? Columbine."

"Jesus, that's right," Derek said. "April twentieth."

April 20, 1999 was Nanette's last birthday. It was also the day of the deadliest school shooting in history, which occurred in Derek's home state of Colorado.

"I was with her that day," Josie said.

"I remember when you went up."

"We brought her an orchid." Josie bit her thumbnail. "And red velvet cake, her favorite. And once my mom and I realized what was going on, we kept the news off, kept the TV on the classic movie channel so she could see all her old pals. So, it's not like she was aware that those sociopaths ruined her birthday. Those sociopaths who had assault rifles. How the hell does that happen?"

"It's a broken world."

"The most tragic day in modern history, and it was her last birthday."

"It was also Hitler's birthday."

"Why do you know that?"

"Because—listen, I owe you some kind of apology."

"For?"

"For not being there for you when it was all going down."

"It's fine, Derek. I was out of town."

"No, it's not fine. I should have checked in with you. Hell, I should have kept you company while you packed. You would have done that for me. For any of us. I should have taken you to the train—"

"Bus."

"Ouch."

"Yeah, insult with a side of injury. But whatever, the bus is direct, I didn't need to change, blah blah blah. Anyway honey, it's okay. You're here for me now. And Jesus, maybe that horrible day will be what finally makes this country stop with the self-serving interpretation of the second amendment."

"Maybe. Look, I have a weird relationship with death and grief."

"I think that's pretty normal. Don't you?" She hadn't known Derek to have any relationship with death and grief. In the six years they'd been close it had rarely come up.

He swirled his glass while he thought. "This is tough to talk about, so I don't. I know." He held up a hand. "That's not healthy, but it's what I've done my whole life. My coping mechanism."

Josie's mind ran through dozens of grisly scenarios.

"I had a brother." He exhaled sharply and looked at her. "He died before I was born."

"Oh my God, Derek! How come you never—" Josie caught herself taking it personally and switched gears. "I'm sorry."

"Thank you. I am, too. And now that you're going through this, I'm sorry I never talked about him. It was just always easier not to."

"What was his name?"

Before he could answer, Sylvie doddered over with an empty champagne flute. Derek looked relieved.

"Good evening, beautiful!" he said, his deep, rich voice spinning the phrase into a lyric. Long before Josie met him, Derek had another brief career doing voiceovers until he decided it wasn't for him. It was lucrative, though, and it baffled her that he'd given it up. It also baffled her that he didn't do more with his writing. And now what baffled her most was the fact that he'd kept his brother from her for so many years. She couldn't imagine harboring a secret of this magnitude for over half a decade. She told him everything.

"Can I get you a refill?" he asked Sylvie.

"No, I think I'd better call it a night. What do I owe you?"

"Nothing, Sylvie. On the house."

"Well thank you, David!"

People had stopped correcting her. She handed him a fifty-dollar bill. "Will you break this? I am allowed to tip, aren't I?" She gave Josie a wink. They often went through this routine.

"If you must, Sylvie."

"Was Maria here earlier? I thought I saw Maria," she asked Josie.

"I don't think I know Maria."

Sylvie laughed. "Of course you do! She works here!"

The lashes on her left eye had come unglued and now hovered over her eyeball like a bent windshield wiper. With her red lipstick caked on heavily and her powdery skin, she reminded Josie of Norma Desmond or Baby Jane.

"I don't think she's here," Josie said gently.

Derek handed over her change, and Sylvie returned it to her pocketbook without leaving a tip. She started to say something then abruptly stopped, looking around the room as though seeing it for the first time.

"Sylvie?" Derek asked.

Her eyes focused again. "All right, then, have a lovely night!" she said.

They watched her leave.

"Oh boy," Josie said.

"I know. I love that kooky dame. Maybe Maria is another one of Andy's invisible hires."

"So. Your brother."

"My brother."

Josie had a dozen questions but waited for him to speak.

"I guess the reason I—" He looked up and blanched. Josie felt someone behind her.

"Hey man!" Derek said. "Josie, I could use a bar back."

This was their code for forgetting a customer's name. Josie turned and her stomach lurched.

"Patrick!" she said, heat shooting up her neck to her face. "You're back!"

Patrick Moore was a photographer from Los Angeles who'd spent the previous summer in New York teaching at The New School. Curtis had referred to him as "so handsome it hurts," and no one had argued. He was in his mid-forties and stood six feet two inches tall with jet-black hair, deep brown eyes, perpetual five o'clock shadow, and a half-sleeve of tattoos. He also, much to Josie's chagrin and Derek's amusement, had a business card that listed him as *Photographer & Bon Vivant*.

And on his last night in New York the previous August, he had taken Josie on a late-night motorcycle ride that ended with a highly charged kiss on the Brooklyn Heights promenade before she insisted on going home alone in a taxi. That he rode a Triumph Bonneville was another source of amusement for Derek, who called it "the mid-life crisis mobile." Josie didn't care. She knew nothing about motorcycles, and when you looked like Patrick Moore you could make a milk truck look dangerous.

Now he stood next to her smelling of musk and cigarettes, helmet under his arm, leather jacket damp from the rain.

"Hey baby," he said with a gravelly voice that almost gave Derek's a run for its money. He nodded to Derek. "Good to see you, man."

"Are you here for the summer?" Josie's voice rose an octave.

"I am." He pulled out the stool next to hers and sat, resting his wet helmet on the bar. Derek looked at it. "Was hoping I'd find *you* here."

"I'm here!" Josie said.

"I see that."

"Do you want a drink?"

"Sure." He turned to Derek. "What kind of gin do you have, man?"

"The usual suspects." He gestured to the shelf behind him. While Patrick studied them, Derek gave Josie a loaded look. He was not a fan. She'd made the mistake of broadcasting what had happened the previous summer, and reactions had varied.

"All right. Tanqueray, rocks, little bit of soda, splash of bitters, two limes."

"What color umbrella?" Derek asked. He laughed, and Patrick joined in. Josie's face flushed again. "Josie, another Pinot?"

"Actually? That sounds good. I'll have what he's having."

"You want to switch to gin? Now?"

"Yes."

She felt for Patrick. It was tough to infiltrate the Bistrot family. The scrutiny was relentless.

Derek picked up the near-empty bottle of Tanqueray. Whistling a bar of a song Josie didn't recognize, he descended to the liquor room.

Patrick leaned in and planted a kiss on her lips. His stubble scraped her cheek. He tasted of cigarettes and something sweet and botanic… gin. It had been years since she'd had gin. "I've thought about you a lot since last year," he said.

"That's nice to hear." That she didn't believe him didn't matter. He was here now, and he was as beautiful as she remembered.

Maybe this was what she needed, something to distract her from her grief. A clean slate who didn't know anything about her but what she chose to present. She could feign levity. She could have a no-strings-attached fling, and she could, when they were together, pretend nothing was wrong in her world. She could escape the burden of sadness. She could take a break from mourning. She could be carefree.

"How've you been?"

"My grandmother died." She closed her eyes.

"Ah," he said with a sound that managed to convey kindness and sympathy. "I'm sorry, baby."

"Thank you. We were very close."

He took her hand between his. On his wrist was a blue-and-black Patek Philippe chronograph watch that wasn't there the previous summer. She would have noticed—her father wore one. It was one of the few of his possessions she could vividly picture.

She looked up at him. "Sorry. That was a pretty weighty answer to your question."

Derek returned and began mixing their drinks, back rigid.

"Nah, it was an honest answer. I appreciate that, baby."

Derek's shoulders tensed.

Josie looked back at Patrick. "Well, anyway, how was your year?"

"My year was great, but I missed this town. And you."

"Enjoy, kids." Derek dropped two lime wedges in each glass and slid them across the bar. When Patrick reached for his wallet, he waved him off. "Welcome back, man."

"Right on."

Josie appreciated Derek's decency. He may have mixed feelings about Patrick, but he knew the right way to do things. He walked down the bar to where the Trinkets had materialized.

Patrick lifted his glass, saluted Derek's retreating back, then toasted Josie. "To your grandma."

"To Nanette."

They sipped their drinks. Josie had a hard time holding eye contact with him.

"So," she began at the same time he started talking. She acquiesced.

"It really is good to be back in this crazy town." He pulled her barstool closer to his and put his legs on either side of hers. "I was hoping you'd still be here. You seeing anyone?"

"I'm not. Are you?"

"Just you now." He took her hand again. "Should we make a move out of here after this drink?"

It was abrupt, but it was late, and she could think of no compelling reason not to.

Chapter Three

❧

FOR A MOMENT on waking, Josie had no recollection to whom the warm body pressed against her back belonged. Then she saw the Patek Philippe on the nightstand, and her stomach fluttered. Disjointed images from the night before flashed through her mind—wearing Patrick's helmet and holding his waist as they sped uptown to Chelsea in the rain, a quick nightcap—more gin—at his local bar, staggering up a flight of stairs, and making out on his landing, fumbling with his belt buckle. Her face flushed. She needed to buy better underwear. She needed to get back to the gym.

"Good morning." His breath against her ear gave her goosebumps.

It was past 9:00 a.m., and Josie had to be at Bistrot in an hour. After extracting herself from the tangle of sheets and Patrick's efforts to keep her there, she collected her clothes from the floor and went into the bathroom. She squeezed his toothpaste onto her finger and swished it around in her mouth, wiping at the smudges under her eyes. A copy of *Vanity Fair* sat on the back of the toilet, and flipping through it, she found a fragrance sample—Allure by Chanel. She tore it out and rubbed it on the insides of her wrists and the back of her neck, shoving the rest of the card into her purse.

Patrick was in the kitchen grinding coffee beans, wearing a pair of grey track pants and no shirt. She glanced at his bare torso and blushed.

"Want some coffee, babe?"

"I can't really stay. I have to get to brunch."

"Ah. Brunch," he said, abandoning his project and putting his hands on her waist. "You smell good."

She tried to channel Mia's easy smile.

"You working tonight?" he asked.

"I am."

He walked her to the front door. "Then I'll see you later." He leaned in for a kiss.

She was glad she'd refreshed her mouth. His breath smelled now of stale cigarettes, and she winced but kissed him back. "Back out into the lovely weather."

"Looks like it's not doing anything yet." Patrick looked through the windows across the room. "I dig the rain. Love the melancholy beauty, the flat light. Reminds me of London."

"I've never been to London."

"Great town. You'd love it. Maybe I'll take you someday."

It was just talk, but it was the right thing to say to put Josie in a good mood on her walk to work.

There was a light mist in the air, and deep gray clouds painted the sky. Patrick's sublet was on 22nd Street between Ninth and Tenth Avenues. Bistrot was on Ninth Street east of Sixth Avenue. Josie calculated her walk and the movement of the clouds and figured she could make it before the rain really came down.

She walked east, admiring the old New York architecture, brownstones and townhouses dripping with ivy and lilac wisteria. Focusing on her surroundings helped stave off the inevitable headache threatening to penetrate her mood. She'd forgotten her sunglasses, and even the dim light was bright to her. On Eighth Avenue she ducked into a bodega and bought an extra-large iced coffee, sweet and light, a portable umbrella, and a packet of Advil, which she swallowed preemptively.

In the mile-long walk the caffeine set in, her headache was thwarted, and she replayed the night. The spontaneity of it gave her a surge of adrenaline, made her feel alive in a way that had eluded her for ages, since long before Nanette's death. Maybe even since her night with Patrick the previous summer. It had not been an exhilarating year. She'd had a few dates of little consequence, but no one as intriguing as Patrick. No one she was pretty sure she wanted to see again. Patrick was a man, not a guy. Guys were still figuring themselves out, works in progress. Men knew themselves. Even the not great ones, like her father.

"Umbrella, lady?"

A street vendor called to her from the edge of the sidewalk. She held up the umbrella she'd just bought but looked at his wares. On his table were racks of sunglasses and a sign with *$5/each* crossed out, and *$3/each* written beneath. Sunglasses would be a tough sell in an overcast, rainy summer. She caught sight of her face in the mirror the vendor had rigged and was mortified Patrick had seen her that way—bloodshot eyes, cheeks puffy and creased with sheet marks. She pulled three crumpled bills from her purse and chose an oversized pair of faux tortoise shells.

By the time she turned the corner toward the restaurant, the rain and wind picked up and blew her umbrella inside out. She tucked it into a trash can and walked inside.

Saturdays at Bistrot began with a pitcher of Bloody Marys before it was time to start prep. Josie took a seat across a table from Curtis.

"Enough with this fucking rain." He held a sweating glass of ice water to his forehead.

"It's too much, man," Derek said. "Trains are all screwed up."

"I'm sick of wet clothes. Everything's wet. Wet shoes, wet socks. I feel like Aquaman. If Aquaman were black. And gay. Actually, he might be gay."

"I'm gonna need to get an umbrella if this doesn't stop," Sam said.

Curtis shot him a look. He had little patience for Sam.

"I kind of like the rain," Josie said, and they all noticed her for the first time. "It's melancholy."

"Good morning, sunshine." Curtis eyed her carefully.

She gave him a wan smile.

He reached over and pulled at the lapel of her rain jacket. "You wore that top yesterday!"

Derek glanced up, then resumed slicing lemons. Josie lowered her glasses and squinted at Curtis.

"The walk of shame! You go girl."

Derek cleared his throat.

Curtis pointed to him and raised his eyebrows.

"God no!" Josie said. "Don't be daft."

"Tell me!"

She waved him off and sipped her coffee.

"Lady!"

Derek put his paring knife down. "Jesus, I'll tell him. Patrick Moore's back in town."

"Holy shit! You go, girl!" Curtis held his hand up for a high five, which Josie refused.

Derek stirred the life out of a fresh pitcher of Bloody Marys.

"What's with the shades?" Curtis asked. "You as hungover as I am?"

"Just a bit."

"No kidding," Derek said. "Who'd have guessed red wine and gin were a bad combo?"

"Hair of the dog, lady." Curtis handed her his glass. "I'm on my second."

"People." Andy emerged from the back and clapped his hands. Josie jumped. "Derek, those better not be strong."

"Just strong enough. You want?"

Andy grimaced and hopped up to sit on a table. "Everyone listen up. We have a couple things to discuss." He held up a wine glass with *Bistrot* engraved in bold, Art Deco font. "One, what is this?"

"A Burgundy glass!" someone shouted.

He sighed. "Fine, but the answer I'm looking for is simply 'wine glass.'"

"Riveting," Curtis said.

Andy held the glass up again. "How full are these supposed to be?"

Silence spread over the crowd.

Sam raised his hand. "Above the B?"

"That's the problem, people. That is the problem. Derek can't pour every single glass of wine we move, and you people are acting like aggressive prom dates. No wonder the coatroom is full of forgotten jackets and umbrellas."

Josie looked over to the coat room. Mia, who was not required at meetings, had just arrived. She waved, and Josie smiled back.

"Between the bumps. Josie, you listening? Between the bumps of the B. That's how full the glass should be, that's how full the glass should always have been."

Curtis slurped the remnants of his drink through its straw and asked aloud for another.

Andy sighed again. "Really, is this a difficult concept?"

"Nope." Curtis leaned his head into his hands. "Loud and clear, Andreas."

"Andy."

"Okay, Andreas. Maybe you should add sommelier to your list of new hires."

"Don't antagonize him!" Josie whispered, taking a sip of Curtis's fresh cocktail.

"But it's so easy," he said under his breath.

"Two, we will be open tomorrow to maximize profit potential."

"On the Fourth of July?!" Curtis shrieked.

"Dude, that's un-American!" one of the line cooks protested.

"People! I know this is not the norm, but neither is this summer. This won't be the usual BBQ-at-the-beach holiday folks are used to, so we're going to offer a festive alternative. Now listen. I don't need all of you, so I'm asking for volunteers to work, and anyone who does will get a holiday bonus."

Every hand in the room shot up.

"Good. Because I do need all of you. We have a lot of covers already."

The front door burst open and in flew Chef, wearing a bike helmet—he navigated the city exclusively by bicycle regardless of weather—and carrying his front wheel. He was drenched, his glasses fogged over, his eyes obscured.

"Chef!" Andy leapt off the table. "Here, let me help you." He grabbed a bar towel and dabbed at his boss.

"Kiss ass," Curtis muttered.

"Let me get this! Did you see the bit in Dining In last week about the—" Andy's voice trailed off as he followed Chef into the dining room, where he dripped rain onto the wooden floor, then up the back staircase to the kitchen.

Mario and another porter ran down the steps with a mop. They were used to this.

Curtis grabbed Josie's hand. "Patrick Moore," he said, drawing out the syllables. "Tell me absolutely everything."

"Absolutely not!" She took another sip of his drink and slid her chair back. "I'm going to make myself presentable."

"You're gorgeous. Isn't she gorgeous, Derek?"

Derek gave her a perfunctory glance and nodded. "Sure."

Josie climbed the stairs to the ladies' room. In daylight it was easier to block the fears that lurked in the shadows.

She frowned at her reflection, tapping her cheeks to will some color into them and tracing her lips with the remnant of a mauve pencil that had melted into itself in her makeup bag. She pulled out her neglected eyelash curler and leaned into the mirror. Invisible fingers ruffled the fine hairs on the back of her neck. In the split-second before the door opened, she yelped.

"Sorry, Josie!" Mia laughed easily. "I didn't mean to startle you."

"You didn't—" Josie clutched the neckline of her blouse. "Sorry, I'm wound a little tight today."

She studied Mia while they primped. They were about the same age, she guessed, and the same height, five foot seven, but Mia was willowy, waiflike, where Josie had curves. Mia's hair was caramel colored, long and wavy, and unlike Josie's, seemingly impervious to the effects of rain and humidity. Everything about Mia was lighter—her skin, her hair, her style. She wore vintage flawlessly, looking like she'd walked off the pages of 1970-something *Vogue*. The same clothes would make Josie look and feel as though she were dressed for a costume party. Today Mia had on a sleeveless minidress the color of avocado flesh and her shiny white rain boots. Gold bangles adorned each wrist, and hoop earrings dangled from her lobes. It was a stark contrast to Josie, who'd taken to shielding herself in black pants and button-down shirts. It had been like this since Nanette's death, ironic since Nanette was always neatly dressed, never left the house without lipstick, and even on her deathbed had perfectly manicured, pale pink nails. Josie looked down at her own ragged, bitten nails. If Patrick Moore was going to be around, she'd need to step up her beauty game. She caught Mia's eyes in the mirror.

"That lipstick's pretty on you," Mia said.

"Thank you." It was a start.

"For what it's worth, girl." Mia's bangles jingled as she blotted her glossy lips with a paper towel. "This one feels like a gentle spirit."

"What?" Josie's throat felt dry.

Mia smiled, not fooled. "I sense them, too."

She patted her arm and walked back out. Josie stared at herself for a beat, then quickly followed.

Saturday brunches could be slow in summer. Despite the weather, the New Yorkers who comprised Bistrot's regulars were still leaving town on weekends, heading to the Hamptons, Fire Island, or the mountains north of the city. This left a clientele of tourists who refused to let the rain dampen their New York experience. Utterly distracted by thoughts of Patrick, and partially distracted by Derek's dead brother, Josie weathered the small talk.

"Sure is a wet one out there!" crowed a ruddy midwestern dad with a perky wife and three sullen teenagers in tow. The man squeezed into the coatroom with Mia and helped himself to hangers. What would have made Josie irritable and claustrophobic, Mia accepted with grace, thanking him for his assistance. Perhaps her Southern roots made her better equipped to handle things politely.

Josie didn't suffer overbearing men easily. She walked the family to a large table and distributed their menus.

"So, what's good here, young lady?" the man asked.

"Everything." Josie's stomach growled. She'd neglected to eat staff dinner the previous night, and breakfast had consisted of iced coffee and sips of Bloody Mary. On the plus side, her clothes were starting to fit better on the grief diet. "All of our produce is from the local farmer's market, and the meat is grass—"

"How's the traitor?"

"The what?"

"The traitor!"

"Dad!" One of the teenagers rolled his heavily lined eyes. "He means the eggs Benedict."

"Clever. Popular choice."

"And the ricotta pancakes?" asked the mother.

"Also excellent." Josie's stomach growled again.

"What's this duck confit hash and poached eggs all about?" the man asked, mispronouncing "confit."

"Well, it's two of our organic, free-range eggs...."

"Organic! You like that, Megan!" the mother said to the oldest kid, who was busy scraping off her nail polish and looking like she wanted to be anywhere but there.

Josie felt for her. "You know what. I'm going to go find your server. He can tell you all about brunch." She wended her way back through the dining room to find Curtis. "A veritable cornucopia of questions at table seventeen."

"Oh dear. Can you give them to Sam? I'm buzzed."

"Too late. They're harmless. Chatty parents and sullen youth." She walked into the bar and poured herself a glass of water.

Derek was trickling prosecco into flutes of orange juice. "Mimosa?"

"Maybe later." She watched him pour and considered how to restart the conversation.

He looked up. "So."

"So."

"His name was Alex. Alex Benjamin Magnus, named after my mom's dad."

"That's a nice name."

"By all accounts he was a nice kid."

"What happened?"

"Hold that thought." He nodded toward the front door. "Customers."

Josie spent the next twenty minutes greeting and seating diners, Alex Benjamin Magnus never far from her thoughts. She was anxious to get back to Derek.

Patience.

The word came out of the ether in the same voice that had whispered her name her first night back, and needles ran up Josie's spine and neck. It was a female voice, so not Derek's brother. When she caught herself trying to apply rational thought to irrational circumstances, she shook her head.

"I'm losing my mind," she muttered, garnering a curious look from a passing diner.

When at last there was a lull, she went back to Derek. "You know, I think I will have a mimosa. Will you join me? Not too strong."

"Just strong enough." He pulled the bottle from the ice trough and poured their drinks.

"To Alex Benjamin Magnus," Josie said, raising her glass.

"To Alex." He touched his glass to hers and took a sip, then placed it on the bar. He exhaled a puff of air. "He made it to eight."

"Eight?"

"Years old."

"Oh, Jesus!"

"Yeah. Riding his bike one night, and a fucking drunk driver took him out."

"Oh!" Josie clapped her hand over her mouth. "The poor little guy!"

"I know. It's awful. And the fucker got off on a technicality. Here's the real fucked up part. My parents thought the only way to get over their grief was to have another kid."

"Wow."

"Yep. I'm the replacement."

"You are *so* much more than that, my love!"

"I know that. But it was a total mind-fuck to live in my dead brother's shadow from the day I was born. And it was a hell of a shadow. He was this amazing kid, so handsome. Blonde curly hair, smiling in every picture you see of him except the baseball ones. He took baseball really seriously." Derek smiled, his eyes focused on a spot in the distance.

"I can't believe you never told me before!" Josie knew it was unfair, but it nagged at her that he hadn't shared any of this in the hours of conversations they'd had about nearly everything. She wondered what other secrets he held.

He was lost in thought, looking at his hands now. They were calloused from years of hoisting kegs and cases and wielding tools. Derek was the go-to when something in the building needed quick fixing. His biceps had gotten bigger, his shoulders broader. Manual labor suited him well. "I'm sorry."

"For what?" she asked more brusquely than she should have.

"For commandeering your grief."

"Please, take it. I don't want it."

Finally, he looked at her. "I know you don't. It's enormous, and what scares me is the examples I grew up with made it seem like it'll never get better. It impacted everything I did, this second-hand grief that I couldn't escape. Living in my dead brother's shadow and mourning someone I loved but never knew. So, I made the decision a long time ago not to let this be part of my psyche. It's why I moved across the country as soon as I could. Not a happy household."

This Josie had known, but without detail. She knew Derek's father was a captain of industry married to his job, and his mother was, as he described it,

"Southern Gothic in the Rockies," prone to histrionics and booze. Now she understood why.

"So, I guess that's why your mom is so—"

"Fucked up?"

"I was going with emotional, but sure."

"Yep. I was born less than a year after he died, and it was way too soon. I was basically raised by the help and my older sister when she was around, which wasn't much. My earliest memories are of my mom lying in bed, shades drawn, bottle of something—vodka, usually—on the nightstand."

"That's dark."

"I can't blame her for grieving hard. Losing a kid has to be the worst thing in the world. It's why I never want one of my own. Or one of the reasons."

Josie shared a lack of desire to procreate, and she now better understood Derek's aversion to the idea. "Do you think about him a lot?"

He smiled spontaneously, but his eyes remained dark. "All the fucking time. I used to fight it, but I lost. So, I gave up. He was with me constantly as a kid. We celebrated his birthday every year and acknowledged the day he died. Which was April twentieth. That's why I know that date."

"What a hell of a thing for you when you were little."

"It was pretty grim. And I've tried really hard to move on from those days, so when the grief thing shows up, I retreat."

"I think next year we should go out and celebrate life on April twentieth. In honor of Nanette and Alex."

"All right, let's do that. I need to rewrite that day. It's funny, but every year when the anniversary rolls by, you're visiting Nanette."

"I had no idea."

"I know that. Because I didn't tell you early on, and then we got close, and it started to feel like it was too late. But maybe if it wasn't Nanette's birthday, and you were in New York every year, I would have told you sooner. It's a hard one for me. Because irrational as it sounds, I feel guilty."

"For what?"

"For living."

"Well, I'm glad you know that that's irrational, but as my Nanette used to say, how you feel is not up to you, how you respond is."

"She was a wise woman."

"Yes she was. And from now on, you and me, April twentieth, we will do something together in honor of her and Alex."

"Thanks, sister."

Josie stayed at the bar while Derek washed glasses and filled drink orders. The implication of her pledge to spend the day with him in the future was that they would still be in each other's lives, likely because they would still be at Bistrot. This was both comforting and depressing. There'd been little forward movement in her life for years. Derek, too. They were both smart, capable people who *should* want more out of life. It made sense now why Derek might be stuck in his job. It was safe, he was valued, it was the opposite of his childhood. Josie's own reasons lay just beneath the surface. The problem was, once she identified them, she'd have to conquer them.

"So, how's the *bon vivant*?" Derek asked. "Did he live up to his name?"

"He's a very nice guy."

"Nice? Uh oh. How inconvenient for you."

Josie smiled. "No one knows me better than you, babe. Not sure why this guy had to walk into my life."

"Of all the gin joints."

Josie held out her glass, and he refilled it, going lighter on the orange juice this time.

"Just be careful," he said. "You're a master at compartmentalizing your relationships."

"Meaning?"

"Meaning just that. The only friends of yours I know are the ones who work here. The only boyfriends I've met are the ones who sat here night after night. I don't get the sense that Patrick Moore is going to do that."

"He isn't. He has a life. And you might want to use the word 'boyfriend' more judiciously if you're referring to the guys I think you're referring to."

"Whatever you want to call them. It's going to be hard for me to get a sense of him, and you're going to be blinded by his looks, so be careful. You've been burned before."

"He is pretty hot, isn't he?"

"You know the answer to that. He's a good-looking guy. And you're fragile right now. I'm looking out for you."

"So, what about you? Are you the fourth Trinket?"

He smiled. "Cute."

"Did you get your honorary tube of glitter?"

"All right, the glitter's a lot."

"They're like bowerbirds. You know what a bowerbird is?"

He chuckled. "Yes. But Alison's a sweetheart. And she's funny. Witty."

"Alison. I thought it was Amanda."

"Amanda's the short one."

"And the nose ring?"

"Danielle." He frowned. "Noelle?"

"Did you sleep with her?"

"With Noelle?"

"Come on."

"You come on. I'm not asking you for details."

"Well, the answer's yes."

"Brilliant. Anyway, she's a good girl."

"As long as you're having fun. And she's not distracting you from other things."

"Such as?"

"Such as your writing!"

"My what? That's in the past. I used to be a writer who tended bar. Now I'm a bartender who kind of likes to write."

"Don't you mean mixologist?"

"Absolutely not."

"Well, I wish you would start writing again because you are supremely talented."

"Thanks for that. And what about you?"

"What about me?"

"What do you really want to do?"

"I don't know." No one had asked her that in a very long time.

"First thing that comes to mind."

"Seriously?" Josie set her glass on the bar. "I think, if I could do anything, off the top of my head…." She paused and considered her response.

"Yeah, you're not so good at this first-thing-that-comes-to-mind thing."

"Well, that's because I haven't given it enough thought, and I'm mad at myself for that."

"Why are you mad at yourself?"

"Because instead of just treading water here for years, I should have been figuring out what I want to do. But I haven't. Maybe I need to move somewhere else, reinvent myself."

"Josie, I can't think of any place better than New York City to do that. It's not going to be easier in some small town or new city where you don't know anyone. But what other industry do you see yourself in?"

"None. I guess I have this crazy fantasy of owning a place someday."

"What's crazy or fantastical about that?"

"Well, going back to the topic of challenging mothers, mine finds this industry frivolous. And it's been long enough that I've started to believe her. We're not curing diseases or saving lives."

"I don't know. We're not curing diseases, but we're feeding people and giving them a place to socialize. So, we're improving lives, and hell, maybe we're curing loneliness. We live in a fucked-up world. Sharing a meal is one of the joys of living. To me, anyway."

"My mom wanted me to be an elementary school teacher."

"Jesus, that does not sound like you at all."

"Thank you. It isn't. But here's the worst part—"

Derek interrupted her. "Hey, you!" he said, his voice stripped of its rawness and cynicism. "What's going on?"

It was Alison, sporting neither glitter nor heels, with an attractive, middle-aged couple in tow. She wore a short red dress and black flats, and Josie noticed that she had very nice legs.

"Hi," she said in her breathy little girl voice. "Derek, these are my parents, Bill and Ellen. And this is Josie."

Josie plastered a smile on her face.

"Ellen, Bill, great to meet you!" Derek sounded like a game show host. Of course he greeted the mom first, the kind of detail that made women love him. "You're joining us for brunch?" He came around the bar and shook their hands. "I'll seat them, Josie."

He walked them into the dining room and Josie went behind the bar to retrieve the pack of cigarettes usually stashed there, abandoned by a bar patron some recent night. She'd never been a regular smoker, but every now and then the craving hit.

"What are you doing Miss Thing?" Curtis, who was vehemently anti-smoking, intercepted her.

"Is sudden irritability one of the stages of grief?"

"Could be. Or maybe you're irritated because people are terrible."

"Not all of them."

Josie stood outside under the awning watching the rain fall on the darkened pavement. A wet newspaper lay helpless in the middle of Ninth Street, turning pulpier with every tire that ran over it. She felt sorry for it. It was the perfect metaphor for something she couldn't name.

The humidity made lighting a match challenging. When she finally did, she took a deep, satisfying pull off her cigarette.

She didn't like the sudden feeling of angst that gripped her. It served no purpose other than to kick the intensity of her grief up a few notches. She resented that she and Derek were finally having a real conversation, the kind they used to have all the time, and it had been interrupted. By Alison. And maybe that was part of her irritability. She was going through something enormous, and Derek was running around with a Trinket when he should have been spending time with her. That's what you did when your close friends were grieving. She wasn't jealous, she was annoyed.

"Ugh," she said aloud.

"Hey, girl."

Josie startled. She hadn't heard Mia come outside. "Hi there," she said, then added, "I don't really smoke."

"I'm not judging." Mia skipped up the three stone steps to the sidewalk and stood in the rain, her face to the sky. "I love this!" she said. She closed her eyes, twirling like a little girl.

"Me, too." Something resembling serotonin kicked in, from the brunch drinks and lack of sleep, and Josie decided she liked rain after all. She rested her cigarette in an ashtray on one of the small patio tables and joined Mia on the sidewalk.

"In New Orleans it rains all summer long, these amazing flash thunderstorms."

"My kind of town!" Josie raised her voice to be heard over the rain, which was falling harder by the moment.

"Hey, are you working on Monday?" Mia asked.

"Well, no, we're closed."

"Let's get together? Go shopping or something?"

Josie was not a shopper. She'd never done it well. But maybe Mia's feedback was what she needed, and she'd certainly welcome the company. She'd been dreading having a day off. "Will you teach me your ways?"

Mia laughed. "I don't think you need me to, but I'll do my best."

Derek poked his head out the front door. "What are you doing up there without an umbrella, crazy lady!"

"We're doing a rain dance!" Josie said.

"Well, bring it inside. Phone's been ringing!"

They walked back down the steps, and Josie took a final pull off her cigarette before stubbing it out.

"You two have history," Mia said in the vestibule, a statement, not a question.

"Minor, and a long time ago. We're good friends. Period."

"I'm not so sure about that." Mia winked.

Chapter Four

❦

ON MONDAY, JOSIE rode the subway into Manhattan, utterly exhausted. Never had she fathomed how all-encompassing grief could be, how even in the moments that her mind and body were elsewhere, it hovered just out of sight, waiting to pounce. It was a strange and fascinating process. Those stages she'd read about were real, except they didn't come in stages. They came in waves in no particular order. Just that morning, in the shower, she'd said aloud, "I cannot believe you're gone!" And later, when the young woman who sold her an iced coffee upgraded her to a large for free, she sniffled, overwhelmed by this tiny act of kindness, and blamed it on allergies.

The most surprising aspect was a tenuous sense of relief. Losing Nanette had long been the worst thing she could imagine. In those last months she lived in constant fear of The Phone Call. Now that it had happened, it could never happen again. The worst day of her life had come and gone, and she'd survived.

She was on the precipice of friendship with Mia, who had a fair amount in common with Nanette. It was as though her grandmother had sent her from New Orleans to pick up where she'd left off and to try to convince Josie to accept her "gift." With the possibility of communicating with Nanette, she almost welcomed it. Almost.

Also fueling her emotions, Patrick hadn't shown up the night before as promised. Josie told herself she didn't care, that whenever they hung out again would be fine. It wouldn't. She was disappointed.

The day promised a break from the rain, and Mia was waiting on the designated corner of 11th Street and Greenwich Avenue. "Hey, girl!" she called when she saw Josie.

They greeted each other with a kiss on the cheek, then entered a vintage store Josie had passed hundreds of times. A sweet mustiness permeated the room, not unpleasant, but strong. The clothing was organized by category and decade.

Mia began rifling through a rack of dresses.

"I am way out of my element," Josie said. "Will you help me shop?"

"It'd be my pleasure." She set to work, feeling fabrics and checking labels, and pointed out a pale gold wrap dress. "This would be real pretty on you!"

"It looks like something you'd wear!"

"We're not shopping for me, baby."

"We're not? This was your idea!"

Mia shrugged. "I know."

Josie held the dress up in the mirror. The tag read *Early 70s*, and the color complemented her olive skin.

Mia continued to flit among the racks making suggestions. She led Josie to a pair of shiny white rain boots just like her own. Josie scooped them up and, arms full, found an empty fitting room.

The gold wrap dress was flattering, as was a chocolate brown mini dress from the same era with short, ruffled sleeves and a deep V-neck. Shopping with another woman—and one with good taste—had its advantages. The third item she tried was a fitted knit in alternating bands of turquoise and purple. She came out to show Mia. "This might be a little bright for me."

"Well, I think you could stand for a little more brightness in your life."

Josie turned and admired the way the fabric clung to her curves. She could get used to dressing up more. Something white caught her eye, a short dress with long, flared sleeves. She pulled it from its hanger. "This is cute."

"Mmmm." Mia rubbed a sleeve between her fingers and frowned. "I'm not sure this is for you—"

"Let me just try it." She pulled the fitting room curtain around her and shimmied into the dress. It was a tight fit. She was asking a lot of the bodice. She turned to the mirror and immediately something was not right.

A sharp tingle started in the back of her neck and radiated downward, enveloping her. She panicked, claustrophobic, as though the air were closing in. A horrible retching sound came from deep in her throat.

"Josie?"

"Something's wrong," she said in a raspy whisper. She sank to the floor.

Mia ripped open the fitting room curtain and knelt beside her. "Let's get rid of this!" She pulled the dress over Josie's head, wrestling with the tight parts.

Josie was too stunned to feel self-conscious in her underwear. She let Mia help her back into her own clothes, take her hand, and lead her toward the front of the store.

An aging hippie with shaggy gray hair and a turquoise Hawaiian shirt stood behind the counter. He'd been watching them, and when Josie caught a glimpse of herself, she understood why. She looked like a madwoman, her face bright red and streaked with sweat, her hair a frizzy mess.

"I'm sorry," she mumbled.

"We're just fixin' to run a quick errand, and we'll be back," Mia said. The man ignored her and kept his eyes on Josie.

The white dress lay abandoned on the fitting room floor.

Josie was lightheaded as they walked back down Greenwich Avenue in the humidity. Mia held her firmly.

"Mia, I'm so sorry."

"Just breathe. Breathe and walk."

"I have no idea what happened. That was terrifying."

"Let's go sit in the park for a spell, okay?"

Josie got herself a bottle of water and a pack of cigarettes from the corner bodega. It had been a while since she'd bought a pack, and the price surprised her—nearly seven dollars. They crossed the street and walked through the wrought iron gates of Jefferson Market Garden. In the tiny, manicured park sat a Victorian building that had been repurposed as a library. Bistrot was across the avenue, the tip of its awning visible.

They walked slowly along the path.

"I'm mortified. I have no idea what that was." Josie lit a cigarette and ignored the disapproving glare from the pair of women walking past them. "I'm not a regular smoker," she said.

Mia waved her away.

They found a dry bench protected by a canopy of trees. Josie exhaled and took in the tranquil oasis in the middle of Greenwich Village. The park's brick paths were lined with rose bushes and wildflowers, their colors vibrant from weeks of rain. There was a woody smell to the air.

"I think I had a panic attack. It felt like that dress was possessed."

Mia paused, taking care with her words. "That's the thing with old clothes. You have to be real careful, 'cause they can hold onto energy from their original owner."

Josie cracked open her water bottle and tilted it back. She was parched. "That was some fucked up energy."

"That's why you got to kind of test the fabric first. See if you get a sense of anything. Use your intuition."

"My intuition is not finely tuned. Clearly."

"You have very strong intuition. You just have to learn to trust it. I should've been more insistent. I felt distress when I touched that dress, but I didn't want you thinkin' I was crazy."

"I don't think you're crazy. But you're tapped into a world I want nothing to do with, if that was any indication."

"Being in touch with the spirit world is a responsibility to be sure. And it's a gift."

"That's what Nanette used to say."

"She sounds like someone I'd get on with."

"She was the best. We talked about visiting New Orleans together some day, but some day didn't come in time." The tears welled up. "Jesus, is the rest of my life just gonna be breaks between bouts of crying?"

"Grief is powerful. But I've learned that if you try and silence it, it'll just get louder."

Josie slid her sunglasses from the top of her head to her eyes and let the tears fall. "It literally hurts."

"I know."

"So, if I get on board with this whole spirit thing, do I get to talk to her again?"

"You get to talk to her whether or not you're on board. She'll hear you."

"It's always scared the hell out of me, maybe because I never needed it. Now I do."

"When did you first realize you had a connection?"

"When I was seven. 1974. My dad had left my mom a few years earlier, when I was four, after cheating on her for months with my now step-monster. We moved from Burlington to New Hampshire to be near Nanette. We rented this crazy old house."

The house had been cobbled together at the turn of the century, one half from an old farmhouse, the other the surviving part of a paper mill that had been badly damaged in a fire. The structures were connected by labyrinthine passages Josie took to exploring while her mother was at work and Nanette was downstairs giving piano lessons. She'd take an assortment of stuffed animals and a flashlight and play school or restaurant.

On a dark, rainy afternoon in late June, she sat in one of the passageways making up songs and singing to her animals. A thunderclap startled her, and she froze in place and held her breath. Her fear turned to relief when she heard footsteps heading toward her.

"Nanette!" she'd called. "Come sing songs with us!"

A moment later she heard the muffled piano scales of a lesson-in-progress coming through the vent. Every muscle in her body tensed except her heart, which pounded furiously. She hugged her sock monkey tight and noticed his mouth was unraveling and an eye was missing. The eye had been there the night before, she was sure of it.

From the darkness behind her a girlish voice sang. "*Rain, rain, go away. Come again another day!*"

Josie shrieked and spun around to empty space and the sound of giggling, and her fight-or-flight mechanism kicked in hard. She scooped up her animals, forgetting the flashlight, and ran out of the passage through an icy patch of air.

She shuddered at the memory of it. "It was the scariest thing I'd ever experienced. Until today."

A couple on a bench across the way stared at her, whispering to each other. She imagined how crazy she looked telling her story.

"When I finally told my grandmother, she told me it runs in the family, that she has it too, but it seems to skip a generation."

"I think that's true."

"Well, my ever-pragmatic mother never believed me. She thought I was looking for attention. To be honest I think she was jealous of this connection to Nanette. We were already close before this. Alice doesn't get close to people. But that's a story for a different day."

"Did it happen again?"

"A few times, feeling like I wasn't alone in a room, hearing these distant voices. Nanette and I called them 'the whispers,' where you can't really tell where they're coming from. Then it faded, I made friends, we moved to a new house, and I figured out how to ignore it all. Or I thought I did." She took a swig of water. "Why is this happening again? And by the way, I don't think the spirit at the restaurant is all that gentle. It's got the same creepy vibe as the one from my childhood."

"Gentle spirits can still be mischievous if they're in the mood. As to why this is happening again? You're going through a big loss, and the portals are open. You're more sensitive to spirit energy."

"Does this stuff ever freak you out?"

"No, girl. The thing about New Orleans is the whole town's haunted. You got no choice. Everyone has a story. Pretty little girls in Creole dress watching you from the top of the stairs, angry servants moving things about your kitchen. Friend of mine used to wonder why her neighbor dressed so weird till she found out he died in the Great War."

"Jesus." Josie rubbed the goosebumps on her arms. "No wonder Nanette loved it there. The last thing I need is to see them."

"If you can hear them and feel them, then I'd be surprised you haven't seen them from time to time. It's not like in the movies. It's not scary. Most of the time it isn't, anyway."

"What if you really don't want to see them?"

"For one thing you can always ask nicely. Like I said, they listen. And for another, it's not nearly as common as it used to be. My grandma used to say that ever since they invented the light bulb, people don't see them as much."

"Is your grandma still alive?"

"No, she passed a long, long time back. She said it takes an awful lot of energy for spirits to reveal themselves in electric light, so most of the time they don't bother."

"And the ones that do?"

"The ones that need to will do whatever it takes."

Josie shuddered again.

"It's not random, you know," Mia said. "There's order to the spirit world. Rules, just like there are in the living world."

"Like it gets cold when there's a ghost around?"

"Not always the case. That's an easy one for the books and the movies. Sometimes rooms are just cold, and it's not a spirit or ghost. And sometimes it's actually warmer where they are."

"Is there a difference between spirits and ghosts?"

"Absolutely. Spirit is in us when we're alive and remains after our bodies die. Some people think we're living beings who have spiritual experiences, but it's the opposite. Right now, your spirit is having a corporeal experience in this particular lifetime. Your grandma's spirit exists always, same as when she was living, even if you can't sense it yet. The girl singing to you? That's a ghost. That's one who still has something to do here, who can't cross over yet. You can still see a spirit that's crossed over, but it's gentler, less urgent. When you get a visit by a ghost, when you see a ghost, it's because they have something to tell you, something they need from you, or something they want you to learn."

"Like *A Christmas Carol.*"

"Exactly. But like I said, takes a lot of energy to be seen clearly, so sometimes you might see a shadow or a flash or a smudge, and that's a being that wants to acknowledge you or wants to come through but doesn't have the energy. But where there's a will—"

"No pun intended."

Mia smiled. "If they're determined, they'll appear as vivid as you and me."

Josie nodded toward a woman sitting on a bench, head tilted back, sun shining on her face. "How do we know she's not a ghost?"

"Once you get used to it, you just know."

Maybe this was what Josie had needed all those years ago, a primer on how the spirit world worked so it didn't seem so haphazard. Nanette surely had all these answers, too, but whenever she'd tried to share them, Josie had resisted. Now all the questions she'd swept under the rug began to reveal themselves.

"How do they decide who can see them? And how do you stop seeing them once you start?"

"You set boundaries, tell 'em when you're ready to see them and when they need to leave you be. And you learn to put on blinders, however you can. On their side, they recognize if you have the gift, same way we recognize them. So, say a spirit wants to get my attention. If I'm in the mood, she can appear to me easy since I been seeing through the veil my whole life. But say she wants to meet you, get a sense of who you are without scaring you, she can appear to you as a living person. And since you're not used to it yet, you wouldn't know the difference."

"So, someone could walk up to us right now and look like flesh and blood to me, but you'd know they were a ghost?"

"That's right."

"Would you tell me if that happened?"

"Would you want to know?"

Josie lit a cigarette. "I don't know what I want. I want Nanette back, but I can't have her."

"I know it's hard, Josie. It's the problem with loving people so much. But the love never goes away."

"Have you lost a lot of people besides your grandma?"

"I have."

Josie had been so consumed by her own grief she'd lost sight of the fact it was a universal experience, that just as Nanette's death had triggered something in Derek, it was likely doing the same for others. Most people her generation had lost a loved one. She was a blissfully late bloomer, a latecomer to a club she'd never wanted to join. "I'm sorry."

"It's part of life. And love. And that's where accepting spirit comes in handy."

"Do the people you've lost visit?"

"Some do. I get visits from my friend Ruby."

"What happened to Ruby?"

Mia shook her head and rolled her eyes to the sky. "Foolish girl took too many pills."

"I'm so sorry! When did this happen?"

"Long time back now, baby."

"Did she"—Josie searched for the right phrase—"was it…?"

"It wasn't on purpose if that's what you're asking. And I know she's sorry. Some quack gave her Seconal, told her to take them when she was edgy or couldn't sleep. Problem was she just got to taking them 'cause she felt like taking them." Mia's mood had shifted, her voice coarser.

"Have you had enough of my questions?" Josie asked.

"No girl. You got the questions, may as well ask them."

"I've been hearing voices at the restaurant. But I've been trying to convince myself it's just my imagination, my mind playing tricks."

"That's you putting on blinders. The thing about the voices is, spirit won't speak to you unless you speak first."

"Then it is my imagination. Because I'm certainly not summoning anyone."

"Ask yourself, what would be so bad about being able to communicate with spirit?"

"After what happened in the store, I can tell you exactly what's so bad about it. It's terrifying!"

"I don't think that was spirit you encountered. I think it was an imprint of the girl who owned that dress, of the energy she felt last time she wore that thing. That's what I sensed, emotion, not spirit."

"So, she got rid of something when she was in a shitty mood, and it kept the mood?"

Mia laughed. "Something like that. Josie, let me ask you something else. Do you believe in God?"

"That's a question I've thought about an awful lot over the years. I don't know what I believe. I don't believe in the white-bearded robed guy, but I don't necessarily *not* believe in him either. I believe in something."

"Does Derek?"

"Why are you asking me about Derek?"

"Only 'cause y'all are close."

"I don't think Derek believes in much. For a creative guy he's got a pretty scientific mind. Early on I started to tell him about the stuff from my childhood—not sure why, or what triggered that conversation—but he wanted nothing to do with it."

As she said it, the pieces fell into place. Of course Derek didn't want to hear about communicating with the afterlife because that meant acknowledging the dead, and that was something he'd packed away in storage when he fled Colorado eighteen years earlier. It made a sad kind of sense now. But just as she might bear her grief better by allowing herself to believe, so might he.

"What do you say we go get the other clothes?" Mia asked.

"Long as you don't leave my side."

Mia took her arm, and they walked out of the gardens and back up Greenwich Avenue. With her head held high, Josie entered the shop, flashing a sheepish smile at the store owner. The dresses were neatly folded on a chair, the boots in a box next to them. The white dress was back on its hanger.

While they waited to pay, Josie looked through the accessories on display—Bakelite bangles and ornate Cameo pins, pocket watches and cat-eye sunglasses.

"You ought to get yourself something pretty to go with your new clothes," Mia said.

"Pick it out for me?"

Mia smiled. "Channel that intuition, girl. You can do it."

Josie lingered over a few pieces, then pulled out a large, oval pendant strung on a bright gold chain. The front of the pendant was white enamel with pressed yellow flowers under glass and a tiny, fake diamond. It was kitschy and beautiful and warm in her hand. "What do you think?"

"I think it's perfect."

Chapter Five

THE SKIES WERE a dusty yellow Tuesday morning when Josie left her apartment in the Carroll Gardens section of Brooklyn. Dressed in her new gold wrap, boots, and necklace, she took the subway into Manhattan and got off one stop early. It wasn't raining yet, and the twenty-minute walk would do her good.

She walked into Washington Square Park, crowded with skateboarders and musicians, chess players, dogs, students, and pot dealers.

"Cool necklace," a teenaged girl with blue hair and a skateboard under her arm said as she passed.

Josie rubbed the pendant and smiled, not caring that the skies were rapidly darkening and threatening to open.

The rain started to fall as she made her way underneath the park's iconic arch and north on Fifth Avenue. All around her, people darted beneath awnings and into taxis. By the time she turned west on Ninth Street, her hair and raincoat were drenched.

A blast of air conditioning assaulted her when she walked into the restaurant. People milled about the front of the dining room waiting for the staff meeting to start. When Josie removed her coat, Derek lingered on her outfit and raised his eyebrows in approval.

"Look at you," he said. "You look beautiful."

"Why thank you, sweet friend." She grabbed a laundered bar towel from a pile and pressed some of the water from her hair, then slid into the booth across from him.

"Okay, folks!" Andy walked up from his back office clapping his hands. "Listen up! Important announcements. One, we're down a busboy. Pedro's wife had the baby."

"Boy or girl?" Josie asked.

Andy consulted the index card in his hand. "Boy. Pedro. Two—"

"Pedro Two?" Curtis asked, and people snickered.

"Two, we need to move the date forward on the renovations. We'll be closing *temporarily* sooner than we thought."

"What? When?!" Josie asked.

"TBD." Andy raised his voice over the murmurs. "This means a couple of things, people. Two A."

"Are you actually speaking in outline form?" Derek asked.

"Two A, if you have any personal items that you store here, like changes of clothes or what have you, it's a good idea to take them home sooner than later. Two B—"

"Or not two B!" Curtis said with dramatic flourish.

"Yeah, yeah. Two B, we all have to pitch in to get the place ready. Josie, you're not needed for set up. What say you get started on the basement this afternoon?"

Josie blinked. "Seriously? I'm kind of dressed up."

"You look fetching. Wear an apron."

"You look beautiful, baby!" Mia said, squeezing into the booth next to her. "I'll help you out down there."

"Okay." Josie shrugged. "Sure, we'll do this."

"Brilliant," Andy said. "Thank you. Finally, three, Chef is a bit anxious these days."

The group laughed nervously.

"Girl, that's like saying it's a bit rainy today," Curtis said.

Andy sighed. "Fine. He's more on edge than normal."

"Why?" Josie asked.

"The renovations, for one, and the fact that it's been slow. We're not turning much of a profit."

"Then, why am I constantly in the weeds?" Curtis asked.

"Because we're short staffed. Justin quit."

"Who?" Josie asked.

"The new guy," Derek said. "We need a new new guy."

"Again?" Curtis whined. "Add him to the list."

"Y'all don't need me here for this," Mia said to Josie. "Why don't I go get started on the basement and you meet me down there?" She slipped back out of the booth and flashed a warm, flirtatious smile at Andy. Though it was the subject of plenty of speculation, no one knew anything about Andy's love life or which team, if any, he played for.

"Anyway," he said, rubbing the back of his neck. "My point is that we need everything to run flawlessly. There's no telling what'll set Chef off."

Something heavy and metallic dropped to the kitchen floor above them, followed by a muffled, expletive-ridden shout.

"I'm going to meditate," Andy announced, walking stiffly back toward his office, muttering under his breath.

"Fasten your seatbelts, folks," Derek said. "This is going to be a bumpy fucking ride."

"You can say that again," Curtis said. "None of y'all were around for the crenshaw incident."

"What's a crenshaw?" Sam asked.

"It's fruit, Sam," Curtis said. "Anyway, some years ago Chef lobbed one at a customer whose steak was too rare. He missed, but the guy sued."

"Jesus," Derek said. "That could have been bad. Death by melon."

"Exactly. And that's when things were going pretty well around here. Now? Who knows what the man is capable of?"

Josie was not in the mood for a worst-case-scenario conversation. She took an apron from a hook by the servers' station and tied it over her dress. She yanked the heavy door to the basement and nearly tumbled down the rickety staircase. The new boots would take some getting used to.

The smell of the cellar reminded her of the passageways in her childhood home in Keene—dank, musty wood that had gotten damp too many times and harbored secrets.

She gripped the handrailing, made her way down the steps in the dim light, and paused at the bottom of the staircase. From across the room came the sound of whispering. Heart pounding, Josie peered around the corner to see Mia standing in the dark in front of one of the old wall safes that hadn't been used since Bistrot had opened.

When Josie shifted her weight, the step beneath her creaked.

Mia spun around. "Oh, Josie!"

"Sorry to startle you," she said a little too shrilly.

"You caught me talking to myself."

Josie wasn't sure she believed her. She flipped a light switch. The shelves and counters were in utter disarray. "Look at all this junk."

Mia picked up a folder and studied its contents. "There's got to be some treasure to be found, don't you think?"

Josie surveyed the mess. Papers in haphazard stacks, mildewed cartons hastily sealed with packing tape and labeled in illegible marker. Dusty sleeves of plastic cups, bloated Nynex Yellow Pages, a calculator with a cracked screen.

She pulled a manila envelope from a pile, and a cloud of dead moths came with it. "Oh gross!" She coughed and brushed her hands on her apron. When she unclasped the envelope, its rusted tabs broke off. She tossed it into the large trash can in the corner and dragged the can closer.

They made their way through the piles. There were pads and notebooks whose pages had been stuck together by time and things no one wanted to contemplate, packets of yellowing paper plates, scraps of newsprint.

"Look at these!" Mia said. "Menus from spring 1987—*Blush!*"

"*Blush!*" Josie took one from her and blew at the coating of dust. "Let's hold onto these."

Over the next twenty minutes they sorted piles, discarding most of what they found.

"Thank you for volunteering for this delightful task with me," Josie said. "Some of this stuff has literally been down here for decades."

"That's why I'm thinking that it can't all be junk. Any idea how to get into those safes?"

"Not a clue. We've never used them."

"Would be a shame if something of value got covered over. Some relic from the past."

Josie fingered the pendant around her neck and rubbed its smooth face. "Thank you so much for yesterday, Mia. I really needed it. Most of it."

"It was my pleasure."

"It's great to have you here. A break from all the testosterone. There's a lot to be said for female energy."

Mia smiled. "We didn't get to talk much about the Bistrot boys yesterday. What are they all about?"

"Let's see. Curtis is cranky and needs a boyfriend. But he's one of my favorite people on this planet and a deeply loyal friend. Sam is sweet but not the sharpest knife in the drawer, which can be maddening. Andy tries too hard, has tons of ideas, and constantly gets in his own way before they come to fruition."

"I think a lot of us do that."

"Can't argue there. Johnny's a conspiracy theorist and probably has ties to the mob. Then again, he puts up with Chef way more than the rest of us have to. As for Chef, I have a soft spot for that weirdo." Josie picked up a three-year-old copy of *New York* magazine with John Kennedy Junior's girlfriend—now wife—on the cover. "Wonder why we kept this?" she asked, flipping through it. "They've actually been in a few times, but I haven't seen them yet this summer."

"Who?"

"John John and Carolyn."

Mia looked over Josie's shoulder. "Who is that?"

Josie started to laugh, then realized she wasn't joking. "That's John Kennedy Junior!"

"The President's son?"

"Yes. I'm weirdly impressed that you don't know this."

"I'm behind on my pop culture I guess."

"That can be a good thing in this business. Means you won't fawn over any celebs like our coat check girl last winter. What was her name? Anyway, yeah, that's Kennedy's son, and he and his wife have been in a few times. They're very nice."

"And Derek?"

"Derek's very nice, too."

Mia smiled. "Tell me about him."

"He has an interesting past. Moved here from Colorado right after high school. Did voiceover work for a while."

"He has a great voice."

"He does, but it wasn't for him. Like I said yesterday, he's a very creative guy. He's a really good writer. Sold a couple of screenplays, but nothing happened with them. Which has to be a bummer. I wish he'd get back to his writing because he's so talented, but like I said he's kind of stymied."

"That's too bad."

"It is, but there's a lot more to the story than I realized." Josie glanced up toward the cellar door, which was closed. "I didn't mention this yesterday, but it explains a lot. Derek had a brother who died before he was born, and that shaped his childhood. It's really sad."

"That is terrible. He seems like a very good guy. And I know y'all are close."

"We are, but it's weird to me. In all these years, he never once mentioned this brother. Alex was his name. I didn't know he existed until last week!"

"I guess he wasn't ready to talk about him?"

"After six years? That's a long time to keep a secret from a close friend. Of course it's his right, but I'm kind of hardwired against duplicity—the whole saga of my dad—and that's what this feels like. I don't like when people in my life keep big, defining things from me. I think back to all these times I probably said things that made him think about his brother, and I feel awful."

"You didn't know!"

"I know, but still. And God do I wish he believed in an afterlife. It would help him so much. So yeah, all this explains why he's stuck in this rut."

"What about you?"

"What about me?"

"Do you ever think you might be stuck in a rut, too?"

Josie's face flushed. "I suppose, sure. I mean, I think everyone does at one point or another. And now with whatever's going on here, I don't know. There's more to it than Andy's letting on. I worry that Chef's losing it. And if he walks away, I don't know what'll happen to this place. He goes away, the restaurant closes, next thing you know this place gets torn down by some developer and turned into a Starbucks or a Duane Reade. Just the idea of that kills me. I complain, but I love this place. It's home. I need it right now."

"That's part of why I need to get back to New Orleans," Mia said. "My family has a restaurant there, and it needs some TLC."

"What's wrong with it?"

"Oh, just the wear and tear of age. But as long as it's there, I'll always have a home." A mistiness crossed her face, and Josie held back her questions. "What do you say we try to open this thing?" Mia ran her hand over one of the wall safes.

The combination lock was so rusted, Josie had a hard time making out the numbers. "Unless you have a crowbar, I'm not sure we'll have much luck."

"I picked a lock or two in my day." Mia gave her a cryptic smile. She cracked her knuckles, a habit Josie would never have guessed she had, and closed her eyes. "Come on," she whispered, rubbing her hands together. She held them over the lock. After a moment she nodded and turned the dial a few times in each direction.

Nothing.

"Damn." She went through the same routine, this time holding her hands over the lock for twice as long. She leaned in and listened carefully as she tried another combination. On the third turn she smiled triumphantly. "Here we go!"

The lock clicked, and the safe opened.

"Holy shit," Josie said.

They peered into the safe, and Mia reached in and felt around. It was empty. "Oh. How disappointing."

"What were you hoping to find?"

"I'm not sure. Something."

Josie felt a chill and wrapped her arms around herself.

"Sometimes places are just cold," Mia said.

They stood in silence until the door at the top of the stairs opened.

"Josephine!" Curtis called. "Emerge from the underworld!"

"Already?" Josie looked at the wall clock, which was frozen on 1:27, its second hand hovering motionless.

"Chef is looking for you!"

"Oh, boy." Josie surveyed the mess they'd made.

"You go on ahead," Mia said. "I'll straighten some."

Josie wiped her hands on her apron and untied it as she trotted up the staircase. She smoothed her hair and squinted in the light. Chef stood at the hostess stand wearing his whites and holding a bouquet of watercress and a bottle of what looked like the house-made limoncello.

"Josephine!" he said with gravitas.

"Chef?"

He stared at her, unblinking, through Coke-bottle glasses. "My condolences on your loss."

"Oh. Thank you, Chef. It's been a few weeks, so hard as it is I'm trying to get used to—"

"One should never in life get used to death!" he said by way of a botched condolence. He looked at the items in his hands as though unsure how they got there, bowed, and scurried out the door.

"What was that?" Curtis asked, pacing up from the dining room.

"That was Chef offering his sympathies. Nanette died."

"Again?"

"No, I think just the once. Why is he leaving before dinner?"

"He put Johnny in charge. We're light tonight."

Though they were light, there was a steady trickle of diners throughout the night, and all seemed content with their meals.

Josie noticed extra flair in the plating. "Johnny's pretty impressive," she said to Curtis after the kitchen closed early.

"He is, but I don't know if it's worth keeping this place going six nights a week long as the weather stays like this. Ain't nobody venturing out in the pouring rain on a Tuesday night if they don't need to. And Sunday was an anomaly."

"Please don't put that out into the universe. I can't afford to have my hours cut."

She followed him into the bar. The last table in the dining room had paid its check, and the usual crew was huddled in their corner. As was Alison, back to her glittery, kittenish self. Josie wasn't in the mood and, despite her fatigue, refused to go home in case Patrick Moore made an appearance. He would eventually, and she'd be there waiting. That was the problem with dating in her line of work—she was low-hanging fruit. A man didn't have to try quite as hard when all he really had to do was show up at the end of her shift.

She found a pack of cigarettes behind the bar and headed to the front.

Mia was putting on her raincoat. "Walking out? I'll join you."

"I'm not really a smoker," Josie said once they were outside under the awning. She cupped her hand around the match she lit.

"I know. You tell me every time."

"I know I do."

"We've all got our vices. Mine was bourbon."

"Was?"

"Still is. Just on special occasions, or if someone else is buyin'."

The front door opened and Sylvie came out, her raincoat inside out. "Maria darling!" she cried, taking Mia's hands. "I knew that was you!"

Mia looked quizzically at Josie, then back to Sylvie. "How do you do? I'm—"

"Where were you?" Sylvie asked. "I've missed you darling!"

"Sylvie," Josie said. "This is Mia. She's joining us for the summer."

"Yes. Of course. I know you!"

"You do now," Mia said graciously, extending a hand. "I'm Mia Boudreaux."

"Oh!" Sylvie shook her head rapidly. "I'm sorry. I must have—" Her voice trailed off, and she looked sad and embarrassed.

Josie put an arm around her. "Sylvie is family," she said to Mia. "I'm so glad you two are finally meeting."

"It's a pleasure to know you, Miss Sylvie."

Curtis walked out of the restaurant with Sylvie's pocketbook over his shoulder and an oversized umbrella in hand. "Miss Sylvie, may I see you to your door?" he asked. "I'm getting sleepy." He often escorted her to her building across the street under the guise of heading home himself.

A flash of disappointment crossed Sylvie's face, and her eyes darted between Curtis, Mia, and Josie. "Have *you* seen Maria?" she asked in a small voice.

"I don't know Maria, sugar." He looped his arm through hers and opened the umbrella. Standing beside his towering physique, Sylvie looked ever frailer. "Come, let me walk you home."

"Good night, Miss Sylvie. I'll see you real soon," Mia said.

As he helped Sylvie up the steps, Curtis turned and mouthed, "*I'm coming back!*"

Once they were out of earshot, Josie turned to Mia. "Poor thing's gotten really confused in the past few months."

"I've seen it before," Mia said. "New Orleans is full of people who live inside their minds."

"Want to come have a nightcap with us?"

"I don't think so darlin'. I'll see you next time."

When Josie walked back inside, the mood was thick.

"I dunno man," Johnny said. "Bad enough we're losing time with these fuckin' renovations. Wouldn't put it past Chef to just close up shop, no warning."

As sous-chef, Johnny Giardino bore the brunt of Chef's mercurial temperament. He was a streetwise kid from Staten Island whose father and brothers were firefighters. He was the renegade who'd carved a different path. Growing up in a firefighter family, to him there were no greater heroes than the FDNY. An ardent conspiracy theorist, Johnny knew "for a fact" the moon landing was staged, Lee Harvey Oswald didn't act alone, and the government was hiding the truth about Roswell. His current obsession was the millennium bug, a tech-induced rapture in which the world's computers would mistake 12:00 a.m. New Year's Day for 1900, go haywire, and reset themselves, causing airplanes to drop from the skies and nuclear missiles to launch. Since the start of 1999, Johnny had sported a red baseball cap with white stitched lettering that read Y2K. All his hometown buddies wore the same cap. Josie and Derek referred to them as the Y2K Boys when they stopped by.

Tonight, Johnny drowned his mood in scotch. "This fucking place is cursed."

"What do you mean?" Josie asked. "This place has amazing history! Dave's was legendary!"

"Yeah, a legendary fuckin' deathtrap!" He pounded his glass on the bar.

"What are you talking about?"

"Josie, are you kidding me? Dave's Continental was practically destroyed in a fire. People died! Come on, this is restaurant lore one-oh-one. Sparks Steakhouse-level trivia."

"Seriously? How do I *not* know this?!" She grabbed Sam as he walked into the bar. "Sammy, do you know the story behind Dave's Continental?"

"What, the fire?"

"Why am I just hearing about this now?"

"I don't know. Jeez, Josie, I learned that, like, my first night here."

"How many people died?" She was incredulous.

"A shitload!" Johnny said. "Well, three, I think. A couple of waitresses and one of my boys, fireman named Tommy Bianco. There's a plaque dedicated to him at my brother's firehouse. I'd say ask Sylvie about it but poor old girl thinks this *is* Dave's."

"Affirmative," Curtis said, sidling up next to Josie. "She just told me she thinks Dave is cheating on Maria."

"This is just crazy." Josie eyed Johnny's scotch.

"Anyways," Johnny said, sliding his glass protectively closer. "Time to start looking for your next gig, folks."

"Next gig? I can't lose this job!" Sam said in a panic.

"Yeah, no kidding," Curtis said. "Like I can?"

"No but you don't understand," he continued, oblivious. "I'm supposed to do so much more than this!"

Curtis flared his nostrils and gave Josie a hard look. She put her hand on his arm.

"I mean I'm not supposed to be a waiter. I'm an actor!"

"Sam," Josie said. "You're an actor whether or not you have this gig, right? Isn't that why you're in New York?"

"Yeah, but you don't understand. If this job ends and I'm not a fulltime actor yet, Dick and Jane are going to cut me off!"

"Who?"

"My parents."

"Your parents' names are Dick and Jane? Are you kidding me?"

"Richard. His real name's Richard. And he was against this whole move to begin with, so I promised them I'd really make a go at it so they'd support me."

"So *that's* how you afford to live on this godforsaken island," Josie said.

Sam lived in a doorman building off Union Square, and Josie had wondered how this was possible.

Sam nodded. "They're paying for me to live here for one year, period. If I'm not acting by January, they'll cut me off! I don't know what I'll do! I can't lose this job!"

"ARGH!" Curtis stomped down to the other end of the bar, leaving his pint of beer behind. Josie took a sip of it. It was hoppy and bitter. She took another.

"I know it's not a great job or anything," Sam said. "But as long as I'm here at least I *have* a job! That's what I thought when I started, and I got sucked into this place and haven't really done much with the acting."

"It happens, this place is the fuckin' Hotel California," Johnny said.

"The what?"

"Never mind," Josie said.

"Gotta up your game, little man," Johnny said.

"Seriously,"—Josie clapped him on the shoulder—"what does being a 'fulltime actor' mean? Even Al Pacino takes time off. As long as you're working at it, you're an actor, right? What was the last thing you auditioned for?"

Sam hung his head.

Josie sighed. "Sam, this is life. Stop wasting time." She was speaking as much to herself as she was to him. He had it easy. He knew what his passion was. Josie didn't have one. She wasn't artistic and had zero business acumen, a point her mother had driven home when Josie was fifteen and dissolving her unsuccessful babysitting referral business. She drained another third of the pint of beer.

"Josephine!" Curtis snapped his fingers from down the bar. "My IPA, please!"

When she brought his glass to him, he held it up and peered through its near emptiness.

"I know Sam can be a little... clueless."

"A little? I have zero patience for anyone over ten complaining about mommy and daddy cutting them off."

"I hear you, but really, my love, does it impact you?"

"Does it impact me? No. But it annoys me. My mama worked three jobs—*three*—so that I wasn't running around naked on the streets of Atlanta."

"And that's admirable, honey. And it was necessary. And your experience is your experience, just like Sam's is his. My mom may not have worked three jobs, but neither is she supporting me in adulthood. And at the same time, you and your mom have a beautiful relationship. My relationship with my mom looks nothing like that. None of our situations is better or worse, they just are."

"I guess. But for Christ's sake, I moved here to go to Parsons and become a fabulous interior designer, and I've been waiting tables for fifteen years."

"That's a choice though. We've talked about this. You could take a class or two every semester if you really wanted to. Sam, too. You both need to just start taking steps toward your goals."

"Sam and I have *nothing* in common. Outside of this place."

"I think we have something in common with just about everyone we encounter. Sometimes you have to dig a little to find it."

"When did you get all Zen?" Curtis sniffed and took a sip of the fresh beer Derek poured for him.

"What's really going on, my love?" Josie asked.

"I don't know. I'm bored. And frustrated. Do you know how long it's been since I've had a man in my—"

"GAH! No details." Josie clapped her palms over her ears. Details about other people's sex lives never appealed to her. She had a hard enough time remembering to care about her own. "Just get back out there. Have you been on one date since you and Nathan broke up?"

"Of course I have!" Curtis said defensively. "Sort of. Ish. What about you missy? Who was the last guy before Patrick Moore?"

"No one worth mentioning. It's a tough town for straight women. I'm a small fish in an enormous ocean."

"You are a beautiful fish, miss. And by the way"—he twirled her around to admire her outfit—"you are working it today! Love this whole thing you've got going."

"Thank you. Mia took me shopping."

"Whoever's responsible, you are fabulous."

"I finally splurged with my birthday money from Nanette."

"Girl, your birthday was last year."

"I know. And I told her I bought myself something, but I didn't. I held onto it. As long as I didn't spend it, I always had at least two hundred dollars to my name. But it was time. I needed to put in more of an effort."

"Good, lady. Because you've been hiding in your own backyard for too long."

Josie reached for his glass. "To personal progress," she said, holding it up.

"You know there's plenty more of this behind the bar. You don't need to drink mine."

"The grass is always greener."

"Fine. In the interest of personal progress, I'm going to flirt with the swarthy gentleman next to Boodles." Curtis's type was swarthy, part of the reason he approved of Josie's involvement with Patrick Moore.

Josie didn't have a type. A friend had once remarked that if she gathered every man she'd ever been involved with in the same room, their only common ground would be her. In an effort to prove that friend wrong, she'd searched for a thread and come up short. Most of them had been placeholders who placated her loneliness. Whatever role they filled was rarely about them at all, nor did their interest in Josie take into account who she really was. The few men who understood her, her friends, did it well.

She looked at Derek, who was talking and laughing with Alison, Boodles, and Bulleit. Judging by the sideways glances the two men kept shooting her, it was clear they still believed she and Derek had a thing.

She studied his profile. It was a face she knew so well it was hard for her to objectively assess his attractiveness anymore. Of course he was handsome— anyone could see that—if not conventionally so. Somewhere over the past six years he'd developed crow's feet around his eyes. He laughed easily now, enjoying the company he was keeping. Josie hadn't seen him this relaxed in a while. She wanted to be happy for him, but something about Alison didn't sit right with her. She was so young. What could she and Derek have in common, really?

Derek sensed her attention and looked at her, then gestured for her to join them.

"Hey, baby."

Josie's stomach lurched. She arranged her face into a breezy smile and turned to Patrick.

"Hey, you!" He looked like a model for God's sake, with damp hair—no helmet tonight—and a Sex Pistols t-shirt under his leather biker jacket.

He leaned down and kissed her. "You look gorgeous. Happy Fourth. What did you do to celebrate the birth of this great nation?"

"I exercised my hard-earned right to work. We were open Sunday, in support of all the stranded Manhattanites who don't get to ride the Hampton Jitney off to better places. If I had the cash, I'd start a helicopter service for that set. They need to feel important, and three hours in a bus can't be helping."

He laughed.

"Want a drink?" Josie looked at Derek, who had turned back to Alison and now had his arms crossed. "Let's grab a table."

She led him to one of the café tables lining the bar, enjoying the fact that her skirt was short, her boots were high, and he had a clear view of her from behind.

"The usual?" she asked with what she hoped was a coy smile.

"Sure, baby."

Josie touched his shoulder as she passed by him and ducked under the bar. Derek was focused intently on a story Alison was telling quite animatedly. Even Boodles and Bulleit seemed enraptured, which made Josie feel betrayed and, just as quickly, ridiculous.

"Get ahold of yourself," she muttered under her breath. She grabbed the gin and pulled a couple of glasses.

"Hey, girl," Mia said, walking up to the bar.

"What are you doing back here?"

"I left something in the coatroom. Wasn't sure y'all would still be here."

Something was missing from her explanation.

"As long as you are here, do you want to stay for a drink?"

Mia scanned the shelves behind Josie.

"Sure. Wild Turkey, neat."

"Right. A bourbon gal."

Mia smiled. "You can take the girl out of the south…."

Josie puzzled over Mia's reappearance while she fixed the drinks. If people hadn't still been there, she wouldn't have been able to get into the restaurant, so why would she take that chance? A spate of petty thefts earlier in the year had prompted Andy to change the locks, and only a few people had keys. Then again, Mia *had* proven adept at breaking into things.

"Course I realized just as I got back that if y'all had gone home I'd be out of luck," she said, reading Josie's mind. She smiled warmly, and Josie felt silly for her runaway imagination. Mia had forgotten something in the coatroom. Period.

She scooted back under the bar and picked up the three drinks, catching Derek's eye.

"Go easy, sister," he said, walking toward her.

"Just having a nightcap, my love." Her cheeks burned with embarrassment.

"Did you eat any of the staff meal?"

"Yes," she lied, turning her back to him.

Mia followed her to the table, and Patrick stood.

"Patrick, this is Mia. Mia, my friend Patrick."

"Pleasure," Patrick said, extending his hand.

"How do you do? Mia Boudreaux."

They launched into the casual banter of two beautiful people who were so at ease in their own skin they never got tongue-tied or stumbled through conversation. Apparently Patrick loved New Orleans and knew it well. They volleyed streets and neighborhoods back and forth while Josie waited for an entry point.

"It is a truly magical place," Mia said.

"What made you leave there anyway?" Josie asked.

"I followed the wrong man," Mia said coldly. "Bless his heart."

"Ah," Patrick said. "Sorry, baby. We're not all bad."

Josie bristled at his calling her "baby." "Mia's family has a restaurant in New Orleans," she said, her delivery forced.

"Great food town." Patrick put his arm around the back of Josie's chair. "What's the name?"

"Esplanade House. Right there by the Faubourg Marigny."

"I know it well! Great spot."

"That's my family," Mia said.

"Place is an institution."

"Yeah, we've had it from the start. My daughter runs it now."

Josie stopped mid-sip. "What? How do you have a daughter old enough—"

"Oh!" Mia laughed and waved her hand in front of her face. "I'm exaggerating. Miss Rita's only four years old, but she's helping my folks out, and they say she's quite a tough little manager."

Four years old, the same age Josie was when her father left her mother—and, by extension, her—for a much younger woman, the neighborhood widow whom he'd gone round to comfort. She knew the impact a vanishing parent had on her younger self and was surprised someone who was so different from her narcissist father would choose to leave her own young daughter—and for a man.

"It must be hard to be away from her."

"It is," Mia said, her voice catching. "Coming up here was the biggest regret of my life. I have to figure out how to get back home soon as I can. It's taking a long time to get the resources together."

Then why are you working as a coat check girl? Josie thought.

Mia looked her square in the eyes. "I reckon I don't have much choice."

Patrick cleared his throat. "Mia, can I photograph you sometime? I'm working on some portraits—"

Josie chomped down on the ice cube in her mouth.

"I don't think so, darlin'. I don't photograph well." She put her hand on Josie's shoulder. "Take pictures of this beauty instead."

"I plan to."

"All right, y'all," Mia said, yawning. "I'm fixin' to call it a night."

"I'll walk you out," Patrick said. "Got to make a quick call." He patted the mobile phone in his pocket. Of course he had one. Josie had no desire to be quite so reachable. "I'll be back, baby," he said.

She finished her drink and, noticing that Mia's bourbon remained nearly untouched, took a swig of it. It burned on its way down before settling into a calming warmth. She felt Derek watching her from the bar and defiantly finished the glass.

Chapter Six

JOSIE WOKE TO a throbbing headache and the sound of rain thrumming on a fire escape. She opened her eyes and saw the exposed brick at the far end of Patrick's apartment.

The grayness of the skies outside his windows made it impossible to gauge the time, and his Patek Philippe, which functioned as his bedroom clock, was not on the nightstand.

Her clothing was folded on a chair, not her doing. By the time they'd gotten home the night before, she'd been in no condition to care about that.

From the kitchen came whistling and the sound of water running.

She sat up, pulled the sheet around her chest, and fake-sneezed to announce herself. The whistling stopped, and a moment later Patrick appeared in the doorway with a mug and a glass of water. His hair was wet from the shower.

"Hydrate and caffeinate?" he asked, holding the beverages toward her.

"Oh my God, you're a superhero." Josie's voice was froggy with her first words of the day. She gulped the water down, and he handed her the coffee and perched on the edge of the bed. She sat up a little straighter, distracted by a clump of mascara in her peripheral vision. "Sorry if I was a little… out of it… last night. I kind of forgot to eat."

"Ah." He sat back down on the bed and squeezed her knee. "No need to apologize, baby. But we got to start feeding you. There's some bread and eggs in the fridge. You want me to make you something?"

She shook her head. "I'm fine."

"That you are."

She smiled into her coffee cup.

"It was a good night, and nice to meet your friend."

"Yeah, I'm thrilled that for once Andy made good on a promise of extra help. That never happens."

"I can't stand people who are untrue to their word."

"He doesn't mean to be, he's just scatterbrained. In the time I've worked there, I can't tell you the number of new hires he's floated and abandoned. 'We might hire a bouncer, we might hire a barback, we might hire an expediter.' It's become a running joke for the rest of us. But Mia's good female energy. She balances things out."

"It is a boys' club, isn't it?"

"It's basically the Lost Boys meets the Island of the Misfit Toys."

Patrick laughed and squeezed her knee again. "You're amazing."

"Go on."

"You're funny and smart. You get people. You've figured all of us out."

"I try. So, if you're around tonight, come by the—"

"Can't tonight." He stood and paced to the window, and Josie felt like throwing the covers over her head. "Have a thing at the school. Do I want to take my bike? Nah, it's already too wet out there."

"Oh! If you're leaving, I can get myself together." Her voice was thin and falsely upbeat.

"You're good, baby. Why don't you just chill here till you have to go in? There's towels in the bathroom." He leaned down and kissed the top of her head. "See you later," he said vaguely, and she panicked.

"Patrick?" The sheet slipped, and she caught it as his eyes drifted downward.

"What's up baby?"

"What did we talk about last night?"

He started to laugh and sat back down. "Really? That bad?"

She shrugged. "Kind of. No dinner, lot of booze. I mean, I remember most," she lied.

"You told me about your dad."

"Oh, Jesus. I'm horrified."

"Don't be. It's okay. What he did isn't okay."

"Which narrative did I tell you?"

"Cheating on your mom with the widow, abandoning you—"

She cringed at the word "abandon." "He's still in my life, kind of, but yeah, he's pretty much a consummate shithead."

"Do you talk to him?"

"Only very occasionally. I did call to tell him about my grandmother, thought he'd want to know."

"And?"

"And he had a really hard time not making it all about himself, but we've had worse conversations to be sure. Anyway, I'm sorry I unloaded that on you."

"You weren't unloading. You told me your deal. It's refreshing. We don't get a lot of that out west. Everyone's trying to pretend to be a perfect version of themselves. That's why I dig this town."

"Maybe you should live here then. This town digs you, too."

"You never know." He patted her knee. "I wish I could hang out with you all morning, but I've really gotta roll. I'm sorry, baby."

"I get it. I'll see you soon?"

"Of course you will. Stay as long as you want, and just pull the door shut on your way out. It'll lock." He kissed her head.

Josie waited until she heard the door click behind him and stood, letting the towel fall. The Sex Pistols shirt he had worn the night before lay on the ground, and she put it on. It smelled like him, musky and smoky with a hint of sweat. More than a hint. She took it off and pulled on a plain gray shirt from his dresser drawer. She carried her empty mug into the kitchen and poured another cup of coffee, then took it to the living room. There was a Bose sound system with an elaborate speaker setup. She hit play, and Al Green filled the apartment, conjuring flashes of the night before.

Patrick had left her alone in his apartment. She had a fleeting image of rifling through his closets and drawers and just as quickly pictured him walking in and catching her. Instead, she pulled the blinds and looked outside.

The apartment was on one of the prettiest blocks in Manhattan. Josie sipped her coffee and watched the foot traffic walking up and down the rainy sidewalks. A dog walker in a transparent hooded slicker tried to wrangle a motley crew of his wards, some in jaunty raincoats. A Burberry-clad businessman with an oversized golf umbrella walked quickly down the sidewalk, veering into the street to get around other pedestrians. A hot dog vendor dragged his rickety cart down the block, splashing through the unpaved craters. It was the bustle of Manhattan even in the rain that reminded Josie how much she loved the town.

She imagined herself doing this regularly, waking up in Patrick's apartment. She'd cook breakfast for him. French toast, or frittatas, bacon extra crisp. Her stomach growled, and she took another sip of coffee. They'd hibernate and listen to music and have sober sex. Sober was key. It would be nice to remember her time with him, and so far she was two for two in not recalling much. This would have to change.

She was surprised she'd told him so much about her father, but he'd responded perfectly this morning, neither pitying her nor unnerved that she'd shared.

She could get used to this.

Patrick sublet from a close friend who "summered in Europe"—a phrase that had made her inwardly roll her eyes when he'd first said it. He'd told her they shared an aesthetic, joked that the apartment would give her some insight into his psyche. At the time it all seemed pretentious and self-congratulatory, but now it didn't bother her.

She looked around the room. There were shelves lined with books, many by or about musicians, and framed black-and-white abstract photographs. She didn't "get" abstract art, though its merit had been explained to her several times. Maybe Patrick could shed light. A stack of his *Bon Vivant* business cards sat on the mantle next to a pile of receipts and a small photo album. Josie flipped it open and saw Patrick standing with a much older man who could be his father. She turned the page, and there he was laughing with a group of people closer to his age, then at a child's birthday party blowing soap bubbles for a little girl in a party hat. On the next page he posed on a sunny deck with a woman—pretty, thin, brunette. Their body language was fairly platonic—he had his hand on her shoulder. Their coloring was similar. Josie pulled the photo from its sleeve and was examining it when the phone rang. She felt like she'd been caught snooping, slid the photo back, and slammed the book shut. After three rings, Patrick's voice came over the answering machine.

"Hey, Josie, it's me, you still there?"

She found the phone and arranged her voice to sound relaxed, as though answering his phone were the most natural thing in the world. "Hey, you. Long time." She paced the perimeter of the room.

"Yeah, I just didn't want to leave things so vague. Sorry about tonight. My schedule's not really my own these days, but I'll try to come by tomorrow."

Josie wandered into the bathroom and made an excited face in the mirror, then noticed how she looked—bleary-eyed, puffy-cheeked, hair that seemed hellbent on fleeing her head in every direction.

"Josie?"

"Yeah, sorry, it's okay! I totally get it."

"Cool. Just wasn't sitting right with me."

"That's sweet. It's all good."

"Good."

"I'll see you soon?"

"Yes you will."

After they hung up, Josie made another face in the mirror. "Jesus, woman," she said to her reflection. "You look awful." She splashed cold water on her face and used spit to remove her mascara streaks.

On the sink were a folded towel and a new toothbrush, still in its packaging. She had never been so happy to see a toothbrush. After she unwrapped it she had a moment of panic—what did she do with it when she was done? Take it with her? She had one at home, and this was technically his. But leaving it there would be presumptuous. Claiming ownership of a portion of his bathroom cabinet was the kind of thing that made men run.

"Stop overthinking!" she admonished her reflection, then turned on the shower.

She stood in the running water and talked herself through the facts. Patrick had come back to the restaurant to see her. She'd opened up to him, had given him insight into her past and her neuroses, and it hadn't made him run. He'd left her alone in his place, he cared that she hadn't eaten dinner, he referenced next time. This wasn't a two-night stand. It was a thing that was not finite.

"Oh my God, you're being ridiculous," she said. "You do not want a relationship."

After her shower, she got dressed in her outfit from the day before, her only option. She'd just have to deflect whatever comments came her way and hope that at least the clientele was different tonight.

At the door she turned around. "Goodbye, apartment. I'll see you soon."

Just as she pulled the door, she saw something streak across the room. If she didn't know better, she'd have thought it was a cat. Instead, the tingling at the back of her neck reminded her of Mia's words. *Sometimes you might see a shadow or a flash or a smudge, and that's a being that wants to acknowledge you or wants to come through but doesn't have the energy.* She scrambled down the stairs and out the front door as quickly as she could, refusing to look back at his window.

The cool rain washed over her hangover as she made her way back down to the West Village. She forced the apparition from her thoughts and focused instead on what she did recall of the night before and how reassuring Patrick had been this morning. She felt womanly and desirable, and the men she passed seemed to notice.

On Seventh Avenue and 14th Street, her nausea kicked in. As she crossed the avenue, a woman with wild gray curls and a bright green rain poncho walked toward her.

"You take care of yourself, child," she said to Josie as she passed by.

The tingling returned. Josie turned to look back, and the woman was gone. *She jumped in a taxi,* she told herself, repeating it like a mantra as she walked to Bistrot.

Sam was the first person she encountered. "Oh, hey Josie, nice dress," he said when she walked in, and for once she was grateful for his obliviousness.

Behind the bar, Derek looked up from his newspaper and shook his head almost imperceptibly.

"Nice to see you, too," Josie said. She walked into the bar and took a seat, resting her head in her hand. "Can I have a pint of water? And a Coke?"

He poured her drinks and slid them across the bar.

"I'm pretty hung. Maybe a little hair of the dog?"

"Josie, no. Come on, you're not a day drinker."

"I know. I think it'll help."

"What would help is if you fucking ate something. I saved you a plate from staff meal, you can heat it up."

"Ugh, I don't want food, I'm nauseous," she said, waving the thought away.

"Yeah, because you haven't been eating. You're getting so thin!"

"Not sure how you meant that, but I take it as a compliment." She sat up straight and grabbed a straw for her Coke. "And besides I *did* eat," she lied. "Patrick and I went to lunch." Might as well acknowledge it. She clearly hadn't been home.

Derek tightened his lips and shook his head again. "I'll be back," he said, pulling up the door to the liquor room.

When he was gone, Josie ducked under the bar and grabbed the rum, pouring a few fingers' worth into her Coke. She mixed it with the straw and took a big sip from the glass. She knew this caliber of hangover, and the only thing that would help right now was a little booze.

"And where did we sleep last night Miss Thing?" Curtis asked, sidling up next to her. "Cause I know you don't have two dresses that look like that."

"Chelsea," she said triumphantly.

"Fancy."

"And you? How was the swarthy fellow?"

"Straight," he said, pouting. "I slept at home." He picked up her Coke and took a sip before she could warn him, then made a face. "Girl!"

"I know, my mixology skills are lacking today. But it's doing the job."

Derek came back up, carrying an armful of bottles that he set on the bar.

"D, make this lady another drink!" Josie tried to shush him, but he kept going. "This thing is flammable."

Derek shot Josie an incredulous look as Curtis walked away, none the wiser to the havoc he'd wreaked. "Are you kidding me Josie?"

"Derek please, stop acting so high and mighty. We all drink, occupational hazard. I don't remember you being judgmental before."

"You just seem to be hitting it harder since what's-his-name came back to town."

Josie sighed an exaggerated sigh. "His name is Patrick."

"I know."

"And anyway, did you notice that his coming to town happens to coincide with my coming back from burying my grandmother?" She said that louder and more crudely than she wanted to. She had been pretty heavy-handed with the rum. She was embarrassed by her outburst, but instead of toning down she doubled down. "So, you can't exactly fault me for coping with my grief like a normal, flawed human being!"

Derek remained calm. "Nope, I can't. You're right. And as long as we're exploiting our personal tragedy to justify our behavior, I might remind you that I *just* told you I grew up with a woman who boozed her way through grief. So, maybe I'm a little jaded." He yanked back open the trap door and descended.

Josie felt ridiculous and selfish. Of course this was a trigger for Derek. How myopic she was being. She felt tears springing up behind her eyeballs and countered them by sucking back more of her boozy drink. "Derek, I'm sorry," she said when he re-emerged. "I wasn't thinking about—"

He waved her away but didn't make eye contact. "Sorry you're having a tough time."

She waited another moment, but the conversation was over.

They avoided each other as best they could, and as afternoon faded into evening, Josie realized she'd opened a Pandora's Box. She needed to maintain a certain level of inebriation or she'd crash. Thankfully it was a busy night, so it wasn't hard to keep a surreptitious buzz going. Derek was often occupied at one end of the bar, giving her access to whatever was at the other—whites and rosés they served by the glass in a trough of ice on the side closest to the dining room, reds and the odd bottle of booze that hadn't been returned to its proper spot at the other end.

Several hours into the night, Derek waved her over. Two flutes of champagne sat on a tray on the bar. "Table fourteen. Proposal." A sparkling diamond ring sat at the bottom of one of the flutes.

"Where's Sammy? That's his section tonight."

"In the weeds, but the gal doesn't want dessert, and her boyfriend's panicking. Can you drop these off?"

"Sure." She picked up the tray and walked into the dining room. A young couple sat at table thirteen holding hands and talking quietly. She'd noticed them when they'd first arrived, an attractive Asian-American couple, both in suits, hers a chic pencil skirt with a fitted short-sleeved jacket. Somehow after a few hours of food and drink her lipstick was still intact. She was bright-eyed and happy. They were in their early to mid-twenties, the same age Josie was when she'd arrived in New York City, and were lightyears more polished than she'd been. They would lend themselves perfectly to the "Vows" section of *The New York Times*.

As Josie approached, she felt a pang of sadness, regret for not having loved and trusted her twenty-four-year-old self enough. For not having been given, much earlier, the confidence needed to turn into a well-adjusted young woman with a loving boyfriend who was about to propose to her.

She plastered on an enormous smile. "Hello there." She winked at the man, who looked confused. "The bartender sent a little something special for you." She placed the flute with the ring in front of the young woman, who stared at it for a few seconds, then looked up at her boyfriend, eyes wide and lip trembling.

"Miss!" A man one booth away waved frantically to get her attention, and when she looked at him, he gestured to the glasses and to himself.

"What did I—" she stuttered.

Fourteen! a voice whispered in her ear, and she felt an icy rush.

"Oh my God, Peter," said the woman with the ring in front of her.

Peter looked as nauseated as Josie felt.

"I'm so sorry. Wrong table," she whispered and swept the glasses away, leaving the young woman slack-jawed and on the verge of tears. She delivered them to the right table, where the man was practically apoplectic, and made the decision to comp their entire meal.

Word traveled stunningly quickly. When she returned to the bar, sheepish, Derek's teeth were clenched. He slid a plate of food and a pint of water toward her.

Chapter Seven

THREE DAYS PASSED without Patrick showing up. Josie told herself it was okay, that this was the way dating in New York was supposed to work. Two busy people meeting up when they could, not clinging to each other for the sake of companionship. She told herself this less because she believed it— she was starting to have a sinking feeling it *had* just been a two-night stand—but because she hoped tricking herself would reflect outwardly, would mask her insecurity. The truth was that the hours ticking by, and the notion of Patrick as a regular distraction growing more remote, augmented her grief. Derek was right. She was drinking more to quiet her mind. If she didn't drink enough, she didn't sleep, and if she lay awake, she cried. It was a relentless cycle.

It didn't help that Alison had been around every night that week.

On Saturday it was raining sideways, and Josie's efforts to use an umbrella proved futile. The air conditioning chilled her wet skin when she walked into work.

People milled about the bar talking in hushed tones.

"What's going on?" she asked.

"We need an exorcist in here!" Johnny said.

"We do not," Curtis said. "We do not have a damn demon. We have a ghost."

Josie's pulse quickened. "What do you mean?" She locked eyes with Mia, who stood off to the side wringing her hands.

"Jeez, Josie," said Sam. "You haven't noticed anything either? Everyone says things've been wicked weird."

Of course she hadn't noticed anything. She'd been dulling her senses, all six of them.

"Okay, people!" Andy walked up from his office clapping his hands. "Focus. We need to talk about the strange things that have allegedly been going on here." He put air quotes around "strange things."

"Girl, there's nothing alleged here," Curtis said.

"Listen," Andy continued. "We've already discussed the fact that Chef is delicate these days. This is not the time for rumors and impractical jokes. If you're orchestrating this, it needs to stop."

"I didn't orchestrate a thing," Curtis insisted. "Swear on a stack of bibles someone ripped that damn pitcher of water right out my hands and dumped it on the floor."

"And I didn't move any of that shit around the kitchen," Johnny said. "Something fucked up is happening up there. I'm keeping my chef's knife on me, man."

Curtis gave an exaggerated look to the ceiling and then turned to him. "And what are you going to do with your chef's knife if you see a ghost, Johnathan?"

"I dunno, but I'm not taking any fuckin' chances." With that, he headed up to the kitchen.

"Have you had anything weird happen, Andy?" Sam asked.

"No," Andy answered quickly. "No."

"'Cause it's kind of cold in some parts of this place, and they say—"

"It's an old building," Derek said, exasperated. "Temperamental cooling system."

Josie looked at him, silently pleading with him to believe. She and Mia exchanged another glance.

"But if anyone can explain to me how my keys wound up on the floor in coat check, that'd be great. Thought I was gonna have to sleep here last night." Derek glanced toward Mia with an expression more concerned than angry.

"Keys to what?" Curtis asked.

"Everything. This place, the cellar, cash register, home…."

"That's interesting, D," Andy said. "Because that's exactly where I found my Palm Pilot a few days ago. Stashed in coat check. Seemed more the work of a thief than a ghost."

Josie blanched. Mia had slinked away and busied herself arranging things in the coatroom. "I wouldn't just start accusing people, guys," she said. "Coat check doubles as lost and found, so maybe you misplaced those things without realizing it, and one of the porters stashed them there."

"Yeah, that's not very effective thievery, to just move shit around," Curtis said. "Definitely the work of a mischievous ghost."

"All I ask, people, is that no one mention any of this nonsense in front of Chef. We need to leave him out of it entirely. So, please keep quiet if you misplace your keys or drop something and don't want to take the blame." Andy looked straight at Curtis, who held his right hand in the air.

"Stack of bibles."

Andy let out a labored sigh. "I'm going to meditate."

"What do you think is really going on?" Sam asked after he left.

"We're haunted," Curtis said with a shrug.

"Come on. You don't really believe in that stuff, do you?"

"It's not about belief, Samson. It's fact."

Sam looked to Josie for help. "What do you think, Josie?"

"What do I think? I think there's something to this. I've gotten some weird feelings here." She didn't want to scare the kid, but she didn't want to lie. "And plus, it kind of makes sense. We know people died here, right?"

"In that fire?" Sam asked.

"Yes."

"They died decades ago," Curtis said. "Why would they just be coming around now? No girl, this is someone else."

"Have you seen a ghost here?" Sam asked her.

"No," she said quickly. "I've never *seen* one anywhere."

"I have." Curtis was matter-of-fact.

"Oh, please," Derek groaned. "I'm not having this conversation." He stomped down the bar and began setting up.

"You've seen a ghost?" Sam asked.

"My Grandma Ethel. The night we buried her. I was seven. Trying to fall asleep, and the woman walked into my room and told me she loved me and to be a good boy and take care of my mama." Curtis clasped his hands and looked upward. "And I do, Grandma Ethel! Love you."

Sam looked at the ceiling, then back at Curtis. "How do you know?"

"Because I was there, Sam."

"How do you know you weren't dreaming?"

Curtis held his palms up. "I wasn't dreaming. It was Grandma Ethel. And when I told my mama the next day she cried and told me that Grandma Ethel had come into her room and kissed her goodnight, too."

"I don't know any dead people." Sam sounded disappointed.

Johnny came running down from the kitchen. "Okay this is fucked up. Huge jar of saffron that I bought yesterday, gone. Like hundreds of dollars-worth!"

"Check the coatroom," Curtis said drily.

"Seriously, I know exactly where I put it. Chef is gonna freak out."

"What did you get hundreds of dollars-worth of saffron for?" Josie asked.

"The bouillabaisse!"

"What's that?" Sam asked.

"It's the freakin' special. Jesus. This is a mess."

While everyone was prepping for dinner, Josie huddled by the coatroom with Mia. "It's not just us anymore."

"I don't think it ever was just us. I think we're just the ones to talk about it. This place has a past."

"That's got to be part of this, right? That people died here?"

"Could be."

"But what I don't get is why this all just started. I've been here for years. Curtis has been here even longer, and he's a believer. Why is this happening now?"

"Maybe it has something to do with Bistrot's future. Maybe they have the same fears you do about Chef leaving and what might happen to this building. If the restaurant goes away, any souls trapped here lose their home, right?"

"That's so sad."

"Maybe *trapped* isn't the right word. From what I've seen, some souls are attached to the places they liked spending time in life. And some linger because they have unfinished business."

"Maybe that's why Nanette's not around. I can't imagine she had any unfinished business."

"Some spirits come around just to look in on their loved ones, but it's awfully recent that Nanette passed. Sometimes it takes a while."

"It's cool and weird to have someone I can talk to about this stuff."

"You can talk to me anytime you want."

Josie wanted to broach the topic of the missing things, but she couldn't figure out how to. Though she wished it weren't the case, the fact that multiple items showed up in coat check was suspicious. Add that to Mia's returning to Bistrot after hours and her safe-cracking skills, and something wasn't sitting well with Josie. Maybe she was so desperate to get home that she was willing to resort to thievery. Or maybe it was all coincidence. Whatever the case, Josie knew she had to defend Mia if accusations flew.

While there were no new reports of paranormal activity during the night, Sam was a man obsessed. He asked Josie every chance he got about her experiences, about what specifically she felt when she got those feelings at the restaurant. He was so wrapped up that he failed to take note of the well-heeled older couple Josie seated in his section. As he breezed past her to deliver their appetizer, she pointed them out.

"Congrats, Sammy. You've got your first VIPs."

"Who?"

"Daphne and Cleaver Dunnehill!"

"Whoa!"

Daphne Lane Dunnehill was the star of decades' worth of iconic films and leading roles on Broadway. At sixty-five she still stunned and oozed with Southern belle sex appeal. She'd been married for an industry record-breaking forty years to British playwright, director, and legendary curmudgeon Cleaver Dunnehill. They had a home on Charles Street in the West Village and stopped into Bistrot from time to time.

Josie stood by while the now panic-stricken Sam delivered their food.

"Enjoy your mussels, please," he said. His voice cracked, and he grimaced.

"Beautiful," Daphne purred.

Cleaver Dunnehill pulled his glasses from his jacket pocket and studied the bowl.

Sam walked away stiffly, with Josie trailing him.

"Oh my God," he said in a stage whisper. "What are they doing here?"

"They're having dinner, Sam."

"They're, like, really famous!"

"I know, honey. Relax. This is not the time to drop off your headshot."

"Can't. I don't have one!"

"Don't tell me these things."

"Your boyfriend's a photographer, right? Does he take headshots?"

"I don't know. He's not my boyfriend."

After seating one of the last reservations of the night, Josie passed a frantic Curtis holding a pot of bouillabaisse and heading toward the kitchen stairs.

"Lady!" he cried when he saw her. "I need your help."

"Please don't tell me you're bringing that back."

He nodded and let out a maniacal laugh. "Chef will be nicer if you're with me."

"Okay. I've got you." She followed him up the steps and into the kitchen, where he signaled to Johnny.

Chef spun from the stove, nostrils flaring. "What is this?" he demanded, lifting the lid. He peered inside.

"It's bouillabaisse, Chef?" Curtis said meekly.

"It's bouillabaisse, Chef," he mimicked. "I know it's fucking bouillabaisse because it's my fucking bouillabaisse!"

"Chef, if I may," Josie said.

His expression softened at her voice. "Yes, Josephine?"

"Apparently the table that ordered this had a change of heart."

"What table, Josephine?"

She looked to Curtis.

"Table eighteen, Chef?" he said. "I've never seen them before, think they're probably tourists—"

Behind Chef's back, Johnny slid his finger across his throat, begging Curtis to stop talking.

"Real unrefined types, obviously," he continued. "Most of us, especially me, think the world of your bouilla—"

Chef wrenched the pot from his hands and kicked open the kitchen doors. Curtis and Josie followed him and stood on the balcony as he marched down the stairs, the entire restaurant watching. He turned right, walked a few paces, and slammed the pot down on table eighteen, startling the quartet that occupied it.

"Who ordered the bouillabaisse?" he asked in a voice that was both inappropriately loud and unnervingly calm. The only sounds in the dining room were flatware clinking and strains of "Stormy Weather" piping through the speakers.

"My wife did!" a man said, rising to look Chef in the eye. He was a good six inches shorter than Chef. "And it's flavorless."

"Do you know who I am?" Chef poked the man in the forehead on the word "know."

"Yes. You're the maniac who runs this place, and your bouillabaisse is disgraceful!"

With that, Chef flipped the dish over, and the seated diners jumped back as broth drenched the tablecloth and clams and mussels clattered to the ground. "Your palates are disgraceful!" he shouted. He stomped toward the front of the restaurant and out into the pouring rain.

The dining room remained dead silent as Mario ran down the stairs with Chef's helmet and the wheel to his bicycle.

Murmurs rose, punctuated by shocked laughter and angry shouts from the denizens of table eighteen, who followed Chef out the door.

Andy dashed into the dining room waving his arms amid the chaos. "I apologize for the disruption!" he shouted over the din. "There's been a misunderstanding. Please, go back to your meals. Ten percent off all your bills." He ushered two of the busboys over to clean up Chef's mess.

The rest of the night consisted of damage control, fumbled explanations, jokes about "dinner and a show," and plenty of drinks. Chef's meltdown had invoked in everyone else a celebratory spirit.

Sam was too mortified to approach the Dunnehills, and he let the runners take care of delivering and clearing their main courses. When it was time for coffee and dessert, Josie followed him over to the table.

"We apologize for the disruption," she said, placing dessert menus in front of them. "Chef's been under a bit of stress lately." She nudged Sam.

"Mister and Missus Dunnehill," he stammered. "I apologize for what happened. That was quite a...." The right word eluding him, he mumbled something that sounded like *shmuss*.

"Oh, darling," Daphne said with a sultry drawl straight out of Tennessee Williams. "We're in show business. We've seen it all. And please, it's Daphne."

Josie beamed while Sam blushed. Cleaver Dunnehill had yet to glance in his direction. Instead, he waved his fingers in the air to signal for the check. Sam stood awkwardly at the table until Josie pulled him away.

"Okay, honey, you know what to do with VIPs, right? Go upstairs and get some cookies." Special customers were gifted a cellophane-wrapped packet of the pastry chef's petit-fours and miniature Linzer tarts.

Sam looked at her, wide-eyed. "But he asked for the check! I don't think he wants dessert!"

"Sam, they're very, very important people. This is how we do things."

"How will they know they're free? What if they—"

"Sam!" He shrunk like a scolded puppy. "Sorry. You can do this. You say, 'These are for you, with our compliments,' or something like that. It's not rocket science."

"These are for you with our compliments?" He frowned on the last word. "Are you sure?"

Josie threw her hands in the air. "No. Say whatever you want."

Sam climbed the staircase to the kitchen, repeating the phrase to himself. Josie waited for him, and when he came back down still mouthing it, she followed him back to the table.

"These are for your compliments!" he said, setting the packet down with the check.

"Isn't that nice," Daphne said. "Look at these, Cleaver! Linzer tarts. My favorite."

Cleaver, studying the bill, peered over his reading glasses at the cookies and grunted.

"What's your name, my dear?" Daphne asked.

It took Sam a moment to remember. "Sam!" he said loudly, then lowered his voice. "I'm Sam. Bothwick. Sam Bothwick."

"Sam joined us in February," Josie said, putting her hand on his shoulder. "And we don't know how we managed without him."

"This has been just a lovely meal, Sam, theatrics aside. We'll certainly be here more now that we're back in the neighborhood. Won't we, darling?" The three of them looked at the top of Cleaver Dunnehill's head as he silently counted out twenty-dollar bills.

"We look forward to seeing you any time," Sam said with uncharacteristic poise and confidence. He started toward the front of the house. Not five steps in, he skidded on a puddle of water left by an umbrella dripping from the back of a chair. Josie reached for him like a mother on a playground. As he landed with a bruising thud, she winced.

"Oh!" A few nearby diners rushed to help him back up.

"I'm fine!" he announced, leaping to his feet, beet-red. This time, Cleaver Dunnehill was looking.

✢

THE BAR WAS packed after dinner with people talking about Chef's meltdown and the Dunnehills' appearance. It was not unheard of for celebrities to dine at Bistrot, with its myriad booths and tucked-away tables, along with the private twelve-top by the kitchen. In the first years after it opened, the restaurant was *the* place to see and be seen. That era ended shortly after Josie came on board.

Still, Bistrot drew famous faces. The staff had become adept at seating the ones who wanted to keep a low profile at the more discreet tables, and the ones who definitely did not—the up-and-coming actresses, the rock-and-roll bad boys, the socialites—in the center where tourists could gawk at them. The Dunnehills fell into the first category, but they were so iconic, so immediately recognizable, they'd never go unnoticed.

Sam was inconsolable.

"Honey, you didn't do anything wrong," Josie said with more patience than she felt. "It's not like you're the one who tried to drown our guests in fish stock."

"I know but it happened. And then I faceplanted in front of them!"

"Actually, you butt-planted."

He hunched his shoulders and hung his head. "What if they never come back?"

"I promise you they are coming back."

When Johnny emerged from the kitchen, he got a round of applause for pulling off the rest of the night with finesse. "Tequila all around." He swung his finger in the air, and Josie ducked under the bar to help Derek pour rounds of shots. He didn't notice. He was at the other end devoting all his attention to Alison and her friends, who seemed to have multiplied.

"Amazing," Josie said aloud.

"What's that?" Mia asked, reassuring Josie with her presence. A thief would keep a lower profile, not stick around after her shift.

"Derek's ever-growing harem."

"Has Patrick been by?" Mia asked gently.

"Nope. But whatever. He knows where to find me. Would be nice if he chose to."

"Bless his heart. I'm fixin' to get out of here. Get home safe, okay?"

"My chariot awaits," Josie said, nodding to Curtis.

Mia waved to the group on her way out.

"What are you mumbling about over there, lady?" Curtis asked.

"Just that you'll see me home tonight."

"Of course I will. But seriously, y'all, what is going on with Chef? He's decibel-eleven crazy. If he hadn't dumped a thirty-dollar dish of food on the floor, I'd think he was going bankrupt."

"He's not going bankrupt, man," Johnny said. "But if he'd splurged on a little more saffron we could have avoided this whole fucking mess. His wife's practically a DuPont."

"What's a DuPont?" Sam asked.

Curtis rolled his eyes skyward and started to answer, but Josie shushed him.

"They're a very wealthy family, honey. She's not a DuPont, but she does come from money."

"Bouillabaisse without saffron," Johnny said, shaking his head at the notion. "Listen, I've been spending a lot of time with him up there, man. He's losing it, plain and simple. *Está loco.*"

"That's Spanish, Sam," Curtis said snippily.

"So, are we in trouble?" Sam asked.

"Yeah, we're in trouble," Johnny said, pounding his fist on the bar. He pointed to the Y2K hat on his head. "The fucking world's about to end. Chef's like one of those wild animals that senses a fucking tsunami and runs inland."

"The world is not about to end," Josie said. She was in no mood for his theories.

"I'm not making this up!" Johnny insisted. "You gotta check out this guy Eric Stone, Media Wars. He knows his shit."

"I don't know who that is, but if he's peddling conspiracy theories, I'll pass. I have enough on my plate."

"Your boyfriend's here, Miss Thing," Curtis said, hitting her thigh.

"Josie!" Sam said. "Headshots?"

Patrick appeared beside her, a Leica camera slung over his shoulder. "Hey, baby." He leaned in and kissed her on the lips.

"Fancy meeting you here." Josie felt self-conscious in front of her coworkers and adamant not to show it. Derek was certainly not being discreet about dating a customer. "You know these fellas, right?"

"Of course." He nodded at them and took her hand.

Curtis and Sam busied themselves in conversation with the people next to them. Johnny wandered down the bar toward Alison and her friends.

"I'm sorry I haven't been around sooner. Putting out fires at the school all week and some family stuff to tend to." Patrick ran his fingers down her arm.

"Everything okay?"

"Getting there. But it's kept me away too many nights. Can I make it up to you?" He managed to make an innocuous questions sound lewd.

"What do you have in mind?" She crossed her legs, blinking up at him. The tequila was weakening her inhibitions. She could think of a dozen ways he could make it up to her once they were back at his place. Hell, she'd take him down to the basement right now if he wanted.

"You're off Monday, yeah? Can I take you to dinner?"

"Oh!" Her face flushed, as though he could read her thoughts and knew how off-base her assessment of the situation was. "Sure, that sounds nice."

"Cool. I can't stick around tonight. Have to help a friend stretch some canvases early tomorrow."

"Cool." Sam waved at Josie behind Patrick's back. "Oh! Do you take headshots?"

"Sure, who needs?"

"Sammy," she called to him. "Patrick takes headshots. You want to set something up?"

"Oh, yeah, cool, um, I need headshots."

Patrick nodded. "Cool, man. I can make that happen. You want to come by my place sometime?"

"For headshots?"

Josie clearly needed to facilitate the operation. "Yes, Sam. Patrick, when would be good for you?"

"We're all off Monday, yeah? Why don't you guys come over in the afternoon, and then you and I can go to—"

"Okay, Sammy?" She cut Patrick off.

"How much does he charge?" Sam asked.

"*He* is right here. Patrick, how much for headshots?"

"Ah," Patrick said. "I'm happy to help out another artist. These are on the house."

"Aren't you wonderful?" Josie said.

He winked at her and pulled out one of his *Photographer & Bon Vivant* business cards.

Josie cringed as he wrote his address on the back and handed it to Sam, who studied it curiously.

"I'll see you Monday, man," Patrick said, punching him lightly in the arm. "Walk me out, babe?"

She cringed again at the coarseness of his phrasing. "I'd love to get some air," she said loudly. If this thing was to be sporadic, at the very least she needed it to look reciprocal to anyone who was paying attention. No one was. Derek was making drinks, Johnny was holding court with Alison's friends, one of whom was twirling her hair and giggling loudly at whatever he was saying. He was eating it up.

"Thank you for being so generous with Sam," Josie said when they got outside. "He's pretty green."

"I know that, baby. I know a lot of Sams."

"Yeah, but you don't really know this one, so I appreciate it."

"Happy to help a friend of yours."

Josie smiled. "Thank you."

"So, you'll swing by with him, yeah? Monday around two?"

Monday was two days away.

"Sure," she said shrilly. "Sounds great!"

He put his arms around her waist and kissed her, holding her for a few moments. She marveled at the mixed messages. "You know I miss you the days I don't see you?"

She shook her head.

"I do. It takes a hell of a lot of willpower not to just roll by here every night so I can wake up next to you. But my mornings start so early, and it wouldn't be fair to you or my students." He kissed her again. "I'll see you Monday, babe."

Josie felt smitten as she walked back inside and glanced into the coat room. Andy was right, there were a lot of abandoned items. But people were forgetful, the weather was unpredictable, and there was a large sign absolving the restaurant—and therefore Mia—of any responsibility for things left behind.

Something red stashed high on a shelf caught her eye. She walked into the room and stood on her toes to reach the shelf, feeling a sense of foreboding as her fingers found the object. She pulled down a tin of saffron and stuffed it in her pocket.

Chapter Eight

"LADY, YOU CAN admit you like the guy." Curtis swayed from the subway pole as they hurtled toward Brooklyn.

"I admit I like the guy."

"You," he slurred, gesturing up and down her body. "Have got your groove back missy."

"Back? I guess I missed it the first time around. Anyway, my buzzed friend...."

"Call me Buzz Aldrin."

"More like Ruth Buzzi."

"Ooooh, girl, wish I'd said that first. Anyway, what?"

"Anyway, ghosts in the restaurant? What do you think?"

"Yeah, girl. Ghosts in the restaurant and Chef gone mad. Coincidence?"

"I don't know. What about things going missing. Ghosts, or...?"

"Now that." He pointed to her and hiccupped. "That I'm not sure about. I suspect human intervention there."

"But you're not accusing...." She stalled, waiting to see if he'd say it first.

He held his hands up and hiccupped again, then grabbed the pole to keep from falling. "Girl, I'm accusing no one. I'm just saying it's odd."

ON SUNDAY, ANDY announced Chef would be taking a few days off, and Johnny would be in charge of the kitchen. This was, as Johnny would tell anyone who asked, "a big fucking deal."

In the ten years since he'd opened Bistrot, Chef had missed exactly one day of work—to attend his mother's funeral. And while he'd always been quick-tempered, fabled crenshaw incident notwithstanding, things had never gone as far as they had the previous night.

Johnny's first official meal at the helm was brunch, which contained few surprises. Between seating guests and answering phones, Josie visited with Mia throughout the day and into dinner.

"Patrick finally came by."

"That's nice, baby."

"It was lovely. Unfortunately Derek can't stop being weird about him."

"He's protective," Mia said with her unreadable smile.

"Maybe so, but it's not necessary. I'm not in love with the guy or anything, I'm just getting to know him. He's a good guy. You met him. What did you think?"

Mia gave a response as non-committal as her smile. "I think things have a way of working out as they're meant to."

The list of missing items, which had grown the previous night, was the elephant in the room. Josie wanted Mia to bring it up. When she didn't, she tried to talk herself out of her suspicion. No one else had come right out and blamed her. And anyway, nothing was actually missing. It had all just been moved.

Johnny entered the bar after dinner to another round of applause and celebratory shots.

Curtis was mid-toast, the third one of the night, when the phone rang.

Josie dashed to the hostess stand to answer. "Good evening, Bistrot."

"Good evening, Bistrot. Who am I speaking with?" a man with an Australian accent asked.

"This is Josie. How may I help you?"

"Right, just a couple questions then, love. What's your role there?"

"My role? I'm the hostess. May I ask what this is in reference—"

"And what was it that someone sent back to the kitchen last night? Was it the boeuf bourguignon?"

"It was bouillabaisse," she said, clapping her hand over her mouth when she realized what was happening. New York had several prominent gossip columns that delighted in scandals in the restaurant world. "Who is this?"

"Marcus Dreyer, love. New York Mirror.*"*

"I have no further comment," Josie said, hanging up.

She flushed with anger and embarrassment. The *Mirror* was one of the city's tabloid papers, and Marcus Dreyer ran its gossip column, "The Dreyer Report." He and his team were known for scathing takedowns of New York personalities. Some were warranted, like the conman real estate moguls who got rich off others' suffering, the wealthy narcissists who'd do anything to see their names in print. But others, like the actress with a drinking problem or, in this case, the chef on the verge of a nervous breakdown, were just cruel. Capitalizing on others' misfortune to sell papers was a soulless enterprise. And Josie had just enabled it to happen.

She took deep breaths and tried to calm herself. She'd hardly said a word. Anyone who was in the room that night could have been the source, and if the story ran, a likelihood she pushed to the back of her mind, she'd deny her involvement.

She went back to the bar, bursting at the seams and needing to tell someone what happened. "If I tell you something, do you promise to keep it between us?" she asked Derek.

"What's going on?"

"You know who Marcus Dreyer is?"

"Sure," Derek said, distracted as he looked past her. He frowned. "Hey, can you cover me for a few?" He ducked under the bar.

Alison stood at the entrance to the room in an oversized rain jacket. Her usually pin straight hair was a wild mess, and her makeup was smeared as though she'd cried much of it off. She looked young and vulnerable. She and Derek spoke for a minute, then he took her hand and led her outside.

For the next ten minutes, Josie ran the bar, managing not to screw up too many drink orders despite being utterly distracted herself. The woman who ordered Shiraz and got Merlot didn't seem to notice, and Josie charged well prices when she mistakenly poured top shelf.

Through the front windows she kept an eye on Derek and Alison as they talked under the awning. Finally, he came back in alone.

"Everything okay?" Josie asked.

"Not exactly." His jaw was tight, and he didn't make eye contact. He took his place behind the bar and made his way toward a customer aggressively waving a large bill. This was the type of person Derek usually ignored.

"Derek, what's going on?" Josie asked him a few minutes later. He wore an expression she didn't recognize and looked like he'd aged five years since the start of the night.

"I can't get into it right now."

Her mind swam with possibilities. He and Alison had split up. She'd cheated on him. He'd cheated on her. They'd had a blowout. Something was clearly wrong between them, and Josie derived no satisfaction from this. Whatever her feelings about the girl, Derek liked her, and he looked stricken. She was not one for schadenfreude. But she could not stand the idea that he was keeping another secret from her. This was not how their friendship was supposed to work.

"Can I do anything?" she asked the next time he came near.

"No, you can't!" he said tersely, then, catching himself, added, "But thanks."

He avoided her for the rest of the night, and she stewed for just as long. By the time she got home and flopped down into bed, she couldn't decide whether she was more hurt or angry at Derek's continued secrecy. At the same time, she knew she had no right to either emotion. She would have to be patient and trust he'd open up to her eventually. He had once, he would again. It was important to her that people saw her as someone they could talk to about anything, someone who would handle their most difficult truths as delicately as if they were spun from glass.

❧

ON MONDAY AFTERNOON, Josie commuted into Manhattan with a small overnight bag she hoped looked like a large purse. She didn't want to appear presumptuous. When she got to Patrick's brownstone, Sam was waiting on the stoop in the rain.

"Did he not give you the apartment number?"

"No, he just said to ring the bell for Goldstein. What's a *Bon Vivant*? And who's Goldstein?"

"This is a sublet, honey. Goldstein's the owner. Why are you standing outside?" She tilted her umbrella over his head.

"'Cause I was waiting for you to get here first!"

"You didn't need to wait for me! You have an appointment!"

"I don't really know the guy, Josie! I didn't want him to think I was, you know, all excited about this."

"Sam, you have a professional photographer shooting your headshots for free. What's not to be excited about? And why didn't you bring a freaking umbrella?"

"I forgot."

"You need to get yourself together. A bad headshot is worse than no headshot at all!" She shook her head and pressed the button next to *Goldstein*.

"—lo!" came Patrick's muffled voice.

"Hi there," she said. "It's—"

The buzzer sounded, and she pushed open the door. She led Sam up the stairs. It was at least two flights up, possibly three. Despite having spent the night a few times, she was foggy on details like which apartment was his. As they neared the top of the third flight, a door opened one floor below.

"Hello!" Patrick called into the hallway.

"Oh! There you are." Josie retraced her steps.

Sam followed too closely, like a newborn foal ambling after its mother.

"Hey, gorgeous," Patrick said when they reached him.

"Hey, gorgeous."

"Sammy, how you doin' man?" He went for a handshake.

Sam misread the gesture and slapped him five.

"Alrighty then," Patrick said with a laugh. "Babe, you want to get Sammy a towel to dry off while I finish setting up?"

Josie relished the proprietary feeling of knowing her way around the apartment. While she got Sam situated, Patrick darted around the room adjusting lights and reflectors. He positioned Sam on a stool in front of a white backdrop and had him hold the light meter.

"Sammy, relax!" Josie said. "Have fun with this!"

"You want a beer or something?" Patrick asked. "Might help loosen you up, yeah?"

"I don't know. Josie?"

"Honey, I don't know if you want a beer."

"Okay, yes. Please."

She went to the kitchen and pulled two from the fridge. "Patrick?"

"Not while I'm on the clock, babe."

She cracked open the bottles and handed one to Sam. "Cheers, Sammy. I'm glad you're finally doing this."

Sam loosened up significantly over the next forty-five minutes. Patrick was a consummate professional, and Josie found the whole thing appealing—his demeanor, his deft handling of the equipment, his art direction.

"Don't stand still man. Keep moving. I'm going to shoot some against the bricks."

David Bowie's "Fame" came on the stereo, and Josie turned up the volume.

"It's a sign!" She danced behind Patrick to energize Sam, who looked like he was starting to fade.

He did his best to move along to the music. What he lacked in rhythm he made up for in enthusiasm. Next came Prince's "1999," a song ridiculously overplayed that summer. But Sam pumped his fist when he heard the opening bars, so she kept it on.

"You having fun honey?"

He gave her a thumbs up.

While they continued to work, she stood in the doorway to the kitchen, watching them.

Every now and then there were moments that Josie knew were leaving an indelible mark in her memory as they unfolded, moments of beauty and purpose. The late-afternoon rain falling outside, the song—an anthem of the year—and bearing witness to this lifechanging step in Sam's career filled her with warmth and love.

And with love came eventual loss. The tears came quickly, overwhelming her. She tried to brush them away but was too late. Never a natural crier before, since Nanette's death she'd become someone who cried even in moments of joy. Joy only reminded her of her pain.

"Josie, are you okay?" Sam asked.

Patrick turned around. "Baby, what's going on?"

"Nothing guys," she said with a laugh no one believed. She heard herself starting to babble. "Sorry. Tears of joy because I'm so proud of you Sammy! This is an amazing step."

"Thanks, Josie, but you don't have to say sorry."

"You know what, I think we got some great shots," Patrick said. "What do you say we wrap for the day?"

"I'm sorry you guys! I don't want you to cut it short."

"No, we definitely have enough. Tell you what Sammy. I'll develop the contact sheet and bring it by this week, and if we think we need a couple more, we can shoot on the weekend. Sound good?"

"Sure, man. Sounds good."

"He did great, didn't he?" Josie said. "Thank you so much."

"He did great," Patrick said, coming toward her. "Come here." He pulled her into a tight hug and stroked the back of her head. "I'm sorry you're hurting so much."

The longer he held her, the higher the likelihood she'd tear up again, so she pulled away. "It's overwhelming. But I've got good support, so that's everything."

"Including me."

"Including you, both of you!" she added to include Sam, who stood awkwardly looking at the books on the shelf. "I'm going to go make myself presentable before we head out."

"You're gorgeous. But do your thing, and then let's go have a nice dinner."

Josie looked at herself in the bathroom mirror, at her lashes wet with tears and the undereye circles shiny beneath her concealer. She sucked in her cheeks. Her nose and upper lip were chapped from so much crying. Yet there was a softness to her face she hadn't seen before, an animal purity, as though Nanette's death had stripped her of some invisible barrier and revealed something new. Her loss anchored her more fully to the world.

She finally saw what Patrick must see because, though she didn't want to admit it, part of her assumed they were one night away from his waking up, looking at her, and realizing it was the booze all along. In the mirror now, she saw a beautiful, grown woman wiser for having experienced the exquisiteness of grief.

Patrick was taking her on a date, and that would have made Nanette happy. Nanette wanted her to find love as fervently as Josie tried to avoid doing so. She'd been raised by two single women and had no model of a husband and white picket fence to which to aspire.

The difference between Josie's mother and grandmother was her mom remained bitter long after her divorce, and Nanette, whose husband had died before Josie was born, accepted her widowhood with grace and strength. Josie grew up believing she shouldn't need a man and created the mythology that craving companionship equated weakness. Love offered no guarantees. Look at her parents, who by all accounts were very much in love when they started dating. By the time Josie was old enough to wonder about this, her mother had sworn off talking about her marriage. So, she asked Nanette, who explained that yes, they had truly loved each other once, but people changed. She impressed in adolescent Josie that one can never fairly judge anyone else's relationship. Things were rarely black and white. When Josie thought about this in later years, she realized her grandmother was taking the onus off her father, upon whom it had been squarely placed by her mother. Josie's mom's version of the narrative was of a victimized woman who rose from the ashes and became a fighter. Nowhere was there room for her father's having been a halfway respectable person. But adult Josie understood people didn't philander because they were happy and getting their needs met. People philandered because something was missing, and they needed an out. While she only really knew her mother as the woman who'd been left by her father, she didn't imagine the bitterness she conjured post-divorce had come out of nowhere. She didn't imagine her pre-divorce mother had somehow been just an easy person to live and get along with, and the sole source of her acridity was that her husband had left.

This gave Josie a newfound sense of compassion for both of her parents, something that had been missing for decades.

When she returned to the living room, the men were sitting on the sofa drinking beers and immersed in conversation. Patrick had changed into black jeans and a black collared shirt.

"Don't you look dashing," Josie said, perching on the arm of the sofa.

"You, too, babe," he said. "You ready? Sammy's going to join us."

Josie's smile stayed plastered on her face.

They walked a few blocks up Tenth Avenue, Josie next to Patrick under his umbrella, Sam on his other side. Patrick held her hand. Sam was buzzed and excitable and babbling about show business, oblivious that he was crashing their date.

"The ultimate goal is L.A. That's where all the action is, right?"

"Not necessarily," Patrick said. "There's a ton of stuff shot here, too. Personally, if I were an actor starting out, I'd probably stay in New York for a while."

He led them into Bottino, a Tuscan restaurant Josie knew was a favorite among the Chelsea art gallery crowd. The hostess, a gorgeous woman with thick, beachy hair and a tan that belied the summer's weather, knew Patrick by name and kissed him on the lips. Under other circumstances, this would have flustered Josie, but that it was so blatant and Patrick neither dropped her hand nor looked uncomfortable rendered it innocuous. The hostess walked them to a table in a covered back garden. With its candles and the rain cascading down the windows, it was painfully romantic for their dinner for three.

"Sorry, babe," Patrick said. Sam was distracted by the hostess and not paying attention. "I told him we were going out, and he thought I was inviting him. Next time will just be the two of us."

Over a celebratory round of prosecco, Sam grilled Patrick about life in L.A.

"Don't get me wrong, man, I love the town," Patrick said after reeling off a half-dozen reasons he didn't. "It's just not New York."

"So, why don't you live in New York?" Sam asked.

"I'm beginning to wonder that myself." He put his hand on Josie's knee, and she took hold of it. It felt sweet and natural.

"Sam," she said. "Let me ask you this. What's next once you have your headshots?"

She could see the wheels cranking as he crafted his response. "I'm going to start auditioning."

"And how are you going to find your auditions?"

He bounced his leg and bit his lip. "You know, all the... you know."

"Hon, it's okay if you need a hand figuring this stuff out. You're not supposed to know it intrinsically."

"I don't know it at all," he said in an exhale. "That's what I've been trying to explain. I got sucked into working at the restaurant and forgot about the rest of my life."

"Well, you just described my life in a nutshell," said the hostess drily as she topped off their glasses.

"Nothing wrong with admitting what you don't know," Patrick said. "Only way to figure out what you need to learn."

"I'd be happy to help you get things started," Josie said. "I'll pick up a copy of *Backstage,* and we can go through it together."

"And I know a couple people here who can give you advice," Patrick said. "Couple pals who are actors."

"Not to mention," Josie said. "Walk into most any bar or restaurant in this town and three-quarters of the staff are in the business. We're kind of an anomaly."

"It's true, man. I also know a manager you can talk to and a casting director. Got to network. We can make it fun."

"Do you think they'd want to talk to me?"

"Of course. I know good people."

Josie was as touched by Sam's innocence as she was Patrick's kindness to him. Sam crashing their dinner turned out to be all right. For one thing, he was thrilled to be included. For another, it gave Josie deeper insight into Patrick, into who he really was, someone talented, wise, and generous.

She looked at him, at his square jaw and beautiful, kind eyes. There was a faint scar on his cheek she'd not noticed before. He was listing off other people for Sam to talk to and absently put his arm around Josie. Aware she was tempting fate, in that very moment she felt everything was all right.

Chapter Nine

A S SHE MADE her way from Chelsea to Bistrot Tuesday morning, Josie felt strong and grounded. She couldn't recall enjoying a day off as much as she had this one. She stopped to buy a large iced coffee, light and sweet, and flipped through a *New York Times Magazine* someone had left behind. There was a profile of a celebrity chef. Seeing it made her stomach lurch. Marcus Dreyer's column ran on Tuesdays. Somehow she'd managed to completely block him from her thoughts, that dubious ability of hers to compartmentalize.

When she walked into the restaurant, the crew was gathered for its meeting. She slipped into a booth opposite Derek, who looked as tense as she felt.

Andy walked swiftly up from his office holding a copy of the *New York Mirror.* Josie felt nauseous.

"Josie, Josie, Josie," he said, shaking his head and pursing his lips. "Josie."

"Oh my God Andy. I didn't tell him anything!"

"Didn't you?"

"I swear!"

"Do you?"

"Yes. I mean, I didn't tell him much."

The others followed the back and forth as though watching a tennis match.

"Really. Let's read this aloud, shall we?" He opened the paper.

"Wait," Curtis said. "Is this about that twat Marcus Dreyer? Did he write about Chef again?"

"Yes and yes."

"That guy's a dick," Johnny said. "Why are you bringing Josie into this?"

Andy began reading. "'Going Down in a Bouillabaisse of Glory,' by Marcus Dreyer."

"Who is a massive twat," Curtis said.

Andy rolled his eyes and looked back at the paper. "'Eriq Villeroy, head chef of tired West Village eatery Bistrot, has never been known for his stoicism in the face of adversity.'"

"Tired?!" Johnny shouted.

Andy held up his index finger. "'Who can forget the crenshaw melon incident of '92?'" He paused and looked around the group, daring anyone to forget it. "'Lest one assume that another several years of restaurant ownership in the food capital of the United States had softened the faux Frenchman, allow us to set the record straight.

"'This reporter had the pleasure of speaking with someone from the front of house, a real 'pussycat,' who confirmed salacious details of Villeroy's latest—and perhaps last—act.'" He looked up again. "Pussycat. As in Josie and the—"

"Yeah, we get it," Curtis said. "Go on."

"'Our Gal Friday confirmed that *l'enfant terrible* dumped an entire pot of bouillabaisse on an unsuspecting diner for reasons unknown. It is rumored he then stormed out of his restaurant *sans culottes*, wielding handfuls of what conflicting reports have named jicama, cilantro, and dill.

"'All of us at 'The Dreyer Report' extend our concern to Chef Villeroy over his apparent troubles. And to the rest of you, whatever Bistrot's dubious fate, this reporter suggests avoiding the garnish at all costs.'" Andy folded the paper and stared at the group, his right eye twitching.

"Tales from the Twat," Curtis said. "Who cares?!"

"Masturbatory hack writer," Derek said. "And *sans culottes* is as pretentious as it is inaccurate."

"What's jicama?" Sam asked.

"Seriously, Andy, he called at the end of the night and asked my name. I was insanely tired. He caught me off guard!"

"But you were alert enough to let him know that it was bouillabaisse."

"Andy," Derek said. "Do you honestly think this story wouldn't have made the rounds anyway? There are no secrets in this town. The gossip vultures feed on this."

"It's true," Johnny said. "I've been in restaurants ten years. These jamokes live for this shit."

"And who even reads that rag?" Derek asked.

"Um, a lot of people?" Andy said. "Including Chef?"

"You should just hire a fixer, Andreas," Curtis said.

"A what?"

"A fixer. A flack. A publicist to address the rumors."

"He's kidding," Derek said, motioning to Curtis to stop talking.

"Did we get a bunch of cancellations or something?"

"I don't know, Josie. I didn't check the reservations line. I believe that would be your job? For the time being?"

Josie bit her lip. Curtis slid into the booth next to her and put his head on her shoulder.

"Anyway," Andy said. "We do have other matters to discuss. Chef is, for better or for worse, taking a 'mental health break.' I think it's safe to say he's been under a great deal of stress lately, and he doesn't respond well to stress."

"Ya think?!" someone said.

"How much time we talking?" Johnny asked, leaning forward in his seat.

"We don't know yet. Which means, of course, that you'll be running the kitchen. Assuming you're up for it, which I, for one, hope you are. I mean, you're a real pro in there." He laughed nervously and his voice rose in pitch. "You are staying, right?"

"Of course you are!" Curtis said. "You're a rock star!" He started to slow clap, and someone joined in, but when it didn't take with the rest of the group, they stopped. Curtis sniffed. "Well, you are."

"I tell you what I'm not up for is a fucking ghost in the kitchen. Can we get like a shaman or someone to come in and cleanse the place?"

"Sage," Curtis said. "We need to smudge the place with sage."

"Johnny, man, this place is not haunted," Derek said.

"How do we know?"

"We don't," Josie said, relieved to be out of the hot seat. "Like I said the other day, there is definitely some kind of weird energy here."

"You can say that again, Lady Love," Curtis said.

"Jeez, has everyone felt it except me?" Sam asked.

"Nope!" Derek said. "Because there's nothing to feel. Right, Andy?"

Andy remained quiet, staring at the notes in his hand. One by one everyone looked at him and waited for him to chime in. When he looked up, he had a half-smile on his face.

"What aren't you telling us, man?" Johnny asked.

"There was, in fact, an incident. And it's a pretty tough one to explain."

"Tougher than hurling shellfish at our guests?" Derek asked, and people laughed.

"Just hear me out, please. I'm only the messenger. But I feel as manager that it's my duty to at least try." He took a deep breath, and Josie held hers. "Apparently Chef came in early yesterday to get some of his personal items. He was the only one here."

Curtis squeezed Josie's shoulder, and she jumped.

"And some pretty strange things happened."

"Like what?" Sam was mesmerized.

"Like knives sliding off their magnetic strips. Like the freezer door popping open by itself. And like a jar of tarragon falling off a shelf and breaking all over the floor."

"It's a crowded kitchen," Derek said. "And he's not the most graceful gazelle in the Serengeti. Things fall."

"There's more." Andy's eye twitched wildly, his face reddening. "According to Chef, when he went to clean up the spilled tarragon, there was a message."

A few people broke into giggles, and Andy shushed them.

"What the fuck!" Johnny said.

"What's tarragon?" Sam asked.

"It's a spice, Sam," Curtis hissed.

"It's actually an herb, brother," Derek said.

"Same difference." Curtis rolled his eyes.

"Actually," Derek said. "Herbs are leaves. Spices are the bark and roots and all the other stuff."

"What was the message?" Josie asked, holding her hand up to quiet the others.

"According to Chef, and I know it sounds implausible, someone had spelled out 'time to go.'"

More uncertain laughter spread around the group.

"He thought it was a prank, so he ran to the walk-in to see who was hiding, and the door slammed behind him. He couldn't open it, like it was locked or something."

"That's terrifying," Curtis said. "How did he get out?"

"He heard a voice whisper the same words, 'time to go.' When he tried the door again, it opened."

Josie took a shaky breath. She could hear her heart pounding, blood roaring in her ears. She looked at everyone else. Sam was ashen, Curtis wide-eyed, Johnny had his elbows on the table and his head in his hands, and Derek whistled and stared at the ceiling.

"Fuck no," Johnny said, shaking his head. "No, no, no, no, and no."

"Look, I'm just telling you what he told me. The bottom line is he needs a break and is taking one."

"Okay, great. Now what?" Derek asked. "He closes shop, and we're all out of work because he believes in the freaking tooth fairy?"

Curtis raised his hand. "I've got an idea, Andy! Maybe you can hire a medium."

"There is no plan to close yet," Andy said to Derek, ignoring Curtis.

"Yet!" someone shrieked.

"Yet. For now, Bistrot will remain open, and Johnny will steer the ship."

"Johnny!" Curtis said. "This is perfect. This is what you've always wanted!"

"Nope. Nyet. No way. Never said I wanted to work with a fucking poltergeist."

"There is no poltergeist," Derek said in a monotone. "Jesus, the man is out of his gourd, and the easiest way to save face after the other night is to invent a boogeyman that communicates via turmeric."

"Tarragon," Andy said.

"Right. Didn't mean to sound crazy there, boss. Folks, you know how many times I've closed this place by myself? Or how many times Mario's come in first thing to open up? Don't you think if it was haunted we'd have noticed by now?"

"Not necessarily," Josie said.

"Okay people, one day at a time. We don't know what's going to happen to the restaurant down the road, but for now we have a couple big groups coming in tonight." Andy caught himself and looked at Josie. "Fine, I did check the reservations, and no, no one canceled."

"Jesus, Andy," she said, exhaling for what felt like the first time since the meeting had begun.

"So, for the time being, Johnny is in charge. I'll send out for some sage to smudge. I'm going—"

"To meditate," Curtis, Derek, and Josie said in unison.

Andy offered everyone a withering look before walking away.

"Jesus effin' Christ," Johnny said.

"Think about it brother," Derek said. "Chef's meltdown didn't exactly happen overnight. You've been running the show up there for months."

"It's true, Johnny. You've saved this place. We need you," Curtis said.

Johnny looked at his watch. "Don't reckon I have much choice. But fuck if I'm going to spend any time alone up there ever."

"You know what," Josie said. "Let me run out and get some sage. They've got to have it at that hippie place on Eighth Street or the health food store down the block."

"Buy a shit load of it," Johnny said.

Josie pulled her rain jacket from the bench. As she put it on, the tin of saffron tumbled to the ground and slid to a stop at Derek's foot. With everything else that had gone on in the past few days—Marcus Dreyer, Derek's mystery problem, her beautiful day and night with Patrick—she'd forgotten about it.

Derek looked at the tin, then up at Josie.

"This is not what it looks like," she said, picking it up.

"It looks like Johnny's missing saffron."

"I know. I found it under one of the banquettes and forgot to give it to him."

"How would it have made its way under one of the banquettes?"

"It just did." She handed it to him. "Do me a favor and bring it upstairs? Just say one of the porters found it and put it on the bar or something." She walked away, aware the optics of the moment were not in her favor, but she would not feed into whatever suspicion might be looming around Mia. A third item showing up in the coatroom was too much.

Josie found sage at the Lifethyme Natural Market on Sixth Avenue and bought several bundles.

As she was rounding the corner on 9th Street, she ran into Mia heading into work.

"How was your day off?" Mia asked her.

"Amazing. I spent it with Patrick. And Sam. Now I'm fully back on the job," she said, holding up her shopping bag.

"What do you have there?"

"Sage. We need to do some serious energy cleansing. There's been an uptick in strange activity at the restaurant." This was the opportunity Josie had been waiting for. She filled Mia in on the Chef anecdote.

"That sounds like someone who wants to force some change around here."

"Yeah, but that's not all. Remember how everyone was talking the other day about things vanishing and winding up in the coatroom?"

"No! What kinds of things?" If Mia thought she was a suspect, she didn't let on.

"Derek's keys, Andy's Palm Pilot."

"His what?"

"That electronic calendar thingy. I don't know, I don't speak tech. And then the weirdest, the other day Johnny couldn't find this expensive tin of saffron."

"I remember him saying that."

"Yeah, and when I was getting my jacket, I found it on one of the coatroom shelves."

"Sounds like some kind of mischief maker to me," Mia said with a laugh.

"A mischievous spirit?"

"Sure, could be that, too," she said. Josie was troubled by the note of relief in her voice. "That's just the kind of thing they do, some of them. Like my darling Ruby—"

"Your friend who overdosed? Have you seen her in the restaurant?"

"No, but you just made me think of her. She loved to play pranks."

She was lying about something, and Josie needed to know what. She'd have to keep Mia talking and hope that the truth came out.

They walked into the restaurant and stood outside the coatroom.

"What was Ruby like?" Josie asked.

"She was a sweetheart. Fiercely loyal. She'd do anything for us girls. The boys loved her, too. But she was a troubled soul. A beautiful, troubled soul."

"What did she look like?"

"Long red hair—that's why we called her Ruby—green eyes, tiny little dancer's body."

"When you've seen her since she died, does she look the same?"

"Yes ma'am, except her troubles are gone. She looks more at peace. That's how it is in the spirit world."

Josie felt a sharp pang of sadness. "God, I wish I'd talked to Nanette about all this when I had the chance. I wish I hadn't let my mom's disbelief impact my own."

"I hear you, girl. I know how hard it is to have people close to you who don't get it. But I've learned if people just don't want to believe, they won't. They'll ignore even the strongest signs or figure out a way to make them fit their comfortable version of reality."

"Yeah, my mom does that, although I don't know how comfortable her version of reality is."

"My mom too, and my daughter."

"But your daughter's so young. Maybe she'll accept it when she's older?"

"Maybe so, but you know well that the sooner you're comfortable with it all, the better. The more peace you can have when you lose people. Because you *can* find peace after, hard as it seems in the moment."

"It seems absolutely impossible right now."

"I know it does. Believe me, Josie. This will get easier."

Josie closed her eyes to keep the tears from reaching them. She needed to accept her gift so Nanette could reach her, and she was filled with regret for not having done so sooner. If she worked hard at it now, if she let Mia continue to guide her through it all, maybe she could find the peace that eluded her. "I really want to talk to Nanette," she said.

"Are you talking to me?"

Her eyes flew open, and Sam stood in front of her. Mia had slipped away and was climbing the stairs to the ladies' room.

"Apparently so."

"About your grandmother?"

"We were having a whole conversation about spirits and missing items and stuff I honestly never thought I'd have a chance to talk about with anyone. Thank God for New Orleans."

Sam frowned. "What does New Orleans have to do with it?"

"It's like the spiritual capital of the world. Or one of them. Anyway, great job yesterday, honey. I can't wait to see the results."

"Yeah, me, too. When do you think he'll bring them in?"

"I don't know, but he will." She handed him the bag of sage. "Give this to Curtis? He'll know what to do. But tell him not to freak out any of our guests." She followed Mia upstairs and found her primping in the mirror. "Thanks for the talk."

"Of course, darlin'. Anytime!"

The door swung open, and a woman entered. "Hello there," she said cheerfully. She was tall and thin with cropped blonde hair, and she spoke with a clipped British accent. "Brrr. Someone's walked over my grave!"

"Pardon me?" Josie asked in a thin voice.

"Oh!" The woman laughed and waved her hand. "Pardon *me*. It's a saying for when you get that ghostly shudder. Nothing to worry about, just the aircon." She entered a stall.

Josie and Mia were silent as they walked out and back downstairs.

DESPITE THE QUESTIONABLE word-of-mouth press, the restaurant had a busy couple of days. Some of the regulars joked with the staff about what had happened, and a few people got the full story. Tourists asked if they could take pictures with Chef. Josie thwarted these requests by describing him as camera-shy.

No other objects went missing, so the incidents that made Mia a suspect faded from people's minds. A few days in the restaurant world were like a few weeks in the real one. Everyone instead recalibrated to a new version of Bistrot without Chef at the helm.

With every day that Patrick didn't show up, Josie grew increasingly despondent. Each day she told herself he *had* to come in that night, that it made no sense for him not to. That it would be so easy for him to do the right thing and not disappoint her. She wouldn't call him. She wouldn't be that girl. She'd be patient.

By the time Friday rolled around, she was miserable.

Johnny taking over the kitchen meant the resurrection of the quality staff meal. Chef had lost interest in the concept years earlier, so staff dinners came to consist of messy casseroles of whatever the kitchen hadn't moved enough of the night before, to be wolfed down when there was a spare moment. Johnny brought back proper sit-down meals and gave them an Italian bent, mimicking the Sunday dinners he'd grown up eating.

Friday night he made seafood Fra Diavolo, an inadvertent nod to the bouillabaisse that precipitated his new role. Josie sat in the dining room with Curtis, Sam, Johnny, and a few other servers after dinner service. Rain pounded the skylight above them and suited her mood. She was raw, vulnerable, and trying to fake it.

While people raved over the food, she smiled and nodded. In truth, she'd hardly touched her plate. She reached for the bottle of red in the middle of the table and filled her glass way above the B.

"This is fabulous," Curtis said. "Not a single complaint since you've taken over. It's been a minute since we've had a stretch like this."

"It's been more than a minute," Sam said, filling his own glass well above the B.

"I tell you what," Johnny said. "Things run a hell of a lot smoother without Chef adding a side of crazy to every order." He put his hand on his heart. "Don't get me wrong, I've got mad respect for that guy. It's just—"

"It's just he's not you." Curtis filled Johnny's glass.

"You see any ghost stuff up there?" Sam asked.

"Fuck no, man. Just some really old-school ways of doing things. Tell you what, I don't know how long the guy's gonna be out for, but if Andy lets me, I'm going to make a few changes around here."

"Meals like this are a great start," Josie said enthusiastically. If she faked it, maybe a good mood would follow.

"Girl, you need to eat more," Curtis said. "You've had, like, two bites of dinner. You're becoming just a slip of a thing."

"It's the grief diet," she said.

"Food is love," Johnny said. "Did your grandma cook?"

"She was a great cook. Lots of Creole and Cajun food, which set her apart from the Durkee onion and cream of mushroom casserole set that was the norm in our neighborhood. Though she made a hell of a meatloaf, too."

"She would most definitely want you to be eating more, missy," Curtis said. "And now we're having these family meals, you got no excuses!"

"What other changes are you thinking about?" Josie deflected the conversation.

"Bunch of things. Happy hour menu with cheap drinks and appetizers, chalkboard with specials, old school French, instead of printing the menu up every fuckin' night, maybe even a prix-fixe like they do in Paris. Depends how much Andy lets me do. You want to work with me on this, Josie?"

"I could stand to do more here than just hand out menus and field complaints. I'm feeling kind of underutilized."

"Word," Curtis said.

After dinner, Johnny grabbed a bottle of Amaro and poured them all digestifs. It had gotten out that he was temporarily in charge, and this lent him celebrity status. He left the others to chat up the women clamoring for his attention.

"Have you guys had any weird things happen?" Sam asked Josie and Curtis.

"Not really, not in the past couple of days," Josie said.

"Same," Curtis said. "I guess the little ghost thief is biding his time."

"His? Why do you say that?" Josie asked.

"No particular reason. Why, you think it's a her?"

"I don't know. But you don't think it's a flesh and blood person?"

"No, I don't. I am not buying into any of that, don't care what evidence people have dangled over the past week."

"Thank you."

"Now, who's the her ghost?"

"No one specific, just a sense I've gotten."

"You have someone in mind, lady, and no poker face."

"Okay, there's a friend of a friend I'm thinking of."

"Who is this friend of a friend, and why do you think she'd have any interest in stealing our saffron?"

"It just kind of goes with her profile. Kind of mischievous in life, so probably that way in death, too, right?"

"How did she die?" Sam asked.

"She overdosed on Seconal."

"Seconal?!" Curtis said. "That's so Valley of the Dolls. I didn't even think they made that anymore."

"You can find pretty much anything nowadays, can't you?"

"I guess. I've never been a pharmaceutical man myself. Now ecstasy. That was my jam back in the day."

"I was never interested in ecstasy," Josie said.

Curtis sniffed. "Doesn't surprise me in the least."

"What's that supposed to mean?"

"You don't strike me as the manufactured joy type, lady." He turned his attention elsewhere but the comment was out there.

Josie was, admittedly, kind of cynical. But she didn't eschew happiness. She craved it. At the same time, it was ingrained within her not to expect it. So, while Patrick's absence was disappointing, she refused to let it make her sad. He clearly cared about her, he just did things his own way. She'd see him again. Diminish expectation, diminish disappointment. She poured herself a glass of the open Malbec that sat on the bar.

Regardless of when she saw him next, Patrick had come along at the right time for the right reason, to help her cope with her grief. He was both comforting and a distraction from the fact that Nanette was dead. *Dead*—a word she'd only allow herself when she was anesthetized by booze. It was otherwise too horrible, too final. No matter what their future held, Patrick was inextricably linked to her grief and the softening of it. For this, she would always be grateful.

Mia, too, had come along at the right time. Through her, Josie was beginning to recognize the value of accepting what she'd rejected for so long.

No, it wasn't that Josie had an aversion to joy, it was that she no longer believed in it. What was joy anyway? How could she genuinely feel it ever again if Nanette was gone? The most she could hope for was comfort, and according to Mia, she could attain this by accepting the existence of the spirit world. So, she would.

She looked at Derek and forgave him for withholding a secret from her. Now that she knew so much more about the events and dynamics that had shaped him for so many years, she understood him better. She'd been too hard on him.

Perhaps he, too, needed to learn the lessons Mia was imparting, to accept that there was life after grief. Perhaps if he were able to accept that his brother might still be around in some form, his misguided guilt would diminish. Perhaps he was one of those people Mia had mentioned who will do their best to ignore even the most obvious signs for the sake of their own comfort. Because Derek didn't accept his brother's death, or else Josie would have known about it long before she did. He'd been a young child not only growing up in his brother's shadow, but in the home where he'd once lived. Young children were open receptors to this sort of thing. Maybe he'd ignored all sorts of communication from Alex because the whole thing was too painful. Because his mother was too distraught to function. Because she resented him for not being Alex. Josie knew a thing or two about maternal resentment. She'd long suspected her mother resented her for her father's leaving, not in any overt way, probably not even consciously. But Josie's mother had been harried and exhausted in the years following her birth, and had gone from thin to zaftig. The woman her father ran off with had the body of a pin-up girl. Post-divorce, Josie's mom had shed every ounce she'd gained and then some and had become a serial dieter. Josie could hardly remember a time she'd seen her mother enjoy a plate of food. The grief diet was a way of life.

She refilled her glass, and Derek turned to her.

"What's going on?" he asked wearily. He had dark circles under his eyes she'd never seen before and several days' worth of stubble.

"Jesus, honey, you okay?"

"Living the dream."

"Listen," Josie said. "I need to talk to you about Alex."

"Yeah, let's talk about him another time, okay? When it's not so busy."

"It's not that busy, and it's really important to talk about this stuff! It's helping me deal with Nanette. And I think there's something that could help you deal…."

"Josie, I've 'dealt' with Alex for thirty-six years."

"I know, but now you've shared him with me, finally, after six years, and now I'm learning more about the grieving process, and I think it's important that you—"

He cut her off. "Not tonight, Josie."

"Why not tonight?"

"Because you've had a lot to drink, and I'm not in the mood."

"No I haven't!"

He sighed. "Okay. It's just"—he shook his head—"never mind."

"What? We all drink!" She heard the defensiveness creeping into her voice.

"Okay, forget it. Let's talk another time."

She slammed her hand on the bar harder than she'd meant to. "No, Derek, you can't just do that!"

"Fine, okay, yeah, you've been acting really weird since this guy came back into your life."

"You know his name."

"I do."

"And we already had this conversation! Patrick showed up right when I got back from New Hampshire. You can't blame him for whatever I'm doing to get through this stretch. He's actually helping."

"Yeah? Where's he been the past few nights?"

"He's been busy!" she said loudly. Curtis looked over at her.

"Yeah? Does he check in with you on the days you don't see him? See how you're holding up?"

"Jesus, Derek! I don't need him to monitor me! He has a life and doesn't need to spend every night here like the bimbo you've been hanging out with!"

She regretted the words as they spilled from her mouth, but it was too late to backtrack. Patrick's disappearing act was having a profound impact on her self-esteem. Derek was right. Why wouldn't he check in with her? He knew what she was going through.

"Bimbo. That's great. She's never been anything but nice to you. Have you ever had a conversation with her?"

"No, and that's fine. I prefer to spend time with adults."

"She's twenty-four years old, Josie. You're being ridiculous."

"Dating a child is ridiculous!" she snapped, taking a hefty gulp of her wine.

"Jesus Christ, Josie!"

"Jesus Christ, Derek!"

He lowered his voice. "Look, I don't want to fight with you. There's just something about Patrick that doesn't sit right with me." He was trying to de-escalate the conversation, but Josie was fast approaching her tipping point. She was annoyed that Derek was being judgmental. She was annoyed that she'd stooped to the level of insulting Alison. She was annoyed that Derek was so protective of Alison. She was jealous of Alison's youth. She was annoyed that she was jealous. And she was drunk. "Easy Josie, stop guzzling your wine!"

She held her glass toward him. "Refill please!"

"No, this is exactly what I'm talking about. This isn't you."

"And this"—she gestured vaguely in his direction—"isn't you, dating some slutty little chick covered in glitter!"

"Enough with the name-calling, Josie."

"You started it!"

"Actually, I didn't. What I did was express concern for you. And now I'm ending this conversation."

"You don't get to just do that!"

"Don't get to do what? End a conversation with an irrational drunk?"

"Irrational drunk!" she slurred. "Great. That's some stellar name-calling, my friend. My pedophile friend!"

"You know what, Josie? Alison may be a lot younger than I am, but she's a refreshing change of pace considering this industry is full of aging party girls desperately clinging to their youth." With that he turned his back on her and started ringing up a tab. The half-dozen people within earshot looked uncomfortable. "Oh, and two more things," he said over his shoulder. "You've been talking to yourself like a madwoman lately, and everyone's noticed. And what's with the fucking saffron? Why would you take it?"

"I didn't!" She slammed her wine glass on the bar. It shattered. "Fuck!"

Derek whipped around. "What the—" He grabbed a rag and started wiping the shards away.

"Like I did that on purpose?"

"Jesus, are you bleeding?" She wasn't. "Pull yourself together, Josie!"

"I'm fine!"

"Hey, you!" Derek said over his shoulder, his demeanor shifting abruptly. Josie didn't need to turn around to know who it was.

"Hi," Alison said. She leaned over the bar and planted a kiss on Derek's lips. "Hi, Josie."

Josie ignored her and looked for Curtis, who was walking over with her raincoat and bag.

"What do you think, lady?" he asked gently. "Ready to hit the road?"

She let him help her off her barstool and avoided eye contact with everyone else as he walked her out the door.

Chapter Ten

⚜

JOSIE WAS DETERMINED to keep her head down the next day, as embarrassed by her own behavior as she was angered by Derek's. Once she arrived at the restaurant though, she knew something else was amiss. Everyone milled about looking distressed.

"What's going on?" she asked Curtis.

"Oh, lady, you didn't hear?" He had tears running down his face. "It's the Kennedys. John-John and Carolyn are missing."

"What do you mean they're missing?" She followed him into the bar where Derek had the radio on. He looked ragged.

"*—search is underway for the Piper Saratoga, which Kennedy was said to be piloting to Martha's Vineyard with his wife, Carolyn Bessette Kennedy and her sister Lauren on board. We will be following this story.*"

"My God." Josie rubbed the goosebumps on her arms. "That's so upsetting."

"Tragic. That poor family." Curtis shook his head.

Andy walked into the restaurant carrying the afternoon edition of the *New York Mirror*. "Guys," he said. "Can you all gather around for a few?"

He looked nervous, and Josie understood. He'd handled many crises before. It was the job. But something about this one felt different. It *was* different.

For once he didn't sit while he lectured the staff. "Everyone, I'm sure you've heard the alarming news, but we still don't have any answers. Of course, many of us have met the Kennedys over the years, which makes this particularly upsetting for us. But we have a job to do tonight, and that's to be a safe and comforting place for our guests to gather. We have to be professional and not let our sadness or worry overshadow our work. Okay?" He looked around the shell-shocked group and blinked a few times, as though he were about to cry. "I'm going to meditate."

While they waited for dinner service to start, everyone hung around the bar discussing the news.

"Why is this hitting me so hard?" Curtis asked. "It's not like I really know them. I've only met them a couple of times, and he's so handsome I got all tongue-tied."

"It's a thing called emotional proximity, man," Derek said. "Even if they didn't come in here, they were—"

"ARE!" Curtis insisted. "I'm not ready to use the past tense about that beautiful couple."

"Okay, they *are* American icons. He was born one. We've literally watched the guy grow up. The whole world has. And she became one."

"My mom is so freaked out," Sam said. "They're a big deal in Boston."

"Of course they are, honey," Josie said. "They're as much a part of Boston as they are New York."

"They might be okay, right?" Sam asked and shrugged. "If they'd crashed, wouldn't they have found them by now?"

"Maybe, Sam." Curtis put an arm around Sam's shoulder in a rare moment of tolerance. "Maybe they're okay."

Josie remained frosty toward Derek as she went about her work, avoiding eye contact, pretending not to hear his attempts at conversation, and it felt disingenuous. What she wanted was to talk to him about the news, to process it together. But his words the night before, anchored in truth though they may have been, still stung. Or maybe they stung because of their truth.

She also wanted to talk to Mia, about the Kennedys, about Patrick, about Derek. If anyone could get through to him, convince him to grieve differently, Mia could. But the rain was light, and she was off that night.

Sam wanted his headshots. He asked Josie four times, in four different ways, when he might get them. "Do you think he's coming by tonight? Do you guys usually get together on Saturdays? Do you know if my photos are ready? How long does it usually take?"

"Sam!" she said, after seating a particularly enervating group who'd rejected the first two tables she'd offered. "I don't know! Stop asking me! You have his phone number. Call him up!"

"I can't do that. It would be super uncool to hound him."

"Well, it's super uncool of him to disappear in the first place. With your headshots." She turned on her heel and stomped away, feeling terribly that she'd been so impatient. Sam had every right to wonder what was going on, and it was not his fault Josie felt ridiculous for not knowing the answer.

All of this had to be hidden behind a veneer of calm projected toward the guests, who were buzzing with conversation about the Kennedys. Josie was annoyed but not surprised by the many people taking ownership of the tragedy, making sure everyone within earshot knew of their six-degree separation from the couple. It was always this way when a famous person died, particularly one of such prominence in New York. And the people who were oblivious to it all and didn't mention them she found equally offensive and tone-deaf. There was no winning for anyone.

Johnny sat at the bar after dinner, too overwhelmed to bask in the adulation he was receiving. He was surrounded by Boodles, Bulleit, and the Trinket with the nose ring, who was wearing his Y2K hat at a coquettish angle.

"Aren't you guys, like, so freaked out about the Kennedys?" she asked, tilting her head like a curious dog and twirling a strand of hair. She wore a pink dress so short Josie hoped she didn't drop anything and had a Merlot stain on her chapped upper lip. Josie chastised herself for dissecting the girl's appearance, then cut herself slack when she noticed the toe ring and Greek letters tattooed on her ankle.

When no one responded, she tried again. "Johnny, are you gonna, like, take over the restaurant now?"

"Depends on Chef," he said with a shrug. "He owns the joint. Can't make any real moves without him."

"I can't wait till you can make some real moves." She crossed one glittery leg over the other and leaned forward too far, slipping off her seat. Bulleit caught her by the elbow and propped her back up.

Johnny remained oblivious. "Yeah man, but fuck. Who knows what the guy has up his sleeve." He stared into his scotch as though it held the answers, shook his head, and took a sip. "Fuck if I know."

"I think we need to toast John-John and Carolyn and celebrate Johnny," Curtis said. "Derek, how 'bout a round of something pink and bubbly."

Derek snorted. "Johnny's a scotch man."

"I'm a scotch man," Johnny said. "Or tequila."

"Then, how 'bout a round of something pink and bubbly for those celebrating the good fortune of working with Johnny?"

Derek shrugged and opened a bottle of rosé champagne. He rationed it to accommodate the crowd and passed glasses around. "Josie?" he asked, extending a liquid olive branch.

She took it without looking at him.

"To the only man cool enough under pressure to step right into Chef's shoes without missing a beat," Curtis said, raising his glass.

"To Johnny," Josie said. Glasses clinked. In her periphery she saw Derek hold his toward her, and she turned the other way.

"Honestly," Johnny said. "I bet Chef would be fucking relieved if someone bought this place off him. He's always talking about wanting to move back to 'the continent.'"

"Puhleeze," Curtis said. "The continent of Michigan? He's from Lansing."

"Wonder how much he'd sell the business for," Derek said to no one in particular.

"Why, man, you sitting on a bunch of extra cash that needs laundering?" Johnny asked.

"Not exactly." He walked down the bar.

Josie's interest was piqued. Maybe those screenplays had been worth something. She bummed a cigarette from the nose ring girl and went outside.

It was almost five days since she'd seen Patrick, and it was embarrassing. It was disrespectful to her, to Sam, in general. He had no problem being affectionate in front of her coworkers and out in public, so it wasn't like he was trying to be discreet about what was going on between them. How did he think this made her look now? She sucked the cigarette straight down to its filter and angrily stubbed it out.

On her way back in, Derek cornered her in the vestibule. "Josie." He held his arm out to keep her from slipping past. "I'm sorry."

"For what?" She crossed her arms over her chest.

"For yesterday."

"For insulting Patrick Moore?"

"No. For insulting you."

"Yeah, you really know how to make a gal feel special. Sorry, not a gal, an 'aging party girl.'" She used air quotes.

He hit the wall with the side of his fist. "Listen, that was a shitty thing to say. And it's not what I think about you."

"Do I have to keep reminding you that maybe I'm drinking too much because I'm sad?"

"No, you don't have to keep reminding me. I get it. I was in a mood, and it was a really awkward way of letting you know I'm looking out for you. Sorry I acted like a prick."

"I'm sorry I called your girlfriend a bimbo."

"Good. Because she's not."

It wasn't Alison's fault she was young, or that Josie feared she was being replaced. There was room for more than one woman at Bistrot. Look at Mia. She was one of the most beautiful women Josie had ever seen, and Josie wasn't threatened by her presence. She'd have to get over her aversion to Alison.

"Why were you in a mood?" she asked for what felt like the hundredth time.

"I can't get into it. Not yet, anyway."

"Okay, you know you can always talk to me—"

He cut her off. "Look, I'm not trying to make you feel bad, but lately I *can't* always talk to you. You're acting strange. You're drinking a lot more, and I know, I know, you're grieving, but it feels like you're acting out in all these other ways. And I can't help but think this guy has something to do with it. I have a responsibility to look out for the people in my life. And that includes you. So, when I see you going off the rails, I worry."

"Why won't you say his name?"

"I don't need to. You know his name."

"Okay. You've made your opinion clear. I still think you're being unnecessarily judgmental, but it's a free country. Besides, if you've noticed, I haven't been spending much time with him lately."

Derek was diplomatic enough to not state the obvious. "All right, Josie, just one question, and answer me straight. Why did you take the saffron?"

"I didn't take the saffron! I found it! Seriously, Derek, I may be self-medicating and acting off, but I am not a klepto!"

"Do you know who might be?"

"No," she said emphatically. "I'm as in the dark as everyone else."

A tingle crept up the back of her neck, and a muted laugh filled the vestibule. By the time she realized what it was, it was gone.

"What's wrong?" Derek shook her shoulder lightly.

"What?" She felt dizzy.

"Where'd you go just now? You looked like you short-circuited."

"Sorry, I'm just overtired."

"Please come drink a glass of water and call it a night."

She nodded and followed him inside.

Thirty minutes later she let herself into her apartment. She turned on her stereo, and Billie Holiday filled the room, singing with resignation about her cheating lover, whom she'd forgive by the end of the bridge. While Josie got ready for bed, she thought about what Derek had said. He was right, she hadn't been all there lately, so he couldn't just talk to her about what was going on with him, and this made her feel bad. This was not who she wanted to be. But it most certainly was not Patrick's fault.

She made herself a cup of chamomile tea and turned on the TV. *Double Indemnity* was playing. Derek had taken her to see a revival of it at Film Forum. She watched it on mute with her own jazz soundtrack playing. The opening chords to "What a Wonderful World" came on, and the tears sprang forth. The song played a profound role in her memories of and with Nanette. It would forever be their song.

When the phone rang at quarter to eleven, she jumped. In the moment before she answered, her mind connected the dots. Patrick had swung by Bistrot, just missing her, and gotten her phone number. But as soon as she touched the receiver, she knew she was wrong.

"Hi, darlin', I hope I'm not calling too late," Mia said when she answered.

"Hi." Josie masked her disappointment. "Are you okay?"

"I'm fine, I just couldn't sleep, and I got the feeling that you couldn't either."

"Did you hear the horrible news?"

"About those Kennedys."

"Yes. I only met them a few times. It's not like they were personal friends, but this is just so upsetting."

"It's a very sad story. That family has been through a tremendous amount."

"I know, it's so awful. I'm really glad you called. I'm having an existential crisis."

"Talk to me."

Josie paced, her tea in one hand, the cordless phone in the other. She told Mia of Patrick's absence, how stupid it made her feel, of her argument with Derek, how stupid *that* made her feel, and of their make-up conversation, in which he called her out for the way she'd been behaving. She left out the part about the saffron.

"And then, remember I told you about what Nanette and I called the whispers? Those disembodied voices?"

"I know them well, girl."

"Yeah, well, they're back. Which is awesome because I don't have enough conflict in my brain right now."

"Look, first of all, you're worried about how Patrick not showing up is gonna make you look? What about him? He's the one who should feel stupid."

"I know," Josie said sadly.

"So, why aren't you angry with him, girl?"

"Because anger's a tough one for me. The way my mind works, if I get mad, some higher power will laugh at my audacity to have expected anything from him in the first place, and I'll never see him again."

"That's one mean higher power."

"I know it must sound ridiculous."

"No, it doesn't. But here's the thing, and here's something I learned the hard way. Remember I told you some about the guy I followed to New York? Turns out he was married, and I was too stunned to get angry. I blamed myself. And I stuck around way longer than I should have."

"Jesus," Josie said. "What a scumbag!"

"If I can give you one piece of advice, girl, it's to respect yourself enough to get angry when somebody wrongs you. Don't do what I did."

"You must hate him!"

"I don't hate him. It's not worth it."

"I can't stand deception!"

"Sometimes people have reasons to keep things hidden. Sometimes they don't tell the truth because they can't accept it themselves. It's not necessarily deception in a vacuum. It can be self-preservation."

This made sense where Derek's withholding Alex was concerned, but lying to a woman about being married was another matter altogether.

"In the case of this guy," Mia said, *"he had his reasons. I didn't agree with them, but they were his. He was tormented. I can't hate him, but I can fault myself for not just walking away when I knew the truth. By the time I was ready to, it was too late, and now I'm stuck here longer than I ever wanted to be. That's why I'm advising you, baby, to let yourself get angry. That's its own kind of self-preservation. If seeing him only every so often doesn't work for you, you don't need to do it."*

"I don't know if it works for me or not. I need to figure that out."

"And you will."

"Can you give me some advice that has nothing to do with him? What do I do about the whispers?"

"Now this is an easy one, and you know the answer. Don't stifle your gifts. But don't let the dead distract you from the living either. Be in the moment."

After they hung up Josie lay in bed. She reached for a sleep mask and just as quickly had a visceral memory of the laughter in the vestibule and no longer felt like being in the dark, even if it meant staying up all night. Her bedside lamp was too bright, so she took her blanket into the living room and flipped through the TV channels, consciously bypassing any stations that might deliver breaking news. She knew in her heart the Kennedys' fate was sealed, and she wasn't ready to absorb this. She put the movie back on mute and let the flickering light dance across her eyelids until she fell asleep.

⚜

SUNDAY SAW BACK-to-back reservations and a restaurant so crowded at brunch and dinner that Josie was hardly alone with her thoughts. Everyone remained in a state of disbelief, and the staff, following Andy's directive, served as grief counselors and cheerleaders.

When Josie had a break, she visited with Mia, whose phone call had been a balm for her soul. She told her as much.

"You know Josie, after we hung up, I had another thought about how you can accept your whispers and everything else that comes along with them."

"How's that?"

"You were a lonely little girl when they first visited. I think maybe you needed the spirits as much as they needed you. And maybe now you need them again, and you just have to learn why."

"How do I do that?"

"I think you just live your life and the reason'll make itself known. Just relax and see what comes. Don't try and figure it out. Let it unfold."

Staff meal that night was *coq au vin*, a Chef specialty Johnny had modified and made his own.

"I'm going to gain twenty pounds by September if you keep doing this," Curtis said.

"No way, man," Johnny said. "You look like you've been hitting the gym pretty hard lately." He squeezed Curtis's bicep for emphasis, and Curtis swooned.

Johnny was not the first vehemently straight man Curtis had fancied at Bistrot, and he would never push the issue but, he'd told Josie, it was fun to have a crush. Still, what Curtis really wanted was love, and Josie didn't want him to lose sight of the fact that New York was rife with eligible bachelors.

"Curtis, love, what happened with that guy last night?"

"Not my type."

"Really? I thought he was cute!"

"He was, at best, friend's out-of-town cousin cute. He was not blind-date cute." Curtis sniffed. "And as Johnny pointed out, I *have* been hitting the gym pretty hard lately, so my standards have risen accordingly."

"Hey, man." Johnny speared his fork into a chicken leg and held it aloft. "Nothing wrong with standards."

"You and that friend of Alison's looked pretty cozy last night," Curtis said.

"Noelle? She's cute," he said with a shrug.

Sam had been quiet since they'd sat down, and Josie felt responsible for his unhappiness, though she had no control over Patrick Moore's comings and goings.

"Sammy, I'm sorry I snapped at you about headshots yesterday. You have every right to be annoyed."

He tilted his head. "When did you snap at me?"

"Never mind."

"Whoa, guys," he said, jutting his chin toward the front of the restaurant.

Everyone turned in their seats to see Sylvie shuffling toward them like a sleepwalker. Her hair hung limp around her bare face, and she wore a quilted blue bathrobe and a pair of yellow rainboots.

She smiled broadly when she reached the table. "Hello," she said, her voice reedy.

Curtis stood and took her elbow. "Miss Sylvie, is everything okay?"

She looked up at him, startled by his height. "I'm Sylvie."

"Oh, dear God," Johnny said under his breath.

"What's your name?"

"I'm Curtis, Sylvie."

"You're so handsome! Such a handsome Black man!" she said flirtatiously.

"Oof," Johnny said.

Josie winced, and Sam's jaw dropped, but Curtis took it in stride.

"Thank you, Miss Sylvie, I think you're very beautiful, too."

"Sylvie, can one of us see you home?" Josie asked.

"No, Frances. Maria wants to go dancing!"

"It's late. Let's take a raincheck." Josie stood and took Curtis's place. "How about if I walk you across the street?" She eased her toward the front door, ignoring the curious looks and snickers from the customers they passed. People's insensitivity astounded her. At her core, Sylvie was a woman of great dignity, and Josie's heart broke for her, for how embarrassed she'd be if she realized what was happening.

As they reached the front, Mia came out of the coatroom.

"Maria! Darling! I thought you said we could dance tonight?"

"Not tonight darlin'," she said, taking Sylvie's other arm. The three walked outside and stood under the awning. "What say we get you home, and then we can make plans to go dancing real soon, okay?"

"Sylvie, do you have an umbrella?" Josie asked.

"I don't think so."

"It's just drizzlin'," Mia said. "We won't melt!"

They crossed the street and stood outside Sylvie's building. Mia rifled through Sylvie's pocketbook and pulled out a set of keys attached to a dyed green "lucky" rabbit's foot.

"Wow, I haven't seen one of those in decades!" Josie said, jarred by its anachronistic gruesomeness.

"Why don't I see you upstairs?" Mia turned to Josie. "I don't mind if you wanna head back."

"You sure you don't need a hand?"

"Positive. Go on over! I'll come say goodbye."

Josie darted across the street, mulling over the fact that Mia, the new girl, was taking the lead with Sylvie. But she seemed relaxed, and Sylvie was comfortable with her, even if she thought she was someone else. Or maybe because she thought she was someone else. Josie wondered fleetingly whether she'd done the right thing, leaving Sylvie alone with someone she barely knew, but everyone seemed to trust Mia. So much so that the mystery of the items in coat check was no longer discussed. This was not a group of people who would hold back if they had suspicions.

Back at the table, the conversation was subdued.

"Oh, Miss Sylvie," Curtis said, shaking his head.

Josie held his hand. "I know, honey. It's really sad. And, about her comment...."

"Fuck PC," Johnny said. He took a swig of wine and sloshed it around his mouth before swallowing. "Curtis can take it."

Curtis held his hand up. "None taken. I *am* a handsome Black man. Wait'll she learns my other deep dark secret, though. She'll have me arrested for inciting the Stonewall riots."

"She was talking like she thinks we're other people," Sam said.

"She *does* think we're other people." Josie could hear Curtis straining to be patient.

"Yeah, in her mind it's 1970-something, and we're at Dave's Continental!" Johnny said.

"I hope she's in good hands with Mia," Josie said.

"She's in good hands with all of us," Curtis said.

They sat in glum silence, Josie's eyes trained on the door waiting for Mia to return.

Change was hard for her, and Sylvie's presence at Bistrot had been a constant. Josie could vividly picture the first time she saw her waltz into the restaurant in a white fur stole, surrounded by a cloud of Chanel Number Five. Moments later she held court at the bar with a flute of champagne and a delighted audience. Josie had never seen anyone like her. She was the kind of person who made the tapestry of New York City what it was meant to be, who infused color into every room she entered.

"God I'm going to miss her," Josie and Curtis said at the same time.

"Jinx, lady," Curtis said without joy.

When Mia returned, she beckoned Josie to follow her to the ladies' room.

"How did it go?"

"Fine. Just walked her inside and got her settled with a cup of tea." She looked in the mirror and wiped at the smudges of kohl under her eyes. "I'm fixin' to call it a night. This was a long one."

"Thanks for helping out with Sylvie," Josie said. "It's a lot for any one of us. This was the worst she's been yet."

"If I had to guess, I'd reckon she's startin' to hear from her ancestors."

Nothing that came out of Mia's mouth would surprise Josie anymore. "Meaning?"

"Meaning some of these people she's talking about or mixin' y'all up with? I'd guess these are people she used to know, people who aren't here anymore, and who are comin' round to help ease her into the next phase."

"The next phase being death?!"

Mia smiled sadly. "I'm not saying she's leaving real soon, but unlikely she'll be coming back to us like she used to. Good she's got others around to keep her company, even if we don't see them."

"But she wasn't just talking to ghosts, she was talking to you and me, except we're Maria and Frances."

"That's just it, at this stage it could be a combination. She is seeing spirit, and she's seeing living people, but it's all jumbled in her mind."

"Memory is a curious bird."

"Sure is."

As they made their way back downstairs, someone waited at the bottom. With the light in her eyes, Josie could only see a silhouette.

"You can be angry, girl," Mia said under her breath as she slipped past. She nodded at Patrick but didn't say hello.

Josie's stomach fluttered when she reached the last step.

"Hey, baby," he said, reaching toward her.

She took a step back. "Hello."

"Got Sammy's headshots." He held up a manila envelope. "Came out great."

"He'll certainly be relieved," she said. She'd meant to be icy, but it came out sounding sincere. "He's been waiting."

"Josie." Patrick absently straightened one of the framed vintage starlet photos lining the stairwell. "I'm sorry I haven't been around. I want to explain. Can we have a drink?"

"This is a bar."

He smiled. "Why don't I go grab us a couple." He held out a pack of cigarettes, and she took them from him.

"I'll be outside." She walked out the front door to wait for him on the patio. Now that he was finally here, all she felt was relief. She knew that Mia was right. She should be angry. She had every reason to be angry, but that wasn't the dominant feeling. The dominant feeling was happiness. And excitement. And gratitude because once again he was making a very tough phase more bearable.

But this was ridiculous. She was letting him off far too easily. He'd completely vanished. And he *knew* that this was an especially tough time for her. For God's sake, she'd wept last time they were together. How did he think his disappearing would make her feel? And not just her. How did he think Sam felt? He had Sam's number, literally and figuratively. Even if he had no interest in continuing things with Josie—and if he didn't, he should be a man and not lead her on—but he could have called Sam to let him know what was happening with the headshots. It was selfish and unprofessional.

"Here you go, baby." Patrick came outside and placed a glass in front of her. "You didn't specify, so I went with our usual."

"What's our usual?" She knew what he meant.

"Sorry. The gin concoction we have here sometimes," he said with a glimmer of self- consciousness she'd not seen before.

Respect yourself enough to be angry.

He held his glass toward her, and she ignored it and took a sip of her drink. "Listen, I'm sorry I didn't mention that I was going out of town—"

"You don't owe me an explanation."

"That's bullshit, Josie, I do owe you an explanation."

"All right, then what is it?"

"It was last minute. I had to run back to L.A."

"Everything okay?"

"Some family stuff going on. My dad needed my help and a few other things. I wanted to call you before I left, but I was running around. And then as soon as I got there I had to hit the ground running. Pretty draining bunch of days. Took the redeye back this morning. I fucking hate the redeye. Least I got to sit up front. Only way to fly across country."

"I've never flown upfront."

Patrick looked embarrassed again. "Sorry."

"That I've never flown first class? Don't be."

"No, that I sounded like a jackass just then. I'm nervous."

"Why are you nervous?"

"Because I like you. I care about you. And I feel like I fucked everything up."

"You didn't 'fuck everything up.' I don't even know what 'everything' we're talking about. But yeah, it was pretty disappointing not hearing from you for almost a week, especially since you were holding Sammy's headshots hostage. Did you give them to him?"

"Yeah, he's looking at them now."

"Okay, cool. And also, not for nothing Patrick, but you know I'm feeling pretty vulnerable these days. So, even though this isn't a defined thing, I could really use some genuine friendship right now."

"You've got that, and more, if it's not too late," he said, cupping the side of her face. "I mean it."

She fought a smile.

"I thought about you a lot because of what I was dealing with. A lot of emotional stuff. With my dad. And it's a different scenario. He just moved into assisted living. But it's emotional, and it's a big change, and I know you're adjusting to a big emotional change, too."

"That's got to be pretty heavy."

"It is. But I'm sorry I disappointed you." He held his hand out, and she caved and took hold of it.

"Want to make it up to me?"

"I would love to," he said, smiling too for the first time since he'd arrived. "And I have this next week off, program's on break. Can we spend it together?"

"If you'd like." Making this happen would be up to him. She would not chase him.

"I'd like." He reached into his pocket and handed her a silky, navy blue bag with silver lettering on it. "I got you a little something."

"You got me something? What's the occasion?"

"I went to visit a friend at her new studio in Venice Beach. She makes jewelry. I hope you like it."

Josie opened the bag and pulled out a hammered gold cuff. She slipped it on her wrist. It was beautiful.

"She has a bunch of different designs, but I picked this one because I thought it would go with your necklace," he said, touching the pendant. "The golds match."

"Thank you, Patrick. This is really sweet."

It had been a very long time since she'd gotten a gift from a man she was dating, and never had she gotten one so thoughtfully chosen.

Patrick leaned in and gave her a long kiss on the lips. "You're welcome."

When he pulled away, Josie looked up at the building across the street, Sylvie's building. There was a light on in one of the windows. Josie thought she saw Mia there, looking out at them. A moment later, she was gone.

Chapter Eleven

✦

PATRICK WAS TRUE to his word. On his week off, Josie saw him every day. He picked her up at the end of each shift, and they spent every night together, cooking late dinners, holding hands on the couch, watching movies. They developed a morning routine where he'd put coffee on and run out for the paper, and they'd read it together over breakfast. They were the picture of temporary domesticity.

Josie played hooky on Thursday so she could spend it with Patrick and attend the opening of a gallery exhibit by one of his former students. She left his place in the morning to go home, pay bills, and get a change of clothes. On her way to the subway, she ducked into a lingerie shop having a sale and splurged on a black lace negligee, a move that was stunningly out of character.

Mia called while she was getting ready to head back into Manhattan.

"He just keeps being amazing," Josie gushed, pacing around the apartment and throwing things into her weekend bag. She bit the price tag off the nightgown and packed it, then decided to wear it under her dress instead. "It's been an incredible week."

"Just protect your heart, girl."

"You sound like Derek, which is precisely why I'm not telling him any of this. No one needs to know why I'm taking today off."

"If I sound like him, it's 'cause we're your friends, and we care about you. One week playing house is not real life. And Patrick's real life isn't in New York anyway, right?"

"Yeah, but people make long distance things work. It's not unheard of. He's talked about getting a place here anyway. Nothing to do with me, but it makes sense for him to be bicoastal. Sometimes you've just got to take a leap of faith, you know?" She was babbling. She was giddy.

"Yes, I do know."

"Shit, of course you do. I'm sorry if I'm being insensitive. I mean, we're not in love or anything. I'll be careful."

At 5:30 p.m. Patrick was waiting for Josie with a large umbrella as she exited the West 23rd Street subway station. "There's my girl," he said, sweeping her in for a hug and kiss. He lifted her bag over his shoulder and held her hand as they walked west toward the gallery.

"So, who is this artist you're taking me to see?"

"Bianca. She took my class a couple summers ago. Talented kid."

"What kind of stuff is it?"

"I haven't seen any of her new work, but she described it as abstract self-portraits. She's done a bit of modeling."

Josie hated it already.

The building was as far west on 25th Street as she'd ever been. It housed several galleries, and they rode a freight elevator to the fourth floor. Ambient crowd sounds directed them down the hall to the space, which was very small and very crowded.

Apparently "abstract" meant erotic black and white—a pierced nipple, a close up of a tongue licking the corner of a mouth.

A leggy blonde accosted them. "Baby!" she cried, slipping between Josie and Patrick and kissing him square on the lips. "You came!"

She was easily five-foot-ten with long blonde hair, hooded eyes, and a sharp nose. She looked to be in her mid-twenties. Josie could not imagine a scenario where it would be appropriate to call one of her teachers "baby." Nor could she imagine one where she'd feel comfortable strutting around in a shredded t-shirt that passed for a dress and a pair of gladiator sandals.

Patrick put his arm around Josie and pulled her close. "Of course I did! I wouldn't miss it. Bianca, I'd like you to meet Josie."

"Hi, Bianca," Josie said.

Her eyes drifted down Josie's body before she turned back to Patrick and took his hand. "Darling, you have to meet my people. I've told them all about you."

Patrick turned back to Josie and motioned for her to follow, but she waved for him to go ahead. She would not play runner-up to a twenty-something who forgot to wear pants.

A young guy with neon orange hair was pouring plastic cups of white wine. Josie took one and sized up the crowd. It was a vastly different ilk than she was used to. Across the room, Patrick and Bianca talked with a tiny Asian woman in thigh high python boots and a hat made of light blue feathers. Patrick again motioned for Josie to join them, but she smiled and shook her head. She knew women like Bianca and didn't need to subject herself to that energy. Plus, it was her night, her show, and if she needed all the attention, she could have it. Patrick Moore was beautiful, and when he talked to you, he made you feel like the only person in the room. Of course his students would lust after him, and the more brazen ones would flirt. Or the more insecure ones. He wouldn't have brought Josie along to this event if Bianca posed any sort of real threat. That's not the kind of man he was.

Josie contemplated a photo of the small of a back tattooed with a Chinese symbol.

"It's upside down." A cute, stocky man in a porkpie hat stood next to her, studying the photograph.

"It is?"

"Yes. It's supposed to say 'Danger,' but it's upside down. And backwards." He pointed to one of the characters. "That one should be on the left, and the point should be facing up. It's gibberish."

"That's amazing," Josie said, laughing. "How edgy."

"Indeed. There's an entire generation of edgy young gals running around with grammatically incorrect Mandarin inked on their coccyges."

"Coccyges! Wow. Do you do a lot of crossword puzzles?"

"Nope, but I didn't drop out of med school for nothing."

They moved onto the next photo, a glistening tongue licking a disembodied swatch of flesh. It was titled, *Hers*.

"Looks like she got hers." The porkpie hat gave Josie a cartoonish, matter-of-fact look.

"Her what, though?" Josie tilted her head and squinted. "Is that a wrist?"

"It's kind of big to be a wrist. I think it's a neck."

"I defer to you. You're the med school dropout."

They spent the next several minutes going through the exhibit and guessing the titles of the photographs, topping each other with suggestions that sounded like hybrids between dime store romances and lipstick shades, *Obsession's Crease* and *Nape of Destiny*. The guy was a bit manic, talked a lot, but Josie appreciated the company.

"So, what are you doing after this shindig? Want to hit a few more shows and grab a bite? There's a Tuscan place just across Tenth—"

"Thank you for the invite. I have plans with my friend."

He looked disappointed. "Maybe another time. I'm Joe, by the way."

"Josie."

"Joe and Josie. Want to give me your number?"

Josie was about to answer when Patrick came up behind her and placed his hands on her hips.

"Hey, baby," he said, kissing her cheek. "You ready to get some dinner?"

"Sure." She turned to him and saw Bianca watching them from across the room, arms crossed, ignoring the people she was standing with. Josie held her hand up to wave, and Bianca looked away. Josie turned the wave into a gesture toward her new friend. "Patrick, this is Joe."

"What's that?"

She spun back around, but Joe wasn't there. She felt a tingling, then saw his retreating figure walking down the hall, ducking into one of the other galleries. He was disappointed, not dead. "Never mind. Sure, let's go eat."

They took the elevator back down and went outside into the rain.

Patrick held the umbrella over their heads and took her hand. "Thanks for coming to this. It means a lot."

"Sure, it was…." She searched for the word. "Something."

He laughed. "Not my thing either, but she's doing it. She's doing what she came to the city to do, and I give her points for that."

"She seems to give you points, too. Somebody's hot for teacher."

"Ah, maybe, but it's harmless. I'd never cross that line with a student."

"Former student."

"Still. She's a nice girl, but I've never been interested. She has some…."

"Daddy issues?"

"Something like that. Anyway, she's not my style. You're my style." He pulled open the door to Bottino and held onto her hand when they stepped inside.

The front bar was crowded with the gallery and fashionista crowd. Josie was glad she'd worn heels. As Patrick steered her through, he greeted a few people by name.

"Patrick!" The attractive hostess who had been there the previous time came around and kissed him hello, then surprised Josie by kissing her on each cheek, too. "Nice to see you again, Josie."

"How're you doing, Nina?" Patrick said, saving Josie, who'd forgotten her name.

"Living the dream." She pulled menus, and they followed her through the dining room toward the back garden where they'd sat the first time. It was far more romantic without Sam in tow.

"Thank you, Nina," Josie said when she sat.

"Can I start you guys off with some bubbly?"

"Babe? You want a cocktail?"

"No, I had some wine at the show. Should probably stick with the bubbly."

"Ooh, gallery wine," Nina said, making a face. "Yeah, we'll take care of you."

"She's lovely," Josie said when she walked away.

"You're lovely."

"Fine, then we're both lovely."

"I mean it, Josie. I'm falling hard for you."

Nina returned with a bottle of prosecco and two glasses. "Cheers guys! Just flag someone down when you're ready to order."

It was a very different style from Bistrot, and Josie appreciated it. It was looser, breezier. She could see herself working in a place like this.

Patrick held his glass up. "Here's to a beautiful week, babe."

"To a beautiful week." Josie tapped his glass and sipped. The cool, minerally bubbles were a welcome replacement for the oaky table wine she'd choked down at the gallery.

"You're going to make it really hard for me to leave New York again."

"When do you head back? And how's your dad?"

"My dad? He's fine." He shifted in his seat and rapped on the table twice. "I don't have my ticket yet, but probably the third week in August."

"Shoot. That's when we'll be closed!"

"Ah, I definitely have to be back sometime around then, but maybe I can stretch it a few days."

"Maybe you can."

The server stopped by, and Josie deferred to Patrick to choose for both of them. She liked sharing food with him. He ordered a burrata appetizer, a pasta course of homemade fettuccini with lobster and rock shrimp, and medallions of beef.

"And we'll take a bottle of the Valpolicella. Nina knows the one I like."

Over dinner they talked about life in New York City versus Los Angeles. Patrick again mentioned finding a place in town so he could be bicoastal.

"If I have time in the next couple weeks, I'll start checking some places out, get a feel for what's out there."

"Maybe I can come out to L.A. sometime."

"I'd love that. Let's plan it. We can make a real vacation out of it. There's a great hotel on the beach in Santa Monica. Shutters. We can stay there when you come." His phone vibrated in his pocket.

"Shit. Sorry. Let me shut this thing off."

While he fumbled with it, Josie imagined visiting him in L.A. She'd never been to California. She'd hardly been anywhere. Staying with him in a hotel on the beach sounded sexy and romantic, and incongruously her eyes welled up with tears. She was grateful the room was candlelit and Patrick was distracted. She did not want to be the buzzed girl crying at the restaurant. She'd had to look after that girl far too many times at Bistrot. She took a sip of wine, then a long sip of water, and waved her hands in front of her face. Only then did Patrick notice her wet eyes.

"What's going on?" he asked with concern, putting his phone back in his pocket.

"Sorry. I don't know where that just came from. This fucking grief. It springs on you at the weirdest times."

"You're missing your grandmother."

"Terribly. Horribly. And I'm going to miss you!"

"Baby," he said, putting his hand on the back of her neck, "I'm still here, and we'll figure this out."

"I hope so. I'm not very good at figuring out this life stuff, if you haven't noticed."

"What do you mean?"

"Like what you said before about Bianca. About how even though her pictures were kind of—whatever—she was doing what she came to New York to do. I feel like I'm not doing what I came to New York to do, and Nanette—that's my grandmother—"

"I know."

"Nanette always wanted me to find something I love, and I let her down."

"Josie, you're an amazing girl." *Girl* gave her pause, but she decided it sounded feminine, not infantilizing. "No way you let her down. Everyone's on a different path. You'll figure yours out."

"Maybe mine isn't in New York at all?"

"Maybe it isn't," he said with a smile. "Maybe we'll both be bicoastal." He wiped the lone tear that was trickling down her cheek and kissed her again.

When they were through with dinner, he paid the check and led her by the hand back through the restaurant. At the hostess stand they stopped to say goodbye to Nina.

"Got to get this lady home," Patrick said, rubbing his thumb on Josie's palm. "It's been a long day."

"This was great. Thank you, Nina."

"Anytime. And thank *you*, Josie."

"For what?"

Nina patted Patrick's arm. "For making this guy happy. I've known him three years and never seen him so relaxed."

"Really? That's nice to hear."

"Yeah, he's usually a miserable mother fucker."

"It's true. My life's gotten a lot better lately." Patrick winked at Josie.

As they headed out the door, "What a Wonderful World" came on the sound system. Josie smiled and thanked Nanette for the validation.

⚜

ON FRIDAY, JOSIE walked to work from Patrick's, an umbrella in one hand and a travel mug filled with coffee in the other. He'd made it light and sweet without her specifying. It was a drizzly day, and she was charmed by the people she passed despite the collective bad mood that followed so many days of rain and the shocking news—now confirmed—about the Kennedys. She was smitten by the realness of the city. By the variety in style and skin tone and language she encountered in her short walk. She was struck by the beauty of Manhattan—the architectural details on the buildings and blocks she'd walked down dozens of times, the lions guarding Chelsea brownstones, the stained-glass entryways, the dormer windows on some of the higher floors. The microscopic gardens people managed to cultivate in their tiny, fenced-in yards. Even the juxtaposition of old New York architecture with some of the shiny, modern buildings, all steel and glass and much maligned by New York purists, was enchanting to her. Every street, every block, had a story. It was a town that welcomed all with open arms. She found herself rooting for the earthworms wriggling to safety on the trampled sidewalks.

She paused outside of Jefferson Market Library and looked up at its gothic spires, the clock tower that watched over Sixth Avenue like a faithful sentry, the green patina at the very top.

"Would you move!" a woman behind her snapped, and Josie stepped aside.

"Sorry! Have a lovely day."

The woman eyed her suspiciously and grumbled something in reply.

Josie got it. Plenty of times she'd been the one in the bad mood or rush getting irritated by oblivious pedestrians.

Once inside Bistrot, her bubble threatened to burst. It seemed everyone there was in a bad mood, too.

"It doesn't bother you, Josephine, that we haven't seen sunlight in months?" Curtis whined. "I feel like one of those people who has that disease where you can only go outside after dark."

"You're not one of those people, honey! So, it's a little gloomy outside. It doesn't have to be gloomy in here," she said, placing her palm on his chest.

He made a face like he'd just tasted spoiled milk. "Did you start taking Prozac or something?"

"Nope. Just having a rare moment of appreciating life."

There was further grumbling about the uncertainty of Bistrot's future. Chef had not been heard from for weeks, and in the meantime the kitchen was working twice as hard for no extra money.

"Guys, we're all in this together," Josie said. "Just say the word, and I'll pitch in."

Johnny pounced on her offer. "I got plenty of stuff you can help out with. Plenty."

The only person not vocally complaining was Derek, who'd been sullen and distracted for weeks. So distracted he hadn't seemed phased by Patrick's constant presence over the week while, in contrast, Alison hadn't been in at all.

Even Sam was in a funk. Sam, who should have been feeling on top of his game now that he had crossed the threshold to actor-with-headshots.

"What are you so glum about?" Josie asked him. "You have your pictures, now it's time to conquer the world!"

"You don't understand, Josie. You can't audition for anything without a decent resumé, and you can't get a decent resumé if you're not in anything, and you can't be *in* something unless you audition for it!"

"What are you talking about? Of course you can audition."

"Not for the big things. You need an agent, or a manager to submit you. Will you be my manager? No casting agent wants to see you if you haven't been cast in anything. That's not how it works."

"Okay, let's not get ahead of ourselves. Maybe you're not quite ready for 'the big things,' but there are plenty of other places to start! You need experience. Look at student films. They're being shot all over town, and they're always looking for talent. You see the flyers!"

"But you don't understand, Josie! I don't want to do student films. I want to go straight to Hollywood! Or at least Broadway."

"Oh, Samuel. Don't ever utter a statement like that to anyone but your reflection or your shrink. Seriously."

"I don't have a shrink. Do I need a shrink?"

Josie patted him on the shoulder and went to help Mario fold the napkins.

Just before 5:00 p.m., Sylvie walked in with a middle-aged couple Josie didn't recognize. She looked like the Sylvie everyone knew, hair and nails done, makeup in place.

The man was in his fifties and wore mirrored sunglasses and a tailored beige suit. He was suspiciously tan with a receding hairline and might have been attractive were it not for the sneer on his face and the wad of gum in his mouth. He had the look of a man who had lost his hair young and never forgiven it. His wife, Josie presumed, had the same suspicious tan and glossy, shoulder-length blonde hair. She wore a floral Lily Pulitzer shift in bright pink and green, pearls, and strappy white sandals. Her birdlike frame reminded Josie of her mother.

"Sylvie!" Josie said, pulling menus. "Are you joining us for an early dinner?"

"James?" Sylvie looked at the man, who was chomping his gum and staring down at his Palm Pilot.

"Yeah, my aunt wanted to come say goodbye," he said, keeping his eyes on his device and cracking his gum in his back teeth. A sweet chemical smell hit Josie's nostrils, and with a Proustian flashback to middle school she identified what he was chewing as grape-flavored bubble gum.

"Goodbye?" Josie asked. "Are you going out of town?

Sylvie's voice was shaky. "I'm going… James?"

He looked up from his Palm Pilot and sighed, then made a show of peering at his watch. "C'mon!" he said with stunning impatience.

Josie wanted to throttle him.

"We're bringing Aunt Sylvie to my sister-in-law in Connecticut," the wife said. She had the high, tight timbre of someone accustomed to holding her breath and keeping the peace.

Curtis chose this moment to attempt to pull himself out of his funk. He tangoed toward them and kissed Sylvie on both cheeks. "Miss Sylvie!" he squealed. "How are you, beautiful?"

The nephew recoiled.

"I'm here to say goodbye. Thank you for all the lovely evenings."

"What do you mean goodbye?"

"It's time to go."

It was the exact message that had been conveyed to Chef before he lost his mind. Josie looked at Curtis to see if he'd noticed, but he was too absorbed with Sylvie, holding her hands in his.

"Where are you going?"

Sylvie looked at her nephew again. He sighed impatiently and pulled his glasses off, revealing flinty, soulless eyes.

"We're taking her to Connecticut to live with my sister until we can find a home for her. Sylvie, we've got to get going, can you finish your goodbyes?"

Sylvie looked embarrassed, whether for her state of mind or her nephew's rudeness it didn't matter.

Curtis put a protective arm around her. "Come say goodbye to Derek." He walked her into the bar.

"Christ," the nephew muttered, looking down at the cellphone he'd pulled from his jacket and flipped open.

"You're a man of many devices," Josie said in a lame attempt to lighten the tension.

"Huh?"

"Honey." The wife put a hand lightly on his arm. He shook her off, and she looked mortified.

"We love Sylvie," Josie said to her. "It must be tough seeing her change and having to move her away from all her—"

"She's old," the nephew said with a shrug, blowing a lavender bubble and sucking it back into his mouth. Josie made a disgusted noise under her breath. "She's senile. She doesn't know what's going on."

"That's not entirely true," Josie said as diplomatically as she could muster. "Yes, her memory's slipped quite a bit, but she's still Sylvie."

"Yeah, well, who knows how much longer that'll last?" He pulled a pack of Bubble Yum from his jacket pocket and replaced the piece he was chewing with a fresh cube, macerating it and sending putrid puffs of faux grape into the air. A sour taste filled Josie's mouth. "Better move her now before she starts soiling herself and walking around in her night clothes or worse. Thank God she's rich. Least we can hire someone."

"James," the wife said quietly, shooting Josie an apologetic look.

James looked at his watch again. "Jesus, how many people does she need to say goodbye to? Let's go already! This is like wrangling a fucking toddler."

Josie's cheeks burned. She took a deep breath. "You know, Sylvie has been a valued member of our family for years. She's a fixture in this neighborhood, and we love her. I think you're doing her a great disservice by speaking to her like that, and by treating her like some kind of invalid."

"Excuse me!" He took a step closer to Josie. She stood up straighter.

"James," the wife pleaded, and he held his hand out at her.

"I don't know who you are outside of some waitress my aunt knows, and frankly I don't care. I care even less about what you think my family should or should not be doing where our private matters are concerned—"

Before he could continue his tirade, and before Josie could match his tone and voice the fury that was roiling inside her, Curtis brought Sylvie back over. He hugged her tight, tears in his eyes.

The nephew gave Josie a withering stare. She stared back. It took all of her will not to mouth obscenities at him.

"Love you, Miss Sylvie. You'll always be welcome here. Always," Curtis said. He pulled away and wiped his nose, then walked back to the dining room to finish his pre-dinner chores.

Now it was just Sylvie, Josie, James, and the wife, who didn't seem to have been given a name.

"Okay?" James said, jingling his car keys at Sylvie as if she were a baby. "We done here?"

"No, wait a minute," Sylvie said, her voice stronger than it had been. She put her hand on Josie's arm. "Where's Maria?"

"Mia is due any minute. Shall we wait for her?"

"Jesus Christ, Sylvie!" James threw his arms in the air. "We have an hour's drive ahead of us!"

"James!" the wife snapped. "Stop it!"

"You've always been so impatient, James! Always." Sylvie scolded her nephew, who looked momentarily stunned. "How dare you speak to me like that! I changed your diapers!"

"We'll be in the car." He took his wife's arm—she yanked it from his grip—and exited the restaurant.

"I'm sorry, Josie," Sylvie said. James's behavior seemed to have jostled her back to lucidity. "Thank God I don't have to live with that one. He's a real jackass."

"I did get that impression."

"And that milquetoast who married him? Personality of a shoelace!" This was the Sylvie who'd been missing for months. Sharp, funny, able to hold her own.

"Are you going to be okay in Connecticut?"

"Yes, dear. My niece is lovely. Don't know what happened to the bad seed."

"I'm going to miss you."

"I'll miss you, too. All of you. Here's my Maria!"

Mia stood inside the door, running her fingers through her hair, reminding Josie of the first moment they'd met.

"Maria, darling!" Sylvie cried, taking her hands. "Darling, how I'll miss you and our conversations!"

"I didn't realize you were leaving us quite so soon, Miss Sylvie!"

"They've come to take me home. Will I see you again?"

Josie hung back to give them privacy. She recognized this process from having seen Nanette go through something similar, morph from strong and stoic to childlike and unsure. Nanette, who'd always had wisdom and advice, bore little resemblance to that version of herself in their final phone calls. She repeatedly asked Josie what was happening to her and why, and it had taken everything Josie had to not break down and admit she had the same questions. With a lump in her throat, she realized she was missing not just Nanette, but suddenly her mother, too.

"Josie," Mia said. "Will you walk to the car with us?"

Josie took an umbrella from the hostess stand, and they walked outside to where James and his milquetoast wife sat in their idling car. James got out of the driver's side and opened the back door for his aunt, glaring at Josie once more.

Sylvie gave Josie a long hug and then turned to Mia. "Come visit me at mother's?"

"All right, Aunt Sylvie, that's enough," he said, practically shoving Mia out of the way. "It's rush hour! Traffic's a bear!"

"I'll speak to you soon, darling," Mia whispered. They stood in the rain and waved as Sylvie was driven off, waving back at them.

"Wow," Josie said. "That guy."

"Bless his heart."

The melancholia that pervaded the restaurant clung to the air for the remainder of the evening. Apparently the nephew had been right about traffic. Josie fielded several calls from people changing or cancelling their reservations because they were stuck in other parts of town. She didn't mind, too distracted to go through the motions of playing hostess at full speed. She was distracted in equal measure by sadness for Sylvie and how closely her demise resembled Nanette's, by pangs of excitement over Patrick, vivid flashbacks from the past week, and by a nagging misgiving about the bond Mia and Sylvie had forged. She'd been so caught up with Patrick Moore she'd forgotten having glimpsed Mia in Sylvie's window that night. And now all the suspicions she'd put on the back burner came flooding back.

Sylvie was a woman of considerable means. Mia needed money to get home. And they'd been spending a lot of time together it seemed. More than Josie realized.

"I hope Sylvie will be okay," Josie said to her later that night.

"Oh, I think she will be. From what I understand her niece is lovely. Lily, her name is."

"I hadn't realized you two spent quite so much time together."

Mia blinked. "We didn't spend all that much time, just some chats here and there. Of course she thought I was someone else the whole time," she added with a laugh. "So, I'm not sure that *I* actually spent any time at all with her!"

This wasn't going as planned. Josie switched tactics. "Goodbyes are hard."

"Yes they are, girl. And your summer started with such a big one."

"Maybe that's why this is hitting me so much. And then you're heading home soon, too, right?"

"Soon as I can. I miss my Rita something awful."

"I bet you do. What's she like?"

"She's a strong girl. Stubborn as all get out but a really sweet soul. She's a little lost without me, I'm afraid." Tears filled her eyes, and she took a deep breath and exhaled. "Which is why I need to get there come hell or highwater. You got customers, baby."

Josie returned to the hostess stand no further enlightened.

Soon the restaurant was busy. It seemed the whole neighborhood had decided to come in. Boodles and Bulleit brought a boisterous group whose energy was in sharp contrast to the mood hovering over Bistrot. Josie was anxious to get back to Mia but couldn't find the opportunity, and Mia slipped away quietly when her shift ended, furthering Josie's sense that something was amiss.

Still, she didn't know for sure that it *was* Mia she'd seen in the window, and she wasn't even certain that was Sylvie's window. It was nighttime, and there was booze involved. Then again, there seemed to always be booze involved these days.

After dinner she sat at the bar ruminating, while Curtis attempted to flirt with a regular in whom he'd never shown interest before, a man who came in alone to drink martinis and read the paper. Derek was still in a mood, wasn't giving her much to work with, but Josie tried. Patrick would be coming in soon, and she refused to sit in sullen silence while she waited.

"It's so weird to know that this is the last time we'll probably see Sylvie," she said.

"Probably? Definitely," Derek said somberly.

"Yes, of course. Jesus, am I such a commitment-phobe that I'm afraid of committing to the *end* of a relationship?" She waited for him to break into a smile. He didn't. "Sylvie practically came with the building. You know what? We should do something to honor her. Like name a drink after her or something."

"She only drank champagne," he said.

"Okay, so we'll dress up a glass of champagne, make a cocktail out of it, and call it the Sylvie."

He nodded.

"Derek," she said. She waited for him to look at her. "You know you can talk to me if you want to, right? I heard what you said the other night and I will get better about listening."

"Thank you. I just—"

The ringing phone interrupted him, and he looked relieved. "Want to get that?"

"Not particularly, but it's my job."

She dashed through the bar to the hostess stand and grabbed the receiver on the fourth ring. "Good evening, Bistrot."

There was a brief pause, then a woman spoke. *"Hello, I'm trying to reach my husband, and I think he spends time at your restaurant."* The woman spoke in an accent Josie couldn't place. She knew most of the customers who were still there, but there were a couple of unfamiliar faces, guests of guests.

"I can certainly ask around. What's his name?"

As the woman spoke, Alison walked in. She'd been crying again. Her eyes were puffy and void of makeup. She paused by the entrance to the bar and looked through Josie toward Derek, who rushed over and ushered her into the vestibule. Josie couldn't hear what they were saying, but it was clear that Alison was agitated, and Derek was trying to calm her down.

"I'm sorry," Josie said. "Can you repeat that?"

"Patrick? Patrick Moore?"

"What about Pat—" Josie said, then heard the rest of the words the woman had said. Her face burned as she gripped the side of the hostess stand so tightly her knuckles hurt and turned white. The oxygen left the room, and her blood felt like it was on fire. "Who is this?"

The woman was patient despite having to repeat herself. *"Yasmin. His wife. I've been trying him for a couple hours, and he isn't picking up his mobile. Do you know him?"*

"Yes."

"Have you seen him tonight?"

"Not tonight." Her breath was shallow and rapid.

The voice on the other end continued to speak. *"...not urgent. Sorry to bother you. Would you give him a message if you do see him?"*

"Yes." Josie ground her teeth so hard she feared they'd crack.

"...Pilar lost a tooth and wanted to tell him."

Josie opened her mouth and closed it again.

The woman—Patrick's *wife*—waited. *"Okay, thank you very much,"* she said finally. *"And what's your name?"*

Josie hung up. She didn't know whether to scream, cry, kick the hostess stand, or storm out of the restaurant. She wanted a shot of tequila. She wanted a cigarette. She wanted to punch Patrick in the teeth.

She wanted to sob.

She walked through the front doors, cutting between Alison and Derek, who abruptly stopped speaking and watched her go by. She stood for a minute in the humid night air and tried to breathe. She'd forgotten how. On one of the patio tables was an ashtray overflowing with half-smoked cigarette butts. She extracted three quarters of one and attempted to light it from a damp book of matches. Each match she struck sparked for a moment and then died. She was numb. She was seething. She was distraught. She was everything at once. Those stages of grief she'd been cycling through for weeks—for months because they'd begun long before Nanette's final breath—hurtled toward her in rapid succession.

The front door opened, and Derek and Alison walked out. She hated the looks of concern in their eyes.

"Josie, I'm walking Alison home. I'll be back in a few."

Josie stared straight ahead into the empty air and nodded.

"Curtis is behind the bar, okay?" She couldn't look at him, but she could feel the worry emanating from him and could hear the uncertainty in his voice. She wanted to weep.

"Bye, Josie," Alison said sweetly.

Derek touched her shoulder and led Alison up the three steps to the sidewalk. Josie sat in thick silence, holding her breath for what felt like an hour but was probably closer to fifteen seconds, then letting it go with a shudder.

People staggered out of the restaurant, and their laugher and upbeat conversation sounded a million miles away. Each time the door opened she heard snippets of other peoples' nights. She wished Mia were there.

She tried in vain to light another match.

"There's my girl." A voice came out of the darkness, accompanied by the flickering flame of a lighter. "Need a light?"

She wouldn't look at him. She couldn't. She started to tremble.

"Josie?" His voice rose and warbled on the second syllable. "What's going on?" He moved the hair off the back of her neck, and she jerked violently.

She stood up and grabbed the lighter from his fingers. Glaring at him, staring through the bewildered and frightened look in his eyes, she lit the bit of cigarette, inhaled, exhaled smoke in his face, and flung the lighter out onto the street without taking her eyes off him. It clattered across the pavement.

Patrick hunched his shoulders and bowed his head. He knew.

"You got a phone call," Josie said through clenched teeth. She pictured herself like a cartoon dragon, fire coming out of her mouth, nostrils flaring with smoke.

"Okay. Okay," he said in a tempered calm that made her want to scream. He stood a little straighter and smiled, but his eyes gave him away. She knew this guy, the despicable man trying to hide behind the cowardly little boy she had caught him being. It was her father redux, only this time she was the cliché, the "other woman" to a man who'd picked up exactly where her father had left off, furthering the damage he'd inflicted so many years earlier.

No kid, I said I'd call today, not yesterday. Not a great time to visit, kid! Sorry kid, I'm married!

"Who called, kid?"

Josie laughed a manic, gurgling laugh that startled Patrick, though he did his best to maintain his composure. He was sickeningly adept at doing so.

A trio of tipsy people stumbled out of the restaurant and onto their scene, and Josie didn't care.

"Yasmin," she said through clenched teeth, waiting for a reaction. "Yasmin called!"

"Who's Yasmin?" one of the guys said as they laughed and walked up toward the sidewalk. They stood there talking, figuring out where to go next. Josie had an audience.

Patrick was good at this. He'd had practice. If you weren't looking for it, you would have missed the twitching of his jaw when he bit the inside of his cheek.

"Your *wife*. Yasmin is your *wife!*"

"Awwwwww shit," one of the guys on the sidewalk said. "Someone got busted!"

Patrick looked at them quickly, and then back at Josie. He let out a sound that was part stutter, part squeak, searched for a word, and stopped.

Josie laughed again, tears spilling out of the corners of her eyes. She wiped them away angrily.

Patrick froze, nothing moving except his mouth, which was still searching for a word that didn't exist.

"Pilar lost a tooth!" she said in a sing-song, mocking voice. "Your wife has a lovely accent. Where's she from?"

"Baby—"

"I asked you a question!"

More people trickled out of the restaurant and on realizing what was going on shuffled away quickly.

Patrick sighed. "She's from Lisbon. Portugal."

"I FUCKING KNOW WHERE LISBON IS!" Josie shouted.

"Josie, baby, it's not what you—"

"IT'S NOT WHAT I THINK?!" Now people inside the restaurant turned and looked at her. "YOU'RE FUCKING MARRIED WITH A KID!"

"*Step* kid," he said, then grimaced.

"So, is this why you were in L.A. last week? To see your lovely wife and *step* kid?"

He looked at the ground, his jaw tense, then back up at her. "It was my father-in-law we had to move. Not my father."

"And you actually gave her the name of the restaurant? The restaurant where I fucking work? What is wrong with you?"

"No. I don't know how she knew. I probably left a book of matches there or something."

"How could you fucking do this to me?" Josie wailed, balling her hands into fists. "What is wrong with you?"

"It's not what you think," he said again. "I mean that. If you'll let me explain—"

Josie took a deep, jagged breath. "No. Turn around, walk up those steps, and don't ever come back here again." She pronounced the words slowly and deliberately. "Ever."

"Josie, you need to give me a chance to explain. If you'll let me come in and talk to you." He put his hand on her arm, and she jerked away.

"Everybody knows," she lied. "And so help me if you follow me back in there you will *not* be treated well." She flicked her lit cigarette at his feet, turned on her heel, and stomped back into the restaurant. She refused to look behind her, to make sure he'd left. She marched up the stairs to the bathroom and shoved the door open. She was trembling, coming unraveled in a way that scared the hell out of her.

How *dare* he? How dare he lie to her, string her along, make a fool out of her? Make her think there was actually something between them? What the hell had the last week been about? What was the point? He put her in a position where she actually had to speak to his *wife*. She dry-heaved into the sink.

The idiot left his trail so poorly concealed that his wife knew the name of the place he hung out, where the woman he was *fucking* all summer worked. And why the hell did he cheat on his wife in the first place?

Now Josie felt sad for the kid. Because she was that kid once, and she had told Patrick that, revealed her demons, which were the very same ones he was now creating for his wife and kid. He'd listened to her, comforted her, feigned disgust at the way her father treated her mother, and sadness at the lonely childhood she'd endured. Maybe he wasn't feigning—maybe he was just a self-loathing loser who knew exactly what he was doing to his kid. Maybe he was painfully aware of the broken spirits he'd left in his wake. No wonder he was so interested in Josie's current relationship—or lack thereof—with her father.

She stared into the mirror. Her eyes were blazing, her cheeks flushed, and she was breathing so furiously she was pulsating.

She would not cry. She'd already started to in front of Patrick, but they were tears of anger. There'd be plenty of time for sadness, and compared to Nanette this was nothing to be sad about. No, she needed to lead with anger. And she had every right to her anger. At that very moment, she held Patrick's marriage in the palm of her hand. Revenge fantasies great and small swirled in her head, ones that ran the gamut of ethics and legality. She could keep it simple, track down his number in L.A., ring *Yasmin* back and introduce herself. Take away Patrick's safe haven.

But what was the point of that? It wouldn't just hurt him, it would hurt the wife and kid, and that she could not do, be complicit in riddling a child with the same isolation and mistrust that had defined her childhood. And her adulthood—fuck—any wonder she had a tough time getting close to men?

She splashed her face and let out a strangled laugh at the crazed look in her eyes. She would not cry. She was mad, not sad. Mad, not sad.

"Pull it together, woman," she commanded her reflection while she patted her face dry. "You will not cry over a man!"

A sound came from the far stall, and Josie froze, heard the blood rushing and pulsing in her ears.

Another sound, quiet gasping like someone trying to catch her breath. Like someone releasing the tears Josie was holding in.

"Hello?" she called in a parched whisper.

It came again, louder this time, and Josie pivoted, put one foot carefully in front of the other and headed toward the noise. Someone was crying, and Josie's addled mind was getting the best of her. This was a real person, not a ghost. A drunk girl crying in the bathroom stall was not unusual at a business that peddled booze in a city where nobody had to drive. She did a mental scan of the customers who were still there.

"Do you need something, honey?" she called, and the person in the stall took a long, creaky breath. The door was slightly ajar, and Josie tapped on it. "What's your name?"

"*Ruby*," came a whisper as Josie pushed the door open and shrieked. The stall was empty, and the room was now silent. She shrieked.

"Oh God, oh God, oh God, not tonight!" She backed away and wrenched open the door, colliding with Derek. She shrieked again, her heart pounding.

"Jesus, Josie, what is happening?"

Now the tears flowed, and she couldn't get down the stairs fast enough. She knew everyone in the place was probably talking about her and the scene she'd made, and she didn't care.

Derek followed her outside where she sat down and put her head between her legs, trying to catch her breath, trying to rationalize the irrational. When she sat up, he was watching her, his mouth hanging open.

"Oh my God, Derek," she said, slumping her head in her hands.

"Josie, what is it?" he asked, panic in his voice. He squatted in front of her so they were eye-level. She couldn't tell him what had happened upstairs. She didn't know that it had, in fact, happened.

"Will you grab me a drink?" she asked, breathless. "And a cigarette? And can you sit with me for a minute? Please? I've had a really rough night."

"I know. Yes, of course. What do you want?"

"Alcohol. And a cigarette."

He pulled a pack of Camel Lights from his pocket and lit one for her. She stepped out of her head and wondered when he'd started smoking again. "I'll be right back," he said, touching her shoulder.

Josie concentrated on her breathing, wiping her eyes with the back of her sleeve so by the time the next couple of patrons trickled out she was almost composed. She could not tell where her fear stopped and her anger began, or whether she'd already reached the sadness stage. She didn't know what was going on.

Ruby was Mia's friend, and if that hadn't been some kind of fucked up fantasy then what was she doing? What did she want from Josie? Maybe all she wanted was to stay by Mia's side, and Josie just happened to be there, too. Maybe she wasn't being haunted after all, she was just in the way. As she grappled with this notion she started to calm down.

Derek returned with a bottle of Pinot Noir, two glasses, and a pint of water that he placed in front of Josie. He took the seat next to her and set to work opening the bottle. "Curtis is calling a car to take you both back to Brooklyn. My treat. He said he'd give us a couple minutes."

"Thank you," Josie said. "You didn't have to do that."

He poured two glasses, and they sipped in silence. "Talk to me sister," he said after a minute.

"You were right about Patrick. He's not an upstanding member of society."

"I'm sorry to hear that."

"Yeah, that phone call before? That was his wife. Yasmin."

Derek put his glass down. "Are you fucking kidding me?"

"Nope." She exhaled smoke. "He's actually married to a woman named Yasmin."

Derek stuck a cigarette in his mouth, shaking his head as he cupped his hand around the lighter's flame. "Jesus."

"I'm an idiot."

He grabbed her hand, cigarette dangling from his lips. "Stop it. No. You are not an idiot. Guy never gave you a reason to think he was married, right?"

"Nope. Or that he had a kid."

"Jesus," he said again. "Sweetheart. I don't know what to say."

"Wait—correction—step kid."

"Well then it's fine." He squeezed her hand.

"Yeah, no big deal," she said glumly. "You know what sucks? I was really starting to like him."

"No, you liked the idea of him, which is totally different from the truth. He's a married man with a kid—"

"Step kid!" Josie pointed out, holding a finger up.

"Step kid, and he's someone who lies easily about pretty major stuff."

"I know. But we had such a good week." The tears started to fall again, and she angrily swatted them away. "Fuck. I miss Nanette."

"I know you do. And I know you're a fucking mess of feelings right now. But don't conflate them. Your grief for Nanette is pure. It's not complicated as far as grief goes. You were there. You did everything right. You know that. This Patrick shit sucks. There's nothing cool about it, and it's entirely on him."

"I was there, too."

"Yes, and do not beat yourself up for one second. Not one. It's not like you had a feeling he was married. You were blindsided."

They held hands and sat in near silence, ambient sounds from the restaurant, the light pattering of the rain, and the occasional whirring of tires on the street punctuated by Josie's sniffles. Derek pulled out another cigarette and lit it, then offered her a drag.

"When did you take up smoking again?"

He let go of her hand and pressed his lips tight together. "Well," he said with a sigh. "Speaking of being blindsided."

A town car pulled up in front of the restaurant.

"Car's here," he said, standing up. "Alison's pregnant."

Josie's mouth dropped open.

"And she wants to keep it." He gave her a loaded look. "Yep."

"Jesus, Derek, what are you going to do?"

He picked the glasses up from the table. "I don't imagine I have much say in the matter. I'll let Curtis know your ride is here. Hang in there, sister." He squeezed her shoulder and walked inside.

Chapter Twelve

***

JOSIE WAS IN no mood to talk on the ride home, and Curtis—either because he wasn't picking up her cues or was and wanted to distract her—filled the time with drunken babbling.

"Sam was on and on about his stuff again tonight, and I wanted to slap him. Some guy in there was a gaffer—a gaffer on commercials—and he cock-blocked me to grill him about the industry. Kid's gotta lose his desperado ingenue act if he's going to have a chance at this. I mean damn, took him long enough to get headshots." He stopped abruptly and shot Josie a sideways glance. "Sorry."

"Why are you apologizing?" she asked wearily.

"Yikes. I don't know. Headshots. I figured it's a sore subject."

"What makes you say that?"

"Josephine. Puhleeze. You look a fright."

"Thank you."

"And Derek treated us to a car home. I know it's not because he felt bad that I was cockblocked."

"Okay, fine. Patrick and I are done. I don't want to talk about it."

"Oh my God, lady, what *happened*?" He swiveled on his seat and took her face in his hands. "You had such a good week! I'm going to weep!"

She wrestled out of his grip. "Yeah, honey, this is why I don't want to talk about it! I'm exhausted. I love you, but I don't need any more histrionics on top of my own. I'll give you details some other time, but it wasn't my doing. And for what it's worth, which is absolutely nothing, this thing was only seven weeks from start to finish."

"That's almost two months!"

"Yes, I know."

"He's married," Curtis said with a decisive nod.

"What the fuck? How do you know that?"

"'Cause I know he didn't beat you, and that's the other horrible thing straight guys do. Sure, it happens in my world, but it's definitely more an angry straight guy thing."

"Wow. Okay. Anyway, I don't want to talk about it. Can I please have the night off from sharing?"

"Of course." He held her hand the rest of the way home and sang a medley of songs about things getting better.

When they reached her place, she kissed him on the cheek. "You're a mensch."

"And you're better off without Patrick Moore."

Once inside, Josie forced herself to go to bed. Otherwise she knew she'd pace and overthink until even in her fatigue she'd be unable to rest. She flipped through the channels on mute and settled on *Casablanca* to fall asleep to. She actively shut her mind off as she'd done so many times before. She'd navigated all the messy bits of childhood—anger, sadness, fear—by repeating a mantra Nanette taught her. *If I don't think about it, it loses power.* Tonight she created a new one. *I don't care. I don't care. I don't care.*

AFTER SEVERAL HOURS of vague, uplifting dreams about Nanette, Josie lay in bed for a few minutes on waking, forgetting her reality. As the fog dissipated, the truth came back.

"Ugh," she said, filled anew with rage. She grabbed a pillow and screamed into it with all her force, the sound muffled and anguished. Nothing made her angrier than people pretending to be something they weren't. Or, in this case, pretending *not* to be something they were.

She took a long, hot shower. In a nod to Nanette, who believed if you looked the part the mood would follow, she got dressed up. She chose a silky red halter she'd bought on sale the previous fall and never worn—it still had its price tag—

and a pair of flowing black pants. She pulled out strappy heeled sandals and looked through her makeup collection, filled mostly with free samples and products she'd bought on a whim. She chose a bright lip gloss that matched her top, a bolder color than she normally wore, and lined her eyes with black pencil, wishing she had Mia's artistry. When she was done, she pursed her lips and examined herself in the mirror.

"Hello, gorgeous," she said, tears threatening her carefully made-up eyes. Her brow furrowed, and she looked away.

Under normal circumstances, if such a thing existed, Josie would be grateful for the distraction of Bistrot and the chance to keep busy. But today she wasn't, nor was she appreciative that it was a cool, sunny day. It didn't match her mood at all. The most appealing thing she could imagine was staying in her apartment and hibernating, opening a bottle of wine much too early, chain smoking, listening to Billie Holiday, watching old movies, and not thinking about anything she didn't want to. Numbing her brain to the empty truth of her life. Because everything she didn't want to think about was waiting for her across the river in Manhattan.

She put on her darkest shades and kept them on throughout the trip into the city. They buffered her from the world.

A young couple sat opposite her, laughing at some inside joke, lazy and in love. The girl draped her bare legs over her boyfriend's lap and played with his hair while he thumbed through a magazine, occasionally tilting it in her direction. They looked so content, bored almost, as though at twenty-two or twenty-three they'd already experienced the once-in-a-lifetime magic of true love, and their future was writ.

Josie wanted to tell them it was an illusion. That whatever bliss they thought they were feeling would be fleeting. One of them would get restless and fuck up, some stranger would enter their world, and their comfort and stability would go up in flames. Hearts would break, tears would be shed, they would end. But they were young enough that neither had to worry about the door forever closing. They would still be able to rebuild their lives and move forward. Josie felt old and irrelevant. She knew thirty-two was still young, but her soul was tired, her heart worn out.

There had to have been all sorts of signs she'd missed. She felt like a forensic scientist combing through seven weeks' worth of evidence, replaying encounters and bits of conversation and mining them for clues. In hindsight, of course there had been some. The furtive glances at his cellphone before he stepped outside to take a call. His evasiveness about his trip home. That he had invited her—sort of—to visit L.A. and stay in a hotel, under the guise that it would be a vacation for both of them. She hadn't questioned his explanation. It had sounded sweet.

In the movies, cheating men had a telltale ring mark on their finger. Josie hadn't noticed one on Patrick. But then, lots of people didn't wear wedding bands.

She wondered what Yasmin looked like and pictured her as tall and effortlessly beautiful. A cool single mom whom Patrick had fallen for so hard he'd married her.

If he had a shred of decency, he would come back in to explain and apologize. He would not let her slip away with this horrible lasting impression of him. Then again, she had made it clear he wasn't welcome at Bistrot, and really, what was there to explain, and what good would an apology do? It was an open and shut situation. He had a wife and didn't respect Josie enough to tell her. She felt stupid and ashamed.

By the time she reached the West 4th Street stop, she was pissed. Forget sadness. Forget feeling sorry for herself. She was pissed. Pissed at her father, pissed at Patrick, pissed at all men everywhere. Men took liberties with women's emotions, played with them, and led them on without paying any mind to the consequences. Then, when they were most needed, they abandoned them.

A man passing by on the sidewalk looked Josie up and down and gave her an appreciative smile. She removed her shades and scowled so hard he crossed the street.

She waited at the crosswalk and looked down Sixth Avenue. With the sun shining she had a clear view of the World Trade Center two and a half miles south, rising from the horizon and anchoring the island. The first time Josie had visited New York was around Christmas, when she was twelve years old. Nanette had brought her for a weekend of sightseeing, ice skating in Wollman Rink, and the musical *Oklahoma*, which had just opened on Broadway. They'd toured lower Manhattan and the Twin Towers, completed only a few years prior. Josie had seen their images so many times by then that finally seeing them in person was at once awe-inspiring and instantly familiar, infusing her with a sense of *déja-vu* that she remembered every time she saw them now. Now they were a touchstone to

Nanette, and seeing them was the only thing grounding her and keeping her from falling to bits. She thanked them silently and made her way to the restaurant.

No rain meant Mia would have the night off, and Josie couldn't talk to her about all that had transpired. Derek had his own demons to contend with, and Curtis was emotional, which wasn't what she needed right now. She needed Mia's calm wisdom, and she would have to channel it herself. She could do this.

But as the evening got under way, she racked up more reasons to begrudge the universe. She was pissed at Derek for not being more careful. She was pissed at Alison for being foolish enough—or manipulative enough—to want to have a kid so young. She was pissed at Chef for leaving the restaurant in shambles so nothing in her life was stable.

And she was pissed at the clientele for being too chipper, or too glum. For needing too much, or for seeming to need nothing. At the parents among them who let their kids run wild as though the staff was there to babysit. There was a certain breed of New York City parent Josie found righteously self-involved, like the dog owners who walked their pets off-leash. These parents would never dream of silencing their children regardless of their surroundings, and so even at a restaurant that, to some people, was the site of a special occasion—an engagement, a celebration, a reunion—smug parents let their kids carry on and run about and use their outside voices. There were several of them that night.

Mid-dinner she marched up the stairs to the ladies' room and realized she was pissed, too, at Ruby for invading her space. So pissed she refused to be afraid.

"Don't fuck with me," she said aloud before shutting herself in a stall. "I am not in the mood, so leave me alone."

"Excuse me?" came a voice from the other stall. Josie looked down and saw shoes.

"Sorry," she mumbled. "Running lines for a play."

When she came out, a woman she'd seated earlier in the evening was washing her hands. She'd come in with three other women, and their shoulder pads and short, frosted hair indicated that they hailed from a part of the country that was a good fifteen years behind in style.

"So, you're an actress then?" the woman asked with the flattened vowel sounds of a midwestern accent.

"Something like that," Josie said, running the water.

"Then it's true that everyone who works in a restaurant in New York City is an actor! Just like in the movies! So funny!" She laughed with delight.

Now Josie was pissed at this woman, too, for belittling her fake career.

"Has anyone famous ever worked here?"

"Sure, Tom Cruise, Kevin Bacon, Sylvester Stallone was a busboy," Josie said. "Off the top of my head."

"How coooool! The girls'll flip! I've got to tell them." She walked out, and Josie rolled her eyes.

"You do that, honey," she said, then paused, half-expecting a response from the empty room. When none came, she exhaled with relief.

In the hallway, she was startled by a little boy loitering outside the men's room. She huffed in annoyance, then the kid looked up at her and she softened. He could be cast as a Dickensian orphan, rosy cheeks, messy blonde curls.

"Do you need something, honey?"

"No, ma'am. I'm just waiting for my brother," he said. He was adorable, and Josie made a mental note to begrudge the parents, not the kids.

Back downstairs, she kept herself as busy as possible to offset the emotion coursing through her veins. Against her best judgment, she hoped Patrick would show up. She didn't want to hope that, but there it was.

When the dining room wrapped up, she helped herself to several glasses of wine, and Derek gave her no grief. It wasn't until she told him she was hoping to see Patrick that he objected.

"No, you don't. Josie, what good would that do?"

"I don't know!" she said, buzzed and belligerent. "Maybe it would kick me out of this weird limbo I'm in. I mean, I don't want to take him back."

"Good."

"For one thing he probably doesn't want that, and for another, he was never mine to begin with."

"Exactly. And you were never his. That's not how it works. It's 1999, not 1950."

"Yeah, well, maybe I wish I could live in 1950 where the only thing women needed to be was fucking barefoot and pregnant." She winced. "Sorry. Not that there's anything wrong with being barefoot and pregnant if that's your bag, but I'm just saying it's not *my* bag, and maybe life would be a lot easier if it was. Not that what you're dealing with is easy. Jesus."

"*Josie*," he said, leaning across the bar to her. "Keep it down. My situation is not public knowledge."

"Okay! Duly noted! Give me a task so I can stop overthinking, please!"

"Yeah, feel free to bring the empties to me." He gestured around the bar, where sweating glasses and crumpled bar napkins lay on the tables.

Josie pried herself off her barstool and made the rounds straightening up. At a small table off to the side sat a very young couple.

The woman was visibly upset, and the man was talking a mile a minute, pleading with her for forgiveness Josie was sure he didn't deserve. They were an unlikely match. She wore a floral dress and ballet flats, her thick, light brown hair tied loosely in a white scrunchie. Her boyfriend, or date, or whatever he was, looked like an East Village musician. A drummer. He was pale-skinned and rakishly disheveled, with tousled black hair, a chip-toothed smile, and a motorcycle jacket that looked as though it had been shredded by one too many collisions with pavement.

"Baby, baby, please!" he begged her, and Josie felt sick remembering Patrick's pleas. "I'm sorry."

The girl wouldn't look at him. Her big blue eyes brimmed with tears. "This is just crazy," she said, shaking her head and staring at her drink. "So stupid."

Josie caught the guy's eye and felt a surge of sympathy for him. He looked sad and helpless.

"Honey," he said to his girlfriend. He was slurring his words. "Please don't leave me."

She shook her head slowly. Finally, she spoke again. "I have to learn how to live without you." She put a few bills on the table and pushed her chair out. "Asshole," she said quietly.

Josie stopped her as she walked by. "Honey, are you okay?" she asked.

"No," she said abruptly, shaking her head against the tears that were falling. She kept walking. Her boyfriend staggered behind and looked at Josie, shrugging.

"Anything we can do?" she asked. "Can we get you guys a cab or something?"

"She's so unhappy with me. I fucked up huge. Now what do I do?"

"I don't know, honey. Just do your best. Good luck."

"Thanks," he said, touching Josie's arm. "Thanks." He followed his girlfriend out the door.

Josie cleared their table and walked over to the bar, where Curtis was standing.

"That poor girl," he said.

"What did he do to her?"

"Who?"

"The boyfriend, or whoever that was?"

"He died!"

Josie stared at the glass she was holding. There was a peach lipstick stain on the rim. "What?" she asked, feeling nauseous. She looked back at the table. There'd only been the one glass.

"That girl who was just in here by herself? In the flowers? Her boyfriend died in a motorcycle accident last month. So sad."

Josie took a step and staggered, tripping in her heels.

"Lady, you okay?" Curtis helped her to a bar stool.

"I need a drink," she whispered.

"I know, it's really sad. On top of so much sad. D, can we have another round?"

Derek pulled the bottle of Sancerre Josie had been drinking from the ice.

"Actually?" she said. "Can I have a chilled shot of vodka?"

"That sounds perfect, lady, I'll join you."

Derek tried to shake his head furtively, but Josie caught him.

"Derek, please. I'm an adult. I've had a rough twenty-four."

"I know, but you've also had a few glasses of wine."

"D, she's had a rough twenty-four," Curtis said, putting his arm around Josie. "Let mama have her vodka."

Derek threw his hands in the air. "Fine. Just looking out for you."

"Then join our pity party," Curtis said. "Have a shot."

He hesitated, shrugged, and pulled out three shot glasses. "I'll have *one*," he said to Josie. "I'd do the same if I were you, but what do I know?"

When he went outside to smoke a cigarette, Curtis shook up another hefty shaker of chilled vodka. He replaced Josie's shot glass with a rocks glass, and she was content.

"Sip it. It's not a shot."

She complied, though she wished she could explain to him, and to Derek, that she was not just drinking her feelings about Patrick, she was anesthetizing herself to the fact that she had just seen a ghost. Each sip took away the panic so she could process what had just happened.

"So, the girl who lost her boyfriend? She was the one sitting right there?"

"Mmmhmm."

"With the white scrunchie and the little flowered dress?"

"It was a romper."

"Romper." In her tipsiness Josie found the word funny and started to laugh. This was another coping mechanism she'd developed when she was scared as a kid, to search for anything she could spin into laughter in hopes of chipping away at the dread in the pit of her stomach. It seldom worked. "Romper."

"Romp her."

"What did she tell you?"

"About her boyfriend? They were high school sweethearts."

With each word Curtis spoke, Josie's skin felt pricklier until she could barely sit still.

"He was a musician, a drummer, she showed me a picture. Handsome young guy, apparently he was riding home from a gig one night after a few too many and he bit it on the BQE."

Josie took a big sip of her vodka.

"Easy there, lady."

"That's really sad."

"That's why you don't drink and drive. Or ride. His poor judgement is the worst thing that's ever happened to her. He got off easy."

"I don't know about that."

"Well, she's really sad and really hurt, and she said she's mad at him, too. I guess they had this issue in the past, and he swore he wouldn't do it again. He broke his promise, and now this."

"Straight men are the worst. You have no idea how lucky you are."

"Girl, you think I've got it any easier?"

"Yeah, but the shit we have to worry about when we meet a guy. Are they married?" She made a sloppy checkmark in the air. "Check!"

"At least y'all can *get* married."

"Yeah, but what's the fucking point? Then they cheat. Or they leave. Or they do both. Or they drink too much and bite it on the BQE."

"I don't know lady, I'm a romantic. I want forever. I want to have a family someday."

"Yeah, well, my mom pretty much convinced me there was no such thing as forever and no point in trying for it."

"That's sad."

"It's fucked up." Josie picked at a small tear in the red leather bar stool she sat on and pulled out a tuft of upholstery. "She literally convinced me not to bother. I had a nice boyfriend in high school. Briefly. And a nice boyfriend in college. Briefly. Even a halfway decent one right after college, before I moved to New York to sell my soul to the restaurant world. And she talked me out of all of it."

"You did not sell your soul. You don't hate this world."

"I don't hate this world. I kind of love it. But that's another brilliant thing Alice drilled into my brain—that this world doesn't count, like it's not an important enough way to make a living or something. And who the hell knows, maybe it isn't. But the point is now that I think about it? My whole adult life has been colored by my mom's negativity. Strong women don't need men, so I'm weak if I ever wanted a boyfriend, and this industry is frivolous. I've been working in this industry for a decade, so that's a decade of frivolous living under my belt." She took a slug of her drink. "And now even my frivolous life is all fucked up because who knows what the hell is going to happen to this place? Chef gets rid of it, we're all out of work, and where do I go from here? Start over doing the same thing somewhere else without my anchors?"

She took another slug and felt the hysteria rise in her voice but couldn't stop it. She knew she'd had too much to drink, but at this point she didn't care that there were still customers in the bar, or that Derek was watching her with disapproval, or that she was unloading onto poor, sweet Curtis. Curtis, who was always there for her and really never asked for anything in return.

"Not to mention I just lost my main anchor, my Nanette. And that's the fucking worst part about this Patrick situation."

"Not that he's married?"

"No, not that he's married, that's his fucking problem. And hers. *Yasmin.*" She said the name with contempt. "*Yasmin Moore.* No, *Yasmin* probably kept her last name. *Yasmin* is probably this, like, high-powered feminist supermodel with a PhD who does Pilates and plays tennis. I bet she drives a Lexus. Do you think she drives a Lexus?" Realizing her own glass was empty, she reached for Curtis's. "Or an Audi. No, a Lexus."

"Girl, you're losing the thread." Curtis tried to rescue his drink. Josie kept a firm grip on it, and he gave up. "This isn't about Yasmin."

"My point exactly!" she said, pointing a finger at him. He cocked his head, confused. "My point is that Patrick was, like, my grief tourniquet. If I hadn't had him to distract me over the last month and a half or whatever the fuck it's been, I would have drowned in tears. Drowned! Wait, that's a mixed metaphor. What did I say before?"

"Tourniquet."

"Right. If I hadn't had him to distract me, I would have bled out. My grief would have bled out. He staunched the flow. He was like the EMS worker to my accident victim, and the blood is my grief."

"Yes, I get it." He tried again to reach for his glass, and Josie moved it to her other hand. "So, now what?"

"So, now you got through the really rough stretch, and he was here for that. It helped. And so even though he turned out to be—"

"A *bastard*!" she snarled, causing Derek to look over at her and motion to her to lower her voice. "*A BASTARD!*" she repeated in an exaggerated whisper that managed to be louder than the first time she said it.

"Okay, even though he turned out to be a bastard, lady love, he served a purpose, right?"

"What damn difference does it make if now he's just ripped the scab off on my grief? It's ten times rawer than it would have been!"

"Is it?"

"Yes. No. I don't know." She took another sip. "I don't know what grief is supposed to feel like."

"I think it's kind of just supposed to feel like whatever it feels—"

"But I do know that Patrick Moore is a bastard!" she steamrolled over him. "And that I am stuck in a rut, and it's my mother's fault! But at least I'm not stuck with a baby!" She glared at Derek, unsure why she was directing any vitriol his way.

He looked up startled, then angry, and started walking down the bar toward her. "Josie," he said calmly. "Put the drink down before you—"

"Before I say something I shouldn't?" She slammed the rest of the vodka and stood up, wobbling into the barstool and knocking it over.

"Josie, it's time to go home," Derek said while Curtis picked her seat back up.

"You're not *my* dad." She felt like some vodka demon had possessed her, like she was having an out-of-body experience. Some small core in her knew she was being irrational and nasty, but the rest of her overpowered it.

"I'm calling you a car. Curtis—"

"I'm on it. Get your things missy. Let's go home."

"I have to go to the bathroom! Gotta go see a friend." Moving unsteadily on her feet, she walked to the staircase, gripped the oak banister, and started up the stairs, feeling stabbing pains in her ankles. She was not used to heels, not used to being this drunk. The combination was a rough one.

Fuck you, Patrick, for making me feel so awful and insecure that I needed to get all dressed up so I could feel less hideous. Fuck you for ruining everything.

She had a sudden sense of blankness, as though she'd missed a stretch of time, and found herself in front of the bathroom door. She wasn't quite sure how she'd gotten there so quickly. She only recalled starting up the stairs.

When she walked into the bathroom, there was a woman drying her hands. She smiled at Josie, oblivious to the absolute rage boiling inside her. "Why it so cold in here?" the woman asked.

"Because this place is fucking haunted!" Josie said, and the woman exited quickly. She stared in the mirror and felt like she was seeing double. "Come at me, Ruby!" she slurred.

There was silence.

"Wait!" She hiccupped and stumbled in a circle but managed not to fall. "If I say your name in the mirror three times you'll appear, right? Isn't that the game?" She leaned into the mirror. "*Ruby, Ruby, Ruby!*" she whispered, waving her hands in the air with the flourish of a magician. "Come on!" she said forcefully. "Where are you now, dead cat got your tongue?" She laughed, a witchy, unfamiliar laugh. "Show me a sign, ghost girl!"

From just outside the bathroom door came the muffled sound of the restaurant's payphone ringing. She pulled open the door and picked it up.

"Josie?"

"Mom?" She pulled the receiver from her ear and looked at it, then hiccupped again. "Why are you calling on this thing?"

"*On what thing?*" came her mother's impatient voice. "*Josie, are you drunk?*"

"Am I what?"

"*You just called me collect and hung up.*"

"I did what?!" Josie tried to steady her voice. "I'm sorry. It must have been a mistake."

"*Is something wrong? Are you all right?*"

"Am I all right? No, I'm not all right!" The words poured out of her mouth before she could stop them. "I'm a fucking mess! I'm a fucking mess because you made me think all men are awful like the one you married, and that girls who want boyfriends are weak, and so I gave up on all those decent guys, and now I'm thirty-two and chasing married men, and I hate my life, and you hate my life 'cause I work in a restaurant, and you think I'm wasting my life—"

"*Josephine you've been drinking. I am not going to have this conver—*"

"And Nanette is gone, and now I have no one who supports my decisions or who thinks I can do anything!" She was sobbing now. "And I'm so pissed off at the world, and I'm turning old and bitter like you!"

"*I'm hanging up now. Call me after you've gotten some sleep.*"

The phone went dead.

"*Bitch!*" Josie screamed, then staggered and started down the steps. She stumbled down the last few to the bottom where Boodles, or Bulleit, caught and steadied her.

"*Josie!*" Someone screamed her name.

Josie turned and saw a beautiful, pale redhead running down the stairs. She vanished before she reached the ground.

Chapter Thirteen

✦

"Josie... Josie...." Derek's voice worked its way into Josie's dream the first three times he whispered her name. When he shook her arm, she woke with a start.

"Whoa." Her eyelashes felt like they were coated in glue, and she had a dried line of drool on her chin. "Did you kidnap me?"

"Not exactly."

"Oh Jesus." She winced, her temples throbbing as bits and pieces came back to her. Vodka. Anger. Vodka-fueled anger. At Patrick, and then at her mother.

She'd called her mother. And yelled at her.

She squeezed her eyes shut and flopped a hand over her head. "Shit."

"Hurting?"

"Like the M14 ran over me."

He held out a glass of water and a couple of aspirin. "Take these."

"What time is it?"

"Time to leave for work."

"Already?" She opened an eye and peered out the window. "It's early."

"It's Sunday. Brunch."

"Fuck." She could not fathom the thought of working a double. Her tailbone hurt. Her right foot was throbbing. One high-heeled sandal lay next to the bed she was sleeping in. She shut her eyes again. Not a bed, a couch. Derek's couch.

She was in Derek's living room in her clothing from the night before, lying on his couch with a comforter over her. It smelled of cedar.

She took the aspirin and drank down the water. "I don't know if I can—"

"Yeah, I called over and told them you weren't coming in. Get some sleep, sister."

He walked out, leaving Josie sad and relieved. And exhausted. She'd done a number on herself and was too tired to try to account for the entirety of her lost evening. She couldn't believe she was taking another day off so soon after playing hooky with Patrick.

She pulled the blanket up higher—the air conditioner was running full force—and closed her eyes again. The aspirin would kick in soon, and it would be as though her headache had never existed.

She'd manage the consequences of the night later.

As she drifted back to sleep, more memories filtered in. The motorcycle accident couple. The woman in the bathroom whom she'd unapologetically freaked out.

Ruby.

She rolled over and put a couch cushion over her head.

Sometime later she was awakened by the sound of a shower running and was confused. And then as she heard the faucets screech off, she realized who it was. Faking awkward conversation was the last thing she felt like doing.

At least the aspirin was doing its job. The shades were drawn, and it was dark in the living room, so she closed her eyes to feign sleep.

A few minutes later there was movement in the kitchen, the sounds of something being prepared. And while Josie wished it were coffee, she knew it probably wouldn't be. She had to pee, which meant passing the kitchen.

"Christ," she muttered. She got up and tried unsuccessfully to sneak by.

"Good morning," Alison said. She looked adorable, sleepy, in a short, pale pink robe and bare feet. Barefoot and pregnant in the kitchen, drinking a cup of herbal tea.

"Hey, there. Sorry for intruding. I'm going to take off in a few."

"Do you want some coffee, Josie? I can make you some coffee." She sounded so earnest and hopeful that Josie felt bad declining. And she sure as hell needed the caffeine.

"That'd be great. Thank you."

Derek's bathroom was filled with women's products. She helped herself to Alison's eye makeup remover and face wash.

She wondered how much Alison knew about her—about her past with Derek. That's the sort of thing that would have bothered Josie at that age, but Alison never really seemed threatened by her, only shy. Obviously she understood that she and Derek were friends, but she had to find the fact that Josie had spent the night even mildly threatening, didn't she?

One look in the mirror quickly dispelled that theory. She looked haggard and tired. Nothing remotely threatening to the fresh-faced young woman who was making her coffee.

Back in the living room, Josie pulled the curtains open and looked out onto the nexus of 1st Street and First Avenue. It was pouring, and she was glad. She had an excuse to hibernate when she got home. Now she regretted accepting Alison's offer because with coffee would come obligatory conversation.

"Cream and sugar?" Alison called from the kitchen like a post-war housewife.

"Yes, please." Josie folded the blanket and sat on the couch.

Alison emerged with the two cups and sat next to her, handing her a spoon. There was a very comfortable armchair in the room and an ottoman, but she chose to sit so close their legs were touching.

Josie smiled a strained smile and took a sip of her coffee. It was very good.

"You're so pretty, Josie," Alison said, disarming her.

"Thanks." Josie made a face at her reflection in the back of her spoon. "I've seen better days."

"But even so you're just so pretty. How are you feeling today?"

"I'm fine," Josie said, trying to read her tone and body language. "How are you?"

"I'm sorry you were so upset last night. Sounded like a really bad night."

Oh dear God.

"I can't believe Patrick turned out to be married!"

Josie froze.

"You don't remember seeing me last night," Alison said, nodding. She blew into her teacup.

"No, I do," Josie lied. "Conversational details are just a little foggy. I don't remember telling you that particular gem."

Alison smiled. "You told me a lot of things."

"Oh, dear." Josie took a sip of her coffee and held up the mug. "Hence the need for this."

"Do you really think you saw a ghost?"

"Jesus. Did I mention that in front of Derek?"

"No, he was in the shower. But do you think you saw one?"

"Kind of. I've always had this ghost thing. Don't think I'm nuts."

"I don't!" Alison said excitedly. "I totally believe in ghosts! I'm pretty sure the house I grew up in was haunted."

Josie raised her mug. "Cheers, sister. That makes two of us."

Alison smiled, and for the moment Josie was happy for the company. She didn't know what would happen once she was home alone and no longer had to keep up appearances.

"So, what other secrets did I reveal?"

"Nothing really. And I went to bed soon after you guys got home. You and Derek stayed up a while."

They sipped their beverages, and Josie enjoyed the silence. Alison really was pretty, too, petite, high cheekbones, big brown doe eyes with thick lashes. Josie understood the appeal. And then—

"Can I ask you a question, Josie?"

"Shoot."

Alison twirled a strand of hair, a nervous habit that usually got under Josie's skin. "Does Derek talk about me?"

"Does he talk about you? Sure, he mentions you all the time."

"Do you think he likes me?"

"Of course he likes you!"

"Like, do you think he thinks of me as his girlfriend?"

It was becoming clear Josie wasn't meant to know about the pregnancy. "Yes, I mean, don't you think of him as your boyfriend?"

"Oh my God, yes!" She gripped Josie's arm too tightly. "He's amazing! He's perfect."

Josie gently pulled herself from Alison's grasp, unsure whether she was witnessing immaturity, insecurity, or pregnancy hormones. "Okay. Glad you're happy. Just remember, he's human, and there is no such thing as a perfect human."

"Except Derek."

"Nope, I'm afraid he's not perfect either."

"No, but you don't understand, it's like he was a gift from God!"

Josie desperately wished she were back in Brooklyn.

"Because in high school? I went to this psychic? And she told me that I would meet my husband at twenty-three, and that his name would begin with an *M*, or an *R*, or a *D*."

"Wow."

"Right? *DeRek Magnus*. How bananas is that? And I know I'm twenty-four, but I literally *just* turned twenty-four."

"Bananas." Josie was simultaneously hooked and horrified. She sipped her coffee and waited for the monologue to continue.

"And she told me I'd meet him at work. She didn't say specifically that it would be *his* work. And she told me that he'd be tall with light brown wavy hair, and that we'd fall in love and get married and have babies! I've always wanted to be a mother ever since I was a little girl." She put her hand protectively over her stomach. "And I've always wanted to have four kids, two boys and two girls, and this lady told me that I would, and that this guy I met at twenty-three—twenty-four in my case—would be the one! Isn't that amazing?"

She was beaming, and Josie realized she was meant to respond. "Honey, if I can offer a bit of unsolicited advice, I would be cautious about planning your life around a psychic's prediction. Maybe think of it more as a guideline than a roadmap, you know?"

"I mean there are certain things that would need to change, of course. Like I can't marry a bartender, obvs," she said, gesturing to herself. "But he's so much more than that. My dad? He works on Wall Street? And I know he could help Derek out. Derek could even work for him!"

"Are we talking about the same Derek? You know he's a writer, too, don't you?"

Alison waved her hand in the air. "Yeah, but he needs a real job."

"He's a really good writer. Have you read any of his stuff?"

"Oh, Josie." Alison pouted and put down her teacup. She took Josie's hands in hers, and Josie felt her headache coming back. "I'm being insensitive in broadcasting my bliss when you're hurting so badly over Patrick."

"Honey, I'm not hurting. I'm pissed off."

"Of course you are. What a lousy thing to hide from you. And the horrible thing is now *you're* the bad guy."

"Come again?"

"Like of course it was his fault *first*. And you didn't know. But now that you do know? It's like,"—she leaned in close as though she were telling a secret—"you slept with someone's *husband*. I can't imagine how awful you must feel!"

Josie could not believe the words that were coming out of this girl's mouth. And the worst part of it was she was being empathetic. She was trying to be supportive. Alison didn't seem to have a catty bone in her body.

"I know you must be furious with yourself, but be gentle. You *have* to forgive yourself."

"I do forgive myself. I didn't do anything wrong."

"No, you did, but you didn't realize at the time, right? Please tell me you had no idea. Actually! Don't answer that, I'm just going to tell myself that you didn't."

Josie stood. "Okay, then. Thanks for the coffee and the pep talk. I'm needed in Brooklyn."

Alison stood, too, and put her arm awkwardly around Josie's shoulders. "Anytime, Josie. I mean it. Derek and I are here for you. We love you."

Josie left the apartment certain Derek was making an enormous, life-changing mistake and would be forever saddled with a woman who viewed him as a psychic prediction who needed help from her father. And who might just be a little nuts.

Back in her own apartment, she felt like a caged animal, only there was nothing to escape because the cage was inside her. All of the angst and negativity were roiling and growing like a cancerous mass.

She opened a bottle of wine and poured a glass to let it breathe. Just in case. Wedged in the cushions of her couch, she found a flattened, half-filled pack of Parliaments.

She smoked a cigarette and turned on the television, Turner Classic Movies. In addition to their love of film, she and Nanette loved the station's elegant host, with his rich, silky voice and infectious passion for film. Today he was introducing *Rear Window*, starring Nanette's favorite actor. She used to say Jimmy Stewart was "the type of man who would just make everything better." Josie needed to find one of those.

Instead, what she'd found in the first man she'd let herself develop feelings for in a very long while was quite the opposite. Maybe he'd "made everything better" by filling a void when Nanette died, but it was smoke and mirrors, nothing more, and the aftermath was far worse than being alone would have been.

Because now Josie was both grieving and feeling stupid for not having figured Patrick out.

Who the hell would invite someone to their hometown and put them up in a *hotel*? A man with a wife, that's who.

Now, like the woman who'd come between Josie's parents, a woman she refused to acknowledge by name, or by the false title of *step-mother*—they shared a profound lack of interest in each other—she'd become the catalyst for a family's disintegration. Because Patrick may have been immoral and dishonest, but he was not without feeling, and he would wear his guilt like an albatross. It would inform his interactions with his family for a very long time. There was no way he married a woman who wasn't smart, so Yasmin would pick up on things. And kids? Kids *always* picked up on things.

Though she'd been unable to articulate it at the time, at four years old Josie knew. She knew her mother was sad, and mad, and her father had caused it. Neither parent was a yeller, so their most combative arguments had taken place in furious, hushed tones that ripped right through the walls of the house into Josie's bedroom. She'd picked up on the threat of the other woman even before it came to fruition. One of her earliest memories was a July Fourth party in the neighborhood, where she recalled trying in vain to get her father's attention. He'd been busy talking to the woman he'd one day marry while that woman's ill-fated husband looked on, baggie swim trunks, pasty skin, handlebar mustache, can of Schaeffer in hand. Something about the whole scene had seemed off to Josie. It's impossible to hide truth from a sensitive kid.

She had spent years after her father left feeling like it was somehow all her fault. As a little girl this had manifested as magical thinking, as believing that, had she been better, had she not been so messy or so afraid of spiders and snakes, had she been more adventuresome, he'd have been happier and wouldn't have left. As though it were her responsibility to hold her family together. And while her mother had never outright blamed her, nor had she gone out of her way to convince her young daughter it had nothing to do with her.

Of course it had something to do with her. Dynamics change when kids are born. Women's bodies change. Their needs change. Grass looks greener.

In retrospect, she wondered if Mia was right, if she had come to believe in ghosts out of need. Out of need to forge connections with an afterlife because she felt so alien in this one. And then when she realized it was something she shared with Nanette, the need strengthened their bond, set them apart from her mother. It was Nanette and her against the world, a world that was much smaller in her young eyes, much easier to conquer with a single ally.

At thirty-two the world looked very different. The world was full of married men who cheat, of dreamy young women who have babies to keep men, of so many more lonely people than Josie ever imagined. Everyone was lonely.

The whole marriage-and-kids thing had always struck her as arbitrary. You meet because you go to the same school or live in the same town or walk into the same restaurant. What if you hadn't? What if you'd made a left turn instead of a right and wound up on a completely different life path? How did everyone not wake up one day and look at their spouse and their job and think, *Why is this my life? Did I design this?*

She could understand why Alison wanted to believe her psychic. How comforting it would be to have these decisions made for you. How comforting for Josie to be told by some higher power, *Yes, you are supposed to be single at thirty-two and living in Brooklyn and working at Bistrot. This is the plan. You're exactly where you're supposed to be, and someday it will all make sense.*

Right now, nothing made sense. None of it. Of all the thousands of restaurants in Manhattan, why did Patrick walk into Bistrot?

As Alison had so earnestly pointed out, for the rest of her life, Josie will have at one time been The Other Woman. She could join a convent and become Mother Superior, and it wouldn't change the fact that she had an affair with a married man.

"God damn it!" she seethed. She stalked her apartment, gathering all the tangible Patrick evidence she had, which admittedly was not a lot. Into a trash bag went his Ramones t-shirt, a pair of socks, the razor and soap he'd left there, marking his territory. A book of matches from Bottino and a couple of notes he'd left her that she'd saved because she thought they were *cute*. And the bracelet. The beautiful bracelet he'd bought her in L.A.

Fuck it. She'd keep that. She deserved it.

She went to take a sip of wine and realized it was a bottle he'd brought over. That was all the impetus she needed to pour it down the drain.

As she did, she felt a wave of something wash over her, tingling, gentle, maternal. There was a faint smell of lavender in the air.

"Nanette," she whispered. Tears started down her face, warm and welcome, and she knew that they would continue. That this was the big one. And she would survive it.

Chapter Fourteen

On Tuesday, Josie walked into Bistrot with her tail between her legs. She figured she should just dole out apologies to everyone she saw, but she didn't want to draw the attention of anyone who might have been spared her vodka-fueled rage. The one person she knew for a fact she needed to contact was her mother, but she would put that on hold until she could muster the wherewithal.

The first person she saw was Mia.

"I missed you Sunday, girl!" Mia said, coming out of the coatroom and giving Josie a kiss. "You feelin' all right darlin'?"

"Physically, yes. Emotionally, not even close, though I had a long overdue weep yesterday. I have a shitload to tell you. You're not going to believe it."

People were gathered in the bar, and Andy called her name. "Josie, whenever you're ready. Important announcement!"

"Can you give me the quick version?" Mia asked.

"Patrick is married, Ruby is haunting this place, and I might have written myself out of my mother's will."

"Wow."

"I think I need a break from this town. When you going back to New Orleans?"

"Soon as I can, girl. Would love if you came down."

"Josie!" Andy called. "Anytime you feel like joining us."

Josie rolled her eyes. "So good to be back," she said.

Mia smiled.

Curtis wrapped his arms around Josie when she walked into the bar. She felt sheepish. "I love you, beautiful miss."

"I think you mean mess. I don't even remember half of what happened."

"We'll talk."

"All right people," Andy said. He jumped up and sat on the bar, motioning to the others to gather around. "There's no easy way to do this, so I'll just give it to you straight. Chef is not coming back."

"At all?" someone asked.

"At all. He's left the city."

"Where is he?" Sam asked.

"Upstate. He's at a facility. Resting."

"He's in a mental hospital?" Curtis asked.

"A resting facility!" Andy tossed him a hard glance. "Voluntarily. However, that is less our business than this." He took a dramatic pause and looked at the group.

"We're closing," Curtis said.

"We are?" Sam asked, panicked.

"Let the man speak," Derek said. "He needs to go meditate!"

Josie smiled at Derek. He winked at her, and she felt an unexpected surge of something.

"Thank you, D. We are not *necessarily* closing, but we are not necessarily *not* closing."

"Well, that's helpful. Now I know what to pack," Curtis said.

"People. I'm doing the best I can here. What happens next is that I have a conversation with the investors, and they are not easy to track down in summer. So, we need to prepare for the fact that we may be on break a bit longer than the few weeks we'd allotted for renovations. However, we still have to operate on all cylinders for now. We need to work together. There's strength in numbers, and there's survival in strength." He paused, pleased with the maxim he'd created. "For the time being, Johnny will remain in charge. Josie, he mentioned that you two have been brainstorming, so please keep that up."

She caught Derek's eye again, and he raised his eyebrows and silently applauded.

"A-games, people. A-games." He jumped down from the bar and walked back to his office.

Throughout the night, Josie tried to piece together just how bad things had been two nights earlier. People were being overly kind to her, including Boodles and Bulleit, who'd apparently watched her skid down the stairs, which accounted for the bruised tailbone. The kindness was embarrassing to her, such that she didn't want to ask any direct questions of the people she'd spent the most time with that night. She wasn't yet ready for the play by play.

Focusing on her embarrassment took away from what Josie would otherwise be obsessing over, which was the restaurant's possible closure. Focusing on that took energy away from her anger and, she allowed herself to admit, her sadness about Patrick. And focusing on him detracted from her sadness over Nanette. Of all these thoughts though, her feelings about Nanette were the only ones she could really articulate. And the only ones that really mattered.

She certainly couldn't articulate the vision she'd had of Ruby, and of the young motorcyclist, nor could she explain how it wasn't exactly fear she was feeling anymore. It was different. Because yesterday she'd felt Nanette's presence. She was certain it was Nanette's presence, warm and nurturing and lavender-scented. That made her feel safe. Safe that this life is not all there is. That the afterlife need not always be daunting and heavy.

There was even something comforting about the image she had of Ruby reaching for her as she fell, being protective, trying to help.

She explained this to Mia when they finally had a chance to talk, just before Mia left for the night.

"I can't say I'm awfully surprised about Patrick," Mia said, then added off Josie's reaction, "I'm sorry, girl. I just got a sense he was hiding something."

"And you didn't think to tell me?" Josie was more bewildered than angered. Granted she was not terribly well-versed in the art of female friendship, but she thought this was the kind of thing women told one another.

Mia smiled. "I never think there's much point in airing suspicions, do you? In trying to talk people out of their happiness?"

It was as though she knew of Josie's plan to speak to Derek. "I supposed it depends on how big a mistake they're making."

"I'm glad you made amends with Miss Ruby," Mia said.

"I wouldn't exactly call it 'amends.' It just felt like she was on my side somehow."

"That's Ruby. She could be teasing and a troublemaker, but her friends are everything to her. I reckon she considers you a friend by now."

"You're not surprised to hear that I saw her here when you haven't?"

Mia shook her head. "No, and now all the mischief of the things turning up in the coatroom make perfect sense. She was framing me. Like a practical joke."

This made some strange kind of sense. It didn't dispel Josie's feeling that there was something strange about Mia's friendship with Sylvie, but it vindicated Mia of being a thief.

"I'm honored that she considers me a friend, but could you ask her maybe to back off? I need to get used to this slowly."

"Of course darlin'. In fact, I bet you just asked her yourself."

JOSIE WENT THROUGH the motions of the rest of the night, seeing people out, retrieving the few items left in the coatroom, then finally joining the others at the bar to lament their uncertain fate. She needed to talk to Derek, and much as she tried to plan how to initiate the conversation, she knew she'd have to do so extemporaneously. Over preparation would make her come on too strong. This was to be handled as delicately and sincerely as possible.

"It's not like I wanted to be here forever," Curtis said. "I'm just not ready to leave yet. I have nowhere to go."

"None of us do, man," Johnny said. "Just hang tight. Maybe he'll decide to hold onto this place. Besides, none of this shit is gonna matter soon." He pointed to his Y2K hat.

"Chef holding onto this place? That would be an extremely odd decision, wouldn't it?"

"An extremely odd decision," Johnny repeated with a snort, swirling the ice around his glass of scotch. "You talk like the man ever makes any other kind. He could stay on as silent owner or something. I don't know."

"I've got to get my act together," Sam said. "It's on."

Josie turned to him and sighed. "Sam, my love, we've had this conversation. It's *been* on. You're one of the lucky ones. You know what you want to do next. I told you, I'm happy to help you start. Give me something to do while I'm looking for work."

"Nah, fuck that, Josie," Johnny said. "You're a restaurant professional. I go, you come with me. I need your mind."

The house phone rang, and Josie knew who it was. She felt it in her gut. "Good evening, Bistrot," she said in as neutral a tone as she could muster.

There was a pause and the sound of his throat clearing. Her heart thumped against her ribcage. *"Josie."*

She didn't say anything, just picked up a pen and began tracing letters in the reservations book.

"Josie?" He tried again.

"This is Josie."

"It's Patrick."

She remained silent.

"Josie?" he asked with such trepidation that she felt sorry for him. It was a hard habit to break, feeling apologetic for other people's missteps.

"What can I do for you, Patrick?"

"You can listen to me for a minute, please. I need to explain something. And first I need to apologize for not being completely upfront with you."

She fake-laughed. "Ha! Completely upfront? Are you kidding me, Patrick? You weren't even *remotely* upfront."

"I know baby, I know."

"Please don't call me baby. You've lost the right to do that. You actually never had it in the first place."

"I know," he said again.

"And truly? The people you should be apologizing to are your wife and kid."

"Step kid. Stepdaughter, not that it makes a difference. You have every right to be mad at me."

"Yes, I know I do. And you do realize that we have caller ID here, right? And that I have your *wife's* phone number?"

In fact Chef had refused Josie's request to get Caller ID based on a conspiracy theory Johnny had touted. She'd stopped listening to his explanation once he'd mentioned NASA.

"Josie, listen, please don't do anything rash—" He sounded so panicked that she felt another fleeting dose of sympathy for him, followed quickly by rage.

Exhaustion and rage. She wanted to hug him one second and spit in his face the next.

"Don't do anything rash like what, Patrick? Like get involved with someone's husband and father? Sorry, *step*father?"

"Please, just listen to me. It's not that simple. Yes, Yasmin and I are married, technically. And yes, I am technically Pilar's stepfather. But it hasn't really been a marriage for a couple of years. We sleep in separate rooms, and we have separate lives. How else could I spend three months here every year?"

"When's the last time you were intimate with her?"

He took too long to answer.

"Lovely, Patrick."

"We've been talking about separating, and that's most likely what's going to happen. Doesn't mean I don't care about her—about them—and I needed to be there to help with her dad."

"Let me ask you something. Does she think you're more than technically married?"

"I'm not sure anymore."

"Would she be all right with the fact that you've been fucking another woman all summer?"

He hesitated again. *"Probably not,"* he admitted.

"Then you're an asshole."

"Josie, I fucked up, but I really care about you. Even when I was out there, I couldn't get you out of my mind. I told her I want to move to New York because I do. And that would be that. Her life is in Los Angeles. That would be the end of our marriage."

"Patrick, you have a child."

"Stepchild."

"A child is a child, and a stepfather is a father. Wow. So, you're not just a shitty boyfriend and husband, you're also a horrible father. *Step*father."

"I'm so sorry."

"I'm sure you are, my dear." She hung up, regretted it, and looked at the receiver. No, she wouldn't do anything rash, there'd be no point, and she was better than that. But she was disgusted with him. He'd been intimate with his wife while he was home—of course he had, she was his wife—and then returned to

New York and picked right back up with Josie. And now he'd finish out his summer and go home, and Yasmin would be none the wiser, and he'd go back to playing the dutiful husband and stepfather, and he'd probably find himself another little side fling somewhere along the line. Men like him didn't do this sort of thing once and get it out of their systems. She didn't believe the bullshit that they slept in separate rooms. All married men claimed that. It was straight out of the infidelity playbook.

She returned to the bar and took a seat near Derek.

"How are you doing, sister?"

"He just called."

"I had a feeling he would eventually."

"Yeah, he gave me all the textbook bullshit about his marriage being transactional and nearing its end. I'm so pathetic and weak. I can't believe I let him get to me so much that I fell apart."

"You didn't fall apart. You were emotional, and you have every reason to be."

"So sayeth the man who refuses to emote."

"*Touché.* I could learn a lot from you. And what's this bullshit about being weak? You're one of the strongest people I know. And funny. And beautiful. You don't need to apologize for anything."

"Even my craziness the other night?"

"Even your craziness the other night. You don't need to apologize, you just need to start taking better care of yourself."

"I know. Thank you for taking such good care of me instead."

"The last thing I wanted was to send you home alone like that. I'm glad you got to sleep in."

This was her opportunity to segue. She bit her lip and trod cautiously. "Alison made me coffee, which was sweet."

"She's a sweet woman."

"How are you doing with everything?"

He considered his answer and shook his head. "I'm terrified. Really terrified."

She hadn't anticipated his blunt response. It took a lot for Derek to admit vulnerability. "Is part of you happy?"

"Happy? I don't think that's the word I'd go with. Curious, I guess, but that turns right into nausea. This isn't what I wanted, Josie."

"I know."

"But it's not up to me."

"Ultimately, of course it's her choice, but do you have to stay with her if she has this kid?"

"Don't I?"

His question took her by surprise. "No, Derek! You didn't sign up for this. You have rights here, too!"

"She doesn't know you know. I probably should have told you that."

"I figured it out pretty quick. But she did talk a lot about you, and I have a few thoughts."

"Such as?"

"Can I be totally blunt?"

"Yep."

"I think she's a wee bit nutso." She cringed, knowing she'd likely overstepped her bounds.

"She's… we're very different," Derek said, "As are you two."

"Yes, that's become increasingly obvious." He laughed, and Josie continued. "After gushing about you and how perfect you are, she apologized to me for, and this is a direct quote, 'broadcasting her bliss' in light of what happened with Patrick and me."

"Yeah, that sounds about right."

"Don't get me wrong. She is sweet and incredibly earnest. And she's beautiful. But I'm worried that she doesn't know you as well as she thinks she does, and that she's expecting to have a life with you that looks even less like what you want than you might realize."

"You realize—well no, you probably don't. But the other night you said all this to me almost verbatim after she went to bed."

"That was prophetic of me because it was pretty much confirmed during our conversation the next day."

"Okay."

"Do I want to know what else we talked about?"

Derek blushed, actually blushed, and looked down at the bar, then back at Josie. "Maybe, but this might not be the right night."

"You're blushing!"

"We had a pretty intense talk, sister. And by the way, you need to call your mom."

"I know." Josie groaned. "I've been pretending I don't, but I know I do. I'll call her. Can you throw me a bone about our intense conversation?"

He thought for a moment. "Let's just say you know me better than just about anyone else in this world."

Now Josie blushed. "Is that a good thing?"

"It's a very good thing," he said, smiling and looking away.

Chapter Fifteen

J OSIE SPENT THE remainder of the week sober and sad. "I finally understand why I drink," she said to Derek one night. "I drink so that I don't have to think about the reasons I drink."

"Yes, sister, it's a rare phenomenon known as 'self-medicating.'"

"I feel deflated. Now instead of passing out, I lie in bed missing Nanette, being freaked out about the Kennedys, hating Patrick, worrying about the restaurant, and feeling guilty about my mom. And that's just the first five minutes."

"You haven't talked to her yet?"

"Nope. I called when I knew she wouldn't be home. Left a message that I was sorry and was traveling—like I travel, she'll see right through that—and that I'd call her when I'm back in town."

"Okay, maybe a little cool-down time will diffuse things."

"I'm an asshole."

"You are not. Sure, your delivery was intense, but from what I heard—"

"Oh dear God, you *heard*?"

"Just a little. It sounds to me like you got a lot of the things you've been sitting on for years out of your system. All the things holding you back, keeping you from seeing the person I described the other night."

"Which person is that?"

"Are we fishing for compliments? The one who's strong, funny, beautiful."

"Go on."

"Easy. Smart, empathetic, open-minded...."

"*Easy?* Thanks a lot."

"Witty, wise, pretty much my favorite person in the world."

"Derek Magnus, if I didn't know better, I'd think you were flirting with me!" Josie said with mock outrage.

He shrugged. "Maybe I am."

"But anyway, the immediate issue isn't just great! I finally got this off my chest! It's entirely my delivery, and I'm mortified."

"Sometimes it takes a dose of *pot-valor* to get to the hard truth."

"Okay, man-who-should-be-writing, what does that mean?"

"Liquid courage, sister. Just a pretentious way of saying liquid courage."

It wasn't until she was home that night and getting ready for bed that Derek's statement came back to her. *Maybe I am.* Since their fling years earlier, they'd just been friends, and she didn't think about him in any other way. Every now and then in the early years she'd have to remind herself that she didn't think about him in any other way, but those brief flirtations were few and far between. And then, like the whispers of her childhood, she stopped having them altogether. Now they, too, were back, or some strange, wiser version of them was, anyway.

She felt lighter as she made her way to work the next day. She blushed when Derek joked with her and noticed him looking at her more intently than he had in a while. Something had shifted for both of them, and as wildly unexpected as it seemed, she could feel it chipping away at the gnawing heartsickness she'd been walking around with all summer.

And then Alison came in, fresh-faced and pretty, and sat at the bar sipping club soda with lime, making moon eyes at Derek. When Etta James came on the stereo singing "Good Morning Heartache," Josie decided to end her sobriety streak.

She stayed in a funk and wallowed away her day off, sleeping till noon, chain smoking and listening to all the songs that captured and broke her heart. She drank an entire bottle of Pinot Noir and ate stale leftover Chinese food for dinner.

Week two post-Patrick passed in a blur of rain, work, and Kennedy talk.

On Sunday, Mia suggested they see a movie on their day off, saving Josie from a repeat of the previous week. *The Sixth Sense* had just come out and was the film everyone was talking about, the one about ghosts with the shocking twist that no one sees coming. Reviewers were begrudgingly impressed by its rookie filmmaker, and audiences were dumbfounded by how seamlessly he wove in the film's secret.

They met at the Union Square multiplex. It was their second time hanging out outside of Bistrot, and the irony of seeking out a ghost story after what happened the first time was not lost on Josie.

Mia offered to save seats while Josie waited in line for a Diet Coke.

When she walked into the darkened theater, previews were beginning. Mia had taken the first two seats of a row, leaving the aisle open for Josie. She sat, and the guy on the other side of Mia leaned forward and smiled at her. He was about their age and had kind eyes and an unforgiving profile. He was thin and toothy, with a wispy beard and mustache and a backward baseball cap.

"God it feels good to just sit in a dark, air-conditioned room, with nowhere else to be," Josie said.

"I hear you, girl," Mia said. The guy next to her smiled and nodded, non-threatening and thrilled to be in the presence of attractive women.

"I can't remember the last movie I saw in the theater," Josie said. "I never go to the movies."

"Been ages," Mia said.

"Same. Mine was *Episode One*!" the guy enthused, referring to the new *Star Wars* franchise, which had come out in the winter. "But the talk this one's getting? They say it'll almost make you believe in ghosts."

Mia squeezed Josie's hand and smirked, and Josie nodded.

"It sounds amazing," she said. "A ghost story!"

"How implausible," Mia said.

"I'd love to hang out after this," Josie whispered.

"Sure." Mia nodded toward the screen where the film was about to begin.

Josie was intrigued from the opening scene, Bruce Willis and his wife returning from an event, celebratory and in love. Then, the guy from New Kids on the Block, naked, shockingly thin, traumatized, confronts him in his home and shoots and kills him. Josie and Mia startled at the gun shot, and the guy looked over.

"You okay?" he whispered.

"Yes, we're fine!" she whispered back, staring at the screen. Josie kicked Mia, and she nodded imperceptibly.

It took a few more scenes for Josie to realize what the twist was. No one knew Bruce Willis had been killed in the beginning. That he was a ghost was obvious, the way everyone but the kid came just-this-side of making contact with him, how no one addressed him directly except the kid. There was a scene in a restaurant where he reached for the check, and his widow grabbed it first, and Josie thought of the couple from Bistrot. She wondered if, like Bruce Willis's character, the young man in the motorcycle accident didn't yet realize he was dead.

Part way through the film she whispered to Mia. "Am I crazy, or is this pretty clear?"

"It's pretty clear," Mia whispered back. "But it's really well done."

"Not to me," the guy said.

"What's not to you?" Josie asked. "That it's clear, or that it's well done?"

"No, of course it's well done!" he said loudly, garnering a few shushes. "I'm a filmmaker. I know good film when I see it."

A filmmaker who didn't see films. That was New York for you. Derek was a writer, Sam was an actor, this thin toothy guy was a filmmaker.

When the twist was finally revealed, the audience gasped, and people whispered excitedly to one another.

"Whoa!" the guy said. "No way you saw that coming."

"We saw it coming," Josie and Mia said simultaneously.

He frowned at them in disbelief. "Shut up. How the hell did you know?"

"It's kind of our thing," Mia said.

Josie nodded. "Kind of our thing."

"Not mine!"

"Anyway, it was nice watching with you," Josie said. "Enjoy your afternoon!"

She and Mia walked up the aisle into the crowd, and he came lumbering after them.

"Wait!" he said when they got into the lobby. They turned around. "What's your name?"

"Josie and Mia," Josie said.

"Josie-Ann, Mia. I'm Kevin. What do you want to do now?"

"We're fixin' to go meet some friends," Mia said politely.

"Yeah, we're running late. Nice meeting you, Kevin."

They walked outside, and he followed them.

"Wait!" he said again, a little more sharply. "I thought you said you wanted to hang out!"

Josie was quickly progressing from annoyed to uncomfortable. "With each other," she said firmly. "Again, it was nice meeting you." She took hold of Mia's arm, and they walked quickly in the direction of the subway.

He followed and grabbed Josie's other arm. She shrieked and pulled away. "You said we were going to hang out!" he insisted and morphed at that instant from sympathetic lonely guy to deranged stalker.

"Leave us alone!" Josie hissed.

"What do you mean *leave us alone*?" he repeated. Now people on the sidewalk were looking at them. "Crazy bitch! You led me on!"

"Do you need help?" a man asked.

"No, we're fine!" Josie said, hailing a cab. They spilled into the taxi, and Josie trembled with rage. "Jesus!" she said, on the verge of tears. "I don't even know where to go."

The driver started the meter and looked at them in the rearview mirror.

"Why don't you give him your address, baby. Let's get you home to relax."

Josie practically shouted her address, still trembling.

"Miss, are you all right?" the driver asked.

"Yes!"

Mia put a hand gently on her arm. "She's had a fright. We're fine, thank you, sir."

Josie leaned back and closed her eyes. "Any wonder I don't leave my apartment on my days off? This city is full of nut jobs. We're lucky that guy didn't have a gun."

"You sure you're all right?" the driver asked.

"We're fine, sir," Mia said with far more patience than Josie could have.

"Sorry, I didn't sleep last night."

"Why don't you just close your eyes and relax for a few," Mia said.

Josie complied and focused on her breathing to calm her nerves. At a stoplight she opened her eyes. The driver was watching her in the rearview mirror, strengthening her desire to never leave home again.

When they pulled in front of Josie's apartment, she insisted on paying. "Thanks for coming all the way out here," she said as they walked up the steps to her front door. She unlocked the door and ushered Mia in. "Welcome to my humble abode."

"It's lovely, Josie! It's a beautiful home."

Josie had lived there for so long she could no longer see it. It *was* a lovely place, though. Shiny, honey-colored hardwood floors, a cozy living room, pass-through kitchen, and quiet bedroom. As it was the ground floor the windows had latticed bars over them, but the place still managed to filter in light. At an Urban Outfitters clearance sale, she'd found filmy, jewel-toned curtains for the living room and bedroom, and at a Tibetan shop on Greenwich Avenue she'd bought colorful throw pillows to offset the muddy gray sofa, a hand-me-down from her mother.

The living room had built-in shelves on which she'd placed candles, vases, and other objects she'd collected over the years. The end result was cozy and charming, like a jewel box with splashes of color and sparkle throughout.

"It's so colorful and whimsical," Mia said, admiring a turquoise glass elephant an old boyfriend had gotten Josie in Thailand. "Reminds me of New Orleans."

"I love color. Not that you'd know it by my wardrobe!"

"You've gotten better. Lots."

"Have a seat," Josie said, and Mia perched on the sofa against a crimson and gold pillow. "Would you mind terribly if I had some wine? That guy frazzled me."

"You don't need to explain yourself, darlin'."

Josie took a bottle of rosé—a reasonable afternoon choice, she figured—from the fridge. She pulled two juice glasses from her cupboard. No dishwasher and a shallow sink had made quick work of her stemware. On her counter was a half-pack of Camel Lights.

She brought the wine over to the coffee table and poured two glasses, though she knew Mia was unlikely to join her. The coffee table was an old wooden trunk, a gift from Nanette's in-laws when she and Josie's grandfather got married. Shortly after Josie acquired it, she'd filled it with spare sheets and pillows, then promptly lost the key. No locksmith could touch it without destroying it, and so it remained a time capsule of cheap bedding and whatever else may have fallen in before it was locked forever.

"Music?"

"Of course!"

Billie Holiday, Ella Fitzgerald, and Louis Armstrong occupied Josie's three-disc player. Soon the sounds of old Greenwich Village and New Orleans filled the room.

Josie cracked a window and stood by it with her wine and a cigarette. "So, that movie," she said, carefully blowing smoke through the bars. "Did it seem plausible to you?"

"Sure, in a movie way. All the rules kind of go out the window in fiction, don't they?"

"I guess. The idea that a spirit could not know they were dead is heartbreaking to me."

"It's rare, but it happens."

Josie thought again about the young motorcyclist, how he'd pleaded with his girlfriend not to leave. She gave Mia a brief synopsis of what had happened. "It was really sad, his demeanor and how helpless he seemed, how frantically he was trying to apologize. Could that have been what was going on?"

"Sure, something sudden like that, and he wasn't in his right head when it happened."

"Jesus." Josie took a long drag of her cigarette. "That's so tragic. And the eeriest part is he looked just as vivid as you and me. And then Ruby. Does this mean I broke the seal, and now it's just a fact that *I see dead people*?"

"No, darlin', not necessarily. That was a particularly traumatic night for you. That's why they all came around probably. You're tapped into it, and you were vulnerable, and your channels were open. Trauma can do that. And then you learn how to shut it off when you need to, if you want to."

"I want to."

"Once you start to accept it, and it seems to me that you're starting to, then you'll get to a point where you can tell when you're around spirit, and you can access those blinders I've told you about. It all comes down to acceptance."

"Okay, I'm not quite there yet."

"And that's all right."

Josie stubbed out her cigarette and drained her glass, then refilled it.

"Is that a young Nanette?" Mia asked, pointing to the single framed photo on the shelf.

"That's Nanette."

It was a colorized portrait taken when Nanette was in her mid-forties, though she'd aged so beautifully she looked virtually as Josie still pictured her. In the photo, she sat on the powder blue velvet sofa Josie knew well, the one now in her mother's living room. She wore a white cotton dress with short sleeves and a red belt. Her legs were crossed daintily at the knee, and her red heels matched her belt and lipstick. She was smiling, almost laughing, and had always been very secretive about who the photographer was. All Josie knew for certain was that it wasn't her grandfather. Her wavy dark hair was held partially back in a clip, the rest falling to her shoulders. She was old Hollywood glamorous.

"She's so beautiful," Mia said. "And you look just like her."

"She was the best." Josie stared into her grandmother's eyes.

On cue, Louis Armstrong began to sing about trees of green and red roses, too.

"This song. Brings me right back to a decades-old memory."

"A happy one?" Mia asked.

"A comforting one. It was after the second time I encountered something inexplicable. A few weeks after that terrifying afternoon in the passageways at my house? I was setting the table for dinner—that was one of my chores—and there was a knock on the door." Josie knocked on the trunk. "Clear as that. And I told my mom, and she went to answer, and no one was there. Nanette gave me *the look*, the one that meant that she believed me.

"After dinner I got upset because I didn't understand why those things were happening, and because my dad had said he'd call me that night—I'd passed some kind of swimming test at camp or something—and of course he didn't. So, I was weepy, and Nanette brought me over to the piano and taught me the song. We used to sing it together. So many times Nanette saved lonely little me with that song."

"I'm sorry your childhood was so lonely."

Josie thought about Rita, a four-year-old girl without her mother around. It was a tough age to comprehend change of that magnitude. She attributed the sadness she saw in Mia sometimes to the guilt she must feel for having followed the wrong man to New York and not being able to get back to her daughter right away.

"I thought if it worked out, I'd have brought her back up here," Mia said, as ever unfazed by her intuition, if she even realized it was happening.

"You'd have left New Orleans?"

"For love? I would've done damn near anything."

"But the bastard turned out to be married."

Mia nodded. "And then some."

Josie supposed she should be grateful that she'd learned the truth about Patrick before she'd started rearranging her life. "New York is still New York. Couldn't you go get her and move back up here anyway?"

Mia shook her head. "It's too late now."

"Why?"

"For one, I have to get back down there and help save Esplanade."

"Save it from what?"

"New Orleans has gotten so much pricier. Not like New York or anything, but it's gone up for sure. And the current management can't really keep up with the times. Got to make some changes, and they're slow to change."

"What about your folks?"

"They're getting on in years. Another reason I need to get back. Rita's a handful anyway, and they don't have as much stamina as they did." She shook her head and sighed. "Puttin' a man before my little girl? Worst thing I ever did."

"You talk to her, though, right?"

"All the time. And I tell her how sorry I am that I'm not back there with her. But she doesn't have many people left besides my parents. And the folks at Esplanade. Her father—" She paused.

Josie poured more wine into their glasses despite the fact Mia's was nearly full. "You know," she said. "I've never asked you about him. I have no idea who he is."

Mia smiled joylessly. "Turns out I didn't know who he was either." She looked at Josie now. "You ever want to have kids?"

"No. No, I don't. I've never felt cut out for it. Never felt maternal, which I know makes me a freak of nature."

"Not at all, Josie. Makes you human. We've evolved. That's what that ERA is all about, right? Turns out women aren't just here to make babies, and the world is finally startin' to realize that. And besides, I think you're more maternal than you know. You take great care of everybody. There's lots of ways to be a mother."

"That's one of the things Derek and I bonded about early on, once we got past whatever little pseudo-romance we had. He never wanted to be a dad either. Which is pretty ironic." As soon as she said it, she realized she'd come close to betraying his confidence. Mia didn't seem to notice, which Josie attributed to the fact that "ironic" was one of those descriptors people used too liberally.

"Interesting bond."

"Yeah, I think I get why we share it. Neither of us really had a chance to forge our own identities because we had to exist around our mothers. Tiptoe around their fragility. His was blatantly fragile, grief stricken, and mine was so determined to pretend she was strong that she grew bitter." She took another sip of wine and walked to the window for a cigarette.

"So, why is it ironic?" Mia asked, picking up on the one word Josie had hoped would go unnoticed.

A cinematic clap of thunder made her jump. "Fuck."

"Derek's girlfriend. She's pregnant?"

Forgetting herself, Josie exhaled a stream of smoke into the room. "Yes! She's pregnant, and she wants to keep it! And this has nothing to do with any past between Derek and me. This has nothing to do with me, period! But I talked to her the night I stayed over. She's slightly unhinged…."

"And if she weren't?"

"You're right. It has nothing to do with that either. It has nothing to do with her at all, really. I know Derek, and he has never wanted to have kids. Plus, he barely knows this woman, and now he's going to be trapped!"

Mia sat quietly for a moment, considering this. "Like I always say, I think things have a way of working out as they're meant to."

"I hope you're right," Josie said, waving at the smoke in the air. "If not, we have a baby shower to plan."

Mia laughed. "Actually, I'm fixin' to head back to New Orleans real soon."

"How soon?"

"With the restaurant closing for a spell, I think it's about near time."

This meant she'd found the means to travel, which puzzled Josie. "I'm happy for you, but I'll miss you!"

"How 'bout coming for a visit when y'all shut down?"

"That would be a dream. If I can round up the funds, maybe. And assuming I have a job to come back to."

"You could always buy a one-way ticket. Lot of folks come visit for the first time and never even use their return. The Marie Laveau spell."

"Intriguing concept. Not like there's much anchoring me to this place."

"Isn't there?" Mia gave her a sly smile.

Josie's phone rang. "Okay, that's either Derek or Curtis calling to check up on me," she said, picking up the cordless receiver.

"Josie, it's Mom," Alice said.

Josie felt like she'd been kicked in the gut.

"Hi," she said meekly. "My mother," she mouthed to Mia, who nodded. Josie picked up her wine and paced into her room. "Mom, listen, I'm so sorry about the other night. I don't know what to say."

"Sorry is a promising start."

"I know. I know. I shouldn't have called when I was so emotional—"

"And drunk."

"Yeah, that too." She absently picked up the bracelet Patrick had given her and held it in her hand. She felt teary and squeezed it.

"What is going on with you?" her mother asked in a tone that, did Josie not know the speaker, might have conveyed nonjudgmental empathy. There was nothing to do but err on the side of honesty.

"I'm sad. I really miss Nanette. And I haven't been handling it well." She waited for Alice's at times awe-inspiring steeliness to rear its head. She prepared to nod and agree, nod and agree, until she could comfortably get off the phone.

"I know you are, honey. Of course you are," Alice said instead. Josie made a face in the mirror. *"Losing Nanette is terrible for both of us, and I'm well aware that what you two shared is irreplaceable. I wish I could take your sadness away."*

Josie felt horribly. Nanette was Alice's own mother, and she was consoling Josie on her loss. "Oh, Mom!" she said, tears flowing down her cheeks. "I'm sorry I haven't been more sensitive to what you're going through, too! I've been so selfish."

"It's very different for me, Josie. Of course I'm sad, but I'm relieved, too. I was with her every day, and it was a lot. She was not herself anymore, really."

"And I should have been more sensitive to that, too! To the fact that you were shouldering all of this alone. Uncle Stuart's on the other side of the country, I'm in New York. You've had a lot on your plate."

"Josie, I haven't exactly made it easy for you to be sensitive toward me over the years."

"How do you mean?"

Her mother sighed, then sniffed, and Josie realized she was crying. *"Honey, I may not have appreciated your delivery the other night, but everything you said has merit. You're right that I've been bitter. Your father leaving was a big blow to me, to everything I'd planned for my life, and the fact that he's been such a shitty father to you in the years since is unforgiveable."*

"But that's not your fault."

"No, of course that's not my fault, but I could certainly have done a better job of picking up the pieces. I didn't need to convince you that men are terrible. Because they aren't all terrible. My father was one of the greatest men that ever lived."

"I know he was," Josie said. "You and Nanette have helped me to 'know' him even though I never got to meet him. And don't worry, I'm not done with men. There are a lot of shitty ones out there, but I'm not giving up. I just need better instincts."

"You just need to listen to your instincts," her mother corrected her. *"But then what do I know? My instinct was not to marry your father in the first place."*

"What do you mean?"

"I didn't want to marry him. I didn't want to marry anyone, but he convinced me, and Nanette convinced me. Josie, you come from a long line of women who dole out advice based on their own realities. That's what my mother did to me, and that's what I've done to you. And I'm sorry."

"But if you hadn't, then I wouldn't be here!"

"That's not true. I wanted to be a mom, I just didn't want the husband."

"Wow, Mom, I had no idea."

"Of course you didn't. Now what is this about chasing married men?"

"That was just the wine talking," Josie lied.

"All right, then. And for the record, I don't think you're wasting your life. I just want you to be happy, Josie."

It was the simplest of concepts, and the most obvious—of course a mother just wants her daughter to be happy. And yet this was groundbreaking in Josie's world.

She wandered into the living room while her mother spoke. Mia was gone, as was the wine bottle. She hadn't heard the door close, but there was a note on the trunk.

Wanted to give you some privacy. Thanks for a great day! See you tomorrow. Love, Mia.

Josie realized her mother was in the middle of saying something she should be paying attention to.

"...a sense of responsibility, however, and what you do with it is really up to you. Anyway, I've just come from Alan Siegel's office." Alan Siegel was the family's attorney, a handsome divorcé, and Josie had long suspected he had the hots for her mother.

"Ooh la la, hot date?"

"No, Josie." Her mother sighed and put on the slow, patient voice Josie had heard so often growing up. *"We needed to go over Nanette's estate and what she's left to you."*

Nanette's estate. It took a moment for the phrase to register. Nanette's estate must have been decent. Josie's grandfather had left her a bit of money, and Nanette herself came from a solid background. In all likelihood, Josie would receive the lion's share. Her mother was vehemently self-sufficient and had one brother who lived in San Francisco with his partner. They both worked in finance, had no children, and were not wanting for extra cash.

Josie went to the kitchen and found that Mia had made her a cup of peppermint tea before she left. It was exactly what she needed at that moment, and she took a sip. As she walked over to the window she acknowledged that her mother was speaking. "Right," she said, pulling a cigarette from the pack and looking for a light.

"...of money," her mother said.

"Sorry, what was that?"

"What Nanette left you. We've transferred a bit into your checking account, and the rest should go into savings. You can do a lot with that figure."

"That figure being...."

"Josie," Alice sighed at having to repeat herself. *"This is important. She left you about one seventy-five after taxes."*

"One—" Josie tried to conceptualize this.

"One hundred seventy-five thousand dollars."

The cigarette dropped to the floor.

Chapter Sixteen

⚜

JOSIE WOKE TO sunlight streaming through her windows and piercing her eyeballs. Her television was on, and the chipper local news anchor was issuing a warning to the good people of New York.

"...stretch of dry, hot weather means a citywide surge of air conditioning and a possible overload to the electricity grids. And this, folks, could spell power outages, so take precautions!"

Through her early morning haze, she pieced together the previous day. *The Sixth Sense*, the strange filmmaker, an afternoon of rosé, and trips down memory lane. It had wound up being a nice day overall, so why had she needed to inure herself to it with wine? The answer was she hadn't, but old habits die hard.

She cased her apartment, stumbling past empty, stained glasses. In the kitchen, she downed two pints of water in quick succession. She wouldn't feel so badly had she eaten, but that was the responsibility she shirked most these days.

How nice it was, though, in the middle of this chaotic summer, to have made a friend in Mia. When she needed most to be able to talk about grief and ghosts and blind affairs with married men, all of which she might have discussed with Nanette, along came beautiful, sparkly Mia, who understood. It was as though Nanette had designed her the perfect friend and placed her in Josie's path at the perfect time.

After a cooling shower, she chose the lightest thing she could find in her closet, a white sundress she'd bought months earlier and forgotten about. When she'd first tried it on it had skimmed her figure. Today it was big on her.

She walked barefoot into the living room looking for her sandals and stepped on something—an unlit cigarette. In an instant, she recalled talking to her mother. It was an important conversation, one that had begun with an apology and finished with a vital piece of information. She'd inherited money, and a decent amount of it. It being Alice, of course, the information had been accompanied by a lecture.

This was the foggy part.

Before she was halfway down the steps of the subway station, she was assaulted by the thick air, sour and redolent with something neither chemical nor organic, just stale. She bought a Coke at the underground bodega and took small sips, willing herself to feel less horrible.

The canned air conditioning of the train was a welcome relief from the temperatures outside, and Josie leaned back in her seat, eyes closed behind her dark glasses, gritting her teeth through the lurching and swaying of the subway car.

When the ride ended, she made her way out of the West 4th Street station past the steely sounds of the resident busker and his insufficiently strung guitar. The sun, making a triumphant total appearance, beat down on her as she walked to work. Something cold and wet dripped on her head—condensation from an air conditioner, or worse. Her stomach rumbled.

A frenzy of activity greeted her when she got to Bistrot, people rushing about as though President Clinton were coming in to dine. She was relieved to see Mia, hadn't expected her on a dry day.

"How are you feeling, darling? How was the rest of your day?"

"I kind of feel like someone's pounding me with a mallet. I'm sorry if I got a little—"

"Josie!" Andy accosted her mid-sentence. "We need you on serious basement duty this afternoon. We're running out of time, and if the weather keeps up like they said it will, we're gonna be slammed the next few days."

"Oh, for God's sake!" Josie said in a panic. "I don't want to go down there alone!"

"You don't have to, girl," Mia said. "I'll go with you."

"All right. I need to hydrate first."

Still wearing her sunglasses, Josie wandered into the bar where Derek and Mario were rearranging tables.

"Hey, you," Derek said. "Bloody Mary?" He cocked his head toward the pitcher on the bar. "I know it's Tuesday, but it's hot as hell out there."

"Ugh." Josie waved her hand. "I don't think so. Not yet, anyway."

"You sure? Little hair of the dog?"

She stopped in her tracks and looked at him. "What makes you think I need that?"

He smiled a tightlipped, loaded smile.

"What?"

"Josie," he said, lowering his voice. "We talked last night."

She flushed. "Oh dear. I called you?"

"No, I called you. It's okay, sister. You have a lot going on right now."

She dropped her forehead against his shoulder. "I guess it doesn't surprise you that I'm now oh for two in remembering our substantive conversations."

"You had the floor for most of this one. And you needed it. You went off on the *bon vivant*."

Josie groaned. "Please tell me I didn't call him, too."

"Doubt it. Sounded like you were ready to drift off at the end."

"Good." She picked her head up.

"Do you remember talking to Alice?"

Josie nodded.

"So, that's a game changer. Guess it's a pretty tough thing to digest."

"I don't even think I've taken the first bite."

"Do you remember details?"

"Not entirely. I'm sorry."

"Don't be sorry. Just start eating, please. You're so thin."

"I know," she admitted.

"Beautiful, but thin."

Andy zipped through the bar, rubbing his hands like a praying mantis. He pointed to Josie, and she flinched. "Josie, basement please! D, what's happening with the wine, you going to update it?" He gestured to the handwritten list of wines-by-the-glass etched on the chalkboard next to the bar.

"I'm on it," Derek said. He saluted Andy and touched Josie's elbow. "We'll talk about it all later."

Josie wanted to talk about it *now*. She was embarrassed she'd monopolized a conversation she didn't recall having when Derek had enormous things going on in his life, too, and she was embarrassed she'd told him about the money. She was raised not to talk about money, in part because she hadn't really had much to talk about. What did finally having it even mean?

It meant no longer living paycheck to paycheck, or relying on the bit of padding that came from annual gifts from Nanette and occasional guilt gifts from her father. Guilt or tax write-off—she didn't question the specifics. She wasn't foolish with money, always paid her rent on time, wasn't an impulsive shopper, had no student loans. Nanette had insisted on paying for college. But Josie didn't know what it meant to have money.

This was, as Derek said, a game changer. This meant she could indulge a little, if she could bring herself to do so. And real indulgence, like travel, not just getting drunk on better wine. Traveling to New Orleans was something she could actually do.

This also meant that regardless of Bistrot's uncertain future, she'd be okay. She could put some time into figuring out what she wanted to do next.

She walked to the cellar. On pulling open the door, she was ambushed by a rush of damp, mildewed air that made her sneeze. She creaked down the flight of stairs and surveyed the room, which was vastly improved from earlier in the summer. The staff had made slow and steady progress. The mess of papers and supplies in the front room had been whittled down to a select few items that sat on the shelves in neat piles. The thick coating of dust was gone, but the stillness of the air meant a lighter layer had settled in its place.

She walked a few paces, and a chill ran down the back of her neck when she heard Mia, on the other side of the partition, whispering.

"I knew there were more! I knew it!"

As Josie's eyes adjusted to the dim light, she saw Mia standing by another wall safe that had been previously obscured from view.

Mia turned quickly and gasped. "Josie!"

"Who are you talking to?" Josie asked.

"No one, baby."

"You sure?" The air around Mia was warm.

"Look what I found," Mia said. "It was covered up by this weird sign." She pointed to an old laminated first aid poster, an early version of the kind now mandatory in restaurants.

The bottom half of the safe was still blocked, and it looked as though the area had been ransacked.

"What the hell happened here?" Josie asked. "It wasn't like this last time we were down here!"

"Looks like someone was lookin' for something."

They sifted through the junk, tossing old magazines and inventory forms, catalogues from kitchen supply stores and unopened mail. Underneath it all were two packets of cocktail napkins with *Dave's Continental* printed around a logo of a martini glass.

"How cool!" Josie said. She handed a packet to Mia, who turned it over in her hands and held it to her cheek. "How's the energy on these?"

"Definitely mixed."

"Ready to try your hand at another round of safe cracking?"

Mia put the napkins down and held her hand over the dial. She whispered quietly to herself and after a moment began to turn the lock, her eyes flashing with excitement.

On the third spin, she pulled the handle to no avail. She shook her head, shut her eyes, and concentrated again, turning the knob in tiny increments and listening for clicks.

"Come on, come on, come on," she whispered. Once more she opened her eyes, turned the dial, and pulled. Nothing. "You want to give it a whirl?"

"I don't know how to do this!"

"Just concentrate, see what numbers come to you. Worth a shot, anyway." Mia stepped aside.

Josie emulated her by closing her eyes and holding her hands over the dial. Numbers ran through her head, and she chose a few and turned the lock. Nothing happened. She tried again and again, then gave up in frustration.

"Damn!" She hit the safe with the side of her fist.

Just as she did, a burst of cold air blew in her face, and a voice whispered, "*Thirty-seven!*"

Josie shrieked and jumped back. "Did you hear that?" she asked Mia, her heart pounding.

There was a loud popping sound followed by an electric hiss, and the lights above them flickered and died. Josie shrieked again and reached out for Mia in the pitch black of the windowless basement. She couldn't find her.

"Mia!" she whispered, panicked.

"I'm here, girl!" Mia took her hand and squeezed it. "What happened to the lights?"

"I don't know. I must have hit a wire or something! But did you hear that—"

The door at the top of the stairs opened, and Derek called down to the basement. "Josie! Are you down there?"

"Yes! Mia, too! What's happening?" she screamed.

"Power's out. Stay tight. I'm grabbing a flashlight!"

Josie was sweating despite the iciness in the air. Claustrophobia was starting to envelop her. She sneezed.

"*God bless you.*"

"Thank you," she said, her voice timid and warbling.

"For what, baby?" Mia asked.

"Good God! How long does it take to find a fricking flashlight?"

"We're okay," Mia said. "Breathe, girl. He'll be back in a minute."

"It's so fucking dark down here!"

From somewhere outside came the muffled sounds of sirens.

"We're okay," Mia said again. "Isn't it nice the rain's finally stopped? They said this'd probably happen. They'll get it fixed real quick."

Her attempts to distract Josie were offset by singsong-y chanting.

"*Rain, rain, go away, come again some other day!*"

Josie felt like she was losing her mind. "Make it stop!" she said, near tears.

"Stop it, Ruby!" Mia hissed, swatting at the air around Josie and finally acknowledging what she'd been denying for months.

"It *is* her! You hear, her too!"

"*The itsy bitsy spider went up the water spout,*" Ruby sang right behind Josie, out of Mia's reach.

Josie clapped her free hand over her ear and hummed loudly to drown her out. A fragment of a poem lodged in the recesses of her memory popped into her mind.

Those long childhood hours when you were so afraid....

Through the cacophony inside and all around her, Josie realized she recognized Ruby's voice, her timbre, rhythm, and intonation. It was the voice that had haunted her so many years earlier. It was impossible.

She hummed louder, certain she was on the verge of a full-blown panic attack that would erupt if Derek didn't get to them fast.

The door at the top of the stairs opened, and he called down, shining a light. "I'm coming. Hang on."

As he barreled down the steps, all the sound stopped at once—Mia, the spirit, and the high-pitched, indecipherable hum that hovered in the air. Josie followed the beam of the flashlight jostling back and forth as he searched the space.

"Where are you?"

"We're here!" Josie and Mia called in unison.

"*We're here!*" the spirit echoed.

"Ruby!" Mia shouted. "Stop it at once!"

"It's not Ruby!" Josie said, whimpering. "It can't be!"

"Who the fuck is Ruby?" Derek asked.

"Nobody!" Josie said.

"*Hey!*" came Ruby's voice in protest.

"I'm here." Derek shined his light on his hand and reached toward Josie. "God damn it's dark down here."

Josie clutched his hand, Mia holding her other one, and together they navigated carefully up the stairs, Derek shining the light back and forth so they could see where they were going. Disembodied giggling surrounded them as they made their way back above ground.

Chapter Seventeen

⚜

O NCE UPSTAIRS IN the natural light of the restaurant, Josie flooded with relief—a sensation quickly assuaged by the stagnant air and nausea she felt. There was no sign or sense of the spirit, as though they'd shut her in the basement when they closed the door.

People buzzed about the bar area speculating on what was happening. Andy sent Sam out to gather information.

He sprinted in some time later, red-faced and sweating. "It's bad out there," he said between breaths. "I went all the way up to Fourteenth, over to Eighth Avenue, back down and around to Broadway. Everything's out."

"Did you speak to any authorities?" Andy asked, as though blackout authorities would be posted on every corner handing out information packets and flashlights.

"No, but some dude in Washington Square said it's all over the city and maybe even Jersey."

"Helpful," Andy said. "Shit. People, we need to figure this out."

"Figure this out?" Curtis repeated. "How exactly are we supposed to do that? It's not like we can watch the news!"

"Is there a hand crank radio around here?" Derek asked.

"D, excellent idea," Andy said. "Sam, run to the Radio Shack and get a hand crank radio, and see if you can get any more updates."

Sam, bent at the waist, hands on his knees, still trying to catch his breath, looked at Andy with dread.

Josie got him a glass of water. "Sammy, stay hydrated. Apparently you're Paul Revere today."

"Who?"

"Don't worry about it." She glanced at Derek, who winked. He was in a good mood, all things considered.

Josie poured herself a Bloody Mary. For once, Andy didn't seem to care that the staff was drinking on the job. There was too much else going on, and it was keeping spirits up. Josie needed to keep her spirits up to stifle whatever other ones were around.

After Sam set off on his mission, Johnny came down from the kitchen to fill everyone in on his plan. With thousands of dollars of food in peril, the guys in the kitchen would salvage what they could. That meant packing as much into the freezer as possible and surrounding it with all the ice, which was in scarce supply. People were deployed to the local markets and delis to scoop what ice they could before the other neighborhood restaurants depleted it all.

They would cook and serve everything that had already been prepped or would not last unrefrigerated—like seafood and chicken—and focus on the dishes that could be easily and quickly thrown together.

"Johnny, I implore you to be selective," Andy said. "We can't serve any spoiled food!"

"No kidding, boss? Then I guess I need a fucking Plan B. Anyways, we have the door propped open, so the skylight's helping, but once the sun goes down I am fuckin' out of there. No way I'm staying up there in the dark."

"I don't blame you. Ghosts love blackouts," Curtis said with a sly smile.

Josie looked at Mia, who couldn't meet her eyes. She leaned against the wall biting her lip and looking worried.

"There are no ghosts," Andy said robotically. "Anyway, what are you going to serve?"

"Got a shitload of fresh shellfish this morning. We've got to serve that half-price and early. Gotta be the first to go. Fryers are electric, so that's out. Gonna cook up and slice a bunch of fuckin' steaks and some other stuff. We'll do this buffet style."

A loud thud and a shout from the kitchen interrupted him, and he looked up at the ceiling.

"Shit. That sound okay?"

"That sounds perfect," Curtis said. "Like we're in agile hands." He caught Josie's eye and shrugged.

"Okay, boss?" Johnny asked Andy.

"Okay. Yes. Thank you." Andy waved him back to his post and wrung his hands.

"We've got this under control," Josie said. "Don't worry Andy. I bet we're more prepared than a lot of places around here."

"Wait," Curtis said. "How are we going to charge people when credit card machines hook up to nonworking phone lines?"

Andy blinked several times. "We'll have to be cash only tonight."

"Banks are closed, and ATMs aren't working," Derek said. "Everything's computerized. We've got to have a manual card reader around here somewhere."

"We do!" Josie said. "I remember seeing it in the basement a while ago."

As soon as the words were out of her mouth, she feared she'd be asked to retrieve it.

Andy looked sick to his stomach.

"You threw it away," she said, relieved.

"I threw it away. Didn't know why we'd held onto it so long since we never used it, so... damn technology."

"It's okay, Andy," Derek said. "Look, it's probably going to be a bunch of regulars tonight, right? We'll let people pay what they can, or we'll start tabs. Our customers are good for it."

"Isn't that risky?" Andy asked. "What if it's not just people we know?"

"What else are we going to do? Let all the food go to waste? Might as well feed people. If it's a buffet, we can make it easy, flat fee, drinks are extra."

When Sam returned with the radio, he was sent out a third time to stock up on candles. He came back with all the votives that were left at the nearby bodegas—Jesus candles, Virgins de Guadalupe, Saint Theresas—as well as several bulbous, pastel-colored numbers meant for birthday cakes and a few novelties from the party store.

One Bloody Mary and a significant amount of water later, Josie's hangover—and the residual tension from the incident in the cellar—was forgotten. She was enjoying the strange energy of the day, the excitement of everyone trying to prep and plan for what promised to be a memorable night.

She walked outside and breathed in the strange stillness in the air. There were fewer cars on the road than there should have been, and despite the fact that the traffic lights were all out, they seemed to be coexisting peacefully. Sometimes New York managed its chaos well. The drivers Josie observed were displaying unprecedented amounts of patience and politeness with one another.

"Josie?" Mia came outside and stood next to her. "Will you take a walk with me? It's still a while till opening, right?"

"Sure. Want to go sit in the park for a bit?"

"Perfect."

Josie took Mia's arm, and they crossed Sixth Avenue. It wasn't humid, it was hot and perfect, and she'd forgotten how she relished the sun. There was a palpable energy among the people they passed, and an electricity in the air, as though the whole city were waiting for the day to unfold. It felt like they were on a movie set, the sounds of traffic muffled, action suspended in time. From the distance came the plaintive wail of a firetruck and the staccato rasps of its horn as it made its way through the streets.

It wasn't until they walked into Jefferson Market Garden that she realized Mia was shaking. "Are you okay?"

"I can't take that sound."

"Which sound?"

"The fire trucks." Mia looked as panicked as Josie had felt when the lights went out. She was usually the calm and comforting one, not the one trembling in fear.

The sound faded, and Mia released her breath. "I'm sorry, girl. That's what haunts *me*, the sound of those sirens."

"I'm afraid there are probably going to be a lot more where that came from. Par for the course in an event like this."

"I know. It'll be better once we're back inside. I just needed some air."

They stopped in front of the pond and watched the Day-Glo orange koi nosing the lily pads.

"I wonder how these guys fared with all the rain," Josie said. "They're cute little things, aren't they?"

When she looked up, the expression on Mia's face gave her pause. She had tears in her eyes. This wasn't just a walk.

"Mia, what's going on?" Josie asked, bracing herself.

"Sylvie passed last night."

"Oh my God!" Josie's hand flew to her mouth. "That's so sad! Does Curtis know?"

"No one does. I only just found out."

"Did the niece call you?"

"Not exactly." Mia led her over to the bench they'd sat at the first time they visited the park together. "Okay, girl, yes, that was Ruby. And she told me."

"But that's impossible! That can't be Ruby. I swear that was the same exact thing that happened to me when I was a kid! The same voice taunting me."

"Now I know it doesn't make much sense now, but it will. Like I've said, time moves different on the other side."

"I'm so confused. How is this possible? And how did she know about Sylvie?"

"Sylvie had the ability, too, not sure if she had it her whole life or just toward the end. But one night I was getting ready to walk her home and Ruby appeared. Sylvie greeted her. They already knew each other."

"How?"

"There's a thing that happens with someone like Sylvie, darlin', when they get to that point near the end. When they're ready to cross over the bridge into the other world, sometimes there's folks like Ruby who come 'round to help out, to usher them in."

"So, Ruby's been around for a while then. And you *have* seen her."

Mia nodded.

"The whole time you've been with us?"

"No, just a little while. I'm sorry for not telling the truth. She's grown awful fond of Bistrot and the action there. That's how some spirits do, they get energy from energy. It's why restaurants and theaters and places with a lot of people in them every night are haunted."

"Lucky us."

"For what it's worth, she doesn't mean you harm. She just likes to play is all. Always had a sense of humor, like I said."

"She's hilarious."

"She promises me that Miss Sylvie is at peace."

"I'm glad she's at peace." These were the sort of words Josie had scoffed at in the aftermath of Nanette's death, when so many people had offered them up. At that time, she didn't care what others wanted to believe, she was consumed by raw grief. Now, though, she got it. Now it *was* a comforting concept.

"Josie, listen, there's something else I wanted to let you know. I'm going back to New Orleans in the next couple days."

Josie knew this was coming but hadn't expected it quite this soon.

"My girl needs me. But y'all are gonna be closed for a stretch. Won't you just come down, like we said?"

"How much warning do you need?"

"I don't need any warning at all. I love surprises."

"That makes one of us."

"If you're gonna spend time in New Orleans, you're gonna have to get used to expecting the unexpected. There's surprises 'round every corner." She looped her arm through Josie's. "I'm gonna miss you, girl!"

"I'm going to miss you so much! But I will come visit, and maybe someday you can come back up here with Rita?"

"Maybe so."

They walked slowly back around the path in silence. The gardens were rain-lush and vibrant.

"I have a question," Josie said as they exited the gates. "Why are you so fascinated by those old wall safes?"

Mia shrugged. "I don't know, really, guess I just feel like they have to hold some kind of answers."

"To what?"

"Well, any other questions about the restaurant come to mind?"

"Sure. If Ruby's only been there a short while, who else is haunting this place? You think that answer's in the safe?"

"I think it could be. We should get on back there."

As they made their way back, Josie held Mia's arm, gripping it tightly when the sounds of sirens again echoed in the distance.

The lack of electricity cast the restaurant in a bewitching light. Dust floated in the bands of sunlight that streamed through the windows, a welcome sight after so many dark days. Josie once read that a large percentage of dust was comprised of fragments of human hair and skin, a particularly intriguing notion to her now that she'd found evidence of people who'd once walked the earth and ceased to exist in the tangible sense of the word. Who knew to whom these dust particles had once belonged?

Sylvie's seat at the bar was empty, the absence of its longtime resident ever more striking in the sunlight, and with the knowledge she was truly gone. Josie wondered how long it would be before she would come back to claim it. There was nowhere else she imagined Sylvie spending eternity.

The first few intrepid diners trickled in around 5:30 p.m., relieved to find a restaurant that was open. Gradually, the room began to fill with people who wanted to be anywhere but home alone in the dark. There was boisterous camaraderie, everyone eager to share where they were the exact moment the lights went out. It was like Kennedy's airplane crash, or the Columbine shootings in April—a year of personal connection to public events, of everyone wanting to tell their version of the story. In the excitement of the blackout, strangers became acquaintances and acquaintances friends.

Andy kept vigil by hand-cranked radio and updated the crowd on what was going on and how much worse it was than had been previously announced. "It's everywhere, people!" he bellowed dramatically to the fifteen or so guests in the dining room and bar. "Up and down the eastern seaboard!"

As more people filtered in, rumors abounded as to what it all meant, how long they would have to live without electricity. Predictions ranged from a couple of hours to several weeks.

Toward seven o'clock, the staff started to light candles, placing them in illogical groupings throughout the room—Saint Anthony next to a sky-blue number three and an owl in a graduation cap. They lent the room a festive air. People visited the buffet and table-hopped.

Derek kept the wine and shots coming. His own supply of ice running low and everything the busboys bought having been dedicated to preserving the food, mixed drinks were not an option. The draft beers he served got progressively warmer as the night wore on.

The scene was fast becoming a Bacchanalian free-for-all, and Josie stood in the entrance to the dining room watching it unfold. A man and woman who'd come in separately were now sitting together, eating off the same plate. Boodles and Bulleit were entertaining friends and celebrating a birthday, complete with party hats, kazoos, and a melting Carvel whale. A neighborhood couple who often ended their evenings bickering in the vestibule were halfway through a bottle of wine and pawing at each other, madly in love.

Something was shifting in Josie, though it was hard to say what. The night marked a new beginning, and her financial freedom played a significant role in that.

She could walk out of Bistrot and never return, a thought at once thrilling and terrifying. More than that, it was bittersweet because while she may not have been realizing her full potential in her current situation, she loved the world she was working in. She loved the people she worked with. There was much to be said for getting out and exploring the world, but equally appealing was the notion of staying put, rearranging her schedule, and exploring New York City. Even that would be a step in the right direction. In the near-decade she'd lived there, she'd grown complacent about all the city had to offer. Now she had no excuses. She could see a Broadway play every week. She could dine in five-star restaurants every now and then. She could get memberships to museums, go to the opera, do all the things people came to New York to do. That she had come to New York to do.

The restaurant would be closed for a little while at least, and this would be a great time to start living. Now she had the freedom to admit to herself that she loved the industry. That she wasn't "less than" for doing so, wasn't staying there only because she had no other options. That was the old narrative.

She walked over to the coatroom to find Mia. There were no coats and umbrellas to check, yet Mia was standing guard outside her post.

"You don't need to stay up here, you know!" Josie said.

"I'll come join y'all in a bit."

"You need a little light! Let me grab you some candles."

Mia's hands flew in front of her face like a vampire facing a wooden stake. "No, that's okay!"

"*No!*" came a second voice.

Josie spun around to icy nothingness. "What the—"

"Sorry," Mia said. "Open flames make me nervous." She waved her hand in the vicinity of the voice. "And sorry about her."

"*Boo!*"

"Ruby!" Mia said sharply. "I'm sorry, Josie. She's trying to be funny."

From behind Josie came an eruption of giggles.

"Seriously?"

"I'm afraid we're stuck with her tonight."

Sam rushed over in a panic. "Josie!" he said breathlessly, nearly colliding with Mia in the dimness. "They're here! The Dunnehills!"

"Okay honey, relax and watch where you're going."

"What should I do?"

"You should welcome them and explain how we're working things tonight. It's an unusual one." She turned to Mia. "Clearly."

Mia shrugged. "I'm sorry, girl."

"Can you do it?" Sam asked.

"I can help, but I'm teaching you to fish, Sammy. We'll seat them, and then you offer them something from the bar."

He followed Josie to the hostess stand where Daphne and Cleaver Dunnehill stood waiting, she in a brightly patterned Pucci dress with her customary warm smile, he in a dark gray suit with his customary grimace.

"Good evening," Daphne purred when Josie greeted her. "Isn't this terribly exciting? We're so pleased that you're open."

"We're pleased that you're joining us," Josie said.

"You're serving food?" Cleaver asked.

"We are indeed, buffet style." She escorted them through the room, noting the curious stares and whispers they garnered along the way, and seated them at one of Sam's tables away from the fray. Cleaver looked curiously at the Saint Christopher candle in the middle of the table.

"We had to do some improvising," Josie explained. She grabbed a wax frog from a vacant booth. "Here's a little more light for you."

"It looks beautiful in here. Thank you, Josie," Daphne said, and Josie felt a burst of pride that they were on a first-name basis.

"Sam?" Josie nudged him. He was a deer in headlights.

"Yeah? Oh! Do you want drinks?"

"What do you think, Cleave?" Daphne asked her husband, who had donned his glasses to read the inscription on the back of the Virgin de Guadalupe. "Something celebratory? Champagne?"

"Champagne," he repeated.

"Wonderful," Josie said. "What are you celebrating tonight?"

Daphne beamed and took Cleaver's hand across the table. "We're celebrating Cleaver's new theater company, the Barrow Street Playhouse! Official as of this morning and right in the neighborhood, which means we'll be seeing a lot more of you!"

"Yeah, as long as we don't clo—" Sam started, and Josie clapped him on the shoulder with more force than she'd meant to.

"That is fantastic news!" she said. "Congrats, Mister Dunnehill!"

He waved his hand without looking at her. "Please, call me Cleaver." he said.

Josie looked at Daphne, surprised. Daphne winked.

"Sam, isn't that great news for Mister—Cleaver? A theater company!" Josie said.

"You're an actor, aren't you, Sam?" Daphne asked.

Josie slipped away to get the champagne, knowing this conversation would be awkward enough for Sam without her hovering. Knowing, too, that he needed to be thrust into these situations so he could go about the business of being an actor, which meant constantly stepping out of his comfort zone.

The crowd in the bar was even rowdier than the folks in the dining room, and Derek was fully invested in the festivities. A young guy from the neighborhood had brought in a guitar and sat in the corner taking requests and encouraging singalongs. As Josie walked in, he was finishing "Who'll Stop the Rain."

"'Freebird!'" someone shouted.

"'1999!'" someone else yelled.

"'Here Comes the Sun it is!'" the guy said, strumming the first few chords.

There were a few hyper kids spinning around like tops. The only one Josie recognized was the little boy with the blond curls she'd seen the night of her meltdown.

"Hey, you!" Derek said. "Enjoying the chaos?"

"I think we're doing a pretty stellar job tonight."

"Troop morale is high. What can I get you?"

"A bottle of bubbly for the VIPs." She pronounced it with one syllable.

"Ah. Josie, probably not the best choice. Been opening the fridge all night, and you can't serve them warm champagne."

"Okay, let me just go back over and tell Cleaver Dunnehill no. This one's non-negotiable, love."

Derek shook his head and carefully extracted a bottle from the refrigerator. "Be extra careful opening it. Seriously, that's a lethal weapon in the wrong hands."

"I've got it, fret not."

When she got back to the Dunnehills' table, Sam was still there listening intently to Daphne.

"It could be a wonderful opportunity for you, and for us," she said. "We need bright young people who want to hone their craft."

"Okay, yeah. Sure," Sam said, sounding utterly confused and unsure as to what she was proposing.

"Why don't you come over to see the space and meet the others? Isn't that a good idea, Cleave?"

"Call Henry to set it up once all this is over," Cleaver said, gesturing to the ceiling. "This business with the lights."

"I'll make sure you have Henry's number before we leave, Sam," Daphne said.

"Okay, yeah! Sure!" he said again with the enthusiasm that was missing the first time.

"Here we are!" Josie presented the bottle. "Now, Derek wants me to warn you that this isn't terribly cold, so if you would rather—"

"Chilled or not," Cleaver said, holding a fuchsia 5 toward the bottle so he could read the label in the light of its flame. "My wife has never met a bottle of bubbly she didn't love."

Filled with fresh and unbridled confidence, Sam laughed too loudly and grabbed the bottle from Josie's hands.

"Be careful, Sam," she warned him, placing two flutes on the table. "Open it slowly."

"Josie, I know how to open champagne," he said cockily, shooting a lopsided grin at Daphne.

"Yes, I know you do. But Derek has been opening the fridge all night, so it's warmer—"

Ignoring her, he peeled the foil off and began to untwist the wire caging that held the cork in place.

"Sammy." She tried again, reaching toward the bottle. "Please hold your hand over the—"

"*Sam, it's too warm!*" Ruby shrieked, and Josie swatted at the air next to her as Sam succeeded in pulling the wire off.

A resounding pop followed, along with a celebratory yelp and several enthusiastic cheers.

Someone shouted, "Happy New Year!" from across the room.

Sam tried frantically to control the overflowing bottle. "Sorry! Sorry!"

Josie took the bottle from him and got it under control.

"*Sam was careless!*" Ruby said.

"Shush," Josie said. "Not helpful!"

"But I'm so sorry!" Sam said, wringing his hands.

"It's all right dear, we're fine!" Daphne looked at her husband and giggled. "Well, I'm fine, anyway."

Cleaver sat perfectly still, champagne dripping from the front of his hairline down his glasses.

"Sammy," Josie said with exaggerated patience. "Get Mister—Cleaver—a towel please."

As he shuffled away with his tail between his legs, Josie filled their glasses. "I hope it goes without saying that this one's on the house."

"Please, that's not necessary! It was an accident," Daphne said. "Right, Cleave?"

Wordlessly, Cleaver took the napkin Sam had been dabbing him with and finished the job himself.

Josie wiped the bottle and set it down before following Sam to the bar for a towel.

"Oh my God, Josie, I totally blew it!" He was on the verge of tears, and Josie put her arm around him.

"Honey, you didn't blow it. It was an accident. Just listen next time I give you a tip like 'be careful, Sam.' Okay?"

"I'm an idiot!"

"No, you're not," Josie said.

"*No you're not, Sammy!*"

Josie decided in that moment to stop fighting the fact of Ruby. She was, at the very least, being a kinder version of herself.

Sam wrapped his arms around himself. "Why is it so cold in here?"

"It's the A/C," Josie said out of habit.

"In a blackout?"

"It's the lack of A/C," she said, recovering. "What were they talking to you about anyway?"

"His theater company. I don't know, some kind of apprentice thing they want me to do."

"Honey, that's amazing!"

"*Sam's a star!*" Ruby said, cooing flirtatiously. The notion of conveying this to Sam made her laugh.

"Yeah, well, there goes that," Sam said. "Like they want to work with me now."

"Sammy, look on the bright side. You've just proven you're cut out for something other than the restaurant business."

Josie was stuck with Ruby, who followed her on her rounds with a running commentary on everyone they encountered. She was funny and a busybody.

"*She's too good for him!*" she said of one couple. "*What an unhappy woman!*" she astutely observed of Mrs. Guilfoyle. "*I don't think they're gonna last,*" she said of a pair on an awkward first date.

Derek moved several more bottles of champagne that night, the festivity of it all having caught on. Sam slowly mastered the art of opening champagne without dousing the clientele.

As Josie walked into the bar with a couple of empty glasses, Mia intercepted her.

"Josie," she said. "You have company."

Josie's stomach somersaulted.

"*It's that louse!*" Ruby said. "*Patrick.*"

Josie set the glasses on the bar.

By the look on Derek's face, she knew he'd seen him, too. "You want me to bounce him?"

"No." She sighed. "I can do this." She walked toward the front where he stood nervously drumming his fingers on the hostess stand. He was clean-shaven and handsome. Josie had been so busy hating him that she'd forgotten just how handsome he was. When he saw her, a smile spread on his face.

"Josie," he said, leaning in to kiss her. She moved her head so he wound up with a mouthful of hair. "How are you?"

She crossed her arms over her chest in a display of defensiveness. Feeling ridiculous, she uncrossed them. "I'm all right. We're very busy. Do you need something?"

"Yes," he said, laughing nervously. "Yes. I need to talk to you. Can you give me just a minute?"

She looked around. Everything seemed to be running fine. She could spare a couple of minutes. She led him toward the front door so they could sit outside, away from prying eyes and ears.

As she passed the coatroom, Mia whispered to her. "Be strong, girl."

"Do you have a cigarette?" she asked when they reached the little table under the awning.

"Actually, I quit."

"Congratulations. I'm so proud of you," Josie responded with intended sarcasm and accidental sincerity.

"Thanks. That's just the start. I'm making some pretty big changes."

"How wonderful for you."

"Josie, will you just look at me? Please?"

She turned and faced him, and the look in his eyes was so sad and hopeful that she felt herself softening. He reached across the table and took her hand. She let him.

"I am so incredibly sorry that I hurt you."

"You didn't *hurt* me," she said, even though he had. "You're a fucking liar."

"I know, and I'm sorry."

"I'm not the one you need to apologize to, Patrick. I have a lot less at stake here than you do. Always have."

"I get it. I get what you're saying. But please listen. The reason I didn't tell you was in part because my marriage, like I said, hasn't really been a marriage for a while. On paper, sure. But like I said we've been talking about separating—"

She pulled her hand away. "Remind me when the last time you fucked your wife was?"

He dropped his head, then looked back up at her. "We had a moment when I was home during that week. And it was a mistake. It had been a long time."

"Yeah, and that's still gross. You were with me, like, the day before and the day after that trip!"

"I know. And honestly, the whole time I was home I knew I needed to get out of that relationship."

"That *marriage*," Josie corrected him. "You are married to a woman named Yasmin, and you have a daughter named Pilar. *Step*daughter."

"Yep, you're right. And you're right that it was wrong that we were together when I was back in L.A., but not just because of you. It was wrong because neither of us really wants to be in this marriage any longer. We've both moved on, we just haven't made it official."

"You've moved on but you slept together."

"Josie, I was helping her through a really tough process. And we stayed up late one night drinking and talking and reminiscing and it happened. I told you that I've been thinking about spending more time in New York, and I told her that, too. And yesterday I was offered a job at The New School for the full year."

Josie was quiet while she processed this. Patrick reached for her hand again. She felt nauseous. "Wait, so you mean...."

"I'm staying in New York, baby. Yasmin and I are officially separating."

"But why?"

"Because I'm happier here. My marriage is over. We were never the right fit, and I could never really explain why until I met you. She's wrong for me. She's the opposite of you."

"What does that even mean?"

"It means she's cold. She has a selfish streak. You're not. You're warm and kind, and you care about people so deeply—about everyone, not just the people who can do something for you. Like Sammy, like everyone you work with, every busboy and bartender we've encountered—you see people the way they want to be seen. You see me. Most girls only see the exterior," he said, gesturing up and down his torso. "And that's fine for them. You actually care about my mind."

Josie's mind was made up, but she let him continue.

"And you're so beautiful. You have no idea how beautiful you are. We look right together."

"We *look right* together?"

He was staring at her intently, and she noticed for the first time that his ears stuck out too far.

"Did you get a haircut?"

He frowned and ran his hand over his head. "Yes. But Josie, listen to me. I couldn't stop thinking about you while I was home—even the night she and I were together, I was thinking about you, picturing you, wishing it was you lying underneath—"

"Okay, I'm done." She stood.

Patrick laughed, actually laughed, and grabbed her hand. "What are you talking about? You can't be done."

She pulled her hand from his, and he stood, too. "I'm done with this conversation. I wish you well—"

"Josie!" His nostrils flared in indignation. "What are you talking about? I'm telling you I want to be with you. I'm staying in New York!"

"I heard you, yes. And I'm telling you that I do not want to be with you. I'm done with this conversation, I'm done with this relationship, no bad feelings between us, I wish you all the best."

He shifted his jaw from side to side, seemingly vacillating between confusion and ire. "But did you hear anything I said?"

"I heard everything you said. You have a lot on your plate right now, and I wish you well with all of it. I don't want to be part of any of it. Goodbye."

She turned and walked back into Bistrot and toward the bar, feeling at once resolute, horrified, and empowered.

"Girl." Curtis headed her off at the pass. "You okay?"

"You will not believe what just came out of that man's mouth."

"Talk to me." He put his arm around her and walked her toward the bar.

"The nutshell version, I don't know what I was thinking."

"What you were thinking? Girl, you don't need to think all the time. Sometimes it's okay to just react. Right D?"

"Right," Derek said.

"Lady, sit down. I'll go check on things." He walked back to the dining room, and Derek took her hand across the bar.

"You okay?"

"I feel like an idiot. Not only is he married, he's completely full of himself. I can usually spot that kind of thing a mile away!"

"Josie, you've been grieving," Derek reminded her. "Grief makes people do things that don't make sense. And he was lying to you. Thing about a guy like that, he's probably really fucking good at lying by now."

Now Josie felt strangely protective of Patrick. "I don't think that's necessarily true. I don't think he was just using me. I think he actually had feelings for me. I feel sorry for him."

"Why? He doesn't deserve your compassion."

"He's not all bad, Derek. Obviously he's unhappy in his marriage. Happy men don't cheat."

"They don't, but I don't care about his happiness. I care about yours."

He went to wait on a customer and Josie thought about what she'd just said. Happy men didn't cheat, unless they were full-blown sociopaths or sex addicts. Patrick was neither.

In retrospect, she was certain what had happened between her parents wasn't entirely her father's fault. He had been unhappy, and he left, and her mother had launched a smear campaign that had soured Josie on him. Sure, he hadn't stepped all the way up to the plate in the aftermath of their divorce, but her mother, in her own version of grief, hadn't welcomed his involvement. There was never a visit or an arrangement that wasn't negotiated within an inch of its life. In the earliest years, the ones Josie had all but blocked out, he had made concerted efforts. There had been summer trips to the lake, boat rides, county fairs. There had been some semblance of balance that fell away with each passing year as her mother made it more and more difficult for him to see Josie. She'd cashed the checks and sacrificed the bond that might otherwise have been strengthened, pitting Josie against her father in the process.

Too much time had passed now, too many years had bled together without substantial attention paid to their relationship, and it was unlikely much could be salvaged. But maybe a new version of it could take its place, a civil, adult relationship, now that she didn't need anything from him. The empathy that Patrick had described in her could be the tool she needed to forgive and move forward.

"I think I'm having some kind of blackout-induced catharsis," Josie said when Derek returned. "Seriously. Weird things are happening in my head."

"It's been a weird summer."

"Extremely."

He came around the bar and took the seat next to her. "So, what are you going to do with your newfound freedom?"

"For one thing, I'm not going to drunk-babble about it to anyone because that's supremely tacky."

"It wasn't to me, Josie. You can tell me anything. I'm guessing you don't recall my big revelation last night either." Off her blank look he continued, "I came into a bunch of money myself some years ago. When I turned twenty-five. Got a double trust fund, mine and my brother's."

"What? You're a trust fund kid?!"

"Guilty."

"Aren't you supposed to be a douchebag living in a doorman building and taking cabs everywhere?"

"I am definitely, one hundred percent not supposed to be that."

"I know. I kid. Look at us, a couple o' rich folk drinking warm table wine."

"To the good life," Derek said, raising his glass to Josie's.

"So, why do you work here?"

He paused, thought it through before answering. "Because I like it here. And because if I don't then I have no excuse not to get back to my damn writing. Turn my demons into something more."

"Derek, I would love that for you. Truly. You are so talented."

"Thanks, but writing is a pretty lonely endeavor. I'm not good at lonely. And I've got this other matter on my hands. Don't imagine this leaves much time for creative pursuits."

Josie knew she should let him talk about it all, but she didn't feel like hearing Alison's name. In that moment she didn't care about Alison and Alison-and-Derek and this pregnancy, and something was definitely shifting. In both of them.

"I don't want to talk about me," Derek said. "Let's focus on you. What do you want to do now that you can do anything?"

"'Anything' is a stretch, but I can certainly do more. And I don't know because now that I can't blame lack of money for holding me back, looks like that was never really the problem in the first place. The problem is that I don't know what I want to do because I don't know who or where I'm supposed to be. Sometimes *I* feel like the ghost."

"You're supposed to be exactly where you are. This is the life we're living. This is who we are right now."

"To quote Curtis, when did you get all Zen?"

"When we talked the last two times, we really talked, and I know you don't remember but those conversations—those were everything to me."

"How so?" Josie asked, stalling for time to calm her heart palpitations and the knowledge hurtling toward her that life was about to change forever.

"Josie, I love you."

"I love you, too, honey! You're family."

He smiled and shook his head. "That didn't go as planned. Remember that *pot-valor* concept? The night you stayed over, we talked for a long time. We talked about Alison, we talked about the *bon vivant*, and we talked about the fact that you're in love with me, and I'm in love with you."

"I'm in love with you?!" She glanced around to make sure nobody could hear. "Holy shit... am I in love with you?"

They were both laughing now.

"You told me that the Patrick thing had been a fine diversion because it kept you from having to think about Alison and me. But you said that now that it was over, you had to tell me how you felt before I made a 'life-changing decision.'"

This was starting to sound familiar, and Josie was grateful Derek couldn't see her face reddening in the candlelight. "Well... am I too late?"

"No. We'll figure this out. Whatever it means. I'm not going to force Alison into doing anything, and I'll step up to the plate if I need to, but I can't do that the way she wants me to. It's you, Josie. There's a reason I fell so hard so many years ago. And if you buy into the whole higher purpose thing?"

"I do."

"Okay, then there's also a reason you put me on hold and we became such good friends. I've fallen in love with my best friend, and that is a ridiculously amazing thing."

"You've got to have a movie quote for this."

Derek pursed his lips and looked at the ceiling, then took Josie's hand and looked into her eyes. "In my time, I've known contessas, milkmaids, courtesans, and novices, whores, gypsies, jades, and little boys, but nowhere in God's western world have I found anyone to love but you."

"Well played, sir."

He took her other hand, his face so close she was caught in the beautiful, gray eyes she'd forgotten to notice for a very long time. "I don't know how the hell I'm going to fix this, but I am."

"It's gonna take some kind of magic, Derek."

"I don't believe in magic. I'll figure this out." He leaned in and kissed her, and she kissed him back. Suddenly, he jolted upright.

Josie turned her head to see Alison's friend, the Trinket with the nose ring, standing with her hands on her hips, venom on her face.

"You god damn bastard!" she slurred at Derek, then turned to Josie, eyes blazing. "Filthy whore!"

Chapter Eighteen

❧

THREE DAYS AFTER the power returned, Josie was in a first-class seat on the first airplane she'd been on in nearly a decade.

She had rushed out the door the night of the blackout into a miracle taxi idling in front of Bistrot. Once at home, she'd sat on her sofa staring into nothingness, trying to sift through the wreckage of the night. Nothing made sense. She was in love with Derek, he was in love with her, and there was nothing they could do about it. He was going to be a father, and she refused to get in the way of that. She needed out of New York City.

Rifling through her purse to find a cigarette—which she didn't have—she found instead a note from Mia. Mia, who had slipped away sometime in the night like the elusive creature she was.

Dear Josie,

I'm not good with goodbyes, so I didn't want to make a deal of my own. Guess because I said too many of them, it's easier for me like this. By the time you read this, I'll have left New York.

I hope and think you'll come down to New Orleans sooner than later. I want you to visit my family's place, to see where I come from, to meet my Rita. It's most important to me that you are in her life. In the short time we've been friends, you've made a huge difference, more than you'll know until we meet again.

There's a saying in New Orleans that once you drink the water, you've no choice but to come back. They say it's because Marie Laveau, the Voodoo queen, cast a hex on the water. You must visit her grave when you come to New Orleans. For good luck.

The combination on that second safe is 37-4-16. Open it, and you'll find a package meant for Rita I didn't get to bring to the post office. I know it's weird, and I bet you have questions. I guess I put it there because you're meant to visit. You'll love New Orleans, Josie, I know you will. And maybe once you experience it, you'll figure a way to bring a bit of that magic to wherever you go next.

Finally, Josie, the necklace—the one you're probably wearing right now. There's a tiny pin on the bottom. Pull it halfway out and slide the two halves apart. It's a locket. I think you'll like what you find in it.

Thank you for a wonderful friendship. Thank you for letting me in when I most needed you. I will see you soon, and I will know you always.

Mia

She read through the note twice. It didn't surprise her that Mia had gone without saying goodbye, but it made no sense she'd left Rita's package behind.

She found the pin at the bottom of the locket and pried the halves apart. Mia had placed two tiny photos inside, one of her and one of a little girl with the same beautiful eyes—this had to be Rita. Since Josie always wore the necklace to work, Mia must have found it in her apartment when she'd visited and added the pictures then.

Josie knew what she'd do when the power came back on. She would get away from Derek and their messy situation. She'd just have to stuff the feelings she now realized she'd had for a very long time as far down as she could until they didn't matter anymore. He was not available to her. He would do the right thing. He always did.

The power was restored a little less than twenty-four hours after it had gone out, and on Thursday, Josie rode the train into town to buy her ticket, then to stop by the restaurant to retrieve Rita's gift. God willing, she'd slip in and out unnoticed.

On 8th Street was a brightly lit storefront she'd passed many times with glossy posters of palm trees and sand, cobblestone streets and centuries-old cathedrals. She'd never taken much notice of the specifics, never wondered where the pictures were taken because she'd never needed to. Travelling was something other people did.

She walked inside and was greeted by a tall, pleasant looking man with pale hair and features and a Scandinavian accent.

"And how may I help you today?" he asked, offering her a seat across from his desk.

"I'd like to book a ticket to New Orleans."

"The Big Easy!" He entered information on his keyboard. "When would you like to go?"

Right now, Josie thought. "As soon as possible. Tomorrow?"

"Is this for business, or—"

"Just a visit. To see friends."

"I hope your friends have warned you that the Gulf Coast is extra steamy this time of year. And that it rains." He laughed. "Which we're certainly used to by now."

He clicked a few more buttons and gave her the prices for direct coach flights from LaGuardia to New Orleans.

"Out of curiosity," Josie asked, trying to sound nonchalant. "How much is first class?"

Swallowing her doubt, she committed to a five-hundred-dollar ticket, and then it was time to find lodging.

"Now we could put you up in a hotel," the agent said. "But to me one of the joys of traveling to a place like New Orleans is its people and its neighborhoods. There are many informal bed and breakfasts that will allow you to experience the city like a local."

He pulled out a binder of listings and handed it to Josie. She leafed through, not really knowing what she was doing. The only neighborhoods she'd heard of were the French Quarter and the Garden District. She was about to suggest that he choose when she came across a listing in the Faubourg Marigny, the neighborhood where Mia's restaurant was located.

Authentic New Orleans, in the heart of the Faubourg Marigny, the city's best neighborhood! Charming, colorful three rooms with private entrance and bath, air conditioning. Steps away from the music and flavor of Frenchmen Street, and just a short walk to the historic French Quarter. $75 per night.

She studied the photos. There was something both familiar and foreign about it. The décor—and there was a lot of it—was eclectic and charming. The outside of the house was painted forest green and a shade of lilac, Josie's favorite color when she was a little girl, a shade she associated with Nanette. This was it.

She left the travel agent, ticket in hand, feeling elated. This would be the most independent thing she'd ever done, taking herself on vacation to a place she'd never been. No one knew she was leaving New York, and the one person she knew in New Orleans was not yet expecting her.

It wasn't until she was about to walk into Bistrot that she felt a nervous, sinking feeling in the pit of her stomach, the aftermath of having done something wrong. She did not want to run into Derek, or Curtis, or Andy, or anyone who might have seen what happened.

She braced herself and opened the door. The only people she saw were the porters and busboys who were working overtime to clean the place up. As far as she knew, none of these guys had still been there at the end of the night.

"Senorita Josie!" Mario greeted her. He'd always watched over her with an avuncular protectiveness, and she was happy to see him. "We're not opening today, you know?"

"Yes," she said, thinking on the fly. "I left my bag down in the basement the other night, and in the chaos I forgot to pick it up."

He looked quizzically at her purse. "Let me go get it for you."

"That's okay! I'm not sure exactly where I put it," she said, reaching for the door handle.

"Please be careful down there, Josita."

She was halfway down the stairs when it dawned on her to wonder what he meant.

Despite her trepidation, though, the basement felt warm and safe. She reached into her bag for Mia's note and pictured it where she'd left it—on her dresser. She closed her eyes and tried to visualize Mia's handwriting. The figures *4* and *16* came to mind, but that was all. She tried them frontwards and back, striving to employ the intuition Mia had taught her to trust. The lock wouldn't budge.

She took a deep breath and closed her eyes again when something else Mia taught her came to mind.

Spirits won't speak unless spoken to.

"Okay, then," she said aloud. "Will you please tell me what the third number is?"

She waited. With Mia gone, Ruby had no reason to hang around there anymore.

"Will you please tell me what the third number is, *Ruby*?"

The air around her shifted, growing thick and kinetic. She stretched her arms out and focused on her breath. The sound of giggling filled the air, and this time Josie wasn't afraid.

"*Thirty-seven*," came the response.

Josie smiled. "Thank you, Ruby. You may go now."

The air softened and warmed, and a sense of peace washed over Josie, like the one she'd experienced when she was sure Nanette had come through. She turned the dial right, then left, then right again. The safe clicked open.

Inside was a small package wrapped in brown paper, addressed to Margarita Boudreaux on Louisa Street in New Orleans. She felt triumphant as she trotted back up the stairs and closed the basement door for what may well have been the final time.

⚜

THE NEXT MORNING, Josie got to the airport with plenty of time to spare and learned that flying first class had its advantages, from the lounge where she ate breakfast and leafed through *The New York Times* to the fact that she was first to board. Once on the plane, she hoped to sleep. However, her seatmate, Eleanor, was a chatty woman in her sixties who smelled like Dove soap, a New Orleans native returning home from a brief—and unexpectedly exciting—visit to New York.

"Y'all have such a lovely city," she said in a languid drawl. "Even in a crisis, y'all sure know how to make a gal feel welcome."

"I'm glad you enjoyed yourself. I've heard nothing but great things about your town, too."

"Y'all are brave comin' down for the first time in August!"

"So I hear."

"I always say there's two seasons on the Gulf coast, summer and August."

"After the crazy summer we've just had in New York, I'll take my chances. I'm going to visit a friend, and this was the best time for both of us."

"Your friend is from there?"

"Yeah, her family owns the Esplanade House."

"I know it very well! The owners are gettin' on in years."

"That's what she tells me. I'm friends with their daughter, Mia. Do you know her?"

"Hmmmm. No, I don't think I knew they had another daughter. I know Rita, the granddaughter."

Josie slid open the locket and showed the photos to Eleanor. "Look familiar?"

"Yes, that's Rita," Eleanor said. "Beautiful girl. She's really like a daughter to me."

"I look forward to meeting her. I've been wanting to see New Orleans for years."

"Everyone should. They say there's plenty of folks who don't get there during their lifetimes but who sure as heck do when they're dead."

"Okay, so what can you tell me about this alleged ghost culture?"

"It's not alleged honey. It's fact. But it's nothin' to be scared of. Most of the ghosts are real friendly. They'll help you out if they can." She frowned, thinking over what she'd just said. "Not that they can do much."

"It's funny, I used to be scared, but I'm pretty sure the place where Mia and I worked together is haunted, and I think I'm done being afraid."

"And Esplanade House, they say that one's haunted, too."

"I'm not surprised."

"They've gone through some tough times, some tragedies way back when and now financially. I hope they survive, but it'd likely take some kind of miracle."

Josie was delighted to realize she could be the miracle. She could use some of her money to help save Esplanade House. It was exactly the sort of thing Nanette would want her to do. Mia had helped Josie through the toughest few months of her life, and now she could return the favor. She could find an apartment in town and work with Mia at Esplanade, help her family get it back on its feet. Make a fresh start in a new city. A new very old city that she was certain she'd love—it was in her DNA.

It was perfect. It was all unfolding, the meaning behind this crazy summer. Maybe this was the "higher purpose" Derek had spoken of. Derek—she didn't want to think about him.

Eleanor was babbling about all of the things to see in the city, and Josie was half-listening until she heard the words "spiritual medium."

"What was that?"

"My friend Vivian, at the Bottom of the Cup Tea Room," Eleanor said without missing a beat. "She's the best in the city."

"She contacts spirits?"

"She does it all. She's a psychic, reads cards, and yes, she's a very talented medium. Got lots of loyal clients."

"I wonder how long I'd have to wait to get an appointment?"

Eleanor smiled and patted Josie's hand. "I think you'll find things have a way of working out down here."

It was a statement so familiar that Josie was starting to believe it.

As the plane descended, Josie got her first glimpse of the Mississippi and the brackish Lake Pontchartrain. Louisiana was thick with heat and humidity. You could see it through the airplane window, feel it in the airport.

Before they parted ways, Josie and Eleanor made vague plans to meet at Esplanade House later that night.

Once outside, Josie was assaulted by a blast of air so hot it felt like exhaust from a fleet of city buses. She pulled her hair into a thick knot and fanned the back of her neck. The line at the taxi stand was mercifully short.

"Where you going, baby girl?" the dispatcher asked her.

"To the Faubourg Marigny," she said, and the woman scribbled on a pad and handed the sheet of paper to her.

She gave the address—Burgundy Street—to the driver.

"Bur*GUN*dy," he corrected her.

"Bur*GUN*dy?"

"Bur*GUN*dy. You're in New Orleans now. Forget what you know, young lady."

"I'll get the hang of it. This my first time here."

"You gonna pass a good time den, *cher*."

On the ride in he gave her a tour and history lesson. People from New Orleans loved to talk about New Orleans and did so with a different kind of pride than New Yorkers celebrating their town.

Josie had anticipated the city looking immediately foreign. The texture of the air and the spiky palm trees confirmed she was in a different part of the world, but otherwise the earliest part of the drive was not unlike most trips from the airport, warehouses, car dealerships, motels, and fast-food chains. Then, within a few minutes, everything changed. Billboards advertised swamp tours, beignets, and jazz.

As they drove, they passed more palms and beautiful flowered trees—crepe myrtle, the driver said—in brilliant shades of red, orange, purple, and pink. The further they got from the airport, the more the landscape began to look as she expected, exotic and colorful, the architecture a mix of the Creole cottages and shotgun shacks she'd read up on. Even with the metropolitan skyline soaring in the background, the structures at eye level resembled the city she had dreamt so many times, the one in the photos Nanette had shown her. It was beautiful, gritty, and full of magic.

Twenty-five minutes later, they arrived at the lavender double-shotgun shack, one half of which would be her home for the next few days.

As they parted ways, the cabdriver added a "*Laissez les bons temps rouler!*"

Once alone, standing outside on Bur*GUN*dy Street, Josie was gripped with melancholy for a place to which she'd just arrived, as though New Orleans had already worked its way into her bones.

The proprietor of the house, a Mr. Medley, was out of town for the week. He'd left Josie's key in the mailbox. It was right out in the open, and while anyone *could* have taken it, he'd assured her no one would. It was a tight-knit neighborhood, he'd explained, and people looked after one another. The key was attached to a strand of purple Mardi Gras beads. Josie pried open the pine green shutters that covered the door and wrestled with the rickety lock.

It was like walking into a dream. Dark wooden floors and twelve-foot ceilings framed the three-room space, which was filled with beautiful, mismatched furniture that looked as though it had been handed down for generations. The ceiling fans were on, and there was a handwritten note on the coffee table welcoming her and explaining where things were.

Throughout the rooms were daybeds, real beds, decorative lamps, area rugs that had faded in the sun, an ornate mantle that held local memorabilia and photographs, and a large, mirrored armoire. Josie did a double take when she saw her reflection—in the humidity, her hair had curled and now hung in a springy ponytail of perfect ringlets. She looked like a different person from the one who'd boarded the plane in New York, relaxed, the frown lines she'd thought permanently etched between her eyebrows softened. She smiled. She was prettier in New Orleans.

And she missed Derek. She was prettier in love, even if this love could never work.

Goldilocks-style, she tested each room before choosing the antique brass bed in the middle one. In her private bathroom at the back of the house was a clawfoot tub and no shower. She couldn't recall the last time she'd taken a bath.

It was a lovely, welcoming home, perfect for a first visit to New Orleans. Josie walked back through the rooms to examine the photos and knickknacks. There were Mardi Gras beads dangling from headboards and light fixtures, New Orleans guidebooks, books about Louisiana history, a few by Medley himself. She was staying in a writer's home, and this seemed right, as though the distance between Derek and her were not quite so far. She thought about calling him and shoved the idea to the back of her mind. Mia believed things worked out as they were meant to, and she was on Mia's turf. She'd strive to adopt the same mindset.

The framed photos scattered about the place were a hodgepodge, many taken on the front porch of the house, of fellow travelers she guessed. Fellow travelers—how rich that sounded, different from the life she'd known before this day. Her life had been embarrassingly short on adventure, in part because she'd never felt anchored enough to anything to need to escape it, in part because adventure cost money. Money may not buy happiness, but it could sure make the ride more interesting.

How nice it would be to have someone with whom to share the interesting ride.

She did not need to spend her first day in New Orleans thinking about the grand scheme of life and Derek, what it all meant and if they would manage, and if not, how she'd move forward. She had a different assignment for the day, to get out and explore before it was time to find the Esplanade House and Mia. And the most liberating part about it all, nobody knew she was there. Nobody knew where to find her. She had only herself to answer to. She was on her own schedule.

She filled the tub and added bubble bath from a bottle a previous visitor had left behind. While she soaked, she leafed through a copy of *Lagniappe*, which listed the live music calendar for the week. The first thing she learned was that the word "lagniappe" roughly translated to "a little something extra for free," and was often used in restaurant settings, when the chef offered an *amuse-bouche* or a thirteenth oyster on the house.

She read through the venues, Tipitina's, Preservation Hall, Checkpoint Charlie's, which that night featured a Zydeco band named Dirty Water Dogs. The name was New York slang for street-cart hot dogs, making this another bridge to life back home.

Wistfulness lurked, but this trip was about her newfound independence, and who knew? Maybe she'd go out and meet someone to help take her mind off the someone she wasn't supposed to be thinking about. The future was unwritten.

She bolted upright and sent a cascade of soapy bubbles down the side of the tub. The psychic Eleanor had mentioned—she had to find her. This would be the perfect way to kick off her visit.

She dried off and got dressed, then leafed through one of the guidebooks in the front parlor. She found the address for the Bottom of the Cup Tea Room, located in the heart of the French Quarter.

Back outside under the blanket of heat, Josie walked the uneven sidewalks of Frenchmen Street past New Orleans's Washington Square. The ties to home continued to pile up. Walking through the Marigny, she passed homes of every color decorated for Mardi Gras, Halloween, Christmas, the fact it was August an irrelevant detail.

Further down, Frenchmen Street was lined with cafés, bars, and music venues. On a left-hand corner several blocks in was Café Brasil, a sizeable building painted in cornflower blue and yellow. A handsome man with dark wavy hair stood outside smoking a cigarette, and when he raised his eyebrows and smiled at her, Josie made a note to stop back in later. There were new men in this town, and that was a very good thing.

Frenchmen ended at Esplanade, where Mia's restaurant was located. It was every bit as beautiful as Mia had described, a wide boulevard whose medians—which she'd called "neutral ground"—were lined in majestic oak trees dripping with Spanish moss. Everywhere, the delicate crepe myrtle bloomed. In her haste to pack and leave town, Josie had forgotten to bring her camera and now wished she had it. But it would be impossible to capture even a modicum of what she was witnessing. New Orleans was as visually stunning as it was engaging all her senses, from the warm air that enveloped her to the wind chimes in the trees and the pungent scent of fermenting flowers and river water.

She crossed Esplanade and entered the French Quarter. Decatur Street was as touristy as the books had warned her but Josie was fine with that. She walked through the French Market and perused the stalls of souvenirs—petrified alligator heads, Mardi Gras masks, gumbo mix, hot sauce. She passed the green-

and-white striped awning of the Café du Monde, where tourists stood in long lines to get coffee and beignets—those in the know, she'd read, just walked inside.

She walked further into the Quarter, the heat enough to make her want to stop for one of the icy cocktails everyone was walking around with, but she'd resist the neon signs offering frozen daiquiris on every corner. She needed her wits about her for her mission. A sign hanging on a doorway advertised an apartment to rent and a broker's phone number—an additional sign hinged beneath it advised, "Apartment Haunted."

She got to Chartres Street—pronounced *Charters* according to the shopkeeper who confirmed she was heading in the right direction—and reached Jackson Square. Here street musicians and palm readers vied for the attention and dollars of the crowds. She passed a trio singing "Iko Iko." There was a singer, an accordion player, and a washboard player who stopped what he was doing to blow her a kiss. She kept going to Royal and made a left. A few blocks in, she came upon the sign for Bottom of the Cup Tea Room.

Chimes that festooned the door jingled as she walked in. A haze of spicy incense hung in the air. Sunlight streamed through the lace curtains and crystal ornaments hanging around the shop, making prisms on the walls. A pretty woman about Josie's age with a dramatic black bob looked up from behind the counter and smiled.

"How can I help you, doll?" she asked.

"I was hoping to get a reading."

The glass counter held a display of beaded and crystal jewelry, as well as a vast assortment of healing stones, their properties listed on index cards.

"Any particular type of reading you're looking for?" the woman asked, stumping Josie.

"Not entirely sure, but a friend recommended I see Vivian. Is she by chance available?"

The woman ran her finger down the page of her appointment book and looked at Josie with a smile. "Somebody's looking out for you, baby! She had a cancellation and can see you in about ten minutes."

Josie paid for her session and browsed the shop. There were shelves lined with books on astrology, creative visualization, past lives, and spirit animals. There were tarot cards, healing candles, and boxes of tea with names like *Dragon Moon* and *Serene Wisdom*. Amulets of all varieties were available as pendants, earrings, and ornaments. She picked up a tourmaline turtle, then a heart-shaped piece of rose quartz whose properties, the signage read, were meant to heal the heart and invite new love into one's life. It fit perfectly in the palm of her hand and had a nice heft to it, with smooth, rounded edges.

"That's a great piece," the woman said. "A real powerful quartz."

"Does it work? I could use a boost in this department."

"I got one when I was single, and within a year I was pregnant. And married. True story," she said, holding her hand in oath.

Josie put the heart back in its bin.

The door opened with the jangling of chimes.

"Here's Miss Vivian!"

Vivian looked to be in her eighties, soft and grandmotherly, with a cloud of white hair and wire rimmed glasses—an off-season Mrs. Claus. She wore a long, light blue cotton dress and turquoise jewelry. "Are you Gwendolyn, dear?" she asked in a pleasant, chirpy voice.

"Gwendolyn had to cancel, Viv. This is"—the woman checked the credit card slip in front of her—"Miss Josephine."

"Pleased to meet you, Miss Josephine. Won't you come on back?"

Josie followed her into one of the curtained-off booths in the back of the store. She could hear voices coming from some of the others, dulcet murmurings of people, like her, seeking answers.

Vivian took her seat at a small table draped in royal blue cloth and motioned for Josie to sit across from her. She unwrapped a cassette and placed it into a tape recorder, then wrote the date and their names on the sleeve of its case. There were thank you notes and photographs taped to the wall, and one framed photo in the center of it all.

Josie squinted at it. "Is that Tony Curtis?"

Vivian sighed wistfully. "That's Tony Curtis. What a dear man. I've read him twice."

If it was good enough for Tony, it was good enough for Josie.

"Now dear," Vivian said. "Tell me what you want to cover today."

"I guess I'm just curious to see what kind of insights you get."

Vivian placed a stack of tarot cards in front of Josie and instructed her to shuffle them and make two piles. "Wonderful, now touch each pile and tell me which one you're drawn to."

Josie held her hand over each. She wanted it to be obvious, wanted one to be markedly warmer or vibrating. They felt identical, so she chose the one on the left. Vivian picked it up and began turning cards over, forming a pattern. There were old fashioned illustrations of different characters, celestial bodies, a wheel of fortune, a high priestess, kings and queens.

"You're at a crossroads," Vivian said, studying the cards. She reached for Josie's left hand and traced the lines on her palm. "A real crossroads in every area!"

"Such as?"

"Career certainly." Vivian turned over a few more cards. "Is your company closing?"

Josie felt goosebumps rise. "Very possibly. It's a bit unclear."

"I don't think you need worry about it,"—she pointed to a symbol—"because it looks as though whatever happens, you are going to land on your feet. And it looks as though this might actually be the best thing that *could* happen, a forced change like this." She turned another card—The Hanging Man. This did not sound promising. "You've certainly been betrayed, my dear."

"That I have."

"And more than once, by more than one man."

"Also true."

"There's someone else in the picture, and this one would not betray you, but there's something standing in the way of your being together. Is he expecting a child?"

Josie was hooked. For the next twenty minutes, Vivian delved into her life, describing aspects of her childhood, her difficult-to-please mother, and the second mother figure who helped her through feelings of isolation and otherness. She described her uncertainty about her life's purpose and her fear that she didn't have one. And she assured her that she did.

"Do you have any questions for me?" she asked, midway through.

"Yes, actually," Josie said with a nervous laugh. "I have an interesting relationship with the spirit world, and I'm wondering if you're picking anything up about that?"

Vivian beamed, and Josie shifted in her seat. "I am, and I'm glad you've asked. Not everyone is receptive to these kinds of readings."

"I know. I've met a lot of resistant people."

"I think you might have been a resistant person, too, once?"

Josie nodded. "Guilty. But I'm ready. I think."

"All right." Vivian pulled a notepad from a shelf under the table and started scribbling linear pen marks on it, like the lines of a heartbeat monitor. "I do this to keep my mind focused."

Josie was quiet while Vivian concentrated. Then the energy in the room shifted, and she felt tingly. Not scared, but intrigued.

"There are a lot of spirits coming through," Vivian said.

"That's strange because I haven't lost that many people."

"It's possible they are coming through for people in your life. For friends. Because you're a portal now between both worlds. You've always been, but now you're open. You've lost someone quite recently. Who is Annette?"

"Nanette. My grandmother," Josie said, her voice breaking, goosebumps rising all over.

"And she's crossed over?"

"Yes."

"She's with her husband, who crossed a long time ago, yes?" Josie nodded. "She loves you very much. She's telling me you're exactly where you're supposed to be right now, physically. Does this make sense?"

"Yes," Josie said, tears warming her cheeks.

"She's telling you you're not alone. That there are others watching over you. Other women."

"Okay."

"I'm getting female friend energy, too, maybe someone your generation. Is there an R name who has passed?"

Ruby.

"Yes, but I didn't really know her in life."

Vivian looked skeptical. "She's saying you know her. And she's telling you to relax. Does that resonate?"

Josie laughed through her tears. "I can't believe I'm saying this, but yes."

"Good, dear. There's a male energy here. Did you lose a child?"

"A child? No!"

"Okay. We'll get back to him if we need to. Now I'm hearing an M name."

"I have an M friend who's alive. And an M who's my stepmother, who's also alive. I think."

"Now remember that sometimes spirit uses the name of someone living for association, a mutual friend or a family member who would remind you of them. I'm hearing Mariah or Maria."

"Maria! That's got to be my friend Sylvie, who's passed."

"Okay, then Sylvie is here."

"Does she have a message for me?"

Vivian scribbled on the pad, nodding as she listened to whatever she was listening to. "She wants you to know that your gift to connect to spirit is strong, even stronger than you realize. And she's saying there's a connection to fire in your gift, does that make sense?"

"Yes. Not directly, but I grew up in a place that once had a fire, and I worked in a place that did, too. And I've felt spirit in both those places."

"That's right. And much like your grandmother, your friend Sylvie is telling you that it will all work out as it is meant to."

Josie smiled. "I think she's quoting our mutual friend."

"Then, yes," Vivian said. "That's Sylvie's way of making sure you know it's her. She says she loves you, and she says that you can accept your gift even if you don't understand it all. She's asking you to promise to try to do just that."

"Okay. I promise to try."

"Do you know who your spirit guides are, dear?"

"I have spirit guides?"

Vivian laughed. "Of course you do, we all do. These are ancestors and higher powers who've been with you since birth."

"Are mine here today?"

"Yes they are, dear, and they have a message for you. They're telling me that God knew your face long before your parents knew your name."

That God concept again.

"And now remember, God is different things to different people. Whatever your belief system, whether it's the Christian God or another religion, or whether it's the universe or an unknown higher power, it's all God."

"So, what does that mean that God knew my face long before?"

"It means you are on the right path."

"Wow. I feel like I've meandered off the path altogether."

"You haven't. Your path is one of empathy. Your purpose in this lifetime is to make people feel less alone."

Josie left the Bottom of the Cup alive with energy and purpose. This was real. This was verified contact with the spirit world, a clarion call to accept her gift. And this was validation that she could and would relax and let things play out as they were meant to.

As she made her way back down Chartres Street, she decided she'd have a drink in the French Quarter before heading to Mia. She had a list of the places Nanette had frequented that still existed. One of them was Harry's Bar, which a guidebook informed her had been renamed Harry's Corner. She didn't know the address but figured she could ask someone, and just as she was about to cross Dumaine Street, she saw it.

"Thank you, Nanette!" she said, looking to the sky.

Harry's was delightfully void of the neon lights of Bourbon Street and looked as though it hadn't gotten a facelift since Nanette's days in New Orleans. A half-dozen patrons sat around the small bar drinking Blue Moons, Abita ales, and Bloody Marys. A woman in the corner had a wiry, one-eyed mutt on her lap, and further down the bar, an old shepherd mix slept at its owner's feet. This would not be a wine kind of place. This was not a wine kind of trip.

Josie looked over the booze selection and felt someone's eyes on her. Across the bar sat an attractive man with shoulder length brown hair and a black straw fedora. He smiled at her, his light eyes sparkling. He looked like a handsome, mischievous warlock. She smiled back.

"What can I do for ya, hon?" The bartender was a middle-aged woman with bleached hair and the face of a dedicated smoker.

"I'll have a Bloody Mary, spicy, please." There was a handwritten out-of-order sign taped to the air conditioner, and Josie needed to splash cold water on her face. The heat was as intense as she'd been warned.

The ladies' room was out of order as well. Josie locked the door in the men's room and turned on the faucet, holding her wrists underneath until it was cold enough. She splashed her face and as she straightened back up and looked at her reflection the back of her neck tingled.

Welcome to New Orleans, she thought. This time it wasn't scary, it was exciting.

When she opened the door, the warlock was waiting. Josie's stomach fluttered.

"Howdy," he said, tipping his hat. "Welcome to New Orleans."

She giggled. "Is it that obvious?"

"If you've lived here long enough." His accent was refined, gentlemanly. "Where do you hail from?"

"I'm visiting from New York. I'm Josie, by the way." She held out her hand, and he kissed it.

"William Carter, by the way," he said with a wink. He was very attractive. It was hard to gauge his age—he had the same timeless, ethereal quality as Mia.

"Are you a native?"

"Native of the south, other parts. But this placed claimed me long ago. This your first time in town, Miss Josie?"

"Yes, been wanting to visit forever. Finally getting around to it. I have a friend who lives in town."

"And now you have two."

Josie laughed, lightheaded from heat and flirtation and a bit of dehydration. She needed to stay on top of her water consumption. "You're awfully dressed up for this weather," she said. He wore all black, fitted slacks and a billowy jacket.

"You get used to it. This ain't nothing compared to the real hot days."

A woman walked up to them. "Are you in line?" she asked Josie.

"No, but"—she gestured to William Carter.

He tipped his hat. "Ma'am," he said, holding his hand toward the bathroom. The woman shrugged and passed by. Maybe William Carter types were not an anomaly here.

"So, what do you plan on doin' while you're in town, Miss Josie-by-the-way?"

"Just going to explore, really. Visit with my friend. Her family owns a place here, the Esplanade House."

"The magnificent Boudreaux family."

"Right. I'm friends with Mia. We worked together in New York this summer."

"That explains it. Was wondering where that girl had gone off to."

Josie recognized the look on his face as the one most red-blooded men got in the presence of a beautiful woman or, in this case, the mention of Mia's name. He eyed Josie, and she felt like Little Red Riding Hood encountering the Big Bad Wolf.

He pulled a pocket watch from his belt loop and checked the time, then looked back at her with a lascivious grin. Good. This was what she needed. "I'm afraid I have to get going. Would you like to join me?"

She'd expected more subtlety from a southerner, but his directness was enticing. "I really want to go see Mia. She doesn't even know I'm here yet. I'm guessing I'll spend a lot of time at Esplanade House this week. Why don't you stop by?"

"I just might do." He kissed her hand again, then slipped into the bathroom the woman had just exited.

The Bloody Mary was waiting for her at the bar, and she took a long sip. It was savory and spicy, adorned with a pickled string bean. She took a bite, the first solid food she'd had since breakfast at the airport, and looked around the room at all the people unabashedly drinking during the day. Granted it was nearing late afternoon, but some of these folks were long past their first glasses.

William Carter reemerged and touched Josie's shoulder on the way out. "Hope to see you later, Miss Josie-by-the-way. You tell Miss Mia that Will sends his love. Bye now."

She watched him leave. His was a carefully cultivated look, one she would scoff at on a man in New York. But she was in New Orleans now. To forget what she knew.

While she sipped her drink, she chatted with a couple sitting at the corner of the bar. They were locals impressed she was visiting for the first time in August.

"Most of y'all can't stand it down here, what with the humidity an' all," the woman said. "Yankees anyway. Southerners are used to it."

"You staying in the Quarter?" They managed to pronounce both "Southerner" and "Quarter" as though neither contained the letter *R*.

Josie repeated the words to herself. "I'm in the Marigny."

"Fancy," the woman said, raising her glass. The place on Burgundy was not particularly fancy, but they were nonetheless impressed.

When Josie drained her drink, the bartender brought over a second. "Oh, I didn't order—"

"Happy hour, baby," she said, pointing to the sign. Happy hour ran from two until eight. It was nearly 5:30 p.m., and Josie was anxious to get to Mia. She offered her extra drink to the couple.

"Y'all can get a go-cup," the woman said. She reached across the bar for a plastic cup and transferred the contents of Josie's glass. "Voy-a-la."

Josie said goodbye, tipped the bartender, and continued back down Chartres toward Esplanade. Down one of the side streets she saw a ragtag gang of alley cats.

"Look at you!" she cooed, walking over to them. The smallest of the lot, pale gray with bright yellow eyes and an ear chewed in half long ago, rubbed against her leg. "You're so cute, little one! Are you my familiar?"

They pooled around her feet, mewling in harmony until the apparent leader, a fat tabby, leapt into a nearby alley and the rest followed. Josie's cat turned once to meow before joining the others.

This was a particularly charming block, the homes pastel-colored stucco with Spanish tile roofs, iron gates guarding the driveways. The residents had gotten creative in their security systems. At the tops of some of the gates were colorful shards of broken glass meant to keep people from jumping over. Through the alleyways next to the homes she could see courtyards and fountains.

The sky grew darker at a pace unlike any impending storm Josie had witnessed before. The crepe myrtle petals glowed brighter. From deep in the trees came a churning chorus of cicadas and tree frogs.

In trying to get back to Chartres Street, Josie made a wrong turn somewhere along the way. Nothing was familiar. Her instinct told her to make a right, so she did, and was back on Esplanade. She made a left on the avenue, walked two blocks and, just as the first fat raindrops began to fall, found herself directly in front of Esplanade House. She yelped in surprise.

It was a grand, two-story red brick house with black shutters and white trim. She sought brief cover under the wraparound, wrought iron porch on the second floor and watched the deluge. It was a movie-set storm with thunderclaps that made her bones vibrate and crackling lightening that pierced the sky.

"Oh my God!" she said aloud, watching people who looked like they'd just emerged from the bayou run down the street. In a summer of rain, in thirty-two years of it, she'd never witnessed anything quite like this.

And then just as quickly as it had started, it stopped, as though the power had been cut. No easing up, no lingering drizzle, the rain had made its point and left. Now steam rose from the smoldering sidewalks, and the chorus of wildlife grew louder in the trees. It was only a modicum less hot and humid than it had been before the rain.

The restaurant's name was written in Art Deco lettering on a white sign hung over the entrance. It was nearly six—the evening would be getting started, and Mia would surely be there.

Josie walked inside, her eyes slow to adjust to the dimly lit room. There was a horseshoe-shaped bar in the middle and a few tables along the wall. A larger dining room sat to the left. People were scattered about the front room, eating and drinking.

"Josie!" someone called. Through the relative dark she saw Eleanor sipping a cocktail at the bar. And standing next to her, holding menus and a tray, was Mia.

Josie let out another yelp of giddy laughter. "Surprise!" She rushed over and screeched to a halt just as she reached them. This wasn't Mia, but it was a woman such the spitting image that they had to be close relatives. This was Mia, an inch or two shorter with slightly darker hair. Same kaleidoscope eyes, same alabaster skin, same beauty, a whole lot more makeup.

"We were just talking about you!" Eleanor said. "Here's your friend's daughter."

Josie laughed, embarrassed. "I think there's been a mix-up. Hi, I'm Josie."

"And you knew my mother," the woman said without a shred of belief in her voice.

"No," Josie said, smiling. "No. I'm a friend of Mia Boudreaux."

"Mia Boudreaux was my mother," the woman said in a deep, slow drawl. "And unless you found the damn fountain of youth, you couldn't have known her."

"Rita!" Eleanor said. "Be a lady."

"She's been dead since I was four."

A buzzing sound enveloped the room as the words floated through the air and rearranged themselves. Rita—*Rita*—was still talking, and Josie couldn't make out a single word. She watched her mouth move and her eyes twitch with emotion, and the buzzing sound grew higher and louder, drowning her out, while the room grew so small and dark Josie saw it only through a pinhole of light.

My daughter runs it now, she heard Mia say, her words repeating and echoing as Josie's legs buckled.

Chapter Nineteen

❧

WHEN SHE OPENED her eyes, Josie was slumped on the floor against a barstool, a small crowd surrounding her. Someone squatted at her side with a glass of water, another held ice to her forehead.

"Did I fall?" she asked, her tongue thick in her mouth.

"You started to, an' we caught you."

As Josie's blurred vision cleared, she saw Mia speaking and wondered why she sounded so strange.

"You all right?" Mia asked. She sounded annoyed.

Josie nodded, and someone helped her off the floor and eased her into a chair with a back.

"Now you just sit for a spell, dear," another woman said. Eleanor. This was Eleanor from the airplane. "You're not accustomed to the heat down here."

In fact Josie felt an icy chill. And self-conscious—there were too many people watching her. "I'm sorry," she said, her voice raspy. She took a sip of water, then another.

"It's okay, baby!" the burly, bearded bartender answered her. "You ain't our first customer to faint, you ain't our last."

"Knock it off, Bobby," Mia said. Josie could not make any sense of the scene in front of her. "Y'all may want somethin' stiffer than water to wake you back up."

"Can I have a Coke?" Josie asked Bobby.

"Hell, girl, I meant even stiffer n' that."

"Let the girl have what she wants, Rita!" Bobby said.

Rita.

This couldn't be real. This was a mix-up. Because if this were Rita, and Rita were Mia's daughter—

"Are there two Ritas?" Josie asked hoarsely.

Bobby guffawed. "Hell no! We got our hands plenty full with this one." He chuckled as he fixed her Coke. "Two Ritas. 'Magine that?"

"Yeah, so, seeing as I'm Rita, and you say you knew my mama, guess you was a kid when you knew her."

"Your mother was Mia."

"Mmmmm. Set off for New York City when I was a girl, never saw her again. She died there. Was burned in a fire."

Josie nearly choked on her Coke. "Actually, Bobby? I think I will have something a little stronger in here."

The facts, as they were, would not work here. Mia had made it clear that Rita—her daughter—was closed to the spirit world. If everything else followed suit, if Mia were Rita's mother, and Rita's mother were dead, then it stood to reason that the Mia she knew was, quite unbelievably, a ghost. Explaining this to Rita was not an option.

"So, again," Rita said a little more aggressively. "Less you was a tiny thing then, how'd you know my mama?"

Josie could do this. She could think on her feet and sort through her own mental chaos later. She took a swig of her drink, to which Bobby had added something brown. "I didn't mean I knew her personally." Rita was not a blinker, and Josie started speaking faster. "I meant that I knew people who knew her back then. I guess that heat messed up my thoughts some."

"It's a dense heat if you're not used to it," Eleanor said.

Rita just kept eyeing Josie, waiting for more.

"Yeah, and I misspoke on the plane," she said, grateful for Eleanor's acceptance, which stood in stark contrast to Rita's suspicion. "I didn't know your mom personally, of course, but I'd heard about Esplanade House from someone who'd stopped into the restaurant where I worked, and who knew Mia from all those years ago."

"Was it Miss Sylvie from New York City?" Rita asked. "From Dave's Continental?"

Shivers ran down Josie's spine. Mia and Sylvie *had* known each other... in 1974.

"Yes. Yes, it was Sylvie."

"God rest her soul," Rita said. Josie nodded. "Woman saved our asses, that's for sure."

"For heaven's sake, Rita," Eleanor scolded her. "Language!"

"For fuck's sake, Eleanor!" Rita said like a petulant teenager.

Eleanor just tsked and shook her head.

"How did she do that?" Josie asked.

"Guess she knew somehow we was in trouble. This place was gonna have to close. After Miss Sylvie passed, her niece wrote us a letter with a check—huge check, enough to get us some new equipment and pay off some debt. We got more work to do, but now we know we can stay. We still have a home. Course in her confusion Miss Sylvie did put Mama's name on the check, but it was no matter. We got it sorted."

All those nights they were convinced Sylvie had lost her mind she was telling the truth. She did know Mia. She had her name wrong, but she recognized her. And like the denouement of the movie they'd watched together, when all those puzzle pieces came together, Josie thought back on the nights Mia was or wasn't around. Thought about how she'd wondered why no one else seemed to have gotten close to her—tried to rack her brain to recall Mia coming up in conversation. But this was impossible—of course Mia had interacted with the others. She'd been there all summer. Josie vividly remembered introducing her to Andy, along with the moments that Derek, Sam, and the men who frequented the place all noticed her for the first time. This didn't make sense. And Patrick—they'd absolutely met. He and Josie had talked about her after that, she was sure of it.

She didn't object as Bobby refilled her drink.

Rita kept talking. "Niece said Mama and Miss Sylvie were real close in the day. That she'd wait at Dave's for Mama to get off work, and then they'd paint the town."

Mia worked at Dave's. Mia died twenty-five years ago, one of the waitresses who was in the fire. Profound sadness surged through Josie. For Mia, for Rita, for Sylvie.

How frustrating it must have been for her, to be certain she knew Mia while everyone else was trying to convince her otherwise. Had Mia played into it somehow? Was she like Josie's mother had been in those lonely childhood hours when she was so afraid and her mother would tell her it was all in her head?

"What was your mother's full name?"

"Maria. Maria Louise Boudreaux."

Each detail just brought with it more questions. Why this summer? Why Josie? What had Mia needed from her? She'd expressed sorrow at Rita's unwillingness to tap into the spirit world, and now this fit. If she wouldn't tap into it, her mother couldn't reach her. She could only watch from afar.

Josie was missing a key piece of information, the one that tied all the loose ends. Because this wasn't random. It was not an accident that Mia had chosen this summer, the aftermath of Nanette's passing, to visit Bistrot, to befriend Josie and invite her to New Orleans. Josie was on some sort of scavenger hunt, and the person who likely held the answers was Rita. Rita, to whom she couldn't explain any of this. Fortunately a career in hospitality and a mother who couldn't handle the real her had equipped Josie with the ability to mask her feelings, navigate different personalities, and think on the fly.

"You want another?" Rita asked, and Josie realized she'd drained her glass. So much for maintaining her wits, she was in vastly uncharted territory. Rita signaled Bobby for a round.

"I'm glad to hear you guys are going to be able to keep this place going," Josie said. "It's really special."

"Sure is. Miss Sylvie was lookin' out for us."

Soon they were seated at one of the small tables in the barroom so Rita could keep an eye on things while they talked over drinks and food. Eleanor bid them goodnight, and now they sat with a pitcher of Abita and a plate of buttery, chargrilled oysters in front of them. Her anger and mistrust diffused, Rita seemed to enjoy talking to someone who was loosely—she thought—connected to her mother.

"Sounds like Miss Sylvie was like my grandparents. They're both senile, but still real sweet and kind."

Mia's parents—Josie tried to calculate how old they might be. "How old was your mom when she passed?"

"Twenty-nine. My age."

"And where are your grandparents now?"

"They're in Metairie, in an old folks' home."

"So, you grew up with them."

"Yup." Rita picked up an oyster shell and slurped its meat. "Seeing as how Mama lit out when I was four, I couldn't exactly manage on my own. I need a shot." She sprang from the table and went to the bar.

This was not going to be easy. Rita may look like her mother, but their personalities could hardly have been more different. Where Mia was open, kind, compassionate, Rita was closed, gruff, hard-edged. And alive.

Unless Mia planned to materialize and explain, Josie would have to be strategic in determining why she'd been sent to New Orleans to meet her daughter. She tried again to sort through the ostensible facts of her summer, tried to recall what Mia had said about spirits who could make their presence known to multiple people at once. The booze—and admittedly she was in the process of consuming more than would serve her—was mitigating her shock and grief and discomfort. It was quieting everything and letting her exist in the very weird now.

"Keep 'em coming, Bobby?" Rita called over her shoulder as she placed a shot of bourbon—her mother's daughter—in front of Josie.

"These must be tough memories for you," Josie said.

"That's why I need to get drunk tonight and take you with me. I don't talk about Mama much anymore."

They sipped their drinks. It was smoother than Josie had anticipated, woody with a hint of caramel.

A server delivered several dishes to the table.

"Gotta eat," Rita said, scooping food onto Josie's plate. "Don't need anyone passing out again."

Josie took a forkful of jambalaya and realized she was ravenous. They set upon their feast, which included gumbo, alligator sausage, and something called mirliton, a dense, meaty squash Rita said was a staple in Creole cooking.

She doused everything in Crystal hot sauce, and Josie followed suit. It was the perfect blend of heat and flavor.

"So," Rita said after a few minutes. "I'm guessin' you wanted to come by to talk about Mama? Guessin' Miss Sylvie said some stuff about her, and you want to tell it to me?"

Josie spoke carefully, "I really just wanted to meet you and see the restaurant. I've heard so much over—"

"'Cause I think I know everything I need to about my mama," Rita said, cutting her off.

"But—how could you? You were so young!"

"That's right, and I've spent a lot more time with her gravestone than I ever did with her."

Her gravestone… of course that was here.

"Where is your mama buried?" Josie asked. She took a sip of beer and held back a hiccup.

"Saint Louis Cemetery. Why, you want to meet her?" Rita laughed mirthlessly and signaled the bartender for another round, which Josie was certain she didn't need.

"Rita, you seem angry."

Rita responded by downing the shot placed in front of her.

Josie took a small sip of her own.

"Used to be a lot angrier. But yeah, it'll never go away."

"My dad left when I was really young, too. Believe me, the abandonment? I get it. But the anger doesn't serve—"

"You still see your daddy?"

"Once or twice a year."

"At least you get that, Josie. At least it ain't over."

"But your mom didn't just leave you on purpose! She died." Josie flinched at her own coarseness, at having to put this new and terrible knowledge into words. "She didn't set out to abandon you."

Rita's expression was dark. "No, she was supposed to come back after that summer. Or that's what my Gram says, anyway. It was just supposed to be a couple months. She went there for some guy, and he dumped her ass."

He didn't just dump her, Josie thought, he was married.

"And she was too broke to come back to me right away."

"Can you have some sympathy for her, then? Knowing she was trying to—"

"Of course I can, Josie!" Rita said, raising her voice. "You don't think I'm sad, too, on top of it all? I miss my mama. Always have and always will. Don't mean she was a saint. Don't mean she didn't choose some man over her kid! What would have happened if the guy hadn't dumped her? Then what? She'd have stayed?"

"Wouldn't she have likely sent for you, or come back and brought you up?" Josie had to assume Mia had been telling her the truth which, under the circumstances, seemed an absurd assumption.

But Rita nodded, looking down at the chipped, red polish on her fingernails. "That's what she said before she left, that she was going to see what New York City was like, and if she liked it she'd find us a nice place to live. My grandparents was much younger then, they could have run this place just fine. I guess I'm just mad that she left in the first place."

"I understand," Josie said, reaching over to touch Rita's hand. "And your anger is perfectly valid."

"I never said it wasn't!" Rita jerked her hand away. How disconcerting to look at Mia's face, beautiful, gentle Mia, and see reflected back so much darkness and anger. Children who lost their parents often got stuck in a sort of arrested development, and Josie could see in Rita the stubborn, angry, and confused child Mia had described.

In Mia there was pain, too, a quiet, bittersweet resignation that came, Josie had thought, from missing her daughter. And it did, but now Josie knew it was far more complex than that.

"Did you get to talk to her on the phone while she was up there?"

"Some. Not too much. It was expensive, one, and two, I guess she was going through the breakup and didn't want me to hear her sad. That's what Gram explained after. But try and make sense of that when you're a little girl who's just missin' her mama."

"Wow, Rita, that must have been really hard."

"And then I sent her this package, this present, this real special present, and I thought for sure she'd call then. Or write. Every day I ran to the mailbox to check for a letter."

"Maybe she never got it?"

"Maybe. But I sent it a good month before she died."

"What was it?"

"My grandma had taken me to this crafts fair, and I saw this beautiful necklace, this locket, that reminded me of Mama. Gram said Mama would love it and that we'd fill it with pictures so she'd have me with her whenever she wore it. So, we put a picture of me and a picture of Mama inside, and we got it engraved with this poem my Gram said Mama liked."

It took a few seconds for Rita's words to land, and when they did, Josie's exhausted, addled brain forgot to remind her not to say too much. "It's engraved? Really?"

"What?"

"The locket—it's a gold pendant with white and yellow flowers—" She ignored Rita's frown and flared nostrils—or maybe she didn't notice them—and barreled on. "Rita, honey, she did get it! And she gave it to me, sort of!" Josie fingered her collarbone where the pendant should have been—she'd forgotten to put it back on after her bath. "Shit—shoot—I always wear it! I must have left it on—" She stopped abruptly and bit her lip, hard. Rita stared her down, fury in her eyes, her mouth open.

"What are you talkin' about?" She pronounced each word slowly. "What in the hell are you talkin' about?"

Josie wanted to disappear. She cycled through outlandish explanations to save the moment—maybe she could say that the "she" who'd given her the necklace was Sylvie. Maybe she could pretend she was out-of-her-mind drunk or clinically insane. But it was too late. Rita knew where she was going with this, and she was not at all happy about it.

"Rita," Josie said, her voice quivering. "I know this sounds crazy, and I know you don't believe in this stuff—and I know this 'cause your mom told me. She was with us this summer, in New York."

Rita just stared, livid and unblinking, while Josie babbled.

"Your mom—Mia—she came to us at the beginning of summer to work in coat check—we had all this rain. Well, I thought she came to *us*, but it turns out she came to *me* because I have this thing with spirits. I didn't realize she was one. How could I? I'd never seen one before, only felt them and then started hearing them. But it had been a while, years. And just around the time she came I started feeling all these creepy tingly feelings, and at first I thought it was because my Nanette—my Gram—had just died, then I thought maybe it was my friend Derek's brother, Alex—holy shit, that's the little boy Vivian was talking about! Then Ruby, and actually I guess it was all of them, *and* your mom!" She paused and took a sip of her beer. "We were really good friends," she added in a tiny voice.

Rita downed a shot. "Please leave," she said, her eyes flickering with fury. "I don't know who the heck you are coming into my restaurant like some crazy fortune teller and shaking up all these memories."

"Rita—"

Rita stood. "Get up, turn around, and walk out that door."

"But Rita," Josie pleaded, choking back tears. She stood and looked into Rita's eyes. "I know you don't want to believe me. I don't want to believe me either because of what this means about my friend, but I'm telling you that—"

"Get out of here now!" Rita said in a sharp tone similar to the one Mia used when she was cross with Ruby.

"I'm sorry," Josie said with a whimper. "I'm so sorry." She picked up her things and looked around the room. Rita had spoken quietly enough that no one had heard the specifics of their conversation, but Josie could tell by the way the patrons and bartender were eyeing them that they knew there'd been an altercation. And that Josie had caused it.

Her eyes blinded with tears, she ran out the door so quickly she almost tripped. She'd failed in her mission. She'd failed Mia.

Chapter Twenty

❧

JOSIE WATCHED THE ceiling fan spin in the morning light. She'd known where she was even before she opened her eyes, the entirety of the previous day's events flooding her thoughts as soon as she was conscious.

Raw grief enveloped her now in more manifestations than she'd ever dreamt possible. Despair, depression, anger, guilt, shock, incredulousness, all of it. She regretted her drunken blunder but had to forgive herself. It's not like she'd blurted out, "*I know your dead mother!*" She'd listened, she'd empathized, and after too much of whatever Bobby was pouring, she'd responded as best she could, which was not very well.

She wanted to lie in bed with the covers over her head weeping, for herself, for Rita, and most of all for Mia.

But she couldn't. She was in New Orleans for a reason, and she needed to find it. She paced the rooms like a widow atop a lighthouse, then ran water in the tub. While she waited for it to fill, she sat at the mirrored vanity. The deep sadness she felt showed through the shadows in her eyes. This was a messy, impossible situation she'd managed to make even worse.

The necklace lay in a coil on the mantel. What might have happened had she been wearing it when she met Rita? Would she have recognized it straight away? She flipped it over, and the back of the locket, which had been tarnished, was now shiny and gold. On it was engraved,

To her whose heart is my heart's quiet home.

Love from Rita

Josie held the pendant to her lips. She would no longer wear it. It did not belong to her.

She lowered herself into the tub and closed her eyes. Anything she thought she knew about the laws of physics and spirituality was in question. Mia *had* worked at Bistrot—she was sure of it. She was there from the start.

Wasn't she?

Josie cycled through a slide show of the summer. If the coatroom had been in use, why would Sam have slipped in front of the Dunnehills? Why would there have been an umbrella on a chair dripping rainwater on the floor? And why, now that she thought of it, did so many people cram themselves into the coatroom with Mia?

Hadn't anyone else besides Sylvie and Patrick mentioned her by name?

She knew what she had to do. She had to find Mia. But first she needed a proper breakfast.

Josie wrapped the necklace in a bandana and packed it in her tote bag along with one of the guidebooks. She headed down Burgundy in a new direction, turned left on Touro, and walked the block to Dauphine. Her New York pace was ill-suited for the uneven sidewalks.

At the corner of Dauphine and Touro was La Peniche restaurant. The bells on the door signaled her arrival.

"Anywhere you like honey." A large woman with a high-pitched voice and a gold tooth greeted her.

Josie chose a small table by the window. It was an uncomplicated menu. "I'll have the veggie omelette, coffee, and a Bloody Mary, please?"

"Kick?

"Pardon?"

"You want some spice with your Bloody, sugar?"

"Yes, please." Josie leafed through the travel guide and honed in on the section about cemeteries. Rita had mentioned Saint Louis Cemetery—there were three of them.

Girl, please make this easier on me, she silently pleaded. She picked the closest one and mapped her route.

After breakfast, she left La Peniche and walked to the Quarter, then down Bourbon Street to see what all the fuss was about. The French Quarter was teeming with tourists, lending credence to the myth of the loud, obnoxious American. They were everywhere with their maps and cameras, turkey legs and frozen drinks. The streets were lined with daiquiri shops, strip clubs, and live music. It was barely 11:00 a.m. and everything was packed.

She stopped to read a sign advertising Ghost Tours.

A tall, thin man with shaggy brown hair and big eyes emerged from the doorway in a top hat. "Welcome, milady, are you interested in exploring our haunted city?"

"I think I'm already doing that. But what is this all about?"

"This is about taking a walk through some of the most haunted spots in the Quarter, plus a graveyard tour in the middle of it all."

"What are the most haunted spots?"

"There's the Lafitte Blacksmith Shop, for one." He pointed in the direction she'd just come from. "Oldest bar in the country. The original piano player still hangs around, along with Monsieur Lafitte *lui-même*. A visit to Miriam's on Jackson Square. They set a place every day for their resident ghost, Cyril. Down on Pirate's Alley there's Faulkner House Books, where William Faulkner himself still… resides."

"Sounds like the whole Quarter is haunted."

"Sure is. Plenty of famous ghosts roaming these streets." He counted them off on his fingers. "Mad Madame LaLaurie, the socialite serial killer. You've got General Beauregard, of course."

"Of course."

"Julie, the octoroon mistress. And everyone's favorite rake, the devilishly handsome Will Carter."

Josie's stomach lurched. "Who?"

"Ha! Thought that one would get your attention. William Carter. Left broken hearts all over the Quarter back in the roarin' twenties."

"What happened to him?"

"Seduced the wrong woman. She fell hard, and when he didn't marry her, slipped a healthy dose of arsenic into his Gin Rickey. They say he still frequents the bars looking for beautiful women to seduce."

In spite of the goosebumps covering her body, Josie was flattered.

"You okay, miss? These tales are pretty spooky, but I promise you you'll be perfectly safe on my tour. We also visit Saint Louis Number One, home to some of the city's most famous ghosts, Homer Plessy, Bernard de Marigny, Marie Laveau."

Marie Laveau, the Voodoo Queen.

You must visit her grave when you come to New Orleans. For good luck.

Mia had been dropping hints all along the way.

"We have a group fixin' to set out in about five minutes."

"I can't today, but maybe another time."

The man produced a card out of thin air. "Take this and give us a call another time then."

Josie pocketed the card and continued on her way. She needed to see Mia, and now she knew where to find her.

According to the map, Saint Louis Number One was too great a hike given the heat and unfamiliar terrain. Josie hailed a taxi and, once inside, started to laugh at the sheer absurdity of it all. The one man she'd met in Louisiana had been dead since the twenties, and her best girlfriend since the seventies.

"You enjoying yourself, baby?" the female taxi driver asked, smiling at her in the rearview mirror.

"It's certainly been interesting."

"It always is."

The driver let her out on the corner, and there was Saint Louis Number One, rising up like an ancient walled city populated by the dead. It was unlike any cemetery Josie had seen, elaborate, above-ground tombs peeking over the brick wall surrounding the grounds.

She stalked the perimeter and found the entry gate. The cemetery was about one square city block and so crowded with tombs she'd no idea where to begin. She wandered among the vaults, which were in varying stages of decrepitude, some pristine and white as though they'd just been built, others with broken windows and graffiti, like neglected public housing for the departed.

Josie wove in and out of the rows, reading names and dates. "How the hell am I going to find you, woman?" she asked aloud.

In the distance, an elderly man swept the grounds around one of the crypts. She walked toward him, and as she got close, he turned and looked at her. He was like a painting—creviced, onyx skin, white hair, kind, deep-brown eyes steeped in decades of sadness.

"Afternoon, ma'am," he said in a gravelly voice that sounded as though it hadn't had a conversation partner in a while.

"Good afternoon, sir. How are you?"

He looked up at the skies. "No complaints. Got work that matters, got loved ones. Ain't much more to it all. Just enjoy the here and now."

Josie's heart swelled. "This place is beautiful," she said. And it was, a beautiful tribute to the dead in a town that honored them deeply.

"You lookin' for someone particular?"

"No, just looking around—"

The man eyed her carefully, nodded and said in a low voice, "If it's yo friend, she's over there." He gestured behind Josie, and her skin tingled.

She thanked him, turned and walked down a path parallel to the one she'd come in on.

And there was Mia, leaning against a gravestone, waiting for her. She looked beautiful, even more so than she had in New York, which Josie could not have thought possible. She wore a sheer, flowing sundress with a pattern of yellow and turquoise chevrons, her hair loose, the sun glowing behind her like a halo.

As she got close, Josie could read the words etched into the vault behind Mia.

Maria Louise Boudreaux
October 10, 1944 – June 29, 1974
Mother, Daughter, Friend

"We have the same birthday," Josie said.

"I know we do."

"Maria."

"Mia's my nickname." Her voice sounded exactly the same, which shouldn't have surprised Josie but did.

"I know. Rita told me. Which explains why Sylvie kept calling you that."

Mia nodded. "I tried to reinvent myself in New York, went back to my full name."

"And we all thought she was crazy."

Mia just looked at her, her face open, pleading, beautiful. And very sad. "I'm sorry, Josie."

"For what?"

"For so many things."

"I don't even know where to start. I'm feeling so much. But why is anger the first thing bubbling up?"

"Because, Josie, betrayal and deception have marked your life and have made you unhappy, and I added another layer to it all."

"Hell of a layer." Something churned in Josie. She wanted to yell, to weep, to hug Mia and never let her go. She turned to see if the man who'd sent her over was watching, but he was no longer in sight. "You lied to me, Mia!" It came out with more anger than she intended.

"I know, and I'm sorry." Mia stepped closer and touched Josie's arm, like she had so many times before, and it felt just as tangible. "This was the only way I could make it work."

Josie did nothing to stanch the tears that flowed. "I mean, you *really* lied. Who are you? What happened to my friend?"

Mia was crying now, too, but unlike Josie, who was red faced and runny-nosed, Mia looked as though glitter was spilling from her eyes and disappearing into the air. "I'm me, Josie, I'm your friend. Except I'm not who you thought I was. I'm the fool who came to New York and died in that goddamn fire."

"The fire at Dave's Continental. In 1974."

"Yes, baby."

"Why did you come to New York in the first place? Why did you leave Rita? And what do you mean this was the only way you could 'make it work?' Make what work?"

"Like I told you, I came to follow a man who turned out to be married, and that man was Dave."

"Dave Dave?"

"Yes. Dave who owned the joint."

"Okay." Josie wiped her nose with the back of her wrist. "Why did you come back? And why this summer?"

"Actually, girl, I'd come by a bunch. You weren't ready. 'Member one of the first things I told you about the spirit world? Spirits only speak when spoken to. And so though I'd been right in front of you lots of times over the years, you never saw me until that day you looked up and said hello. That's when I knew you were ready."

"Ready for what? Why me?"

"Well now, Josie, it works two ways. One, you needed a friend this summer. And more so, I needed you. I needed you to come down to New Orleans and meet my girl, help her understand."

"Yeah, that went well. I think we really hit it off."

"Hear me out, Josie!" Mia implored her. "I'd been trying to get back into Dave's—Bistrot—for a spell, and I never could."

"How come?"

"At first I wasn't ready. I couldn't bring myself to go back in there. Then, by the time I could, well, the eighties weren't a particularly spiritual decade."

Josie laughed in spite of herself.

"And once Chef took over the place, he was so easily spooked that I didn't know where to begin with him. But then you came along, and I knew."

"You knew what?"

"That you had the ability. I stood in front of you so many times over the years, and I'd see this flicker pass through you—could tell you had the ability but were determined to shut it down. And then Nanette passed. And it was like they say, a perfect storm. You needed a friend, and I needed to be in that space more than ever before."

"Why?"

"Because." Mia's southern drawl was more pronounced on her home turf. "Y'all are renovating. Y'all are gonna cover those safes. Josie, that necklace—"

"The one Rita sent you. That you never thanked her for."

"That's just it, girl, I did thank her. I wrote her back. Only it never got sent, and that's what the package I asked you to get was. It's a thank you letter and a bunch of gifts for my little girl, and the damn thing was never sent. Ruby was supposed to mail it, and she didn't."

"How did it wind up there?"

Mia was quiet for a minute but kept her eyes trained on Josie. "They gave it to Sylvie after we died."

Hearing the words aloud was shocking. Josie reached out to steady herself and grabbed the edge of Mia's tombstone. "Then why was it in the store?"

"She was getting mixed up, as you know, and started giving a lot of her clothes and things away or selling them. In her confusion, she forgot how much that necklace meant to her. She never wore it, just kept it on her dresser next to a picture of the three of us, Ruby, her, and me. It was her shrine."

"Poor Sylvie."

"She lost both of us that night."

"You and Ruby were both close with her?"

"We were. Course she was a good fifteen years older than us girls. She looked out for us like a big sister. We were two foolish young things who didn't know New York City like she did. But she was good to us. She loved us. It took her a long, long time to get over, and I'm not sure she ever did."

"She must have been devastated."

"She felt guilty, too, because she'd have been with us that night. She happened to be out of town visiting her sister in Connecticut. Otherwise, it'd have been the three of us up there, two of us trying to rouse Ruby. Ruby had a drug problem."

"Seconal."

"Among other things, yes. And the night it happened—the night of the fire—she was passed out upstairs."

"In the bathroom."

Mia nodded. "I tried to drag her out. Foolish girl was passed out cold."

"Do you remember it clearly?"

"Clear as anything up till near the end. I tried to scream, and no one heard me."

"Why didn't you just leave?"

"Leave my friend?" Mia shook her head. "No, girl, you don't do that."

"Can you talk me through what you remember?"

"If you want to hear it, yeah." She took Josie's hand and pulled her down to sit against the grave. The cool stone felt good on Josie's skin. "When I think about that night, I hear the fire engines shrieking up Sixth Avenue."

"That's why you were so scared of them the night of the blackout! And of the candle flames!"

"Yep."

"Do you remember the fire?"

"I remember this muffled explosion. Course my first thought was an A-bomb, we grew up half-expecting one to drop at any minute. But once I heard the shouting, I knew we were in a different kind of trouble.

"And then I realized she was missing, she hadn't gone home yet—she never went home this early—and she wasn't sitting with us. So, I ran upstairs to the girls' room, and there she was, pretty baby, half asleep with her head on the toilet seat. I told her we had to leave. I told her we were in trouble. I tried to pull her up, and she said it hurt, but what I really think is she wanted to sleep it off."

"Poor thing."

"Poor thing. And yeah, you're right, I could have, I *should* have, left her there to save my own life. But I couldn't." Mia shook her head, staring into a scene that Josie couldn't see. She reached out her hand and gripped at the air. "I tugged at her a few more times. Thought about running downstairs so one of the guys could help me get her up, but it was too late. I knew it was too late. No matter what would happen to us, it would happen to us together."

"What did you do?"

"I sat with her. I played with her hair, which she always loved." Mia continued to pantomime the scene. "She smiled and said my name and babbled something. And soon, the smell of smoke and something worse, the horrible sound, the horrible crackling sound with this high-pitched whizzing noise. The warmth, at first it tricked me into thinking it felt good, and then it became unbearable. The metal on my necklace heated up too quick, and I pulled it off." She touched her clavicle. "That's why you couldn't read that inscription," Mia said, turning to Josie as though just remembering she were there. "Until I cleaned it off for you yesterday."

"Did Ruby know what was going on?"

"Once she realized something was wrong, it was too late. There was nothing left to do but wait for it to be over."

"My God. I can't imagine."

"It was terrible. I sang to her to try and calm her, sang 'Time in a Bottle'—she loved that song. The smoke seeped in slowly at first, and then much too quickly. It got so that I couldn't see her, could barely make out my hand holding her head." She held her hand in front of her face. "I heard shouting coming closer and this loud boom, and someone had kicked in the door to the girls' room."

"The fireman who died?"

"The fireman who died. Tommy Bianco. A very good man who gave his life trying to help us. As he came closer, for a second I thought we might be okay, but when he threw himself over us, I knew we were done. Worst part of it all, as it was happening, I just kept thinking how I'd never see my little girl again, never be able to hug her." She clutched Josie's hands, tears flowing steadily. "Will you bring her the necklace and explain? Tell her I love it! And that I love her more than anything else in the world."

"But Mia, *you* can tell her yourself, can't you? You can appear to her like you have to me, so why don't you?"

"Because, Josie, she doesn't want that. I told you way back you can't force this on people!"

"I didn't exactly want it either!" Josie shouted. She looked around to see if anyone could hear, but still the only other person there was the old man cleaning graves. He was weaving in and out of sight as he worked.

"No, but you can handle it. And Nanette knew you could. She knew you'd come around when you needed to." She reached out and wiped at the tears running down Josie's cheek. Her fingertips were soft and warm. "Baby, you needed a friend to help you get through this stretch. And now, my Rita needs someone in her life to help her get past everything that happened. And the key to all of that is the necklace. And the package from the safe. That'll be a start, but it's not enough. Yeah, I could try and force the issue, but she doesn't need a phantom. She needs a living person. Someone she can see and know for a very long time."

"Rita doesn't want to see me, Mia! You think she wants to hear what I have to say after last night?"

Mia nodded emphatically. "Yes, Josie, she does want to believe you. She just needs to cool down—hotheaded girl. But once she sees that necklace, she'll know, baby! She'll know you were telling her the truth. And she'll know that her mama loves her and watches over her. She's not like you, she needs a living person to convey all this. Lots of folks do. But if she doesn't get over her anger about everything that happened, or start to anyway, she'll run that restaurant into the ground and check out early. We Boudreaux women don't do well with twenty-nine. I'd like her to make it a long, long time."

"How did you know I'd pick that necklace? How did you know where it was?"

"Ruby told me where it was. And I knew you'd pick it. I just knew."

"Was that Ruby's dress I tried on?"

"No, baby. I don't know whose that was."

"When did you clean the pendant up?"

"Last night, while you were at Esplanade. I was so nervous and fidgety."

"This is just crazy, Mia!"

"This is your life, Josie. This is your gift." She paused. "Like Vivian said."

"Jesus, are you following me?"

"Just checkin' in from time to time. It's a weird town."

"Oh, that reminds me, Will Carter sends his love."

Mia shook her head. "Stay away from that one."

"Not to worry. I prefer my horrible men to be currently living."

"Girl, I'm sorry about that. I should have warned you about Patrick. Ruby kept telling me there was something wrong, and she didn't like him for you, and that's why I met him. That's why I appeared to him. I needed to see for myself."

"You didn't appear to all of us?"

Mia shook her head again. "No. Only you, and Patrick, and Sylvie. Patrick, he's a photographer, he 'sees' things different than most. I realized that one night when I passed him outside and he smiled and said hello to me. I knew I could come back 'round and check in on you and him."

"What about Curtis? How come he wouldn't have seen you? He's a believer."

"Girl, you know Curtis. He didn't need to see me. He'd never have been able to keep his mouth shut, so my plan wouldn't have worked. He doesn't keep things separate in his head like you do. No, no one else saw me. All those afternoons in the cellar, or the park, all those conversations late at night, it was just us."

"And that's why everyone thought I was talking to myself?"

"Maybe so."

"Who terrorized Chef? Ruby?"

Mia nodded. "It was time for that place to change hands again. It wouldn't have ended well otherwise."

"And that's up to the dead to decide?"

"Sometimes the living don't realize how stuck they are. Don't know how to move forward without some assistance."

"What about Sylvie? She was seeing you all those nights. And you let us all think she was losing it."

"What choice did I have? If I'd validated what she was saying, you'd have tried to have us both committed. I visited with her nights after she left Bistrot. We spent lots of hours talking and reminiscing. I was with her in those last days."

"I saw you one night in her window."

"I know."

"I thought I was losing my mind. And then I thought you were up to no good. I had no idea what was going on."

"Josie, I'm sorry I lied. I'm sorry I couldn't tell you everything. But I couldn't. I needed your help, and you needed to get out of Dodge no matter the cost. I saw what happened the night of the blackout. You think you'd be better off moping around your apartment about Patrick and Derek? Hell no, girl! You needed to spread those great big wings you pretend you don't have and find yourself. It's not just that I need you to reach through to Rita. I needed your friendship, too, and I like to think mine helped you through some dark days."

"Of course it did, Mia! That's what's so horrible now. I'm so sad to know the truth!"

"This isn't the end, I promise you that. We will stay in each other's lives."

"How?"

"Do you really have to ask that? Once you let go of what you think you know, you'll see that many things are possible."

"I hate that you've been walking around with decades of guilt."

"It's not like that. Time moves different. And I knew I'd just have to be patient, and that eventually, somehow, this would work itself out. That's what I want you to learn, too, Josie. That old saying it's about the journey and not the destination? It's the truth. And the journey is yours and is up to you, not some manmade time table."

A loud voice interrupted them from across the cemetery. It was the tour guide, talking to a crowd of people.

"And here, ladies and gents, is the tomb of the Queen of Voodoo herself, Madame Marie Laveau."

"Will *they* be able to see you?"

"No, baby." Mia looked at the tour group and then back at Josie. She stood and held her hand out to help Josie off the ground. "You need to get going, girl, okay?"

"Wait. I have so many more questions! What about Ruby? How was the voice I heard in the basement the same one I heard as a kid?"

"'Those long childhood hours when you were so afraid,'" Mia quoted.

"Yes! What is that from?"

"All will become clear. I promise you. And I promise you I will see you again."

"Okay. Okay. I'm scared, but I guess I can't do anything but believe you, so I'll try."

"Please do. And Josie?"

"Yes?"

"On your way back to Rita, I want you to stop by two places, okay? The Faulkner House on Pirate's Alley, and Miriam's on Jackson Square. You'll find 'em easy, and you'll find the answers to some of your questions. I promise."

"I love you!"

"I love you too, girl." Mia stepped forward and hugged Josie, tears streaming down both their faces. "Go, baby," she whispered. "It's time."

Josie nodded and let her go. She wiped her face and started to walk away. When she turned back, Mia was gone.

As Josie passed the tour the man was talking.

"…they say that once you drink the waters of New Orleans, you'll always consider it home." He noticed her and doffed his hat.

A few paces ahead was the grave sweeper. "I'm glad you found yo friend," he said. "She was waiting for you."

Josie walked through the steamy afternoon as though through a dream. Everything was both impossible and overflowing with possibility. It would take her a while to sort through all that had happened, all she was meant to understand. And maybe she never would, but this was part of the lesson—she could accept her gift without fully understanding it all.

She found a taxi and had it drop her at the edge of the Quarter, then wandered until she found Pirate's Alley and the Faulkner House bookstore. The meticulously curated shop felt charged with energy. Mia had sent her here for a specific reason.

Use your intuition, girl.

There were works by Southern writers contemporary and classic, as well as scores of poetry books. She found herself drawn to one shelf in the corner and there, side by side and out of order, wedged between Collins and Cummings, were two books—one by Rainer Maria Rilke and one by Christina Rossetti. The first name she knew, the second she didn't, but she was certain she was meant to get them.

When she paid, the clerk stuck a bookmark in each and put them into a paper bag.

Josie headed back up to Jackson Square to find Miriam's. She stood on the corner outside the restaurant listening to the music playing in the square. She wasn't hungry, but she'd go in for a drink because she was supposed to. It was part of the unraveling of the mystery.

The hostess directed her past the dining rooms to a bright, sun-drenched area with a long bar at one end. She took a seat in the middle and looked at the cocktail menu, deciding on a *Fleur de Lys* cocktail.

While the bartender prepared her drink, Josie pulled the books from her bag. She liked poetry, had studied it in school. She looked first at the Christina Rossetti, learning she was a nineteenth century British poet. The bookmark led her to a poem called "Sonnets are full of love," and four lines in she found the passage she was meant to.

To her whose heart is my heart's quiet home,

To my first Love, my Mother....

Josie reached to her collarbone where the pendant no longer sat and felt a sharp pang as she thought of her own mother.

Next she opened the Rilke to the bookmark, and there it was, "Before Summer Rain," with its final verse.

And reflected on the faded tapestries now;

the chill, uncertain sunlight of those long

childhood hours when you were so afraid.

It was no wonder the line had stayed with her. It captured it perfectly, her haunted childhood. When she'd read it in college, she was too close to it still, too deeply in denial of all that had transpired—and yet she'd held onto that line. It would take this incredible summer and meeting Mia for her to fully appreciate how deftly this poet who died forty years before she was born had put into words her experiences.

"How's your day going so far?" the bartender asked. She was a young woman with dark red hair and a gritty accent. Her name tag said Megan.

"Pretty impossible to put into words," Josie said.

Megan smiled. "Happens down here."

"I've heard you guys have a resident ghost?"

"Yep. Good ol' Cyril. Bought this place when it was restored after the Good Friday fire of 1788," she said.

Of course there had been a fire.

Megan launched into a speech Josie knew she probably had to deliver several times a day. Such was the price one paid for working in a famously haunted restaurant in a town full of tourists.

"A whole bunch of buildings were destroyed in that fire, including part of this one. This was a private house, and a family of plantation owners used it as their city place. Used to keep the slaves in the courtyard there while they waited for auction in the square. So, there's a lot of real tough energy over there, a lot of sadness, part of the ugly fact of this country's history. This town's history."

"Those poor souls."

"Mister Cyril bought the place after the fire and restored it and turned it into his dream home. Then, in 1817 he got arrested and was going to lose the place. And the night before he was supposed to move out, he went upstairs and hung himself. He's been hanging 'round ever since," she said, rolling her eyes at her own pun.

"That's tragic," Josie said. "Do you ever see him around here?"

"Sure do, sweetheart. He's not like other ghosts. He's this kinda purplish shimmery orb."

"Do you see other ghosts in town?"

Megan laughed. "Of course, baby. This place is a refuge for lost souls. You can go upstairs and take a look at the rooms, maybe you'll see him yourself. Head on up to the séance lounge. They say he died in the second room in."

Josie stepped through a curtain to a wooden staircase. Underneath the stairs was a small round table with two place settings, two glasses of red wine, and a basket of bread. A framed sign on the table read, *Reserved for Cyril and Guest.* There was a faint pink lipstick trace on one of the glasses. Cyril was on a date.

Sunlight filtered through the windows and bounced off the wooden steps. Josie walked upstairs and wandered the hall until she found the séance lounge.

It looked like a Victorian brothel, bathed in red light and filled with sumptuous velvet sofas and chairs, quilted wall coverings, tasseled lamps, and oil paintings. Josie wandered around looking at the décor, then walked into the back room. Against one wall was propped a full sized, cloudy mirror. On an adjacent wall was a painting of a woman, a young woman with dark wavy hair and full lips, dressed in garb from long ago. Josie walked toward it, transfixed.

"She does look like you, doesn't she, dear?"

She froze in place. The voice was the most beautiful sound she'd ever known. She turned and, seated on a crimson love seat at the far end of the room, looking as vibrant as ever, was Nanette.

"Oh my God!" Josie whispered. Her knees started to give out, but she caught herself. She ran across the room and crumpled next to her grandmother, hugging her tight, inhaling the scent of lavender and weeping into her shoulder. When she could speak she sat up. "Nanette! I love you so much!"

Nanette held her warm hand over Josie's cheek. "I know you do, dear, and I love you, too. I'm so pleased you took Mia up on her invitation."

"This is so crazy!"

"She found me as soon as she could. Will you help her, dear? Will you bring those things to her sad, lost Rita and help them both find some peace?"

"What about you, Nanette? Can I help you find peace?"

"Darling, I'm already at peace. It was time for me. Mia is not, poor girl, and hasn't been for twenty-five years."

"But you know what happened when I met Rita, right?"

"Yes, and you can make things better. You have the power to do that and so much more. That's why you're here. Go, before the night gets underway."

"I don't want to leave you!"

Nanette smiled. "Josephine, I've always told you that we're the lucky ones. You will see me again. You have the gift. And for right now you need to use that gift to help others."

"Okay." Josie tried to smile through her tears. "But God, I miss you. I love you."

"And I you, darling. And I know she's not easy, but please, dear, your mother could use your love and empathy, even if she doesn't always know how to provide the same."

"Okay," Josie said, hiccupping with a sob. "I don't want to leave you."

"You're not leaving me. You're going to someone who needs our help. This is why you're here." Nanette stood with more ease and agility than she had in a decade. She threaded her arm through Josie's and led her toward the staircase.

Josie wanted to hold onto her forever.

Nanette wiped her tears. "Have faith, my girl. I will see you soon. I promise." She kissed Josie on the cheek. "You must go now and do this, for all of us."

Josie started down the stairs, reluctant.

"And Josephine, darling?"

"Yes, Nanette?"

"Wine is a privilege. It's not a way of life. You're not a sommelier, dear. Respect the grape and yourself."

"I know."

"If I'm the one asking you this, I can no longer be the excuse."

Josie smiled. Her sadness gave way to a sense of tranquility and optimism.

She walked back down Chartres toward Esplanade feeling buoyant. She was on her clearest mission ever. She wended her way through the Marigny, which was starting to pick up with the promise of nightlife, and went to Burgundy to retrieve Rita's gifts. Walking back toward the Esplanade House, she didn't need a map or to second guess herself. Her tiny pocket of New Orleans was familiar now.

"Okay, Mia, this is for you," she said when she reached the restaurant. She took a deep breath. This is why she was in New Orleans.

She pulled open the door and immediately spotted Rita across the room, her back to Josie, talking to a table of customers.

Josie sidled up to the bar and took a seat, wondering how much Bobby knew.

"Well, hi there, darlin'!" he said. "You're lookin' bright eyed and bushy tailed after last night. What can I get you?"

"Just a club soda for now. Thanks, Bobby."

"And how're you enjoying your stay in our fine town?" he asked as he shot soda water into a glass.

"Full of surprises, this place."

They locked eyes for a moment—he knew something.

"Josie."

She jumped.

"I didn't expect we'd see you back here anytime soon." Rita sounded more surprised than angry.

"I know. Rita, if you don't want me here, I understand. But I can't leave town without at least trying—"

"I'm not gonna kick you out."

You sure didn't have a problem doing that last night, Josie thought.

"What I *mean* is it'd be impolite to kick you out two nights in a row," Rita said impatiently, reading Josie's mind. Just like her mother.

"Can we maybe talk in private?"

Rita puffed out her cheeks. "It's busy right now." She gestured around the half-empty room. "Maybe in a bit."

Josie spent the next several minutes making small talk and waiting. She fielded questions about New York from the people at the bar and stuck to club soda.

Finally, Rita led her back to the table they'd occupied the night before. She went to the bar and came back with a pitcher of beer and two glasses.

Bobby followed with two double-shots of bourbon. "On the house, ladies." He winked at Josie.

Rita kept her eyes on Josie while she took a long sip of her bourbon.

Josie touched the rim of her glass to her lips. "Listen, Rita, I'm sorry I scared you. That was certainly not my—"

"You didn't scare me, Josie. You pissed me off."

"I know, and I'm sorry." She took a modest sip of her drink and coughed.

Rita slapped the table and gave Josie a long, flinty stare. "You really think you're the first one to do this? To talk about seeing my mama? I even believe them. Some of them."

"I know what it's like to lose someone."

"It ain't about that, Josie. It's about all these damn people claim to get to see my mama, and I don't. Half of them are lying. How the hell do I know you ain't one of them?"

Josie pulled the necklace out of her purse and handed it to Rita.

"What is this?"

"You'll know when you see it."

Rita took it from her and held it in her hand. She exhaled slowly, staring down at the necklace, turning it over and rubbing her thumb on the engraving. She looked up at Josie, her face transformed. "Where'd you get this?"

"In New York. I told you, Rita."

"How do I know that for sure? How do I know you didn't steal it somehow?"

"I didn't. I know your mom. I know you gave it to her. Do you remember how it works?"

Rita nodded and mouthed something to herself as she slid it apart, revealing the photos inside. She put her fingers to her lip. "Mama," she whispered. "You did get it."

"That's what I tried to tell you last night, honey. She got it and she loved it. And she loves you."

Rita nodded again, staring at the photos.

Josie didn't give her the package right away, didn't want to overwhelm the moment. She sipped her drink slowly and waited.

"Why didn't she tell me she got it?" Rita asked, her voice soft and high.

"She tried to. She wrote you a letter, but it wasn't sent out in time."

"And then she died," Rita said.

"Then she died."

"Oh, Mama. I love you, too. I love you so much." She kissed the pendant and clasped it around her neck.

Josie took the package from her bag and handed it to Rita. "This is what she wanted to send you."

Rita stared down at it.

"It was locked in a safe at Bistrot—Dave's Continental. It had been there for twenty-five years, and we finally got it out."

"Should I open it?"

"That's up to you."

"I don't know if I'm ready. Thing is, Josie, Mama has tried to reach out to me over the years. Lots of times, and I never let her. I'm stubborn, I guess." Her voice was all sadness and regret.

"That's not stubbornness, Rita. It's a hard thing to accept. Trust me. I understand."

"And like I said, you're not the first person I know who can see ghosts, or who claims to know Mama. People are always tellin' me 'bout some lady looks like me who hangs out here. Easy to make that up—her picture's all over the place. But this—this is proof I never got before."

For the first time, Josie had not a shred of doubt that what she had was a gift.

"It *is* a gift," Rita confirmed without knowing it.

"Do you remember her well?"

"I remember she was beautiful."

"And you look just like her."

Rita shrugged. "Guess I do know that. I remember she'd sing to me and play with my hair. And we had this little make-believe language." She smiled at the thought. "She talk about me?"

"All the time. She was—she is—so proud of you."

"Don't know why. I haven't done anything with my life."

"That's not true, Rita. You've kept this place going. You've become this beautiful, wonderful woman like your mom, and you'll continue to be."

"It was a long time before my grandparents told me what happened to her. They just said she decided to stay in New York."

"Oh, Rita! No wonder you were so angry!"

"They just did what they thought would be easier for me to hear. It wasn't until I was lookin' for something years later in my Gram's papers and I found the article."

"The article?"

Rita stood and motioned for Josie to follow her. They walked through the main dining room to a small office in the back of the restaurant. She pulled an album from a shelf and opened to an article from the *New Orleans Times Picayune*, dated July 1, 1974.

A fire at a restaurant in New York City took the life of a Bywater woman. Maria Louise Boudreaux, age 29, died at her place of employment, the restaurant Dave's Continental located on 9th Street in the borough of Manhattan. A kitchen fire broke out after business hours on the night of June 29 and claimed the lives of three people: Boudreaux, who was a waitress, Frances "Ruby" Samuels, 27, another waitress who hailed from Keene, New Hampshire, and Thomas Bianco, 33, a fireman from the Canarsie neighborhood of Brooklyn, New York.

Josie stopped reading. Frances, Keene, 1974. It was all coming together in the most stunning of ways. And the coincidences couldn't be coincidences. This was how things were supposed to unfold.

Boudreaux leaves behind her parents, Charles and Lola Boudreaux, proprietors of The Esplanade House in the Faubourg Marigny, as well as a four-year-old daughter, Marguerita Collette Boudreaux. Details on services for Miss Boudreaux to follow.

"Wow," Josie whispered.

"Kind of a tough thing to just find. But I'm not mad at them. They meant to do right."

"Thank you for sharing this with me."

"Yep." She held up the package. "You think I should open this?"

"Do you want to?"

"Yeah, I think I need to open it with you here."

Josie felt she could weep with joy. She'd broken through to Rita.

Rita tore the brown wrapping away, and there was a small box inside with three tissue-wrapped gifts and a card in an envelope. Her hands shaking, she opened the first gift, a refrigerator magnet in the shape of an apple with *New York City* written across it.

"The Big Apple," she said, and Josie smiled.

The second was a miniature version of a yellow checker cab, boxy and quaint.

"Y'all ride around in taxis all the time, huh?"

"Sometimes. But they don't look as cool as that anymore."

Rita ran its wheels across the palm of her hand. The package was a perfect time capsule of early-seventies New York and made Josie nostalgic. She knew this version of the city from movies and television.

The last gift was a domed snow globe with a truncated Manhattan skyline, the Chrysler Building, Empire State Building, Brooklyn Bridge, and Statue of Liberty. The Twin Towers were so new they hadn't made it into this tableau. Half the water had evaporated, leaving an air bubble at the top.

"We can get you a new one."

Rita shook it and glitter billowed about. "How pretty," she whispered. "Thank you, Mama." She handed it to Josie to look at and picked up the envelope, turning it over and running her fingertips across Mia's handwriting. She looked at Josie with tears in her eyes. "I dunno. I dunno about this one yet."

"Maybe you want to save it for later, when you're home?"

Rita nodded. "Yeah, that's what I want to do. I love my presents, though, that's for sure."

"Rita, you mentioned that there are photos of your mom here?"

"Sure, you wanna see them?"

"I would love that."

She piled her gifts up with the envelope and led Josie back into the dining room, where one wall was lined with framed photos. They were all taken at the Esplanade House over the years, starting when it opened in the 1920s. It had hardly changed. Even the clientele looked the same.

Rita walked her through the chronology, pointing out her grandparents, then a very young Mia—who looked just like Rita did in the photo in the locket—at various celebrations, birthdays, Halloween, Mardi Gras. How strange to see her in the old-fashioned black-and-white photos. There was adolescent Mia in a poodle skirt and saddle shoes, her hair in a high ponytail. Josie watched her grow into a wisp of a teenager, trying out the styles of the sixties, getting bolder and brighter, her skirts shorter, as she blossomed into the beautiful version of herself whom Josie knew. There were photos of her pregnant and Bohemian, then of her with Rita as a baby, a toddler, and finally a little girl.

"You two look so much alike."

"I know."

In the final, color photo of Mia, she sat at the bar, looking over her shoulder and smiling at someone or something. It was a candid, and it was beautiful.

"That was right before she left," Rita said, touching the glass. "That's Dave from Dave's Continental she's smilin' at, Gram says. That's the last picture I have of her."

Mia was wearing the gold wrap dress that now hung in Josie's closet.

There were more photos of Rita and her grandparents after Mia left, but Rita had lost the spark and joy she had in the earlier shots. There was a deadening to her eyes in the post-Mia period. Josie looked at her now. She was much lighter than she'd been the previous day. Softer and younger, a twenty-five-year burden having lifted.

Josie could have stayed all night, but she knew she should quit while she was ahead. She'd accomplished what she'd set out to do.

"Rita, I'm going to get going, but I'm really glad you let me back in."

"I'm really glad I did, too."

"Will you come visit me in New York sometime?"

"You're leaving town already?"

"I'm not sure. Maybe in a couple days."

"Then don't say goodbye now, Josie. Just say you'll be back."

Josie understood why Rita needed to hear this and, more important, why she needed to stick to her word and come back in. "I absolutely will."

"Maybe we can even have dinner or something?" Rita asked shyly. "There's other places right nearby."

"That sounds wonderful. Why don't I come back in when you open tomorrow afternoon, and if you're not too busy we'll have dinner."

Rita smiled, really smiled, for the first time. "Thank you, Josie."

They hugged, a brief and awkward hug they both needed. Josie said goodbye to Bobby and walked out.

The first few drops of rain were falling, and she calculated she'd have just enough time to get back to Burgundy to wait out the storm before setting out to explore more of the city. She turned to look back through the window.

There was Mia, at the table where she and Rita had sat, watching her daughter. Oblivious, Rita bussed the table and reset it for the next guests. Mia looked at Josie and smiled, holding her hand up. Josie held hers up, too. She watched her for a moment, saw the tenderness on Mia's face as she observed her daughter, then started to walk away. When she turned back, Mia was still there.

Josie made her way back through the Marigny feeling elated and purposeful. She greeted people on the street as she walked the length of Frenchmen, passing Washington Square. She'd misjudged the timing of the rain but didn't care. She crossed Burgundy and made a left, then started toward the steps to her porch and stopped suddenly, her heart pounding as the rain cascaded around her. Lightening crackled, illuminating the front of the house.

Someone stood on the porch shaking a mess of umbrella spokes and running his fingers through damp hair. It was Derek.

Josie stared at him, speechless.

He walked down the steps so they were both in the rain and took her hands. "Hi," he said.

"How did you find me?"

"I decided to start believing in magic."

Chapter Twenty-One

❧

THE NEW MILLENNIUM dawned, and the world did not end.

Josie sat at a table in the front of Miss Sylvie's Bistrot, sipping iced tea and sorting through paperwork. Derek, leaning on the bar, transcribed the night's specials onto a chalkboard.

Billie Holiday's "Crazy He Calls Me" came on the sound system, and they looked up at the same time.

"Excited?" Derek asked.

"Nervous!"

"But excited, too, yeah?"

"Excited for you to meet her. And for her to experience New York. Nervous about what all it might bring up, if she's ready to see this place. If this is the right move."

"Josie, I don't think it's up to you at this point."

"Meaning?"

"Meaning, it's kismet. You wander into a random spot in a city you've never been to and strike up a conversation with a woman whose dead mother turns out to be part of Bistrot's history. And who knew Sylvie. *That*, love, is divine intervention. Whether she's ready or not, she's supposed to be here."

"Holy shit, Derek Magnus believes in divine intervention?"

"Maybe I do." Derek still didn't believe in ghosts, but he was broadening his mind and starting to believe in what he called magic after thirty-six years without evidence of it. All the evidence he needed came the previous August, when a beautiful woman visited him in a fitful night of fever dreams and told him where to find Josie. He woke in a panic and wrote down the address she'd repeated. Ignoring his persistent rationale, he'd hopped a plane to New Orleans. When he reached the house on Burgundy Street, he knew—this was where he'd find her.

After he waited on the porch for close to an hour, she came strolling up the street in the rain as though simply running late for their planned meeting.

Ten months later they sat in the restaurant they now owned—turned out Josie did have some business acumen, despite decades spent believing she didn't. They'd renamed the place after the woman they affectionately referred to as their patron saint and remodeled it in the style of Esplanade House, hiring a young chef from New Orleans. Among the evening's specials, blackened snapper, shrimp and grits, seafood jambalaya.

"Is this her?"

Josie turned around.

Rita stood in the vestibule holding a small suitcase and looking entirely out of her element.

"Yes it is!" Josie leapt from her seat. "Rita!" She ran to the front door and pulled her friend in for a hug.

"Y'all are a sight for sore eyes," Rita said shyly. She wore the locket Josie had given her the previous summer.

"How was your flight?"

"I was nervous as all get out."

"But you made it!"

"By the skin of my teeth. I ordered some of them tiny bottles of booze to calm my nerves, had two Bloody Marys and, son of a gun, about to pour my third and that little bottle of vodka slides right off my tray and dumps onto the guy next to me. Thank God he was sleeping."

Josie laughed. A tingle like static electricity began in the back of her neck and radiated, enveloping her. She knew what was coming and was not afraid.

Hello, beautiful friend.

"I am so happy to see you," she said to Rita and Mia, who now stood just behind her daughter. "My God, I've missed you so much."

All three had tears in their eyes.

"I've missed you, too, Miss Josie. This place is like home already." Rita took in the room—same café-style tables and chairs as Esplanade, same tiny white fairy lights strung around the perimeter, same Victorian lamps on each table. And on the walls, vintage posters of Jazz Fest, Mardi Gras, an old Café du Monde sign.

Josie couldn't take her eyes off Mia. Though she'd visited New Orleans two more times over the year, they'd not seen each other since August. She laughed and shook her head.

"Surprise, girl. Let's go somewhere we can talk!" Mia said.

"Come." Josie took Rita's hand. "Meet my better half."

They walked into the bar, and Derek stood to greet them.

"Derek, my love, this is Rita."

"Rita!" He kissed her on the cheek and stepped back. "Wow. You look really familiar."

Josie's eyes widened, and she looked at Mia.

"Guess it's because Josie's painted such a strong picture. It's great to finally meet you!"

"Nice to meet you, too, Derek. Thank you for having me."

"Can I get you a glass of water, or a beverage?"

"Actually, honey," Josie said. "Would you mind taking Rita down the block to drop her stuff off and freshen up? I'll finish up my paperwork so we can spend the rest of the day together, no interruptions."

"Sure thing. Sound good, Rita?"

"Well, yeah, if it ain't too much trouble."

"No trouble at all." He took Rita's suitcase and led her to the front door.

"Am I dreaming?" Josie asked Mia. She couldn't stop laughing.

"No, girl!" Mia was just as excited. "I told you you'd see me again. Look at this place! It's beautiful."

"That visit last summer introduced me to a world I've needed for a long, long time. Visiting New Orleans felt like coming home. And so I tried to recreate it here."

"It's just perfect, Josie."

They walked through the dining room and took a booth at the far end by the office. Josie and Derek's office.

"Now tell me everything," Mia said.

"Where do I begin?"

"What's down the block?"

"Our apartment."

When they decided they were together, when they forged their plan to buy Bistrot, Josie and Derek gave up their apartments and signed a lease on a one-bedroom on the corner of Ninth Street and Fifth Avenue. It was an old building with lots of history and ghosts.

"And does Derek have any idea?"

"Derek respects that I have a connection to the afterlife, and he doesn't ask specifics. But he doesn't roll his eyes and leave the room anymore, either. Not always, anyway."

"Now what about the rest of the crew?"

Josie filled Mia in on everything that happened since that August night. It turned out Alison wasn't pregnant after all, it was a false alarm. But she was plenty pissed about what transpired between Derek and Josie the night of the blackout, and she told Derek as much, said it was Josie or her. That Josie had to be out of the picture completely if Derek wanted to keep her around.

It didn't take him long to decide what to do there.

"I told you this would work out!" Mia said.

"You sure did."

"And the other guys?"

"Curtis finally met his Mister Wonderful, Henry, and the guy is loaded. He owns an art gallery, and he's putting Curtis through school. They come in for dinner sometimes, and they're adorable."

"And Sam?"

"Ready for this? Turns out Sammy has some acting chops after all! He's a member of Cleaver Dunnehill's theater company. Not a leading man yet, but he's working hard at it."

"What wonderful news on both of them. Who else?"

"Andy left New York, moved back home to Ohio, no one's heard from him. We have a brand-new chef and she's wonderful. A New Orleans transplant named Naomi. We're having a hard time finding a sous-chef, though."

"What happened to Johnny?"

"Johnny. When he survived the new year's rapture, he had this come-to-Jesus moment and decided to follow his dad and brother and join the FDNY. Says he feels called to do it. He's with a firehouse way downtown by Wall Street."

Mia was quiet, and Josie understood why. "May God bless him," Mia whispered. They sat in silence for a moment.

"Josie, it is so good to be here with you," Mia said finally.

"How come I never saw you the other times I visited New Orleans?"

"Because I wanted you to have your time to get to know Rita, just Rita, without the distractions. And it worked. Y'all forged a beautiful friendship."

"She's really come a long way since we first met."

"And that has everything to do with her knowing you, girl."

"Actually, it has everything to do with my knowing *you*."

"You're happy, Josie?"

"Happy? Certainly happier. It's not always easy, being business partners *and* romantic partners. We have our moments. But I love Derek, and I love this place. And I have a surprise for you."

Mia followed her up the staircase toward the kitchen. The twelve-top was gone, and in its place was a round table, currently set for six but easily expandable. It was a ghost table, inspired by the one at Miriam's, and the six place settings were to honor the three victims of the fire at Dave's Continental, along with Sylvie, Nanette, and Alex.

"My goodness!" Mia's eyes filled with tears. "Josie, this is beautiful!"

"It's yours."

"Do they come here?"

Josie laughed. "I can't believe I'm saying this, but yes, they do, once in a while. Ruby comes the most, of course. Come up here tonight. I bet they'll be so happy to see you!"

Mia hugged her. "Thank you. Thank you so much." She walked around the table, ran her hand over the charger, admired the cut crystal stemware. The ghost table was the most finely appointed in the restaurant. Josie had made sure of it. And though Derek didn't really buy into the project, he appreciated that it mattered to her.

"Josie!" he called from downstairs.

"That was quick," she said, then called out, "Be right down!"

"I'm just going to sit here a spell, okay?" Mia said.

"Of course. Take your time." Josie went back downstairs where Derek had chilled a bottle of champagne. She'd worked hard on herself over the past year and had become much more moderate and respectful of the grape.

He poured three glasses, and they toasted.

Rita spoke excitedly about all of the things she wanted to do and see while in New York.

When Mia came back down a few minutes later, only Josie was facing her. Serene and beautiful, she walked behind her daughter and listened.

"And I wish I could go all the places my mama went to, but I don't know what they are."

Mia put a hand on her shoulder, and Rita stopped suddenly, looking puzzled. Then, her expression softened, and she smiled.

"But somehow I think I'll find them. Somehow I think things'll work out just as they're meant to."

"What a Wonderful World" came on the stereo.

"So do I," Mia and Josie said at the same time.

Epilogue

June 29, 2000

IT'S BEEN ONE year since the new coat check girl showed up at Bistrot, and twenty-six years to the day since a fire broke out at Dave's Continental, killing three—Tommy Bianco, Ruby Samuels, and me.

"And here we are," Nanette says, patting my hand.

"And here we are."

We're at Miss Sylvie's waiting for the others, while our girls have dinner downstairs. Seeing Rita and Josie laughing and talking and bonding makes the ache of everything that came before this moment easier to bear.

"It certainly does," Nanette says. "Did you ever think you'd see either of them quite so light?"

"Didn't know my Rita had a 'light' option till she met Josie." I'm not joking. Josie saved her. All the confusion and hurt Rita felt when she revealed the truth has faded from her memory. Now she just knows she's made a friend who was connected to her mother through Miss Sylvie. She thinks it was Miss Sylvie gave Josie the necklace and package of gifts.

"Didn't know Josie had a light option until Derek," Nanette says. "And I've been meaning to ask you about your role in all that."

"My role in all that." I'm smiling at the memory of it. "I knew right away what I needed to do, soon as I realized Josie was hightailing it down to New Orleans.

That boy spent two days looking for her, pining for her, weeping harder than he'd ever wept before. I had to help."

"So, you visited with him?"

"I visited with him in his dream and told him where to find her. Kept on repeating that address till I was sure it took. And the rest is history."

"And the rest is history. We have company!"

I turn and look. Here comes Miss Sylvie herself, leading the charge, followed by Tommy and Ruby, who's holding hands with a beautiful young boy. Josie knows, now, that it was Alex she encountered last summer. He'd been hanging around the restaurant after all.

After we all exchange greetings, our dinner party gets under way. Alex is a wonderful boy, sweet and curious and funny, like his brother.

Josie comes by to visit with us, but she has to do so on the sly, under the guise of checking on things in the kitchen. Things in the kitchen are just fine. Everything is just fine, finer than I could have imagined. You might not believe in happily ever after, but you ought to believe in things working out just as they're meant to.

Course there's one thing that would make it all better, and that's if Derek could find a way to believe. Knowing Alex would be good for him. For both of them.

And so we'll work on it. We'll get there.

Acknowledgments

I began writing this book many moons ago—in fact, the first line came to mind sometime around 2006. In the years since, I've started and stopped it several times, and somehow these characters wouldn't let me abandon them altogether. Because it has been such a marathon, I have a great many people to thank for helping me get to the finish line.

First and foremost, to my wonderful agent Jessica Reino—whose belief in this book sustained me through times of great doubt, and who never stopped promising me that we would find it a good home. Everyone should have a Jessica rooting for them.

To my editor, Staci Troilo, and everyone else at Roan & Weatherford, thank you for welcoming me into the family and for helping me to shape this story. You are a pleasure to work with.

I had two excellent writing coaches at different points in the process. First, the inimitable Jill Dearman who, when I was vacillating between ideas told me to "just pick one." I did. Next, Ginger Moran, who encouraged me to move part of the story to New Orleans, which meant taking many trips to that magical, haunted town.

To my incredible writing group: Maggie Buchwald, Michel Morin, Hannah Bos, Devin Burnam—as well as to Wendy Bozzolasco from my short-lived *other* writing group—thank you for your feedback and encouragement as I workshopped these pages over and over and over again.

To my fabulous beta readers: Elena Perez, Tarajean Sullivan, Tim McBride, Lisa Roberts, and my unofficial betas, Ana Goncalves, Tim Halpern, Diane McCammon, Stacey Kolba, Tracey Gutierrez, Sybil Rosen, Lauren Fisch—thank you for your support and feedback, and Tim M., for helping me make sure the details of the restaurant world are somewhat accurate. For that matter, to the staff of the former Village restaurant, which is where this all began, thank you for keeping me company during many nights of "research" and for corroborating the fact that your ladies' room was, in fact, haunted. To the staff of Bottino—your place may not be haunted, but you have played a major role in my dining life and have inspired some of the quirky scenarios in this book.

To all who came to hear me read my first chapter way back when—Erika Nanartowicz, Brian Niemietz, Neil Thomas, Rory Hayden, Diane McCammon, Cheech, my parents—thanks for supporting me from the very start.

It is so important to have other writers in one's corner, and these next two people are vital members of my writing community.

First, to Claudia Zuluaga, who never lets me lose hope, who inspires me to keep honing my craft, and whose own writing is among the most beautiful I've read—I'm so glad we found each other again after so many years.

To my podcast partner and friend, the prolific novelist John Matthews—thanks for riding the highs and lows of this crazy writing life with me.

To Josephine Bono, who cooked for me and listened to my pages at the end of many a long writing day, and who shares her beautiful name with my protagonist.

To Claudia Latorre for allowing me to pace through my stuck moments and to talk out my ideas until they began to make sense.

To my NOLA family—Karen Calcagno, Tracy Foxworth, Gary Ptak, Cordula Roser Gray, Emily Schoenbaum, and Melissa Huguenot, my own personal spirit advisor—thanks for always welcoming me to your beautiful town. To Keith Medley, whose home became my second one during much of the writing of this book—thank you for your hospitality and friendship. Love you, K-Med.

To everyone who has shared with me their own ghostly experiences, many of which wound up in some form or other on these pages.

To my parents, Maggie and Don Buchwald and my sister, Julia Buchwald—for always believing in me and cheering me on through this process. I love you three with all my heart.

To Scarlett and Sebastian, for being two of the best people on the planet. Yes, Lini, "everybody clapped."

To my wonderful in-laws, Bill and Linda, and the entire Smith family, thank you for your love and support.

To the four-legged friends who kept me company in my writing room, our sweet Pago, Banksy, and the late, great Louie and Wilkie.

And finally, to Bryan. Never has anyone believed in me and my abilities quite like you do. I am very, very lucky that we found each other.

Author's Note

While this book is a work of fiction, many of the locations and details come from real life. Bistrot is based on the restaurant Village, which opened in 1999 and occupied the storied building at 62 West 9th Street in Greenwich Village for several years. Bottino is real and is probably where I'll suggest meeting if we make a dinner date in Manhattan. In New Orleans, La Peniche, Harry's, Bottom of the Cup, the Faulkner House, and Café Brasil are or were real. Miriam's is based on Muriel's, which opened—séance room and all—in the year 2000. The building has been there since the eighteenth century and their resident ghost is named Antoine.

Writers collect stories, and most of the details of the spirit world come from ones my friends and acquaintances have told over the years—the "bless you" from the ether after one sneezes in a room they thought empty, little girls in Creole dress peering down from the top of the stairs, a grandmother bidding her grandchild goodnight on the day she's crossed over. Once you start asking, it seems more people have evidence that there is an afterlife than don't. I appreciate this, as I want to believe. So I do.

About the Author

Laura Buchwald is a writer and editor based in New York City. Her strong belief in the afterlife has led her to consult with multiple spiritual mediums, to convincing results. She has spent significant time in New Orleans researching ghosts and restaurant culture—two of her favorite things. She is co-host of the podcast People Who Do Things, a series of conversations about the creative process. Laura lives in Manhattan with her husband and dog.